About the author

Sharon Booth writes uplifting women's fiction - love, laughter, and happy ever after. Happy endings are guaranteed for her main characters, though she likes to make them work for it. Sharon is a member of the Society of Authors, the Romantic Novelists' Association, and an Authorpreneur member of the Alliance of Independent Authors.
She loves Yorkshire Tea, Doctor Who, and Cary Grant movies - not necessarily in that order.
Sharon grew up in the East Riding of Yorkshire, and the Yorkshire coast and countryside feature strongly in her novels. Her stories are set in pretty villages and quirky market towns, by the sea or in the countryside, and feature lots of humour, romance and friendship. If you love gorgeous, kind heroes, and heroines who have far more important things on their minds than buying shoes, you'll love her books.

Books by Sharon Booth

There Must Be an Angel
A Kiss from a Rose
Once Upon a Long Ago

This Other Eden
Being Emerald
The Skimmerdale Collection

Resisting Mr Rochester
Saving Mr Scrooge

Baxter's Christmas Wish
The Other Side of Christmas
Christmas with Cary

New Doctor at Chestnut House
Christmas at the Country Practice
Fresh Starts at Folly Farm
A Merry Bramblewick Christmas
Summer at the Country Practice
Christmas at Cuckoo Nest Cottage
The Bramblewick Collection

Belle, Book and Christmas Candle
My Favourite Witch
To Catch a Witch
The Witches of Castle Clair Complete Collection

SAVING MR SCROOGE

Sharon Booth

Green Ginger
Publishing

First published in 2017 by:
Fabrian Books
Kent, England
Published in 2020 by:
Green Ginger Publishing
Yorkshire, England

Cover design by Berni Stevens. www.bernistevenscoverdesign.com

ISBN: 978-1-9993602-5-2

*For my grandad, George Booth, who was the first person
to make me really believe.
And for DM, who was the second.*

CHAPTER 1

Marley was dead, to begin with. Well, she wasn't breathing, and that was pretty dead, in Kit's opinion.

His father used to joke about stuff like that all the time. Whenever a death was mentioned, someone was bound to say, 'What did he die of?' and his dad would always reply, 'Shortage of breath,' before cackling away to himself.

Kit's mother always said he was heartless, which was a bit rich, come to think of it.

Anyway, ironically, his father had died of a heart attack, so there must have been a heart in there somewhere. Kit wasn't with him when it happened. He was abroad — just about as far away from his parents as it was possible to get without launching himself into outer space — so he hadn't seen him actually die. He'd never seen anyone die, and he wasn't about to start that night.

Looking at Marley, lying so still on the floor of The Blue Lamp public house, he knew he had to do something fast, or she would stay dead. She'd never forgive him for that. Knowing Marley, the shame of dying on the floor of a pub would kill her — so to speak.

Christ, all this on his first night back in Yorkshire, and only his second back in England. A dead body to deal with, and Marley's, of all people!

'Do something. *Please.*'

Hazel eyes — quite like Marley's own, Kit realised with a shock — stared at him, wide with fear. The young woman beside him was pleading with him to act, as if he was the only one who could do so.

Would it sound pathetic to shout for help?

He supposed if there was a doctor in the place they'd already have stepped forward.

He tried to fight the growing panic. That wouldn't help anyone, least of all Marley. He'd already slapped her on the back several times, and then he'd tried abdominal thrusts, but whatever she was choking on had refused to budge. She'd slumped in his arms and, full of desperation, he'd laid her on the floor and tried again.

Part of him thought it was hopeless, but he wasn't about to give up on her. Not this time.

'Come on, Marley,' he muttered. 'Don't do this to me. Breathe!'

Something whizzed by his ear, followed by a faint ping of an object hitting someone's glass.

Marley made a weird sort of noise, and it was Kit's turn to slump — with sheer relief. He felt drained.

She opened her eyes and stared up at him.

His heart thumped. God, those eyes! Without even thinking about it, he brushed back a strand of her hair and smiled down at her. 'It's okay. You'll be fine now.'

'Jesus?'

It was barely a whisper, but Kit's heart fluttered in response. Then he realised what she'd said. She thought he was Jesus? Well, that's what you got for not having a haircut in months, and he still had his beard, too. He knew he should have shaved it off that morning, but he'd got used to it. Getting rid of it would have been like accepting he was back. That life was about to change, and not for the better.

Anyway, he'd rather she thought he was Jesus, to be honest. If she recognised him, things could get very awkward.

'Marley! Oh, thank God you're all right.' The girl with eyes like Marley's crouched beside Kit, placing her hand on his shoulder.

Then another young woman threw herself to her knees and grabbed Marley's hand. 'You scared me to death! Trust you to take all the attention.'

Her enormous breasts were threatening to suffocate Marley. How, Kit wondered, could anyone take the attention from that cleavage? She certainly had it on display for everyone to admire.

Hastily, he stood up. As more people crowded around Marley he bent down and whispered to the first woman, 'I'd get her checked over at the hospital, just to be sure.'

'Yes, yes, I will. Thank you so much.' She nodded, and Kit had an awful feeling she was about to ask who he was.

More women looked away from Marley and towards him, a question in their eyes.

Time to go.

He pushed his way out of the pub, gladly swapping the heat that had grown unbearable, the garish Christmas lights, and the annoying festive songs, for the welcoming, cool, quiet darkness of the village street.

Well, that had been a baptism of fire. He'd only nipped into the pub to have a quiet meal before heading back to Farthingdale. Trust him to pick The Blue Lamp, where a raucous hen party had arrived just after his steak and chips had been placed on the table. He'd intended to eat quickly and leave immediately, but events had scuppered those plans. Marley had scuppered those plans. Marley, of all people!

The memory of the last time he'd seen her made him shiver. But she could have died! He'd almost lost her. Again. Not that she was his to lose — not anymore. Even so, seeing her like that, so lifeless...

Kit's stomach turned over, and he fought back the nausea. It was just the shock, he thought. It had been traumatic, seeing someone — anyone — almost lose their life like that. It didn't mean anything.

Over the years, he'd comforted himself with the thought that, just maybe, she'd grown matronly and plain. No such luck. Even lying on the floor, after nearly choking to death, there'd been something about her. And when she'd opened those hazel eyes, he'd felt something stir within him that had lain dormant for years. How could she still have that effect on him? They'd been little more than kids, really. It was crazy.

Still, he'd known he was going to see her again, and at least this way, the shock was over and done with. And, of course, he had the advantage. She had no idea that he was going to be back in her life.

Yes, Marley would be one very unhappy lady, come Monday morning. Let her have the weekend to recover from the trauma of the evening. She was going to need it.

CHAPTER 2

Olivia made the whole thing sound exciting, as she recounted the story to our mother. I, on the other hand, was fuming. It hadn't been exciting for me. I'd been scared witless, and had really thought my number was up, so I was quite offended by the way Mum just sat there, listening to every word, eyes wide, mouth open, as if she hadn't just almost lost her precious eldest daughter.

Olivia paused for dramatic effect, then added, 'And she wouldn't be sitting here now, if it wasn't for that mysterious stranger and his firm, manly grasp.'

Mum shook her head. 'Fancy that,' she said. 'I wonder who he was?'

'Dunno,' Olivia mused. She tilted her head to one side. 'I know everyone around here. He doesn't live in the village, that's for sure. Mind you, he looked as if he'd just wandered in from the nearest cave. Like he's been living in the wilderness for months. He needed a shave and a haircut, I'll tell you that much.'

Mum pulled a face. 'Did he smell? He had his hands all over our Marley.'

Olivia laughed. 'No, he didn't smell. He was clean, and very smart, apart from all that hair. You know,' she added thoughtfully, 'there was something about him. I'm sure I've seen him before somewhere.'

'Maybe he's off the telly?' Mum suggested.

'A telly star in Moreton Cross?' Olivia laughed. 'Not likely, is it?'

'What a mystery.' Mum shook her head. 'And such a shame you never got the chance to ask his name.'

I'd had just about enough of their conversation. Talk about missing the point!

'Excuse me, what does it matter?' I demanded. 'Didn't you hear what she just said? I died! Dead! Brown bread! Your eldest daughter departed from this world. Does that mean nothing to you?'

'Don't be so dramatic, Marley. You came back quick enough,' Mum said, with astonishing heartlessness. 'And aren't you curious? Surely, you want to know who saved your life?'

Olivia nodded in agreement. 'He was a real hero. Proper hunky, too, underneath all that hair.'

'You're a married woman,' Mum reminded her. 'Pity Marley didn't think to ask, though.'

'No, well, I was a bit busy at the time,' I said pointedly. 'You know, what with dying and everything.'

'How embarrassing.' Mum shook her head. 'Thank God you survived. What would I have told the neighbours? Of all the ways to peg it, that would have been the very worst.'

'Choking on a peppermint penis!' Olivia giggled. 'Trust you, Marley. You were supposed to suck it, not take a bloody big bite out of it.'

'Pity any bloke you end up with.' Mum shuddered. 'No wonder you're single. Still.'

I could hardly believe it. Not only was my demise being talked about in a breathtakingly cavalier fashion, but *I* was being blamed for the cause of my death! 'You do realise what just happened to me? I died, people! *Died*!'

Olivia leaned towards me, her eyes wide. 'What did you see?'

'See?' I shrugged, bemused. 'Stars, mostly. I think that was just before I passed out.'

'But didn't you see anything else? I mean, come on. You'd actually stopped breathing. You were dead. So, did you see — you know — heaven?'

'Or the other place,' Mum added, folding her arms. 'Did you see any flames? Hear any screams? Meet a bloke dressed in red, carrying a pitchfork?'

'Oh, well, thanks very much! Is that what you think of your eldest daughter?'

'Well,' she said, sounding thoughtful, 'you can be a bit selfish, after all.'

'Pardon?'

'And self-centred,' added Olivia. 'Think the whole world revolves around you.'

'And materialistic,' Mum continued. 'You do seem obsessed with possessions. You know, buying things. How many pairs of shoes do you need?'

'That's charming.'

'And two-faced.'

'Two faced?' I spluttered. 'How can you say that?'

'Easily. Think of Great Uncle Charles.'

'He hasn't got anyone else.' I felt a bit uncomfortable. 'I know he's mean and grumpy, and tight as a gnat's bum, but he's lonely and sad, and we should make the effort to see him. It's hardly my fault he's also loaded, and we're his only relatives.'

'There you go,' Mum said triumphantly. 'Two faced *and* materialistic. Don't tell me you'd still visit him if he was skint, because we both know you wouldn't go anywhere near him.'

I bit down a response. It was all very unfair.

'You're quite vain, too.' Olivia settled back in her chair again. 'You can't pass a mirror without checking your reflection.'

'And snobbish,' Mum said, obviously getting into her stride.

'I am *not* snobbish!'

'I beg to differ,' Mum said firmly. 'You look down on other people. You're quite superior.'

'I am not!'

'Yes, you are,' said Olivia. 'You look down on me for working in the factory, for a start.'

'Well, come on,' I said, 'I mean, the production line in a factory! You passed exams. You had a good job. Until you had children,

I mean. Now working in a sweet factory seems to be enough for you. Why?'

'You work in that factory, too,' she reminded me.

'In the office. That's quite different. I'm a PA, remember! You wouldn't catch me in one of those daft hats, standing on the factory floor all day. I can't understand how you could settle for that.'

'Maybe because, unlike you, a career isn't the most important thing to me.'

'It's only important to her because she can't find a man,' Mum said.

Had I travelled back to nineteen-fifty? 'I've had boyfriends!' I glared at them. 'Just because I don't mention them —'

'You have not! I can't remember a single boyfriend. No man would be good enough for you, let's face it,' Olivia said. 'And that's your problem in a nutshell, Marley. Nothing is ever good enough for you. This house, this village, your job, men, your family. You always want more.'

I opened my mouth to protest, but somehow the words died in my throat before I could get them out. Was that what they thought of me? I wanted to defend myself, but I knew the conversation could take me to places I had no wish to revisit.

'There's nothing wrong with a woman wanting a career more than she wants a man,' I managed eventually. 'Just because I want to better myself, it's hardly a crime.'

'No. It's not a crime.' Mum's tone plainly showed that it was hardly something to be proud of, either — at least, in her book.

It was on the tip of my tongue to point out that marriage was hardly something that had worked out for her, and that she, of all people, should be encouraging her daughters to build a life independent of any man, but I didn't. I could never hurt her like that, even if she was pushing me to the limits of my patience.

The fact was they didn't understand, and how could I make them understand without stirring up painful memories and leading us down a path we'd avoided for a long time? I couldn't, and I wouldn't, anyway. They weren't the only ones who would be hurt, and I'd had a rough enough twenty-four hours, thank you very much.

'I reckon if you found the right bloke, you'd think differently,' Olivia said. 'What a shame you didn't get the opportunity to find out who your guardian angel was.'

'Well, yes, but only because I would have liked to thank him.'

He'd practically broken my ribs, according to Sadie, giving me repeated abdominal thrusts, until the offending piece of penis had finally dislodged from my throat.

'Thank him! I'd have liked to snog him,' Olivia said, her eyes twinkling. 'If he'd had a shave first, that is. Can't be doing with beards. Even so, his eyes were absolutely delish. Mind you, he looked pretty horrified at what was going on in the pub before you croaked it. I saw him sitting at a table nearby, and the expression on his face! What?' she demanded, as Mum raised an eyebrow. 'I wasn't eyeing him up. Just people-watching, that's all.'

I wasn't surprised my rescuer had looked horrified. Sadie — another factory worker — had gone all-out to have a hen night to remember, insisting we all wore matching T-shirts, bearing her name and a rather lewd photograph, while she donned a bridal veil and tiara and hung an L plate over her ample chest. I couldn't imagine who she thought she was fooling. Sadie Black needed no L plate when it came to her nuptials, that was certain.

I hadn't even wanted to attend the stupid hen night. Getting plastered with a bunch of raucous girls in the tackiest pub in the village was hardly my idea of fun. The peppermint penises — or was it penii? — had been the final straw.

I'd refused one at first, as, frankly, I thought them quite disgusting, but then a couple of the girls began to chant at me, and the mob mentality took over, with the others joining in, their voices increasing in volume, until I was so desperate to shut them up that I'd pulled the wrapper off and shoved the offending item in my mouth. The bite had been a reflex action, and I still wasn't sure how I'd managed to choke on the chunk I'd bitten off. It was all a horrible blur of panic and noise, which was probably a good thing, and then blackness had descended.

The next thing I remembered was opening my own eyes to gaze into the dark ones of my saviour. I remembered him reaching out and pushing a strand of my hair away from my forehead, as he murmured, 'It's okay. You'll be fine now,' or words to that effect. Most of all, though, I remembered the feeling he'd invoked in me. All my panic had vanished for that moment. I'd felt…safe. Why, I couldn't say.

Then Sadie's infamous cleavage had loomed into view and ruined everything.

'I didn't really see him properly,' I said regretfully. Some handsome hunk had had his arms around me, and I'd been too busy dying to notice. How typical was that?

'He probably wouldn't have been good enough for you, even if you had,' Olivia said. 'So, no information on the other side, then? No glimpse of heaven?'

I shivered. A glimpse of heaven? For a moment, I'd thought that was exactly where I was.

When I was a kid, my grandparents had bought me a book, retelling the New Testament stories in language that children could understand. And the truth was, when I'd opened my eyes, finally, after returning to the land of the living, I'd thought for a moment that I was looking into the face of Jesus himself. He was just like the pictures in that book — not that I'd been fully aware of him, to be honest. It was more of an impression of raven curls, almost to his shoulders, and a full black beard, but there was something else. What was it?

Frustratingly, it was all a blur, but I remembered a feeling of — what? *Familiarity*. That was it. There was something familiar and reassuring, and so, so beautiful about him. It had felt like coming home.

I mentally shook myself. What was I thinking? Maybe I'd had oxygen deprivation, and it had affected my brain.

'No glimpse of heaven,' I said firmly. 'Just Sadie Black's quivering bosom. Very traumatic.'

Olivia pulled a face. 'How disappointing.' She glanced at her watch and heaved a sigh. 'I'd better be going. I've abandoned my family for long enough.'

'Yeah, you have,' I said, rather grumpily. I'd been through a terrible experience, and where was the sympathy? 'David will be wondering where you are. That Sunday dinner won't cook itself you know.'

'You're ever so ungrateful. I was up half the night, waiting at the A&E for you to be checked over. Don't know why I bother. Anyway,' Olivia added, 'you can mock, but I'm going home to my nice little house, the man who loves me, and three gorgeous kids. You, meanwhile, will be spending the afternoon watching telly with your mother. No offence, Mum.'

'I'm not staying here,' I admitted. 'I only popped round for an hour.'

'Oh?' Mum tutted. 'Well, you could have warned me. When you said you'd be coming round this afternoon, I assumed you'd be staying. I've bought two microwave lamb platters for our dinner. If I'd known you were going out, I could have saved myself three quid.'

I suppressed a shudder. 'As much as it pains me to miss out on such culinary delights, I'm going to visit Great Uncle Charles, so you can save mine and have it yourself during the week.' What a treat for her. Two cardboard-tasting meals in one week.

As Mum and Olivia exchanged knowing glances, I tried to quell my irritation. 'I haven't been for ten days. He's all alone in the world! I can't see either of you offering to visit him.'

'Too right!' Olivia pulled a face. 'I can just about manage Christmas and his birthday. And since it's almost December, I'll have the dubious pleasure of his company soon enough, thanks.'

'Well, then, don't blame me when he leaves me everything in his will,' I said, stung.

'You see?' Mum and Olivia flashed me smug grins. 'Two-faced and materialistic.'

I was about to protest, but bit down on the words. Let them think what they liked.

Besides, I had a feeling they'd regret they weren't a bit more like me, when Great Uncle Charles finally shuffled off the mortal coil.

Chapter 3

Moreton Cross was a large village, nestling comfortably between the Yorkshire coast and Farthingdale Moor. Its dominant feature was the church of All Saints which, as was generally agreed, was surprisingly grand for a village church.

The village also had a primary school, which achieved satisfactory Ofsted reports, a quirky selection of independent shops and cafés, three pubs, and a tiny police station.

Mum and Olivia loved it there, often saying it was the best place to live in the world.

Personally, I thought that was a bit of an exaggeration, but I suppose it had its advantages.

Certainly, it was in a picturesque location, with the glorious coastal towns and villages of Whitby, Scarborough, and Kearton Bay not far away, and the beautiful North Yorkshire Moors on the doorstep. Then there was the pretty market town of Helmston just a short drive away, and, if you wanted to go a bit further afield, it didn't take too long to get to the city sights of York or Harrogate, to the west, or even the less attractive, but highly industrial, Oddborough in the north.

Despite the growing population of commuters in the village, my family both lived and worked in Moreton Cross. Lack of choice and — it had to be said — qualifications meant that most of them gravitated towards the only large employer in the area, Carroll's Confectionery Factory.

Like their parents before them, my parents had worked for Carroll's. Mum and Dad's eyes had met across a conveyor belt of violet creams, and it had been love at first sight. One thing had led to another, and the other had led to me — an unexpected development that had, apparently, been about as welcome as a coffee cream in a box of Carroll's Premium Chocolates.

After they got married, Mum left the factory to prepare for full-time motherhood, but Dad had stayed there, making his humdrum life bearable by having a number of sordid flings with various gullible factory girls — a fact Mum only discovered when he finally cleared off to an unknown destination, eager to escape the wrath of a very angry, and rather well-built, cuckolded husband.

Funnily enough, his departure seemed to give everyone else at the factory the green light to confess to my poor mother that they'd known about his shenanigans for years, but hadn't liked to tell her, what with her having two little kiddies and everything. Mum had reluctantly gone back to work there as a cleaner after he'd left — one of a handful of part-time jobs she was forced to take on, to make ends meet.

Olivia had, like me, gone to college at sixteen, where she'd taken a secretarial course, and she'd briefly worked in an office in Whitby. Motherhood had put a stop to that, though, and when her three boys had all started school, or nursery, she'd taken a job as a production operative at the factory, working alongside her husband, much to my disgust. As if she couldn't find a better job than that!

'It's close to home, and it's easy money,' had been Olivia's response.

'It's boring and mind-numbing,' I said. 'Wild horses wouldn't drag me anywhere near Carroll's.'

Famous last words. Just five months after making that statement, I'd been made redundant from my job at an insurance company, and had grudgingly applied for, and accepted, a job working as PA to Jack Carroll. Late twenties and twinkly-eyed, he was the owner of the whole shebang. He was also happily married with a son, so I didn't have to worry about wandering hands and lewd suggestions, the way I had at my previous job.

Jack didn't talk about his wife and child much, preferring to keep his business and private life separate, but there was a photo of a blonde woman and a young boy on his desk, and I often heard him talking on the phone to one or other of them.

I didn't mind working at Carroll's half as much as I'd expected, which had come as a massive surprise. Maybe the fact that Jack didn't discuss his private life helped. I didn't have to deal with tricky conversations, or stir up painful memories, and that suited me fine. The pay was okay, too. Not exceptional, but enough to cover my rent and bills and have a bit left over to treat myself. God knows, I needed a few treats. Nothing too extravagant — or at least, not half as extravagant as I'd like to be — but enough to keep me going for now, since Great Uncle Charles seemed to be immortal. The rate he was going, he'd outlive me.

He almost had, given my recent brush with death.

As I headed to Fox Lodge, his large Victorian house on the outskirts of the village, I imagined what Mum and Olivia would be thinking of my latest visit. I knew they truly believed I only visited him for his cash, and it was pointless trying to persuade them otherwise. There was more to it than that, though. There really was. He was all I had left of Grandad, and that mattered a lot.

Having said that, Great Uncle Charles had to leave his fortune to someone, and it might just as well be to me, as to some charity or other. Not that he'd leave his money to a charity anyway. He didn't hold with charity. He said it merely gave people an excuse not to help themselves, which just showed what sort of man he was. Personally, I often thought I should get some sort of award for putting up with him. If you asked me, being left his worldly goods in his will was the very least I deserved.

Nearing Fox Lodge, I took a deep breath and readied myself. He really was a curmudgeonly old devil. No wonder he'd never married. Rumour had it that he'd once been involved with someone, but I found that hard to believe. I wasn't sure which was least plausible — him actually managing to love someone, or someone actually loving him.

His house, though, was beautiful. At least, it could have been, with a bit of money and love spent on it. It would be beautiful again, one day. I'd make sure of that, I thought, picturing myself living in its renovated and redecorated rooms. It would be unrecognisable once I'd finished with it, and I'd have all that space to myself. I could finally say goodbye to the poky little flat above the hairdressers, where I currently lived, and move into Fox Lodge.

My family didn't see the attraction. Olivia and I had discussed the matter one evening at her house, over a few too many glasses of wine, when my defences were down.

'Why would you want to live in that big old place?' David had asked me, overhearing our conversation and lowering his newspaper to offer his opinion. 'Nothing but hard work and money down the drain, maintaining something as huge as that.'

'If he does leave it to you,' mused Olivia, 'why don't you sell it and buy a two-bedroomed house on our estate? So much easier to look after, and plenty big enough for you.'

'And no character whatsoever,' I pointed out. 'I can see why it suits you. You haven't got much character, either.'

'We're being serious,' David said. 'Think of the maintenance. Wouldn't you be happier in a new-build?'

'No thanks.' I'd shuddered at the thought. 'Fox Lodge may be a bit too big, but it's got loads of original features, and with a bit of work it will scrub up nicely. These houses aren't at all interesting. Besides, old houses were built to last. Not like this poxy little box. It's probably held together with Blu-Tack.'

'Charming.' Olivia had glanced across at David, who'd rolled his eyes and gone back to his newspaper.

'Anyway,' I said hastily, 'it's all speculation. I doubt Great-Uncle Charles will leave it to me.'

'Well, you've got a lot more chance than I have,' Olivia said cheerfully. 'Looks like I'm doomed to live in this poxy little box held together with Blu-Tack.'

I'd felt a bit mean at that. My sister's house was rather nice, in a chaotic, homely sort of way. It just wasn't to my taste, that was all, although it was infinitely preferable to the shoebox of a flat I rented in the village.

Not that it mattered. Great Uncle Charles was bound to leave me some cash, as well as the house, so I would be able to renovate and redecorate Fox Lodge beautifully. I really didn't mean to sound heartless, but the day surely couldn't be too far off. After all, how old was he now?

Must be nearly ninety, surely? How long could he go on for, for goodness' sake?

Arriving at his home, however, I discovered that, today at least, Great Uncle Charles looked as indestructible as ever. Standing tall and straight, he fixed his beady eyes on me and said, 'Oh, it's you.'

'Lovely to see you, too,' I assured him, handing him the gift I'd called into the local shop to buy.

He looked at it, then looked at me disdainfully. 'What's this?'

'What does it look like?' I said cheerfully. 'You told me the other week that you used to love humbugs when you were younger, but your teeth make it, er, difficult now, to eat them.'

His false teeth were terribly loose, and he refused to wear them half the time, which ensured that his already stern face looked rather screwed up and even more cross than it needed to.

'So? What have humbugs got to do with this?'

'I thought if you liked mint so much, you might enjoy it,' I said.

He glanced down at the bar of chocolate in his hand. 'Carroll's Coolmint Choc Bloc,' he read, then tutted in disgust. 'I don't eat their rubbish. You should know that by now.'

I was determined not to show him how annoyed I felt. Bloody ungrateful old so and so! That chocolate had cost me nearly two quid. 'I remember you saying you didn't like that box of chocolates I bought—'

'I don't like Carroll's chocolate full-stop!' he snapped. 'Worst chocolate ever made. Not to mention all the other rubbish they keep churning out. Surprised the place hasn't gone bankrupt.'

'Why do you hate Carroll's so much?' I'd wondered that before. It wasn't as if he had my reasons. I was the one who should hate the place, but I'd managed to overcome my loathing.

Needs must, and all that.

As far as I knew, Great Uncle Charles had no history with the factory, yet he'd never approved of the family working there, and when I took the job as PA to Jack Carroll, he'd told me I'd ruined my life, which I'd thought was a bit strong. It had taken me an awful lot of soothing and grovelling to get back in his good books again. Even so, I didn't see that he needed to take his inexplicable hatred for the company out on the chocolate. They made good stuff. Well, apart from the LuvRocks crap, which was another story entirely. I wasn't the only employee who thoroughly disapproved of those products, that was certain.

'Because I have taste,' he said, thrusting the chocolate back at me and shuffling down the hallway. 'If you want a cup of tea, put the kettle on. I'll have another, while you're at it.'

Lovely chap, Great Uncle Charles. I shoved the chocolate back in my handbag and stomped into the kitchen. Looked like it was going to be another prickly visit. God, I hated going to see him. Why couldn't he be nice? I'd had glimpses, just now and then, of a different side to his nature. A softness in his eye, a wistfulness in his voice, but it never lasted long, and then I'd go from wondering what on earth had happened to make him so harsh, to thinking what a miserable old sod he was and trying to work out how he could possibly be my grandad's brother.

Grandad Jacobs had been lovely. I'd adored him, and my heart had broken when he died suddenly, when I was just seventeen. Great Uncle Charles hadn't even bothered going to the funeral.

Why did I put up with him? Of course, deep down, I knew the answer to that. He was all I had left of Grandad, and I was sure Grandad wouldn't have wanted me to abandon his older brother. He had no one else, after all.

I scooped tea into the teapot, thinking I'd have to pour his out immediately, so he wouldn't realise I'd gone overboard with the tea rations. It was supposed to be one spoonful of tea only, but since he bought the cheapest tea in the shop, that meagre amount produced a drink that was basically mildly-flavoured hot water. I couldn't bear weak tea, and always sneaked more in than I should.

After making sure to pour his drink first, I let the tea mash for a few minutes before pouring my own. Still not great, but better than it would have been if he'd had his way. I carried the two mugs through to the living room and placed his on the coffee table, then sat down on the sofa opposite his armchair.

'So, how have you been?' I said, determined to keep things light and cheerful.

'Oh, God, you're going to talk to me now, I suppose,' he muttered, putting down his newspaper with a loud sigh and roll of the eyes. 'Let's get it over with, then. I'm fine. Same as always. Much to my own bewilderment, and your frustration, no doubt.'

'What do you mean by that?' I said indignantly.

'Oh, come off it,' he said, shaking his head. He waved his hand around, indicating the living room. 'You can't wait to get your hands on it.'

'I beg your pardon?'

'Fox Lodge. You think I'm going to leave it to you in my will.' He chuckled and shook his head again.

I watched him, annoyed both at his perception, and that he'd dared to voice his thoughts like that. 'That's an awful thing to say,' I said coldly. I took a sip of tea. 'And are you?'

He cackled. 'That's for me to know and you to find out,' he said. 'So, go on then. Let's play the game. How are you? How's the family?'

'Because you really care, of course,' I said sarcastically.

'Not particularly,' he admitted. 'Still, it passes the time, and I doubt you'll let me read my newspaper in peace.'

'Mum's fine,' I said, deciding to play him at his own game. 'She sends her regards.'

'I'll bet she does,' he said, pursing his lips. 'And what about your sister? Dropped any more sprogs?'

I tutted. 'No, she hasn't. She's enjoying her job and has no plans for more children.'

He gave me a sly look. 'Enjoys her job, does she? Remind me again, where does she work?'

I felt my cheeks start to burn. 'You know perfectly well she's working at Carroll's.'

'Of course she is. Tell you what, why don't you tell me someone we know who *isn't* working at Carroll's? Probably be a lot quicker.'

I decided to change the subject. 'I died last night,' I informed him.

That shut the old buzzard up. He narrowed his eyes and peered at me suspiciously. 'What are you on about now?'

'I died,' I repeated smugly. 'You weren't expecting that, were you?'

'Have you been sniffing glue?' he said irritably.

'Don't be so rude,' I said. 'I was out with Olivia and some friends, and I choked. I actually, literally died. I would be in a mortuary now, if it hadn't been for some bloke who rushed over and saved me.'

'Oh, yeah?' He looked unimpressed. 'You look fine to me.'

'Careful,' I warned him, 'that was almost a compliment. You'll be turning my head.'

'Well, honestly,' he said. 'You died! What rubbish. You mean, your vodka went down the wrong way, and he patted you on the back. Proper drama queen, you are.'

'I did not choke on my vodka,' I protested. 'My windpipe was actually blocked by a chunk of penis, I'll have you know.'

I really hadn't meant to say that. I stared at him, and he stared back.

'Huh?'

'I mean, a peppermint penis,' I muttered shamefacedly. 'It was a neighbour's hen party. Things got a bit, er, lewd.'

'A peppermint penis?' He looked disgusted. 'I can't believe there's any such thing.'

I decided I'd rather he turned his disgust on Carroll's than focus it on me, so I piped up with, 'Carroll's makes them. They have a contract with LuvRocks — that's a sex toys company. We're making sticks of rock with rude words running through them, too, and er, other things.'

I thought, on balance, it was better not to mention the chocolate willies on a stick, or the raspberry nipples. Great Uncle Charles could only take so much in one day.

He looked appalled. 'Since when?'

'A few months now,' I said. 'Jack said it's an excellent contract and will help spread our name to a wider customer base.'

'Jack Carroll!' He snorted in disgust. 'He knows nothing. Why would you want to be known for such vile things, anyway?' He shook his head, then his face broke into a twisted smile. 'Mind you, I'd like to see what Edwin Carroll would have thought of that.'

'Was Edwin the one who started the company?' I said, surprised.

'Nah. It was his great-grandfather, Edward, who started it,' he said. 'Edwin — that's Jack

Carroll's grandfather — he took it over when *his* father died.'

'And did you know this Edwin Carroll?'

He glared at me. 'Bit nosy for a cabbage, aren't you? If you must know, he was at school with me, and a proper show-off he was, too. Thought he was something clever, did that one, just 'cos the dads of most of the kids in his class worked for *his* dad. Thought that made him special. Well, it didn't. Nothing special about him. Nothing at all. All he cared about was money and the mighty Carroll name. Everything he had, he got handed to him on a plate. Not like me. I worked for what I had, and I worked damn hard. Sounds to me like this Jack Carroll is as money obsessed as his grandfather. By, for the first time ever, I wish the old devil was around to see what his precious company has sunk to.'

'Well, that's not very nice, is it?' I said. 'Drink your tea before it gets cold.'

He growled but picked up his mug. 'I hope you're not staying long,' he said. 'I have got things to do, you know.'

'Now, come on,' I said, trying to sound light-hearted, even though I wanted to throttle him. 'You know you look forward to me coming here.'

'Only because it amuses me to see you grovelling round me, desperate to get in my good books, so you cop for Fox Lodge and all my worldly goods when I've shook a seven and bailed out.'

'You are horrible, saying things like that,' I said crossly. 'I don't know why I keep coming here.'

'Oh, you know, all right,' he said, and took a sip of his tea. 'Thing is,' he added, smacking his lips together, 'is it all going to be worth it? Will Marley get her reward, I wonder? Or has this old man got something of a shock up his sleeve for her?' He cackled to himself, then stopped. 'How many spoonfuls of tea did you put in the pot?' he demanded.

'Three,' I said crossly.

It was a wonder the shock didn't kill him. What a tragedy that would be.

CHAPTER 4

I was glad to get back to work on the Monday morning. Weekends were never that great, anyway. What with visiting Mum and Olivia, and Great Uncle Charles, I barely had any time to myself. Not that I had anything to do if I'd had any time, come to think of it. I'd spent the last few months painstakingly redecorating the flat, unable to bear the magnolia-painted woodchip a moment longer. Trouble was, with the flat done, I had nothing else to fill my time.

I hated to admit it, but I was bored.

Sitting at my desk in the small room adjoining Jack Carroll's office, I sipped coffee and pondered whether or not to risk a biscuit. It was stupid, and something I would have to get over, but I'd been a bit wary of eating anything since my near-death experience in the pub.

Last night had been punctuated by horrific nightmares, and I'd woken up several times, convinced I couldn't breathe. I'd had to open a window at one point, and lean outside, taking deep breaths of cold, night air to convince myself that I was fine. I couldn't shake the awful realisation that, if I'd choked on something while alone in my flat, I would have died. No one to perform abdominal thrusts on me at home.

Life, I'd suddenly realised, was a fragile thing. For the first time in my life, I'd become aware of my own mortality, and it scared me rigid.

Determined to put it out of my mind, I took another sip of coffee and reached into my top drawer, where I'd stashed a glossy interior design magazine. It always soothed me to flick through its pages, choosing the sort of soft furnishings I'd have in Fox Lodge, and trying to decide whether to go for a modern or traditional look. They were important decisions, after all.

Fox Lodge would be a perfect house. A sanctuary from the world. My home.

I glanced up casually when the door opened, expecting to see Jack's smiling face. Instead, a stranger stood there, examining the pictures on the office walls, hands in pockets, looking relaxed and *proprietary*, somehow, as if he had every right to be there.

'Can I help?'

He turned to face me, and I felt a momentary flutter of appreciation. Very nice. Glossy, raven curls, firm chin with a neat coating of rather sexy stubble, dark eyes...

My mouth dropped open in shock, and the flutter turned into a Mexican wave. 'You!'

'Hello, Marley.' Christopher Carroll looked me up and down, frowning a bit, then said uncertainly, 'How are you feeling?'

How am I feeling? I thought bitterly. *You mean, after you broke my heart? After you trampled all over my life? How dare you even ask me that question?*

'Did you go to the hospital? I did say you ought to get checked out, just to make sure.'

My heart thudded as realisation dawned. Seriously? Of course! No wonder he'd seemed so familiar. How had I not recognised him? But then, he seemed taller and a bit thinner than he used to. His face had hollowed out a little, and there were fine lines around those eyes. As for the hair — it had always been cut short. Those unruly curls had been well and truly tamed at his father's orders, unlike how they looked now, as he stood before me.

Besides, I'd hardly been able to focus at the pub, having nearly choked to death. Bloody hell, and I'd thought he was Jesus! He was the very opposite.

Trying hard to steady myself, I swallowed and, taking a deep breath, said coolly, 'So it was you. *You* saved my life.'

'Oh, you know.' He shrugged. 'It was just lucky that I was in the right place at the right time.'

How could he be so calm? I could barely breathe, and he was just standing there, all cool and unflustered, as if our meeting up again hadn't shaken him at all. Well, there was no way I'd be letting him know how much his sudden reappearance had affected me.

I stood up and held out my hand for him to shake, even though I'd rather have wrapped both hands around his neck and squeezed, very tightly. 'I wanted to thank you, but by the time I realised what had happened, you'd already gone. I didn't recognise you at the time, what with the beard and all that hair.'

He shook my hand, with apparent reluctance, and didn't reply. I hoped he couldn't feel me trembling.

Hastily, I withdrew my hand in case it became obvious, and we stood there for a moment, staring at each other in awkward silence. I realised suddenly that I hadn't asked him what he was doing in my office.

'Are you here to see Jack? He's not arrived yet.' I glanced at the clock on the wall, my eyes narrowing as I realised it was half-past eight. He was late. Not like Jack, at all. 'Perhaps I should call him, tell him you're here. Would you like to take a seat, Christopher?'

He winced. 'Kit, please.'

'Huh?'

'My name. No one calls me Christopher anymore. It's Kit.'

Weird, but it felt like a personal attack on me, on our relationship. He'd always been Christopher to me. It was as if he was warning me that that part of our life was well and truly over, and the past was out of bounds. As if I needed any warning.

Christopher's eyes narrowed suddenly. 'I know this must feel a bit awkward. After all, it's been a long time, hasn't it, since our...' He gave an apologetic smile. 'You know — thing?'

A wave of nausea washed over me. I needed to sit down. Without preamble, I plonked myself into the chair and stared at the monitor. 'Sorry, just need to finish this,' I managed, tapping on the keyboard and producing a string of unintelligible words. 'I was in the middle of something. Don't want to forget it.'

'I haven't offended you, have I?' Christopher said. 'Mentioning it, I mean. Perhaps I shouldn't have. It was so long ago — a teenage romance. I expect you're married or engaged or something by now. You never said, by the way, did I hurt you?'

I felt a brick sitting in my chest. *Had he hurt me? He'd almost destroyed me.*

'I had to use a lot of force, I'm afraid. Whatever it was you were choking on took some shifting.'

'That's okay.' I realised my voice sounded croaky and cleared my throat. 'I got a full check-up. No broken bones. Throat was a bit sore yesterday, and I ached a bit, but I'm fine.'

'Excellent.'

'And no, you haven't offended me. Like you said, it was a teenage romance. Nothing serious. You know.'

'Yes.' He nodded. 'I know. I'm sure we're mature enough to put it all behind us — whatever *it* was.'

I stopped typing and stared at the gobbledegook on the screen. Stabbing the delete button, I said coldly, 'As I said, Jack's not here yet. If you'd like to wait in the office I'm sure he won't be long.' I gave him a smile as frosty as the tone of my voice. No way would I let him know what he'd just done.

'Well, that's where you're wrong, I'm afraid,' he said, opening the door to Jack's room and marching in. 'Jack won't be back for a while. A good, long while.'

'What? What do you mean?' I followed him into the office, watching in irritation as he plonked himself down in Jack's chair. 'What's going on? What are you doing here?'

He looked up, no hint of an apology in his face. 'Jack's in America.'

'America?' I dropped into the seat on the opposite side of the desk and stared at him in astonishment. 'What's he doing there?'

Christopher shrugged. 'He decided to treat his wife and son to a holiday. They've hardly seen anything of him lately, he's been working so hard, and they all thought it was time they spent some quality time together. He'll be away for a couple of months, I'm afraid, but don't worry. I'm in charge, in the meantime.'

'I don't believe you.' I really didn't, either. Jack and I had a good working relationship. If he'd been planning to take time off to go on a jaunt to America — America! I'd always wanted to go there — he would have warned me. He'd have given notice, put things in place. 'He wouldn't just take off like that. He'd have informed me, and we'd have gone over plans for while he was away.'

'Maybe it was on a need-to-know basis.'

Okay, he was really getting on my nerves, sitting there all smug and clever.

'Not being funny,' I said, 'but have you any idea how to run a sweet factory?'

The smug look, I noticed with some satisfaction, disappeared. 'Afraid not. Well, not much. Still, chocolate's in my blood — makes things very messy when I cut myself shaving, I must say, hence the stubble — so I'm sure we'll figure it out as we go along.'

There was no *we* about it. It was his problem. If Jack Carroll hadn't even bothered to tell me he was off on holiday, or that his patronising git of a brother would be stepping in to take over, why should I help *Kit* figure it out?

'I can see you're not impressed,' Christopher said, folding his arms and surveying me through eyes so dark they were almost black. 'Nevertheless, Marley, you're going to have to get used to it. From now on, and for the foreseeable future, you're *my* secretary, okay?'

'PA, actually,' I said haughtily.

He raised an eyebrow. 'First I've heard of it. Now, how about you start by putting those magazines away and making me a strong cup of coffee? I've a feeling I'm going to need it.'

I had a feeling he wasn't the only one. In fact, skip the coffee. Right now, I'd give my right arm for a vodka. A very large vodka.

How the hell was I going to work with Christopher Carroll, when just being in the same room with him was bringing back such terrible memories that all I wanted to do was go home, lock the door, and cry?

***

'I can't believe it,' Olivia said, as we sat in the canteen together, tucking into jacket potatoes topped with cheese. 'Jack's usually so responsible. Fancy him clearing off like that, and to America, of all places.'

'Never mind where he is,' I said.

Although, the fact that it was America was galling, to say the least.

He would, Christopher had assured me, be away for Christmas and New Year, so he would be living the dream. My dream. Christmas in New York!

Christopher hadn't actually said he was in New York, but there was no doubt about it, really. Nobody going to America over Christmas avoids New York, do they? It was sickening. I wondered when I'd get the chance to do something so exciting.

'The point is, he didn't tell *me*. I'm his PA. He's supposed to tell me everything when it comes to this place. How stupid do you think I felt when his snotty brother turned up, all smug and cocky? I should have been informed. It's bloody infuriating.'

'Very irresponsible of him,' Olivia repeated. 'I mean, it's Christmas in six weeks! We're a sweet factory, for goodness sake. We should be cracking on with the Easter eggs.' She giggled. 'If you know what I mean. Mind you, we probably won't bother, unless LuvRocks decides to make naughty Easter eggs.'

'Don't talk to me about LuvRocks products,' I said darkly. 'They nearly killed me. If I so much as have to look at one of their penises again, I'll heave.'

'By heck, what sort of conversation are you two having?' Don, a plump, dark-haired man with a cheery face, plonked a plate of egg and chips on the table and sat down beside me, as David sat next to Olivia. They both had huge grins on their faces. Don nudged me, then picked up his knife and fork. 'I hope you're not going to make me blush.'

'Have you not heard about our Marley's brush with death, Don?' Olivia said.

David laughed. 'Everyone's heard about that,' he said, as Don rolled his eyes. 'It's all round the factory, thanks to Sadie.'

'Heard you were saved by a proper hunk,' Don said, winking at Olivia and David. 'Were it him you were on about, eh?'

Olivia nodded. 'In a manner of speaking, I suppose we were.'

'Give over,' I said. 'We were just on about Jack Carroll, swanning off to America for Christmas and leaving his big-headed, arrogant brother to run things.'

'Ah.' He shook his head and squirted tomato ketchup onto his meal. 'Weird. Still, I suppose everyone's entitled to a break, and when you think about it, Jack hasn't been away at all this year. He's really been putting in the hours, hasn't he?'

'Stop defending him,' I said. 'He had a couple of weeks off, not that long ago. He may not have gone away, but he was still absent from this place. And if he was planning this trip to America, he should have told me. He's supposed to confide in me. I'm his right-hand woman.'

'Get you,' Olivia said, laughing.

'It's not all about you,' David pointed out, annoyingly. 'He never told Don here, either, and as a production manager, you'd have thought he'd have known *something*.'

'So, you knew nothing, Don?' Olivia sounded puzzled. 'This is a bit strange, isn't it? Aren't you annoyed?'

Don scooped some peas onto his fork and shrugged. 'Jack's been looking really tired lately, and he's not his usual self. If he needs a holiday, well, good for him. Come on, he's a nice bloke. There are worse bosses we could have.'

'Tell me about it,' I moaned, thinking of the man upstairs in Jack's office. 'Christopher Carroll, for one.'

Olivia tilted her head to one side, surveying me thoughtfully. 'You didn't always think like that about him.'

Uh-oh. I was kind of hoping she wouldn't remember all that.

'He was in your year at primary school, wasn't he?'

'Was he?' I looked at her innocently. 'I don't really recall him.'

Olivia giggled, telling me she'd remembered, and all too clearly. 'Yes, you do! Little Chrissie! He was your first love!'

'What are you talking about?' David put down the salt pot with a thump, as he and Don exchanged amused glances. 'She went out with Christopher Carroll?'

'Of course not!' I snapped. It was only a half-lie, after all. I really hadn't gone out with him when we were at primary school. Given the way things had turned out, there was no need for Olivia, or anyone else for that matter, to know how our relationship had really started when we were sixteen — naïve, innocent, and totally besotted with each other. It had been a lifetime ago.

'Only 'cos he wasn't interested,' Olivia told her husband, with a treacherous lack of discretion. 'She had a crush on him for two years. Used to sit there in the school hall, practically breaking her neck just for a glimpse of him. She was the only kid in school who looked forward to assembly.'

'What rubbish,' I said.

'It's not rubbish!' Olivia said gleefully. 'Debbie Jones, who was in my class, had a sister in your class, and she told us all about it. Besides, I remember Mum saying how sweet it was that you were so besotted with little Chrissie.'

'Little Chrissie.' David shook his head, laughing. 'I'm sure he'd be thrilled to hear you called him that.'

'I didn't,' I assured him. 'It was Mum's pet name for him, not mine.'

'She probably had hopes of you marrying him and becoming part of the confectionery dynasty,' Olivia said.

'I was nine!' For goodness sake, Olivia really could be ridiculous at times.

'And then,' she continued, 'when you were eleven, he was ripped away from you. You cried for ages when you found out he was going to that posh private school.'

'Public school, actually, and don't exaggerate,' I said, thinking that, when I had a spare moment, I really must plot some terrible revenge on my big-mouthed sister.

'I'm not exaggerating. I remember it clearly. Fancy little Chrissie growing up to be such a hunk. And he saved your life, too! How amazing is that?'

'Saved her life?'

'Oh, yes. Turns out, Christopher Carroll was the hunk in The Blue Lamp.'

'Never!' Don's eyes widened, then he grinned. 'Mouth to mouth, were it?'

'Oh, shut up,' I muttered.

Olivia watched me thoughtfully. 'He was the only boy you ever seemed to genuinely care for. You thought your heart was broken when you had to go up to St Hilda's without him.'

I tutted. 'Honestly, where do you get these stories from?' I demanded. 'He was a cute kid and I liked him, that's all. When he left, I never gave him a second thought. You watch too many chick flicks. Besides, he's calling himself Kit these days. How pretentious is that?'

Olivia eyed me shrewdly. 'Hmm. If you say so.'

My face burned. Did Olivia remember the endless nights I'd sobbed into my pillow, devastated that the boy of my dreams was going away, and I'd never see him again? It had felt like the end of the world at the time, but seriously, I was eleven years old. Opening your packed lunch to find your mother's made you fish paste sandwiches, instead of ham or cheese like your best friend has, can feel like the end of the world at eleven. I should know. Dratted Claire Walker and her doorstep granary sandwiches, crisps, and chocolate biscuits. Made my two slices of white bread and an apple look paltry. Serious packed lunch envy. Every. Single. Day.

David shovelled fried egg and chips into his mouth with indecent haste, while Olivia pushed her plate away and said, 'Suppose we'd better be getting back to it.'

'Give us a chance,' he protested. 'I've only just sat down.'

'That's your own fault,' she told him. 'I saw you both over there, having a laugh with your mates. You should have started your dinner earlier. Now you'll have heartburn all evening, and it serves you right.'

'You're all heart,' he told her, shoving chips into a slice of bread and butter and folding it over to make a bulging sandwich.

I watched, appalled at his slovenly eating habits. Honestly! David was a nice enough bloke, but refined he wasn't.

It occurred to me suddenly that I'd eaten my own jacket potato without worrying about choking to death. Christopher Carroll always could distract me from everything else.

'What are you thinking?' Olivia demanded suddenly.

I blushed. Good job she couldn't read my mind. 'Er, I was just wondering what we should get Mum for Christmas.'

Olivia rolled her eyes. 'Crikey, I don't know. Haven't thought about it, really.' She glanced at David and grinned suddenly. 'I think she just wants something to keep her warm at night.'

'Really?' I said, doubtfully. 'Like an electric blanket, you mean? Not very exciting.'

Olivia rolled her eyes. 'Use your imagination, Marley.'

I stared at them all. Don took a large gulp of tea, while David nudged Olivia and winked at me.

'Are you saying — do you mean, Mum has a bloke?'

Olivia tutted. 'Crikey, Marley, you're a bit behind the times, aren't you?'

'What? You mean she has?' Realising I'd squeaked that last sentence, I tried lowering my tone. 'Since when?'

'Not a bloke, exactly,' Olivia backtracked.

'Well, what, then? A boy?'

'No, I mean, it's not just one bloke.'

My mouth dropped open in shock. 'What the hell are you saying? What's been going on?'

Olivia giggled. 'I didn't mean it like that. She's on a dating website. She's been on a few dates, although I don't think any of them have particularly floated her boat, so to speak.'

'What sort of dating website? Is it reputable? Are these men vetted? She could be meeting anyone.'

She shrugged. 'It's very popular and well-known. Stop fretting.'

'Mum's dating?' My voice sounded faint. I'd had no idea. Mum was just…Mum. 'I didn't know.'

'No, well.' Olivia sounded uncomfortable. 'Have you ever asked her?'

'Why would I? Aren't you worried about her?'

'She's a grown woman, Marley,' David said with a sigh. 'Stop trying to control her life and let her get on with it.'

I glared at him. 'I'm not trying to control her life. I'm just looking out for her, that's all.'

Don patted my arm. ''Course you are, love, and quite right, too. Nowt wrong with that, is there?' he said, nodding at David and Olivia. 'But try not to worry, eh? Your mum seems sensible enough to me. I'm sure she'll be fine.'

Really? I wasn't so sure. She was quite innocent, my mum. I didn't want some loser taking advantage of her. If I was being really honest, though, Mum having some kind of love life again was way overdue. She'd been alone for sixteen years, after all, and she was still an attractive woman. Well, she was only in her late forties. She'd had me when she was just nineteen. Far too young to be a mother, although she'd made a pretty good job of it. Much like Olivia, I supposed, who'd only been twenty-two when she had Sam.

I picked up the salt pot, turning it round and round in my hand, deep in thought. What sort of mother would I have made, I wondered wistfully. I probably wouldn't have been anywhere near as competent as my sister. She had the whole maternal thing nailed, and at least she had David to help her, providing he didn't bail on her, of course. Olivia was adamant that David wasn't the type, and I could see why she'd think that. He was dull as ditch-water, but he was as steady and reliable as they came.

But then, hadn't Dad seemed steady and reliable, too? A proper family man, with a neat little council house, and a job, and a pair of slippers and everything. Appearances could be very deceptive. It worried me sometimes that Olivia was taking a huge gamble, saddling herself with three children, in the belief that she would always have David around to help. What would happen if he woke up one day, and realised he was trapped? That maybe kids and a mortgage weren't his idea of heaven, after all? Could any man really be trusted?

'Perhaps we ought to meet this fella of hers,' I began, but Olivia shook her head. 'Oh, no. We leave this well alone.'

'It's none of our business,' David said firmly.

'But—'

Don gently took the salt pot from my hand. 'Maybe leave it with your Mum, eh? When she's ready, I'm sure she'll tell you. Now, what were you saying about getting her a nice Christmas present?' He smiled brightly at my sister. 'Marley's right, you know. Time you gave it some thought. All mums deserve summat nice.'

'Yeah, all right, Don,' Olivia said grumpily. 'I do know.'

'Well, we should put our heads together,' I said, determined to shake off my worries — at least for now — and concentrate on Christmas. 'Not long 'til the big day, you know. We're on a countdown now.'

'Can we get November out of the way before we even start to think about it?' Olivia moaned. 'Honestly, you and your Christmas countdown.'

'But it's Christmas!' I said, suddenly optimistic. 'It takes a lot of planning, a lot of preparation.'

'Do you think you have to tell us that?' David asked, waving his fork in the air as if to emphasise his point. 'We've got three kids under five. We start hearing about Christmas in September. They've ticked just about every toy in the toy shop catalogue, and every advert on the kids' channel is for some other flipping thing they've decided they want. At least let us have another couple of weeks without giving in to the madness.'

'I love Christmas,' I said dreamily. 'It's such a magical time of year.'

'What, with the birth of Baby Jesus, you mean?' Olivia sounded cynical.

'I was thinking new clothes, presents, and piss-ups,' I admitted.

'Thought as much. The only Christmas spirit you care about is Bailey's Irish Cream,' Olivia said. 'I may take longer to get into the festive mood, but at least when I do, it's for the right reasons. You miss the point of Christmas entirely.'

'I do not!' I said indignantly. 'I love it all, everything about it. Just because you two are old miseries, it isn't going to stop me from starting my countdown right now.' I paused. 'I must make a list tonight. Start planning the colour scheme for Mum's tree this year.'

Olivia shook her head. 'Colour scheme!'

'These things have to be done properly,' I protested, though I suspected I was wasting my breath telling my sister that. Olivia's Christmas tree always looked like an explosion in a tinsel factory — clashing colours, garish lights, homemade decorations, and an angel that appeared to have had a stroke, perching lopsidedly on the top branch. No taste, whatsoever. 'Besides,' I added, because the thought had just occurred to me, 'I should celebrate even more this year. Think about it. I've been given another chance at life. I mean, I *died*.'

'Oh, not that again,' said David with a sigh.

'Thank God for Little Chrissie Carroll,' Olivia said, giggling. 'He brought you back from the dead.'

'Oh, shut up,' I said, but I couldn't deny how galling it was that, of all people, he should be the one to save me. The uncomfortable truth was, as sickened as I was that he'd turned up at the factory and taken over, I owed him. I owed him my life. Infuriating, or what?

CHAPTER 5

Kit was glad to get back to his office and close the door behind him. The sweet smell which pervaded the factory floor was making him feel nauseated — although, if he was being really honest, he didn't think that was the only cause.

He sank into his chair and put his head in his hands. Hell, it was worse than he'd suspected. Touring the factory with one of the foremen, he'd been made very much aware of how many lines were given over entirely to LuvRocks products. So much so, it had been a welcome relief to find a section of the factory that was churning out Carroll's own brand of chocolates, and when he reached the line working on their sticks of seaside rock, he could have wept.

That was the Carroll's Confectionery Factory he remembered. What the hell had gone so wrong?

He wrenched the tie from around his neck, unfastened the top button of his shirt, and loosened his collar. Thank God for that.

Wearing a suit and tie made him feel constricted. He was so used to t-shirts and jeans that he felt awkward and uncomfortable in such formal wear. He'd toyed with the idea of wearing his usual clothes to work but had reluctantly concluded that Carroll's needed him to be the sensible corporate boss. He had a responsibility to the company, and if that meant buttoning himself into a starchy shirt, smart suit and tie, so be it. Right now, though, he needed to breathe.

'Good morning, Mr Carroll.' Colin Henry's voice was surprisingly calm when Kit finally plucked up the courage to ring him. No point putting things off any longer. No doubt he'd been expecting his call.

'Kit.' *How many more times?*

'Kit. So, is it as bad as you feared?'

'Worse. I don't understand how Jack could have been so stupid. They haven't paid us in months. Why keep supplying them? How could he have been so gullible?'

'I think Jack thought he had little option. He was in too deep. Besides, he wasn't the only one, was he? Bayford's are in it up to their neck. Why else do you think they applied for the winding up petition?'

'At least they had the guts to do it. Looks like Jack just turned a blind eye.'

'I suppose he's had other things on his mind.'

'I know, I know.' Kit bit his lip, feeling a wave of guilt. It wasn't Jack's fault. He'd done his best, and Kit should have been there a lot sooner to take the burden from him. If he hadn't been so selfish, maybe things wouldn't have got this bad. 'So, what will happen next?'

'We wait for the court hearing. According to *The Gazette*, it's next week. After that, we'll be in a better position to judge what's really happening.'

'Will it go into administration?'

There was a definite hesitation. 'Depends if there's any hope of salvaging the company. Though, from what my contacts have told me, that seems unlikely. If that's the case, Halliwell & Stephenson's will go into liquidation, and that will be the end of LuvRocks.'

And possibly the end of Carroll's. Kit almost said it out loud but couldn't bring himself to do so.

'We'll talk again,' Colin said. 'In the meantime, I'd get on with Plan B. It's not over until it's over, and Carroll's has been through tough times before.'

After he'd ended the call, Kit stared at his phone, his mind a maelstrom of terrifying thoughts.

He needed a strong coffee.

He strode into Marley's office and headed over to the kettle.

She glanced up, her eyes wide. 'I can make you a drink. You only had to ask.'

'It's fine.' To be truthful, he was glad of the distraction. 'Do you want one?'

She stared at him for a moment, then nodded. 'Thanks. White with—'

'No sugar,' he finished without thinking. His face flooded with colour. Damn! At her arched eyebrow, he muttered, 'I've watched you make enough drinks these last few days.'

He didn't want her to know he remembered even that little detail about her. Not after he'd played it so cool so far. He wasn't sure if she believed him or not, but she said nothing.

Relieved, Kit handed her the coffee and sank down into a chair against the wall.

Marley took a sip of her drink but winced like it had scalded her lips. Placing the mug back on her desk, she asked, 'Something I can help you with?'

'Just been for a tour of the factory floor.'

'I know that. And?'

He hesitated. How could he put it without alarm bells going off in her head? 'I'm not very happy with the way things are going.'

'What do you mean?' She sounded defensive already.

'I think we've given over far too much time, money, and manpower to LuvRocks,' he said carefully. 'Everywhere I turned, they were churning out some of their low-grade products. That's not what Carroll's is about.'

She eyed him steadily for a moment, then shrugged. 'I agree.'

She did? 'You do?' Kit couldn't hide the surprise in his voice. The last thing he'd expected was for Marley, of all people, to agree with him.

'I think they're really tacky, and Carroll's is — *was* — a traditional confectionery company. We should go back to doing what we do best — seaside rock and gifts for all the family, and quality chocolates.'

Kit couldn't have put it better himself. He stared at her, open mouthed, and she tutted and flicked back her chestnut hair, a gleam of amusement in her eyes.

'You look surprised.'

'I am. I thought you'd argue with me, even if you didn't want to,' he admitted.

'Well, you know what thought did,' she said primly. After another sip of coffee, she said, 'So, what are you going to do about it?'

'Ease off the LuvRocks products and up production of the Carroll's stuff,' he said thoughtfully. 'We'll start on the Easter eggs this week. I need to make new contacts and find new customers. Maybe an advertising campaign, too.'

She sighed. 'Jack tried all that,' she pointed out. 'It didn't do much good. You need a new angle. Something different.'

'Like what?' He realised he'd sounded a little snappier than he'd intended. He wasn't Jack. Just because his brother hadn't managed to drum up business, didn't mean Kit couldn't. He loved his brother, but he wasn't like him. Marley, of all people, should know that.

'I'm not sure.' She put down her cup and drummed her fingers on the desk. 'Maybe you should call Gina at Clarke and Howell's? They've worked with us on marketing before. I can get you her number?'

'No thanks.' He stood, cupping his mug in one hand, as he opened the door to his office with the other. 'I can sort this out myself.'

'But clearly we need help,' she began. 'If you're going to up production of our stuff, we need to have someone to sell it to, and that being the case—'

'I'll figure it out,' he assured her, and ignoring the look of frustration on her face, he went back into the office and closed the door behind him.

He could picture her expression right then, as he leaned against the door. She would be angry, scornful no doubt. Another black mark against him.

Oh, well, if he was being honest, what Marley thought of him was the least of his worries.

Kit picked up the bundle of papers on his desk and perused them once again, thinking suddenly that a beer seemed a much better idea than coffee.

Sighing, he picked up the telephone receiver and punched out a number. It took about ten rings before Serafina answered. He'd almost given up on her.

Hearing her voice, he felt a stab of relief. 'Serafina?'

'Kit, darling! I thought you'd vanished off the face of the earth. I take it you went back, then?'

'I did. It's good to hear your voice, sweetheart. Look, you know what we were discussing on the phone the other week? Well, how do you fancy a trip to Yorkshire?'

Chapter 6

The shops were already decorated for Christmas and had been for several weeks. Olivia had agreed to go shopping with me, although it was against her better judgement, as she pointed out several times.

'York?' She put her hands on her hips and glared at me. 'What the heck do we have to go all the way to York for? What's wrong with Helmston or Whitby?'

I rolled my eyes. The trouble with Olivia was that she had no aspirations. There was nothing wrong with Helmston or Whitby, but if you wanted a big day out shopping, where was the fun in heading up the road, when you could head to the beautiful city of York, with its medieval walls and ancient, cobbled streets, and masses of shops all teeming with interesting and exciting things that you just couldn't get locally? Olivia needed to think bigger, a fact I pointed out very forcefully, as I motioned for her to fasten her seatbelt.

'And what's the point of that?' Olivia demanded. 'All a trip to York means is more shops, more choice, more temptation, and more money. It's all right for you. You've only got yourself to worry about. I have responsibilities. Three of them. Four, if you count David.'

'Actually,' I said, 'it's my responsibility to decorate Mum's house, and I have a colour scheme to plan, and loads to think about. This isn't going to be easy you know.'

Olivia rolled her eyes. 'It's Mum's house. Why can't you just leave it to her?'

I started the car, my face grim. 'You know why. Since when does Mum bother with Christmas decorations?'

Olivia didn't reply, and feeling that I'd made my point, I didn't expand on the subject.

We both knew that Mum hadn't so much as put up a Christmas tree since Dad left. For one thing, she'd had no money. She had rent to pay, and even five separate cleaning jobs hadn't left her with any spare cash to spend on luxuries. Worse, she hadn't had the heart for it. All the joy had gone out of Mum when Dad abandoned us. It had taken years for her to get back to anything like the woman she'd been before he betrayed her. Christmas was just a painful reminder of everything she'd lost.

It was only when I'd left college and started earning my own money that the house had been trimmed for the festive season once more. It had made Olivia happy, I was sure, whatever she said to the contrary, and it had given me a sense of achievement and purpose. I'd felt I was helping to put the past behind us all, signalling a new start and fresh hope. I was making our house a home again. Mum hadn't said much, but I knew she appreciated the effort, and had enjoyed seeing the place so cheerfully decorated once more.

In recent years, though, both Mum and Olivia had informed me that I was going over the top with it all, which I felt was a bit unfair. All I was trying to do was add a touch of class to the proceedings. It wasn't my fault that my family were stuck in the seventies and had a tinsel obsession. I, on the other hand, read the interior design magazines, and knew that Christmas decorations had moved on a long way since those days. I was determined not to be left behind. My own flat was too small to hold a decent-sized tree, so the family home was where I really went to town and practised my design skills.

'I suppose, at least, I'll have more hope of getting the kids some of the toys they want,' Olivia said at last, as we left Moreton Cross behind and headed towards York. 'Mind you, they've got no chance of getting everything on their lists. You should see the length of them. Toy adverts are an absolute bugger.'

I laughed. 'That's the point of them. About time Carroll's started upping their advertising budget, if you ask me.'

Olivia glanced at me. 'What do you mean?'

I shrugged. 'Just that, well, it seems to me that we need to be attracting new customers. Jack's kind of put all our eggs in one basket with the LuvRocks contract. Easy money, I suppose. I can understand the attraction, but personally, I think it was a big mistake, and Christopher Carroll evidently agrees with me.'

'He does?' Olivia sounded worried. 'But we're doing okay? The factory, I mean. Things are all right?'

I flashed her a reassuring smile. Probably best not to discuss what Christopher Carroll thought. 'Oh, yes, fine. It's not that. It's simply that…well, do you approve of the LuvRocks stuff? Really?'

Olivia frowned. 'It doesn't bother me much, as long as we're getting paid. I know some of the older ones don't like it though.'

'Understandable. It's hardly tasteful, is it?'

Olivia tutted. 'Trust you to think about that. The thing is, Jack knows what he's doing. This LuvRocks contract must be worth a fortune, since he's thrown so much work at it. Most of our production lines are working on those products now, after all.'

'Exactly. What happened to good old-fashioned seaside rock, and our premium chocolates?' I shook my head. 'I just think he's taken Carroll's down a rather dubious path, that's all. We should be classier than that.'

Olivia's face broke into a grin. 'It's all about class with you, isn't it? You're ever so pretentious, Marley. Sometimes, I think you forget where you came from.'

'It's not about where you come from,' I assured her. 'It's where you end up that counts.'

'And to hell with anyone who gets in your way en route?' Olivia raised an eyebrow.

I tutted and put my foot down on the accelerator.

York was heaving. It took us a while to find a parking space, and then we stood beside the car, deciding where to go first. Our breath hung in the air, and Olivia shivered and pulled her coat tighter.

'It's bloody freezing. Can we grab a coffee before we start?'

'We've only just got here,' I said. 'And we have shopping to do. Coffee is our reward when we've finished.'

Olivia sighed. 'Wish I'd put a thicker jumper on,' she muttered. 'Right, where's the nearest Argos?'

'I have no idea. I'm heading to Rochester's. They do an amazing selection of Christmas decorations.'

Olivia gaped at me. 'Rochester's? Are you kidding me?'

'What's wrong with Rochester's?'

'Nothing, if you've got pots of money to spend, which I haven't. Why don't we find a Pound Shop? Honestly, Marley, if you will insist on changing the Christmas decorations every year, you may as well buy the cheapest ones.'

I could barely believe what I was hearing. 'Have you any idea how tacky that would look? Come on, let's start browsing.'

Seeing Olivia's reluctance, I sighed. 'There's a fabulous coffee shop in Rochester's, too. We could do some shopping, then have a drink. And think how lovely and warm it will be in there, and everything under one roof. Better than trawling the streets in this cold weather, going to different shops.'

Olivia looked highly doubtful. 'I wanted to visit The Shambles,' she protested, referring to an ancient, cobbled street in York that looked like something from a Dickens novel.

'So do I,' I assured her, 'but we can do that after Rochester's. What do you say?'

She hesitated, then nodded. 'Okay, but I shouldn't think I'll be buying anything from there. I can't afford those prices, and I'll bet the toys are twice the price of the ones in Argos.'

Rochester's Department Store was lovely and warm, and Olivia unzipped her coat with obvious relief. Even she, for all her cynicism, could hardly deny that the shop was beautifully and tastefully decorated for the festive season. Best of all, there were no cheesy Christmas songs blaring through the speaker system. I was sick to death of hearing the endless round of festive blasts from the past, although Mum loved them. But then, my mother was a child of the seventies. That sort of music was a comfort blanket to her. Instead, gentle orchestral versions of carols soothed and relaxed me and Olivia, as we browsed the selection of tree ornaments, garlands and lights.

'Oh, I love this,' I said, holding up a beautiful bauble in deep purple, with silver filigree.

'What do you think? Purple and silver this year?'

Olivia shrugged. 'It's as good as any,' she said, then caught sight of the price tag and gasped. 'You're kidding me! For one poxy Christmas bauble? Marley, you're crazy. You can't possibly buy everything from here.'

I was uncomfortably aware that she was right. As tempting as it was to fill a basket with a selection of the beautiful goods on display, my budget simply didn't stretch to it.

'Why don't you just get a few pieces from here, and get the rest from the Pound Shop?' Olivia suggested. 'Honestly, Marley, it's a waste of money otherwise, and you still have all your presents to buy, don't forget.'

I sighed. 'I suppose so.' It felt like admitting defeat, but I *did* have to buy a new outfit for the factory Christmas buffet, and then there was my Christmas Day dress to purchase, too.

One day, I thought with renewed determination, I would buy everything from Rochester's. Fox Lodge would be like something from a Christmas advert when it belonged to me.

I knew for a fact that Great Uncle Charles wouldn't so much as put a sprig of holly up this year. He didn't hold with Christmas, which he referred to as 'a great con trick foisted on a gullible public by the manufacturers of gifts and cards'. He said the same thing about Valentine's day. And birthdays. And any sort of event that encouraged people to buy things, come to that.

I glanced around, noting with envy the well-dressed shoppers who blithely filled their baskets with whatever took their fancy.

One day.

Olivia refused point blank to buy any of her presents from the store. 'I can get twice as much somewhere else. I just can't afford this place. Sorry.'

I was determined to carry on, regardless. I belonged in the shop. It was my sort of place. I selected a handful of beautiful and elegant tree decorations and chose my Christmas cards with care.

Olivia didn't see the point. 'I bought a box of forty cards for three quid at the supermarket the other day,' she said. 'Why are you paying all that for ten?'

'Because they're classy,' I replied. 'Besides, I don't need forty.'

'I don't suppose you do,' Olivia said.

I scowled. 'Shut up. Just because you send a card to the world and his wife. Ooh, look. Jenny Kingston handbags. Aren't they gorgeous?'

Olivia followed as I rushed over to examine a selection of rather beautiful bags, each bearing the gold JK emblem. Above them, a large canvas poster hung on the wall, showing a striking model with a bag over her arm, and the slogan, *Are you a Jenny Kingston girl?*

'I would love to be a Jenny Kingston girl,' I said longingly, stroking the leather of the nearest bag in awe.

Olivia looked deeply unimpressed. 'I'm more a tenner-from-the-market girl,' she admitted. 'I've never paid more than that for a bag in my life, and I don't intend to start now.'

'But look at them,' I said, stunned at her indifference. 'Look at the design, the quality. Oh, I'd love one. They're so gorgeous.' I turned over the price tag and winced. 'Ouch.'

'Exactly,' Olivia said. 'Who'd pay that for a bag?'

'That one's only two hundred and seventy.' I pointed to a smaller one, which bore a *Sale* sign.

'*Only* two hundred and seventy?' Olivia gaped at me. 'Seriously, Marley, what planet are you on? I once bought a pasta salad from Rochester's food department and had to lie down to recover from the trauma. You need to forget all about designer brands and face facts. You just don't earn the sort of money that enables you to live the lifestyle you want. You have to accept that and cut your cloth accordingly.'

I didn't reply. In my mind's eye, I was choosing a bag and paying for it with my new credit card — the credit card I would get when Great Uncle Charles left me everything in his will. How much longer would it be?

I felt myself start to blush. What an awful thing to think. I didn't wish my uncle dead, really I didn't. I hadn't meant that the way it sounded in my mind, but after all, he was so old. It couldn't be much longer, could it? He didn't have much of a life, did he? And I could make so much of a life for myself with the money that he just left to rot in a bank somewhere, gaining no pleasure from it whatsoever. There was nothing wrong with that, was there?

'Come on,' I said reluctantly. 'Let's go and get a coffee. We'll need warming through before we leave here. How far away is this Argos branch?'

CHAPTER 7

Kit knew it was serious when the caller ID flashed up Colin Henry's name. It was Saturday. Why else would Colin be calling him at the weekend?

'Mr Carroll—'

'Kit.' He'd told him every time they'd spoken not to call him Mr Carroll. Mr Carroll was his father, and Kit wasn't his father. He wasn't even Christopher. Not anymore. 'I'm guessing it's not good news?'

There was a heavy sigh. 'I'm afraid not. The liquidators have been appointed.'

'Jesus.' Kit dropped down onto the sofa and stared unseeingly at the painting of his grandfather on the wall. Why, he wondered vaguely, was that still hanging up there? It had been his father's pride and joy, showing Edwin Carroll in full country squire mode, surrounded by sycophants as he held court at Fell House, pipe in hand and trusty Labrador at his heels. Surely, Jack didn't want it in full view? He'd bet a pound to a penny that Amanda resented dusting it. Although, knowing Amanda, it was probably Jack who did the dusting.

'Kit? Are you still there?'

Kit blinked, forcing himself to focus. 'I don't really know what to say,' he admitted. 'I sort of knew this was coming, but even so.' He shook his head. 'How bad is it?'

'As I said, we're talking liquidation, not administration. There's no hope of salvaging it.' 'Bloody hell.'

'I know. Halliwell & Stephenson's are a big company. It's quite sad, really.'

Kit felt sick. That was that then. 'What do I do now?'

'We'll need to register to claim the money we're owed. Do you want me to come over to talk things through?'

On a Saturday? Hell, things really were dire.

'If you like. I'm guessing I'm going to need to contact my solicitor?'

'I'd leave that until Monday. Solicitors come at a hefty price, don't you think? Besides, there's nothing he can do until Monday anyway.'

Kit decided that the painting was definitely going into a cupboard somewhere. His grandfather eyed him with contempt, and he shivered. The sooner it went, the better. 'How bad is this, Colin?'

'You toured the factory. You told me yourself how things were. The main thing, right now, is to keep a cool head and not panic. We have to go over the figures, see how things stand.'

'Is there any chance of recouping our money?'

There was a long silence during which Kit could feel the beads of sweat forming on his upper lip.

'We're way down the list,' came the reply at last. 'There'll be a whole queue of people ahead of Carroll's. I'm sorry, Kit.'

Not half as sorry as he was, Kit thought, putting the phone in his pocket and running a hand through his hair. He removed the offending portrait from the wall. There would be enough people looking at him with accusation in their eyes before long. He didn't need his own grandfather to do the same.

***

'You've got to be kidding me!' I looked around in amazement, absorbing the unexpected sight of my mother's living room in all its festive glory. 'What the hell happened? Have you been visited by the Christmas fairies?'

Mum was sitting at the kitchen table, magnifying mirror in front of her, sweeping mascara onto her lashes in her usual fashion —

mouth open, tongue sticking out. She apparently couldn't concentrate with her mouth shut.

'Don't be sarky,' she called through the open door. 'Thought you'd be pleased, anyway. Saved you a job.'

I pulled a face as I scanned the room, noting with distaste the balloons, the cheap foil garlands, and the dreaded singing snowman that sat cheerily on the sideboard, just waiting for Olivia's kids to arrive and start it up. God, hour upon hour of *Let It Snow*, in that dreadful whiny voice. Last year, I'd been driven to take out the batteries and hide them.

It was the tree that upset me the most, though. Every year, I looked forward to going to Helmston Market and buying a real tree, cut from the local forest on the Kearton estate. I always chose the biggest, bushiest tree in the group and paid for delivery.

The scent of pine would fill Mum's house, evoking memories of childhood Christmases, when Dad had been around to cheer us on as we opened our presents, and was always as surprised as we were to discover what Father Christmas had brought us.

Christmas *was* Dad. He may not have contributed much to buying our gifts, but it was Dad who got excited about the big day; Dad who chose the tree and decorated it. It was a standing joke that we weren't allowed to touch it. He liked it done just so, and we were forced to sit on the sofa, watching him wind fairy lights around the tree's bushy branches unaided. The only contribution we'd been allowed to make was shouting out if something looked lopsided, or out of place. We never minded. It made us laugh how seriously he took it.

Mum used to pull a face when he unwrapped the tacky decorations, blew up the balloons, and stuck Christmas cards all over her walls, but we knew she was just glad to see him smiling. Dad was never happier than at Christmas. For a few brief days, there was a respite from the bad moods and strained atmosphere. Olivia and I didn't hear them row much, but only because Mum never argued back, no matter how much he tried to provoke her. She was always trying to appease him, like she was just grateful to have him at all, no matter how appallingly he behaved.

My spirits sank as I gazed at the six-foot artificial tree before me, with its fake pinecones and sprayed-on snow. Multi-coloured lights winked at me, as if to deliberately taunt me. Where were the tasteful clear LED lights that I'd bought for my mother last year? The ones she'd draped around it, I was sure, were the ones I'd shoved in the loft, hoping never to see again. They even had a button on the control unit; one that, when pressed, sent tacky Christmas music blaring out. You could choose from twenty carols and *popular festive songs*. Popular with whom, I couldn't imagine.

'What's with the tree?' I forced myself to sound calm as I re-entered the kitchen, barely noticing that my mother had begun applying lipstick.

Mum glanced up at me. 'Do you like it? It was on sale in my catalogue. Couldn't resist.'

'What do you mean, you couldn't resist?' I felt bewildered. 'Since when did you bother with a tree? And how come you've decorated the room? That's my job.'

She frowned. 'It shouldn't be, though, should it? You're not upset are you, Marley? I thought you'd be pleased. Saved you all that palaver.'

It was on the tip of my tongue to burst out that I liked all that palaver, but I kept my mouth firmly shut. I knew I was overreacting. What did it matter who decorated the house? The only thing that mattered was that it got decorated, and it was great that Mum had felt inclined to make the effort after so many years.

Yet, I felt a strange sort of panic growing inside me and had to fight it off. It felt as if things were slipping out of my control, which was ridiculous. There was no way I was going to let on how upset it had made me. Instead, I sank into the chair opposite my mother and held up the bag I was carrying. 'You could have told me you planned to do it before I spent all this money on decorations for you.'

Mum blotted her lipstick with tissue paper, then reached over and took the bag. 'Bloody hell, love,' she said, scanning the contents in disbelief, 'how many decs do you think we need? You buy new ones every year! What's the point?'

'I thought it would keep things fresh if we changed the colour scheme every year,' I protested. 'That's why I got you the clear lights. Nice and neutral. Not like those things...' My voice trailed off and I sighed, feeling defeated. 'I don't know what to do with these now.'

'Take them back to the shop,' Mum suggested. 'You could get your money back.'

I wasn't about to go back to York to beg a pound shop for a refund, and I certainly wouldn't show myself up by asking for any such thing in Rochester's, of all places. How common would that look?

'Can't you use them in your flat?' Mum asked hopefully.

I laughed. 'Yeah, right. That place is so small I can only have a two-foot tree on my bookcase. Definitely no room for all these baubles, and I've got some quite large ones, too. I was expecting to decorate a seven-foot real tree, remember?'

Mum looked a bit guilty. 'Sorry, love. I didn't think.'

'No, well.' I suddenly realised that it was Saturday afternoon and she was putting on makeup. 'What are you doing? What's with the slap?'

My mother flushed and acted a bit shifty. 'Going out.'

'Well, obviously. Going out where, though?'

'Helmston.' She checked for lipstick on her teeth, then began to put all her cosmetics back into her makeup bag, finally closing the zip after a bit of a struggle with its bulging contents. 'Meeting a friend.'

'Which friend?' I narrowed my eyes. 'And why are you getting all dolled up?'

'Well, honestly, can't I put a bit of makeup on without facing an inquisition?' Mum tried to sound indignant but came across as defensive.

I folded my arms. 'Are you meeting another bloke?'

'*Another* bloke! Charming. You make me sound like a right tart.' Standing, she collected up the various tissues smeared with lipstick, mascara and foundation, and shoved them in the kitchen bin.

'You know what I mean. Olivia told me you've joined a dating website. Why didn't you mention it? And are you sure it's safe? I mean, you could meet any kind of weirdo on there. Are you meeting one today?'

'What, a weirdo?' Mum grinned. 'I don't think so, no. At least, if he is, he's hidden it well.'

'You've already met him?' My stomach fluttered nervously. 'So, this is a second date?'

'Might be.' She shrugged. 'Or it might be the third, or fourth. What's it to you?'

'There's no need to be rude,' I said sulkily. 'I'm just trying to protect you, that's all.'

Mum's face softened. 'I know, love,' she said, patting me on the shoulder. 'Sorry. Just that, well, it's early days, and I don't want to jinx things. I feel a bit daft, to be honest.'

'Daft?' I detected a distinct discomfort in her eyes. 'What's wrong with him?'

'Nothing's wrong with him!' There was a flush of pink on her cheeks. 'He's, er, a bit younger than me, that's all.'

'How much younger?' I knew my voice was loaded with suspicion. Was the bloke some chancer, preying on vulnerable older women? 'Are you sure he can be trusted?'

'Well, he's hardly after my money, is he?' Mum pointed out. 'And yes, I do trust him. He's ever so nice, Marley. Nice enough for me to remove my details from the dating site, any road. I just think, well, what does a bloke like him want with a woman of my age?'

Reluctantly, I had to admit that she was hardly ancient. 'You're only in your late forties, Mum. How old is he?'

She looked a bit vague. 'Late thirties, or thereabouts.'

'Thereabouts?' I eyed her sternly. 'Don't you know?'

'He's thirty-six,' she snapped. 'Go on, say it. He must be blind.'

'Don't be silly.' In spite of my misgivings, I wanted to reassure my mother, who did actually look rather attractive now that I came to think about it. Her long, auburn hair had been blow-dried, and she sported a smart pair of trousers and a pretty rose-patterned tunic top. 'He'd be lucky to have you.'

I realised what I'd said, and blushed. 'I don't mean *have* you. I know you wouldn't—hell, you haven't, have you?'

Mum looked deeply offended. 'No, I bloody haven't! What do you take me for? Besides, he's a gentleman. He's only kissed me once.'

I tried not to feel nauseated at the thought. 'Where are you going then?'

'Told you. Helmston.'

'Yes, but whereabouts? You can't just be walking around the market all afternoon, surely?' 'We're doing some Christmas shopping, and then we're having our tea at The Fox and Hounds.'

'The Fox and Hounds?' I raised an eyebrow, quite impressed. 'Wow. Classy.'

It was, too. The Fox and Hounds had won awards for its cuisine, and you had to book well in advance to stand a chance of eating there. Whoever this man was, he obviously had taste.

'I know. I'm a bit worried. Will it be full of posh people, do you think? Will I have to know which knife and fork to use?'

'Is this bloke posh then?' I enquired, suddenly hopeful.

'You must be joking!' Mum laughed, clearly at ease again. 'He's just an ordinary bloke, like—'

Her voice broke off, and I looked at her sharply. Had she been about to say *like your dad?* I hoped not, given that my father had been an unreliable, heartless rake. The last thing my mother needed was a repeat performance of her marriage. 'Like…?'

'Like David,' Mum finished, giving me a look that showed she knew exactly what I'd been thinking.

'Not much older than David, either,' I said wryly.

'Oh, don't say that!' Mum looked stricken. 'God, that makes me sound awful. Like some sort of cougar.'

I spluttered with laughter. 'Hardly! Anyway, he's thirty-six, Mum, not nineteen. I'm sure he's capable of resisting your obvious charms, if he wanted to. I don't think his irate mother will turn up on the doorstep, demanding you leave her baby boy alone.' I eyed her curiously. 'Have you met his mother?'

'No. His parents live in Bridlington,' Mum said. 'Nice, normal family, from what I can gather. I know he's got an older sister, but she's living in Wolverhampton, so he doesn't see much of her. At least they all sound decent. Not like your father's weird lot.'

I bit my lip. If my mother was basing her prejudice on my father's actions, and Great Uncle Charles's charming personality, I could hardly defend the Jacobs family, even though I hated the thought that Grandad was being lumped in with them. 'So, when will you be meeting them?' I asked.

'It's early days. No need for all that yet.'

'Yet?' It all sounded quite promising. Or worrying, depending on the viewpoint. 'And when do *we* get to meet him?'

A definite tension filled the air. 'Someday. We'll see how things go,' Mum said eventually.

She glanced at her watch. 'Not to be rude, Marley, but I have to get off.'

I stood up, collecting the bag of baubles. 'Right, well, have a lovely time.' I kissed my mother's cheek, noting the whiff of *Anais, Anais*. Things really must be serious. 'Just be careful. Keep your mobile with you at all times. Any sign of trouble, ring me, okay? And don't let him talk you into doing anything you're not comfortable with.' Ugh! What a thought.

Mum laughed and pushed me gently. 'Shouldn't this be the sort of conversation I have with you? Not the other way round. See you soon. Take care.'

'You, too.' I headed to the front door, then turned and hugged her, feeling quite emotional. 'Have a lovely time, Mum.'

Clearly surprised, Mum nodded. 'Thanks, love.'

I stepped outside, stung at the contrast between the biting cold air and the warmth of my mother's cosy kitchen, and shivered. 'And turn those bloody tree lights off before you go out,' I warned. Horrible cheap tat. It wouldn't surprise me if they went pop at any moment.

CHAPTER 8

Kit ended the phone call and leaned back in his chair, feeling drained. He needed some air. He didn't mind how cold it was. He felt stifled, unable to breathe properly. He pulled on his jacket, grabbed the keys, and left the house, not even sure where he was heading.

He'd been longing to talk to Jack for days, but when it came to it, he'd barely said a word. He'd let his brother ramble on, giving him all his news. How could Kit interrupt him, for God's sake? It wasn't the time to tell Jack that he felt like he was suffocating — that he was drowning in panic. He hadn't felt any better when the call ended, either. If anything, he felt worse. And then he'd felt guilty, which only made things seem even darker.

He walked, head down, barely noticing where he was going. It was only when he almost collided with someone's dog that he looked up and realised he was standing at the top of Bay Street in the neighbouring village of Kearton Bay. Bloody hell, it was freezing. Why was he heading towards the sea, in this weather?

Kit hesitated a moment, then thought that maybe the beach was just the place he needed to be. As a kid, he'd loved visiting the sands. The lapping of the waves, the cry of the seagulls, the salty tang in the air — they'd seemed like the perfect remedy for any problem.

Who knew, maybe it would clear his head, put things in perspective? Maybe things weren't as bad as he imagined. Maybe

Jack would come home soon. Maybe there would be good news all round. Maybe.

Rubbish. He was kidding himself, and he knew it.

'Dire straits' was how Colin had put it. There might just be enough money left to cover January's wages.

He strode down the steep road that led to the beach, his hands buried deep inside his jacket pockets. His breath came out in clouds of steam ahead of him, and he was beginning to wish he'd worn a scarf and gloves.

The street was almost empty, although he could see people huddled inside some of the shops. The fish and chip shop was the only one with its door wide open. The tempting aroma of fried food and vinegar made his nose twitch and his stomach growl, and he realised he hadn't eaten all day.

Ten minutes later, bag of chips in hand, he continued his journey toward the beach, walking down the slipway and stepping onto firm sand. There were a few hardy souls around, which didn't really surprise him. They were a tough bunch round here. He sat on a rock, ignoring the moss and seaweed that adorned it, and tucked into his chips, eyeing a nearby seagull warily. He knew how aggressive they could be, and they loved chips. To his relief, it flew away, clearly tempted by something more accessible.

Glancing around, he remembered childhood holidays spent playing on this very beach. He could almost hear the laughter as he and Jack hunted for crabs in the rock pools, plodded up and down the sands on donkeys, and dunked each other in the rolling sea. Kit shivered at the thought. He wouldn't be going anywhere near the sea today, that was for sure. It looked pretty threatening, and he'd bet it was icy cold.

Maybe, he thought, he'd go into the local pub and have a pint. The ancient white building stood atop the sea wall. The Hare and Moon pub. He remembered it served a good selection of local beers — at least, it had the last time he'd gone in there. Although, that was…what, seven years ago? He remembered the landlady. Very attractive. Very sympathetic to a young man in his early twenties, who'd just lost his father and didn't have the first idea how he felt about that.

She'd straightened him out, somehow. Made him see that he had nothing to feel guilty about.

Yes, he decided he'd go in there for a pint after all. He deserved it.

Finishing his chips, Kit closed his eyes and took a deep breath, filling his lungs with sea air. Even now, he didn't feel any grief over his father. What he did feel, in spite of the voice of common sense telling him he was being an idiot, was a kind of fear: the fear that, somehow, his father knew he'd messed everything up, and that he'd been proved right at last. Christopher Carroll would never amount to anything. He was too soft, too stupid. James Carroll had always insisted that his eldest son wasn't fit to be in charge of the factory, and it seemed his warnings had been justified after all.

Screwing up his chip wrapper, Kit stood and headed back up the slipway, dropping the paper into the nearest bin. It was odd how, during all those years when his father had ranted at him to toughen up, to work harder, to be better, he'd hated the factory with a passion. His one consuming thought had been to get away from it. His hatred for the place had given him the courage he'd needed to defy his father and walk away from his university course, leaving everything — and everyone — behind. When his father died, and his mother swanned off to Italy to live in her swanky new home, he'd been relieved to hand the reins over to a willing Jack and disappear. It had taken a lot for him to come home, to step inside that factory and brush aside the ghosts of his father, and his equally domineering grandfather.

Yet now.... He shivered. Now, the factory was facing disaster. He might actually be the one to lose it, just as his father had predicted, and suddenly all he wanted to do was save it. It wasn't just his future in jeopardy, after all. He could go back to his old life any time he wanted. Funny how that no longer seemed appealing. He would give anything to put things right at Carroll's and give all his employees a secure future.

Trouble was, he couldn't see it happening. Not now. Life was looking pretty bleak from where he was standing. As bleak as the North Sea in December, and that was just about as bleak as it got.

God, he needed a drink.

As he moved towards the steps that led up to the bar, a tall, dark-haired man walked around the corner from King's Row, arm in arm with a woman with pink-streaked hair. Just in front of them ran a little girl, pigtails flying, face bright red, eyes sparkling.

'Slow down, sweetheart,' the man said. 'You'll fall if you're not careful.'

The little girl stopped and pointed up to the pub door. 'Want to see Father Christmas!'

Kit glanced up and saw, for the first time, a notice pinned to the door, advertising a personal appearance by Santa himself, that afternoon. So, Father Christmas enjoyed a pint, too? Interesting.

'Hurry up!'

'All right, all right, we're coming. Give me your hand, while we go up those steps. No, Violet, come back here! Give me your hand now.'

The little girl duly obeyed and took her father's hand, and watching them, Kit felt a sudden lump in his throat.

Turning away, he began walking back up Bay Street. The last thing he wanted was to be surrounded by children. He would find another pub. God knows, there were plenty of them around here. If he wanted to drown his sorrows, he was spoilt for choice.

***

David opened the door, looking bleary-eyed and scruffy, his fair hair sticking up on end as if he'd only just got out of bed. I looked him up and down suspiciously. 'Have I interrupted something?' I said warily. 'You weren't — you know — *busy?*'

He looked incredulous. 'Are you kidding? Chance would be a fine thing. Tommy's been sick all night, so it's been a bit of a bugger, to be honest. We're both knackered. Meanwhile, Tommy's now right as rain and demanding chocolate biscuits, so there you go.' He shook his head and opened the door wider. 'Sorry. Come in.'

I hesitated. 'It's not anything contagious, is it?'

He shrugged. 'Well, Sam and Max are fine, and me and Livvy haven't thrown up, so it's up to you. Take your chance or run, but hurry up and decide, because Liv's just dishing up dinner.'

'Dinner?' I stepped inside, and David closed the door behind them. 'Bit late, isn't it? It's nearly three o'clock.'

'We've been a bit preoccupied.' He tutted. 'All right, we fell asleep. Sue us.'

Olivia was at the cooker, looking harassed. Her brown hair was escaping the confines of its ponytail, and her face was bright red, likely due to the steam pouring from various pans on the hob.

'What are you doing here?' she demanded, not looking at all pleased to see her precious big sister.

'Charming.' I placed the bag containing the Christmas decorations on the table. 'I come bearing gifts.'

'What sort of gifts?' David rummaged in the bag and held up a silver cherub. 'Er, thanks.'

'They're the ones I bought for Mum,' I explained, pulling out a chair, despite Olivia's obvious disapproval. 'You won't believe this, but—'

'She decorated the house yesterday.' Olivia reached into the top cupboard and pulled down a colander. 'Sorry. I meant to phone you.'

'You knew!' I sighed. 'I don't get it. Since when did Mum bother with decorations?'

'Since this new bloke went round last night and helped her do it.'

My eyes widened. 'He did? That explains a lot. Who is he? Have you seen him?'

'Nope. Don't even know his name, do you?'

I realised I hadn't even thought to ask. 'He's thirteen years younger than her, did you know that?'

David grinned. 'Good for her. She's got sixteen years of sex to catch up on, after all.'

'I know how she feels,' Olivia muttered.

David looked appalled. 'I was tired! Give me a break.'

'Oh, please, just stop,' I begged. 'Honestly, what with you and our mother, it's disgusting.'

'Jealous,' Olivia said. 'Are you staying for dinner, or do you have to get off?'

'Talk about hinting.' I rattled the bag. 'You haven't even looked at these.'

'I'm busy. Have you eaten?'

'No,' I admitted, 'but don't go to any trouble for me.'

'I always make too much, anyway,' Olivia assured me. 'Tell you what, you put the kettle on and make us a cuppa, while I dish this lot out, okay?'

I removed my coat and handed it to David, who promptly opened the hallway door and threw it on the stairs.

'You really must get a coat hook,' I rebuked him.

'We have. We've got two, actually. They're in the cupboard under the stairs. The drill's broken.'

Tutting, I switched on the kettle and busied myself making tea, while Olivia dished out shepherd's pie and a rather soggy assortment of vegetables in a haphazard manner. After pouring gravy over the lot, she slammed down the jug and yelled, 'Dinner, boys!'

I winced. 'Do they want juice?'

'Ask them,' was Olivia's retort, as she carried plates over to the table before pulling Tommy's highchair over.

Sam, almost five, with his father's fair hair and blue eyes, peered round the door. His eyes widened when he saw me, and he ran to my side, throwing his arms around me. I stood there, rather nonplussed, then ruffled his hair awkwardly.

'What's wrong with him?' I demanded. Sam was always an affable child, but this was a bit over-the-top.

'Dunno. Hope he's not getting whatever Tommy had,' was David's response.

I stepped hastily away from Sam's clasp. 'You feeling all right, Sam?'

He nodded. 'Auntie Marley, have you bought my Christmas present, yet?'

Ah! It was beginning to make sense. I exchanged knowing glances with David. 'No, not yet. Why?'

'Cos there's this super cool new toy on telly, and I want it.'

'Sam, what have we told you?' Olivia placed the salt and pepper pots on the table and eyed him sternly. 'You've already made your list and it's gone to Santa. Too late for any more additions.'

'But Auntie Marley buys us presents, too,' Sam protested.

'Says who?' demanded David. 'All presents come from Father Christmas. You know that.'

Sam shook his head. 'No, they don't. Auntie Marley told me last year that she paid a fortune for my Spiderman, so I wasn't to break it.'

My cheeks burned. Hell, I had, too. Although, to be fair, I'd got it from Rochester's toy department, and I'd been rather miffed to discover that I could have got it a lot cheaper in the sale at the local supermarket. Even so, how had a kid of Sam's age remembered that? Typical.

'Okay, I do like to buy you a little something, just to top up Father Christmas's gifts. That doesn't mean I'll get you whatever you want, though. Anyway, I don't even know if you're on the naughty or nice list yet. If you're on the naughty list, I'm not allowed to get you anything.'

Sam looked horrified. 'Nothing?'

'Nothing.'

'Who says?'

'Father Christmas,' Olivia said firmly. 'Now sit yourself down and tell your dad what you want to drink, while I fetch Tommy and Max, since no one else seems to have offered.'

'Oops.' David shook his head. 'Bad books again.'

I sighed and placed the bag of Christmas decorations under the table.

As David filled plastic beakers with blackcurrant cordial, Olivia came through, carrying two little blond boys, one resting on each hip.

'Glued to the Disney channel again,' she said, putting Max down next to Sam, and strapping Tommy into the highchair.

'You really shouldn't let them watch so much television,' I reproached her. 'And,' I added, as David placed the beakers on the table, 'they shouldn't drink cordial. I hope it's sugar free.'

Olivia visibly gritted her teeth.

'It's a once-a-day treat,' David assured me. 'Usually, they drink milk, or water.'

'You don't have to explain yourself to her,' Olivia snapped. 'When she's got three kids under five, then she can start lecturing us on good parenting.'

There was an awkward silence, broken only when Max knocked over his drink and let out an anguished wail.

'Oh, for God's sake.' Olivia jumped up and pulled sheets of kitchen roll from the holder on the worktop, frantically mopping up the rapidly expanding pool of blackcurrant.

After lecturing David on his failure to give the younger boys beakers with lids, making Max a replacement drink, and throwing the soggy kitchen roll in the bin, Olivia finally sat down, and the meal began. Personally, I thought the shepherd's pie was a bit dry, and the vegetables were practically puréed, but I decided it would be wiser to say nothing, given the mood my sister was in.

Sam started an argument with Max over cauliflower, of all things, and Tommy hurled mashed potato onto the floor, despite Olivia's valiant attempts to catch it before it landed.

'Told you we should get a dog,' David said, grinning. 'You wouldn't have to worry about mash on the floor if we had a dog.'

'Can we have a dog?' Sam said, eyes wide with excitement.

'Did you put it on your Christmas list?' Olivia asked.

'No.' He looked crestfallen.

'Too late then.' She beamed at him and shovelled sprouts into her mouth.

Sam considered that for a moment, then said, 'But Auntie Marley—'

'Forget it,' I said immediately. 'Maybe remember to put it on your list next year, Sam?'

'He can try,' Olivia said darkly.

I said nothing more as the meal progressed, feeling it was wiser to stay out of the various arguments surrounding Christmas presents, dogs, the lumpiness of the gravy, why Sam couldn't have salt on his meal, and why people had to eat vegetables, even though they were apparently *disgusting* and smelled like dirty socks.

Really, it was like feeding time at the zoo, and I wondered, yet again, at Olivia's ability to cope with it all every day. I just couldn't imagine being able to deal with so much chaos. Maybe it was a good thing motherhood had never happened for me, after all.

As David cleared the more-or-less empty plates away, Olivia leaned back in her chair and gave a sigh. She looked worn out, and I felt a pang of sympathy for her.

'I'll do the dishes,' I promised.

Olivia smiled. 'Thanks, Marley, but no need. David and I decided not to buy presents for each other this year. Instead, we clubbed together and bought a dishwasher. Didn't you notice?'

I hadn't, but then, why would I?

'A dishwasher? Not a very romantic present, is it?'

'That's what you think,' David assured me. 'It's saved a lot of arguments, and it's a real blessing. Who needs a games console, anyway?'

Olivia scowled. 'You said you didn't mind.'

'I don't,' he said quickly. 'I was making the point that I prefer a dishwasher any day.'

'Hmm.' She looked unconvinced, and I didn't blame her. If that wasn't a blatant hint, I don't know what was.

'So, do you want these Christmas decorations or not?' I said, to change the subject. I lifted the bag from under the table and handed it over to my sister, who peered inside dubiously.

'Are they for our tree?' Sam had buried his head in the bag, making his voice sound muffled.

He looked up, his eyes eager. 'Are we putting our tree up tonight, Mum?'

'Definitely not.' Olivia shook her head. 'It's only just December.'

'You said Grandma's got *her* tree up,' he said sulkily.

'So she has, but that's got nothing to do with it.'

'Have you opened your advent calendars today?' I asked, changing the subject yet again. I was finding this family meal extremely stressful. Talk about touchy.

Sam and Max looked at each other and wailed. 'Mum, where's our advent calendar?'

Olivia glared at me. 'We haven't bought them any, yet.'

I stared back. 'Why not?'

'I've been busy. Thanks for that, Marley.'

David rolled his eyes. 'Not having much luck today, are you?'

'Sorry.' I bit my lip. I should have thought, really. I could have bought the advent calendars myself. They were only a couple of quid each, and the boys were my nephews, after all. 'I'll nip to the supermarket tomorrow and drop you some off. Promise.'

The boys looked mollified, and Olivia sighed. 'Okay. Thanks.' She handed the carrier bag back. 'Sorry, but these aren't really our thing. Besides, we've got loads of decs in the loft, and the boys will be making stuff at nursery to stick on the tree, so...'

Feeling a bit huffy, I decided it was time to leave, but the boys begged me to stay, so I ended up sitting with the whole family in their messy living room, watching some weird children's programme on the television. Olivia and David were quite right, I realised. Every commercial break was packed with advertisements for some toy or other. It was shocking really.

Before long, the boys were dragging out the local toy shop catalogue to show me every present they'd selected. Sam had even made his mother write the prices down, along with the catalogue number, just to make things easier for Father Christmas, even though Olivia had assured him that the elves made all the presents, and Santa wasn't given to shopping in Helmston.

It was clear that the eldest two, in particular, were beside themselves with excitement at the rapid approach of Christmas, and I saw Olivia's eyes soften as they babbled on about the forthcoming Nativity play, and Max warbled *Away in a Manger*, which he'd apparently been learning at nursery, while Tommy banged his fist on the catalogue as a musical accompaniment. It was all very charming, but I thought my sister and brother-in-law should hand out complimentary paracetamol to their guests. I definitely felt a headache coming on.

When Olivia wandered into the kitchen to make another drink, I followed her, desperate for a respite from the excitement.

'How do you stand it?' I said, feeling quite awestruck that she wasn't on Prozac.

Olivia unscrewed the lid of a coffee jar. 'You get used to it,' she assured me. 'Sometimes, I want to put on my coat and run, but most of the time I just feel blessed. They're a handful, but I love them to bits. I couldn't be without them.'

'Really?'

Olivia laughed. 'Really. I'm happy, Marley. They're my family. You should try it one day. It's different with your own, honestly.'

I felt a familiar lurching in my chest. *Was* it different, as she'd said? I would never know, would I? I forced myself to sound dismissive. 'No thanks. That's not what I want at all.'

Olivia paused, a spoonful of coffee hovering over the open jar. 'So, what do you want? What's the great plan?'

I shrugged. 'I don't know. Own my own house one day. Go on some decent holidays for a change. Buy a Jenny Kingston handbag.' I grinned, but Olivia didn't grin back.

'Don't you think that's all a bit shallow?'

'I don't see why. At least it's peaceful. I couldn't cope with this racket every day.'

'I think you'd be surprised what you can cope with. Don't you want children? A husband? A real home? I don't mean a show house. I mean, a home.'

'Not really.' I thought about Fox Lodge, and how beautiful I could make it look. I certainly didn't want piles of children's clothes and toys cluttering up the place, the way they cluttered up Olivia's three-bedroomed semi. I'd had a lucky escape in that department.

As for a husband.

A pair of glittering dark eyes flashed into my mind, and I almost gasped at the shock of it. Where the hell had that image come from?

'I'm happy alone. No one to please but myself.'

Olivia sighed and collected milk from the fridge. 'Makes me wonder why you were given a second chance.'

'Second chance?' I blinked. 'You mean, when I—'

'When you died and came back from the dead. Like Lazarus,' Olivia said, not at all overdramatically. 'And to be saved by Kit Carroll, of all people.'

'Christopher,' I corrected her automatically.

'Kit,' she repeated firmly. 'He hates Christopher, as he's mentioned several times. I mean, in films, people only get brought back to life for a reason, don't they?' She shrugged. 'I reckon you were saved for a purpose.'

I nudged her, almost causing the milk to slop over the top of the carton. 'Don't be so daft.

Saved for a purpose! Have you been watching *It's a Wonderful Life* again?'

It was my sister's favourite film, and always made her philosophical and a bit soppy.

'Not yet. You know it's my Christmas Eve treat,' Olivia said. 'But the kids wanted to watch *A Muppet Christmas Carol* this morning, and it did get me thinking.'

I tutted and reached for my mug of coffee. 'You're barmy,' I said. '*A Muppet Christmas Carol*, indeed. Well, when I find my divine purpose, I'll let you know. These Christmas films have such a weird effect on you. I was only dead for a few moments. I'm not a ghost. Nor am I an angel. You'll be calling me Clarence next.'

A tinkling sound filled the air, causing me to stare, open-mouthed at my sister. Olivia giggled and nodded, indicating something behind me, and I spun round, to find Max standing there, holding a little silver bell in his hand.

'Can we keep this one for our tree, Mummy?' he enquired.

I swallowed, as Olivia winked at me.

'If you like, Max,' she said, putting the milk back in the fridge. 'I'm sure we've got room for just one special decoration.'

Turning back to me, she leaned over and whispered in my ear. 'That was a sign, if ever I heard one. Maybe it's time you earned your wings, sis. Told you so.'

CHAPTER 9

I flicked through my glossy magazine, only half concentrating on the television, which I'd switched on to mask the ticking of the clock which hung on my living room wall. It was an old-fashioned sort of clock, I thought. Time to get a new one. I'd seen some rather classy ones in Rochester's, come to think of it.

'Mankind was my business; charity, mercy, forbearance, and benevolence were all my business. The deals of my trade were but a drop of water in the comprehensive ocean of my business.'

I glanced up at the television. *A Christmas Carol.* Again. How many film versions had been made of that book, I wondered. The one showing was a rather obscure one, and I had no interest in it really. Still, it was nice to have something on in the background, and at least it was festive — apart from the fact that it was in black and white, and everyone in it looked thoroughly miserable.

As my eyes grew heavier, I yawned and dropped the magazine to the floor, too tired to read any more. I pulled up a cushion, propping it on the arm of the sofa, and lay down, resting my head on its plump warmth. I ought to have visited Great Uncle Charles. I hadn't seen him all week, and he had no one else. No other visitors. I wondered if he would get me anything for Christmas. Not likely, I supposed. He wasn't one for presents.

It occurred to me that I hadn't asked what he was doing for Christmas dinner. I hoped he wouldn't be alone. I couldn't do anything about it if he was, as I was going to Mum's. I always went to Mum's, as did Olivia and David and the kids, and there was no way my mother would want Great Uncle Charles there. I sincerely doubted he'd accept such an invitation, even in the unlikely event one would be issued.

I closed my eyes. A short nap would do me good. I'd visit him later.

'You fear the world too much .... I have seen your nobler aspirations fall off, one by one, until the master passion, Gain, engrosses you...'

I sat up and rubbed my eyes. How long had I been asleep? My heart was thumping. Vague memories flashed across my mind — images of Great Uncle Charles and my father, and coffins and ghosts, and a tall, hooded figure that said nothing, but merely pointed accusingly at me, until it threw back its hood and revealed a pair of dark eyes that were no longer soft and melting like black treacle, but hard and cold like onyx. Accusing eyes. Scornful eyes.

'It was always said of him that he knew how to keep Christmas well, if any man alive possessed the knowledge. May that be truly said of us, and all of us! And so, as Tiny Tim observed, God bless us, every one!'

I shivered and stared at the television set as the credits rolled. What on earth was that dream about, and why had it left me with an overhang of dread? I was being ridiculous! It was just a nightmare, brought about by falling asleep while watching *A Christmas Carol*, and thinking about Olivia's stupid comments the previous day. I needed to put it all from my mind and pull myself together.

Even so, I couldn't shake the thought that, just maybe, Olivia had a point. It was hard to accept, but as I glanced around my tiny but elegant living room, I realised my life was going nowhere. I'd been treading water for a long time, and things seemed to have come to a grinding halt. Certainly, I had a decent enough job in the factory, and an adequate, if unimpressive, flat in the village, but that was basically it. My social life consisted of visiting my sister and brother-in-law, or my mother. My evenings were mainly spent sitting in the living room, watching some programme or other on the television, to the point I was in danger of becoming a Netflix addict.

If I *had* died that evening in the pub, would anyone have known, or cared?

Well, obviously, my family would have cared, but who else? I had no one, really. I was going nowhere. And that being the case, why had I been given a second chance at life, when good, decent people like Grandad hadn't?

Chewing my lip, I contemplated the possibility that Olivia was right. Had I been saved for a purpose? And if that was true, what purpose? It didn't make sense that I'd been saved just to carry on wasting my time, when Grandad had made the most of every day, yet had had his life snatched away from him so cruelly, and at a comparatively young age, too.

Sighing, I padded to the kitchen and opened the fridge door. Too much thinking and puzzling was making me hungry.

My gaze fell upon the bar of Carroll's Coolmint Choc Bloc, sitting on the shelf where I'd placed it after Great Uncle Charles had rejected it.

It occurred to me, suddenly, that maybe my great uncle was the reason behind my stagnation. I hated to admit it, but I *had* kind of put my life on hold. With the promise of Fox Lodge and Great Uncle Charles's money dangling before my eyes, I hadn't really pushed myself to take a better job or improve life for myself. It was all about waiting. Waiting for an old man to die.

Feeling bitterly ashamed of myself, I closed the fridge door. I would go and see him, as I'd promised myself I would. Not because I wanted anything from him, but because he was family, and he deserved better from me — however much he enjoyed winding me up.

***

As I stood at the gate of the large, red-brick, Victorian detached villa, some half-an-hour later, I eyed the house with a frown.

It was Sunday afternoon, but the curtains at every window of Fox Lodge had been drawn.

After clicking the gate shut after me, I walked down the short drive and tried the front door. Locked. Well, of course it was. I lifted the heavy brass knocker and rapped loudly, then put my ear against the door, listening for sounds of life. Nothing. I opened the letterbox and peered inside. The hallway was dark and gloomy. I swallowed nervously. Oh, God. What if?

Fragments of my dream flashed across my mind. A coffin, an open grave, an accusing hand... 'Uncle Charles?' Silence.

I stood up and rapped frantically again, then I crouched down and pushed open the letterbox.

'Uncle Charles? Are you there?'

In the quiet that followed, I could feel the blood pounding in my ears.

Just as I was wondering if I should call the police, an ambulance, the fire brigade — hell, even the coastguard, if necessary — I heard a faint call from upstairs.

'What did you say?'

'I said, *bugger off.*'

Feeling outraged, I straightened, all my guilt and compassion forgotten. I lifted the door knocker and hammered it loudly against the peeling, green paint of the wooden door.

After a moment or two, I heard a window opening above me, and stepping back I looked up, unsure any longer whether I felt relief or fury on seeing my great uncle leaning out. Judging by the thunderous look on his face, it was fury he was feeling.

'Stop banging that bloody door. My head's thumping.'

'Well, let me in then,' I responded, suddenly noticing that he was wearing pyjamas, and his wispy white hair was uncombed. Most unlike him. 'Are you all right?'

'If I was all right, would I be in bed at this time of the day?' He sneezed, and I frowned up at him.

'Have you got a cold?'

'Give the girl a paper hat,' he said. 'No flies on you, are there?'

'Well, let me in, and I'll make you a nice hot drink and something to eat.'

'I don't need anything to eat.'

'Yes, you do. You have to look after yourself at your age. Bet you haven't even got the heating on, have you?'

'Don't need it on. Got blankets, haven't I?'

'Blankets? I hope you're joking.' I shook my head. Who used blankets nowadays? Was the old goat too tight even to buy a duvet? 'Look, let me in. I'm worried about you.'

'Sure you are. Bet you could hardly contain your disappointment when I opened the window just now. Bet you thought I'd finally croaked it, and all your dreams had come true.'

'Stop it.' I felt a prickling of guilt, remembering my earlier thoughts. 'You're a horrible old man, but you're my great uncle, and you're not well. And you shouldn't be hanging out of the window in this freezing weather when you're full of cold.'

'Oh, bugger off home,' he retorted, then gave way to a fit of coughing. I glared up at him. 'Right, that's it. Let me in, or I'll break the window.'

'You wouldn't dare,' he wheezed.

'Watch me.'

He hesitated, then tutted. 'Round the back. Key's under the plant pot on the step.'

The window slammed shut, and I rushed round to the kitchen door. Moving the terracotta plant pot, I discovered the key lying there, plain as day. Had he never heard of burglars?

After unlocking the door, I hurried into the house and hurried straight upstairs. Great Uncle Charles was sitting in his bed, propped up by pillows, and I was relieved to see he did have a duvet after all.

'You said blankets,' I said, nodding at the bed.

'Blankets, duvet, it's all the same.'

Standing closer to him, I was alarmed to see how unwell he actually looked, and his voice was definitely croaky.

'It's freezing in here.' As I spoke, my breath misted the air, and appalled, I pulled the duvet higher over him. 'I'm putting the heating on.'

'No need for that,' he said. 'I'm in bed, aren't I?'

'I don't care,' I replied. 'The cold air isn't going to help your chest. The heating's going on, and that's that. Now, have you eaten today?'

He leaned back on his pillows and sighed, suddenly looking rather pathetic. 'Not very hungry.'

'I'll make you something,' I said. 'Hungry or not, you need to eat. Keep up your strength. I'll bring you a nice hot drink as well.'

He didn't reply, and I hurried onto the landing, to the airing cupboard, where I knew the boiler was situated. Flicking on the central heating, I waited a moment until I heard the click of the boiler kicking into action and the sound of water gurgling in the radiators, then I headed downstairs and back into the kitchen.

Rummaging around in his cupboards, I was dismayed — although not surprised — to find them mostly bare. It occurred to me that I had no idea if he did his own shopping, or if someone else shopped for him. God, I was a horrible person. I really should make more of an effort with him.

Finding a tin of chicken soup, I decided that would suffice for now. Chicken soup was supposed to be good for ill people, wasn't it? He had half a loaf in a bread bin. Maybe he could manage a couple of slices to dip in his soup. I made him a cup of tea, weak and disgusting, just the way he liked it, put everything on a tray, and carried it upstairs.

For a moment I thought he'd fallen asleep, but as I put down the tray, he opened one eye and said, 'Took your time, didn't you?'

'Yep. I did it on purpose, just to piss you off,' I informed him. 'Can you sit up? Do you need any help?'

'I'm not a bloody invalid.' He was clearly struggling to get comfortable, but I knew that if I offered to help again, he would only snap at me, so I stood patiently waiting. 'All right, I'm up. Are you going to hand me that tray, or do I have to beg?'

I scowled and handed him the tray.

'What's this?'

'Chicken soup and bread, plus a cup of tea, made just the way you like it. Got any complaints, put them in writing, and I'll file them under *who gives a crap*.'

'You're all charm,' he muttered, but lifted his spoon just the same. 'Don't just stand there watching me. If you want to make yourself useful, get me a hanky. Nose is running. Top drawer.'

He nodded over to the ugly, dark chest of drawers on the far wall of his bedroom, and I clamped my mouth shut to prevent the rude retort escaping my lips. He was ill, I reminded myself. He was old, vulnerable. He needed looking after. Or shoving in a home.

I didn't mean that, I thought quickly, and yanked open the drawer, pulling a face at the sight of Great Uncle Charles's underwear neatly folded up. What an awful day it was turning out to be. I reached to the back of the drawer and pulled out a handkerchief, plain white with a navy blue CWJ embroidered in the corner, just in case he forgot his name. As I went to close the drawer, I noticed a silver frame sticking out from underneath the pile of pants.

With curiosity winning out over revulsion, I lifted the underwear to reveal a framed photograph of my grandparents.

Carefully, I removed the photo from the drawer. 'Why don't you put this out on display?'

Uncle Charles paused, the spoon halfway to his mouth. 'Huh? What are you on about now?' He clearly registered what I was holding in my hand, because his face darkened, and he scowled.

'Put that back now.'

'But why? Why have you hidden it away in the drawer?'

'What's the point of looking at it every day? They've gone. They've all gone.' He dropped his spoon back into the bowl, causing chicken soup to splash onto his tray. 'You've put me off this now.'

I carried the photograph over to him. 'It would look lovely here,' I said, placing it carefully on his bedside table.

He glared at me. 'Are you deaf? I said, *put it back.*'

'But he was your brother!'

'*Was.* Not anymore. Gone. Dead, in case you'd forgotten.'

'Of course I haven't forgotten. How could I? I loved Grandad. He was the best man in the world. And Grandma was lovely.'

Great Uncle Charles studied me, silent for a moment, then he sighed. 'They were good people.'

Surprised, I nodded. 'They were.'

'Not like your father. God knows what went wrong there. He was a real shit.'

'I can't argue with you about that.'

He raised an eyebrow. 'Can't you? Makes a change. Pass me that hanky, for God's sake. This soup bowl's filling up more with every minute.'

I hastily handed him the handkerchief. 'Shall I take the soup away?'

'Nah. Waste not, want not,' he said. He blew, quite ferociously, into his hanky, then rubbed his nose rather vigorously, leaving it alarmingly red. 'Got in touch with me a couple of years ago.'

I was so grossed out at the thought of the chicken soup with snot seasoning that I didn't register what he'd said for a moment. 'What? Who did?'

'Your father.' He said it so casually, as if his nephew still lived in the village and popped round every day.

'Dad got in touch with you?'

'That's what I said.'

'But when? Why?'

Annoyingly, Great Uncle Charles chose that moment to break off some bread, dip it several times in the soup, then shove the lot in his mouth. Naturally, he took his time chewing, paying no heed to me as I stared at him impatiently.

'Well?'

He swallowed the bread and smacked his lips together. 'Well, what?'

'You said Dad got in touch with you? What did he want?'

He shrugged, then coughed. I struggled to feel sympathy as I watched his shoulders heaving. Finally, fearing he was never going to stop, I reached over and banged him on the back. As his coughing finally subsided, he glared at me. 'What the hell was that for?'

'I was trying to help.'

'What? By breaking my backbone? Nearly shoved my lungs through my chest.' He took a sip of tea and leaned back against his pillows.

'I'll go to the chemist tomorrow and get you some cough medicine, if you like.'

'Waste of money. Tot of whisky will do the job.'

'So, you were saying?'

'Yep. Tot of whisky. Haven't got any honey. You can buy that, if you're in a generous mood.'

'I mean about my dad! What did he want? He never got in touch with us...' My voice trailed off. He hadn't, had he? At least, he hadn't got in touch with me. Olivia would have told me if she'd heard from him, surely? But what about our mother? Would she have kept it to herself?

'I know what you're thinking,' he said. 'Save yourself the bother. He won't have got in touch with your mother, or anyone else in your family. Nothing in it for him. Unless one of you has won the lottery and kept your trap shut about it to me.'

'Money? He wanted money?'

'What else would he want?' He rubbed his nose with his handkerchief again. 'Cheeky devil had the nerve to turn up on my doorstep, asking for a loan. A loan! Like I'd ever get that back again.'

'What did he need money for?'

'Who knows? Who cares? Some woman, probably. He got nothing from me, I can tell you that much. Told him to sling his hook and get a job. Can't believe he dared show his face around here, after the way he behaved. Your poor grandad was heartbroken. The shame of it. Said he was glad your gran hadn't lived to see it. Mind you, your mother didn't make things any easier, blaming your grandad like that. As if he could be held responsible for what his son did. Your father was a grown man. Disgusting.'

'She was devastated when Dad left,' I murmured. 'In shock. She was looking for someone to blame.'

'And turned her back on a good man, who had no one left in the world! How was that fair?'

It hadn't been, and I knew it, but I didn't want to be disloyal to Mum, even though having to keep my relationship with my grandfather secret had seemed desperately unfair at the time.

Grandad hadn't really got on with Dad, and family visits to my grandparents' house had always felt forced and rather strained. After Nan died, my parents rarely took me round to see him at all, and when Dad left, Mum cut all ties with his family, and expected us to do the same.

Olivia hadn't seemed bothered. She'd not formed the bond with Grandad that I had, somehow, always being keener on Mum's side of the family, who lived in Whitby. Without even thinking about it, I'd kept my visits to Grandad a secret.

'Did he say where he was living? Dad, I mean.'

Great Uncle Charles sucked in his cheeks, as if he'd just drunk vinegar. 'No,' he said eventually, 'and why would you care?'

'He's my dad.'

'*Was* your dad. May as well be dead now. As dead as your grandad.'

'Thanks.'

'No point sugar-coating things. Everyone goes in the end. Everyone leaves.'

'Except you, clearly.'

'I hang on just to spite people,' he admitted. 'Mind you, the way I'm feeling right now, this might be your lucky day.'

'Don't say that,' I protested. 'You're awful to think like that.'

'Am I?' He eyed me knowingly. 'So, you're not just waiting for me to pop off, eh? Like your father.'

'My father?'

'Well, he's next in line, isn't he? Said as much when he visited. Reckoned he'd got it all worked out. He thought it would all come to him, anyway, so why shouldn't I give him an advance?'

I gasped, appalled. 'He said that?'

'As good as.' Great Uncle Charles settled back on his pillows, a smug look on his face. 'Soon put him straight, though. Told him I'd changed my will when he buggered off, and there was no way he was getting a penny. Quite glad he went. Never liked him. Gave me a good excuse.'

'Well, I'm so glad things worked out for you,' I said angrily. 'Never mind what we went through. What Mum went through.'

'Your mother was a fool. If she'd opened her eyes, she'd have seen what he was from the start. He was always the same. Sly, devious. Must have got it from your grandma's side.'

'Oh, my God! How can you say that?' Anger flashed through me at him being rude about Grandma. She'd been a lovely lady. Great Uncle Charles was a devil.

'Don't take it personally. Nothing against your grandma. Just that genes will out, and there was no one as rotten as your dad in the Jacobs family.'

'What were you? Adopted?'

'That,' he said, wagging his finger at me, 'was extremely rude.'

'You shouldn't insult Grandma, then. Is there anyone you actually like?'

'Not really. Not anymore.' He sighed. 'All gone. Everyone I ever cared about. Dead.'

Noticing the sudden look of sadness in his eyes and the wistful tone in his voice, I tried hard not to feel offended. It must have been hard to be alone. To lose his parents, and his brother.

'You still have me,' I pointed out. 'And you'd have Olivia and Mum, too, if you were a bit nicer.'

'I wouldn't even have you, if you didn't want this place,' he snapped, all wistfulness vanishing. 'I don't need you. I don't need anyone. I'm better off alone.'

I watched him crossly. He really was an old miser. Just like Ebenezer Scrooge. I felt goose pimples breaking out on my arms at that thought. 'You know the other week, when I said I'd died?'

He stared at me. 'What of it?'

'Olivia thinks I was brought back to life for a reason.'

He rolled his eyes. 'She would. One sandwich short of a picnic, that girl. Why else would she have three kids in three years?'

'Stop being nasty for just one second. My point is, I was trying to figure out my purpose — the reason I was saved.'

'Saved?' He cackled. 'Bloody hell, talk about delusional.'

'I was saved,' I continued firmly, 'for you. I think I have to make you see the error of your ways.'

For a moment, he simply gaped at me. Then he burst out laughing, which led to a prolonged, and rather alarming, bout of coughing. When he'd finally finished, he wiped his mouth with his handkerchief and shook his head. 'You're completely cracked. So, you're some sort of angel, are you? You know who you put me in mind of?'

I bit my lip. I had a feeling that whoever it was, it wouldn't be anyone nice.

'My cousin Sis.'

'Sis?'

'Christine, her name was, but we called her Sistine after the Sistine Chapel, which is nearly as holy as she was. She was a nut-job, too, just like you. Had a near miss with a Bourbon biscuit in nineteen-sixty-four and found God. Poor bugger clearly wasn't hiding from her well enough. After that, she thought her mission in life was to convert us all to her beliefs.'

'What *were* her beliefs?'

'Basically, she believed in anything that made you bloody miserable.'

'I'd have thought you'd have converted immediately. Sounds like a religion tailor-made for you.'

His eyes narrowed. 'You think I'm miserable?'

I spluttered with laughter. 'Are you kidding?'

'You should be flattering me. You'll never get anything from me at this rate.'

'Ah, so you *do* intend to leave me something in your will?'

'I do. I've left you my handkerchief collection. Then you'll have something to cry into when you discover you're going to be skint all your life.'

My heart sank. 'Why can't you just tell me?'

'Because where's the fun in that? I may have left you everything. I may have left you my handkerchief collection. I may not have mentioned you at all. Ooh, exciting, isn't it?'

'You're absolutely awful. I can't think why I imagined I was here to save you. You're beyond saving. You'll never get to heaven at this rate.'

'Stuff heaven,' he said, picking up his mug of tea. 'I'm off to Hell. At least I won't have to pay the heating bill. Take my advice, if you really are barmy enough to believe that you were brought back to life in order to save someone, look elsewhere.' He smirked at me. 'Someone, somewhere, needs your help. Who can it be? The suspense is killing me. But not fast enough, eh?'

I looked away from his smug face, too annoyed to answer. If I *had* been given another chance, it wasn't for Great Uncle Charles's sake, he was right about that. But, if not him, who?

A little voice popped into my head. Olivia's voice. Olivia's annoying, over-dramatic, watched-far-too-many-Christmas-films voice. *And to be saved by Kit Carroll, of all people.*

If Christopher was my reason for being brought back from the dead, my debt to the universe would just have to go unpaid. Besides, what did someone like Christopher need me for? He'd never needed me before, had he? Far from it. Why should anything be different now?

CHAPTER 10

Christmas, it seemed, had arrived at Carroll's Confectionery Factory. As I entered the building that morning, there was a cheerful buzz in the air, and an atmosphere of growing excitement and festive jollity.

The joys of the season seemed to have bypassed Christopher Carroll's office, however. He was in a vile mood, and the morning passed far too slowly for my liking.

As I walked into the canteen that lunchtime, it felt like another world. Cheesy Christmas songs blasted out from the kitchen, and people were singing along as they queued to be served.

One or two people even wore Santa hats, one of them being Don.

'All right, Marley?' he said, grinning widely at me, as I wandered over to stand behind him, tray in hand. 'Soon be Christmas.'

'Still three weeks to go,' I pointed out. 'What on earth are you wearing?'

'Me Father Christmas hat. Do you like it?'

'No. You look a right tosspot.' I glanced around. 'Everyone seems to be in a good mood.'

'Well, a lot of them were out at the weekend, at Sadie's wedding, and had a right good time of it. Talking about what they got up to always cheers them up.'

'Hmm.'

I thought, on balance, it was no wonder I wasn't feeling the festive love. What with my mother's secret date, the disastrous lunch at Olivia's, a bag of expensive baubles no one wanted, and my less-than-successful visit to Great Uncle Charles, it hadn't been much of a weekend.

I did need to pop by Fox Lodge when I left work, though, and make sure that he was all right. He was an awful man, but he was still a human being who needed looking after, whether he wanted to be looked after or not.

'Did you go to the wedding then?' I asked him. It rankled that I hadn't been invited. I knew Olivia and David had been asked to the evening do, although they'd declined, admitting to me that neither of them had the energy. At least they'd had the option, though.

Wild horses wouldn't have dragged me near Sadie Black's wedding, but it would have been nice to be given the chance to refuse. I rarely got invited anywhere by the women at the factory to be honest. Not that it bothered me. They were nearly all married, or engaged, or living with someone, and most of them had kids. I didn't want to hear about their kids. They were more Olivia's type of people than mine.

'No. Had other fish to fry,' he said. 'Had a cracking weekend, me. You don't look too happy, though. What's up?'

'Nothing. Family stuff.'

'Ah. Family stuff.' He nodded. 'That'll do it, every time.' He smiled and nudged me. 'Cheer up, kid. Things are never as black as they're painted.'

'That's all you know.' I sighed. 'Found something out this weekend, and it upset me.'

Why had I said that? I certainly hadn't meant to. I hadn't even realised it was still bothering me.

'Oh, aye? And what's that?' There was a sympathetic tone to his voice, and I trusted Don as much as I trusted anyone, and more than I trusted most. He was a decent, straight-talking sort of fella.

Besides, who else would I confide in?

'My dad got in touch with my great-uncle.'

His smile disappeared. 'Your dad? When?'

'Oh, a couple of years ago,' I said hastily.

He looked baffled. 'So...?'

'So, nothing really,' I admitted. 'It just threw me, that's all. I mean, we haven't heard from him for sixteen years, but he went to see Uncle Charles, asking for money. He never bothered to get in touch with any of us. At least, I don't think he did. Mum never said, and I'm sure she

would have. But can you imagine how she'd feel, if she knew that?' He stayed quiet, chewing his lip.

'How could he do that? How could he come to our village and not contact any of us? We don't mean anything to him at all, do we?'

He sighed and put his arm around me. 'Sorry, Marley. This is shit. He doesn't deserve you. He doesn't deserve any of you.'

'No, well. You won't say anything to David or Olivia, will you? I don't see any point in upsetting things.'

'No, no. 'Course not. I don't see why your uncle had to tell you, to be honest. Just upset you for nowt really.'

'Yeah, well, he has to take his pleasure where he can find it these days,' I said grimly.

We each ordered lunch and carried our trays over to a table in the corner.

'He's not well at the moment,' I told him, as we sat down. 'Uncle Charles, I mean. I went round to his house yesterday, and he was quite poorly. In bed, actually. I'm going again after work, to give him some tea and to make sure he's okay.'

'That's nice of you,' Don said, though he eyed me curiously. 'I gather you're the only one who visits him. Is that right?'

I flushed a little, all too aware what he'd be thinking. 'Yeah. Well, he's got no one else. If I didn't go, he'd be all alone.'

'Hmm.' He dipped a slice of bread and butter into his baked beans and chewed thoughtfully. 'Not a nice man, from what I've heard, though.'

'Not really.' I shrugged. 'He spends all his time pointing out that I'm still single and childless, while Olivia's happily married with kids. As if that's all that matters! And he can talk, for God's sake. He's still family, though.' I hesitated, then gave a self-conscious laugh. 'I thought maybe he was the one I had to save. I'm pretty sure now that I was wrong.'

He blinked. 'Save? What do you mean, *save?*'

Blushing, I told him of my recent conversation with Olivia. 'So, I thought, I mean, I think, that I was given another chance for a reason. You know. A purpose.'

'You don't just think that's...' Don paused, as if searching for the right word.

'Unlikely?'

'Bollocks.'

'Oh, well.' Nonplussed, I took a gulp of tea while considering the matter. 'Maybe it is. Maybe it isn't.'

'You're not serious?' Don laughed. 'Liv's got a vivid imagination, that's all I can say. Either that, or she's winding you up. Come on! You had an accident, and luckily for you, someone was around to save you. Doesn't mean you have to pay the universe back by saving someone else.'

'Suppose not.' I sighed. 'You may be right. It's just that I had this dream afterwards, too, and it all seemed to be pointing me in that direction.'

'Oh, well, if you dreamed it, it must be true.' Don's eyes glittered with amusement. 'Mind you, it may not be out of the question, after all. This *is* the season of miracles, and I mean, think about it. Who saved *you*, eh?'

I frowned. 'You know very well. What's that got to do with it?'

'Well, maybe that has everything to do with it. Maybe Kit Carroll is the reason you were saved.'

'What?' No way in hell would I admit that the same thought had crossed my mind. That would make it all far too real. 'You're crackers. Eat your chop.'

He winked at me, so I wasn't sure if he was serious or not.

'Where's David?' I asked, deciding to change the subject. I glanced around the busy canteen.

'And Olivia, come to that.'

'David's got a dental check-up. He needed Liv to hold his hand,' Don said while digging his knife and fork into a juicy pork chop.

I rolled my eyes. 'Why doesn't that surprise me?'

'So,' Don said, after swallowing a forkful of chips, all smothered in tomato sauce, 'not feeling the Christmas spirit, eh?'

'Would you?' I tried hard not to pull a face on noticing a splodge of ketchup at the corner of Don's lip. 'I've got a bagful of Christmas baubles that no one wants, a poky flat that means I can't have a tree bigger than a pot plant, and a great uncle who needs me to take care of him but makes me feel about as welcome as a chocolate gateau at a Lightweights meeting.'

'I should think a chocolate gateau would be very welcome at a Lightweights meeting,' Don said. 'All them dieters would gnaw your arm off for a slice of cake.'

'You know what I mean.' I sighed. 'And then there's this place. Him.' I cast my eyes toward the ceiling, as if Christopher Carroll was hovering above us, somewhere around the garish fluorescent light.

'Who? God?'

'In his opinion, maybe. Christopher Carroll, of course. Big boss man.'

'Ooh. What's he done now?'

'You mean apart from turn up unannounced and unwanted? He's been in a right mood all day. Talk about miserable. You want the Christmas spirit? Don't go looking in that office, that's all I can say.'

'Things tense up there, are they?'

'He's bossy and arrogant, and he's been snapping my head off all morning.' I pushed my plate away, not feeling hungry. 'I'm fed up.'

'Things will get better,' Don soothed. 'He's just finding his feet. Imagine how it feels for him, having to step into Jack's shoes and carry the burden of this place on his own.'

'Should have made Jack stay then, shouldn't he?' I snapped. 'And Jack's another one that's annoyed me. How could he do that? Just walk away without telling me, without warning...'

My eyes filled with tears, and Don reached over and squeezed my hand.

'Strikes me that this is more about your dad, love. Still hurting, eh? After all this time.'

'Don't be ridiculous,' I said, tucking my hair behind my ears and sitting up straight. 'Why would I miss someone who's a total arsehole?' I shook my head. 'Men are all shits.'

'Charming,' Don said. 'I'll try not to take offence.'

'Well, not you, obviously. You're all right.'

'Cheers.'

'And my grandad was lovely, too.'

'And David.'

'Yeah, I guess David's nice enough.'

'And Jack's a decent bloke. I know he left without warning, but everyone's entitled to a break, and he must have felt he needed it.'

I half-laughed. 'Okay, okay, Jack's all right, too.'

'And Kit's done the decent thing, turning up and stepping into the breach like that,' he pointed out, his eyes twinkling.

I shook my head. 'Oh, no. You've gone too far with that one. I will *never* say that.'

A commotion broke out at the counter, interrupting the conversation, and turning that way, I took in the unlikely sight of Christopher himself, standing by the counter. He was arguing with Liz, one of the canteen ladies, who had paused in her task of serving chips to a couple of men in the queue.

Don frowned. 'What's to do? Hang on a minute, love.'

He stood and hurried over, and after a moment's hesitation, I thought *sod it*, and hurried after him.

'It's Christmas, for God's sake,' one man was saying, sounding quite annoyed. 'You can't be serious.'

'Jack never had a problem with it,' Liz said, her face red, whether with embarrassment or anger I couldn't be sure. 'Nothing wrong with a bit of Christmas music is there?'

She looked appealingly at everyone in the queue, and they all shook their heads and murmured words to the effect that it cheered everyone up and Kit was just being mean.

'All right, folks,' Don soothed, 'let's calm it down, shall we? What's the problem?'

'It's him,' said the man, nodding at Kit. 'Throwing his weight around.'

'I'm sure we can sort it out, whatever the problem is,' Don said. 'Come on, lads, it's nearly Christmas.'

'That's our point,' said Liz. 'It's December. Why shouldn't I bring my *Now That's What I Call Christmas* CD in to play? Cheers everyone up, doesn't it? Puts them all in the mood for it.'

'For God's sake, we've got over three weeks to go,' Christopher snapped. 'You'll be sick of hearing it in a few days. Besides, I can't hear myself think in here.'

'Don't need to, do we?' A factory worker that I vaguely knew glared at him. 'This is our place for recreation. We come here to eat and chat and, yes, to listen to music. If we choose to listen to Christmas songs, that's our business. We do our work, and this doesn't interfere with that, so I don't see what your problem is.'

'My problem,' Christopher snapped, 'is that I want to talk to you all, and I don't intend to compete with bloody Shakin' Stevens to do so.'

Liz tutted. 'Well, you only had to say.' She reached over and switched off the CD player.

A heavy silence descended as everyone stared resentfully at our boss.

I felt uncomfortable. Why had he been so confrontational? He'd only had to ask Liz to turn the music off while he made his announcement. Why did he have to be so high-handed all the time? No wonder he got everyone's back up.

Watching him intently, I noticed that he looked as awkward as I felt. What was all it about?

'I just wanted to say...' Christopher's voice trailed off as he looked around, then he straightened and said, rather defiantly, 'I just wanted to inform you that we will be stopping production of all LuvRocks products, with immediate effect.'

There were gasps as people exchanged incredulous glances.

'We'll be increasing production of our own brands from this point onwards. I'll be calling a meeting with some of you this afternoon, during which I'll outline my plans for where we go from here.'

'But the LuvRocks contract is massive,' protested one man. 'We can't just chuck it out of the window.'

'I can do what I like,' Christopher reminded him. 'In my opinion, the LuvRocks brand was never something Carroll's should have been associated with. It's time to return to the good old-fashioned, high-quality products we were once renowned for.'

'Just 'cos you don't like the LuvRocks stuff, doesn't mean you should ditch it,' said another factory worker angrily. 'That contract's worth a fortune. You're putting all our jobs at risk.'

'I can assure you I'm doing what I think is best for the company,' Christopher said coldly. 'And may I remind you that *I'm* in charge here, and I make the decisions. This isn't up for discussion. This is what's happening. That's all I have to say.' He turned to Liz, who stood there with her mouth wide open. 'You can play your precious Christmas music now. Enjoy.'

He walked out of the canteen without a backward glance, leaving everyone staring after him. As soon as he'd gone, an outburst of indignant cries began, as people digested the huge difference the changes would make to the company and debated whether Kit Carroll actually had the right to effectively tear up the contract that Jack had worked so hard to obtain.

Don and I returned to our seats. 'Well,' Don said, shaking his head, 'there's a turn up for the books.'

'He's crazy,' I said, bewildered. 'I mean, I hate that contract, too. LuvRocks has no class, but it pays the wages. For him to just turn his back on it is financial suicide. What the hell is he playing at?'

'Dodgy move,' Don admitted. 'Could go pear-shaped, and then Jack won't be happy.'

'He'll be furious. I mean, does Christopher even have the authority to go above Jack's head like that?'

'Must have. Wouldn't have done it, otherwise. That's a lot of power to suddenly be handed out of the blue.' Don chewed his chop thoughtfully. 'Reckon he may be feeling the pressure.'

I remembered the look in Christopher's eyes as he started to make his announcement. Had I been imagining it, or had he looked really pensive at first? He had such a lot of responsibility, and so little experience. It must be terrifying for him.

Growing aware that Don was watching me intently, I flushed. 'Still think he's making a mistake,' I muttered, stabbing my jacket potato like it was to blame for it all.

'Seems like he has some problems,' Don mused. 'He's not a happy bunny, is he? I dunno, Marley. I reckon Liv might have been onto something after all. Strikes me, maybe you really are here to save Kit Carroll.'

I almost choked on the piece of tuna I was eating and clutched the table in panic. God, not again! I took a deep breath and steadied myself. 'What the hell are you talking about?'

'Think about it. Who seems the most stressed out of everyone you know? Who's the one person who definitely has no Christmas spirit? Who's been thrown into a life he's not prepared for? Who seems completely out of his depth? Who was it who saved you in the first place?' He sat back and folded his arms, grinning at me. 'And,' he added, 'it was a LuvRocks penis you choked on. Fate.' He picked up his knife and fork again and beamed at me. 'That's what it is. Telling you, girl. Reckon you're here to save Kit Carroll. There's your mission. Best get to it.'

I couldn't think of a reply to that. The last person in the world I'd try to help was that man, even if he did have beautiful eyes, the most divine dark curls, and a voice that could melt ice.

After everything Christopher had done to me, I would rather die than save him, whether he'd saved my life or not.

***

Kit heard Marley's door open, and to his annoyance, his stomach flipped. He'd seen her face when he made his little announcement in the canteen, and knowing Marley, she wouldn't think twice about telling him what she thought of him.

He waited, fingers tapping on the desk. When his own door didn't open, he realised he'd been holding his breath and exhaled slowly. Frowning, he fiddled with a pen, wondering what she was playing at. No reaction? Seriously?

He realised suddenly that he was experiencing a stab of disappointment, and stood up, angry with himself. It was none of Marley's business what he did, and why should he care whether she had an opinion or not anyway?

He rubbed his forehead, staring out of the window at the car park below him. A little blue Corsa caught his eye. It was Marley's. No flash sports car for her, after all. He wouldn't have thought such an ordinary car would have been her style. Come to think of it, shouldn't a little princess arrive by horse and carriage? He'd watched her drive up in the Corsa many times since his return. She had a small, plastic Smurf dangling from her mirror. He even knew the registration number, he realised with a start. God, that was worrying.

The clock on the wall ticked relentlessly on, and Kit cursed under his breath. It was no good. He had to get it over and done with. Determined not to betray his nerves, he threw open the office door and peered round at Marley.

Sitting there typing, she seemed oblivious to his presence, but he knew for a fact that she couldn't have missed the sound of the door opening. So, she was ignoring him, giving him the silent treatment. How childish was that?

'Can you make me a coffee, please?' He could get his own coffee. He usually did in fact, but he was determined to remind her who was boss.

Marley didn't even look at him. 'Won't be a minute. I'll just finish this.' She carried on typing for what seemed like forever, until his nerves jangled.

'I would like a coffee *now*,' he said. 'You can finish that later.'

She shrugged. 'Whatever you say, *boss*.'

Was that sarcasm? Kit was bloody sure that was sarcasm. And she still hadn't looked at him.

Angrily, he withdrew into his office and slammed the door behind him.

When Marley arrived with the coffee, he was very busy. Far too busy to look at her, anyway, so he had no idea if she was trying to make eye contact with him. He'd bet she was. A person couldn't give someone coffee and not look at them, could they? Or maybe she was deliberately looking away, just to wind him up?

Kit wouldn't put it past her.

Unable to help himself, he looked up at her, only to find her staring down at him, a stony expression on her face. Kit swallowed. 'Have you got something to say?'

'What could I possibly have to say?'

He took the coffee from her outstretched hand, dying to challenge her, but unable to bring himself to do so. How did she do that? God, she was an impossible woman. She'd been a nightmare kid, but as an adult...

Marley smiled sweetly at him and turned to leave, and Kit placed his coffee on the desk and forced himself to relax.

'Oh!' Marley's voice cut through his thoughts and set every nerve end jangling again. 'There was one thing.'

He tensed, waiting for it.

'Did you want a biscuit with that?'

Kit glared at her. 'Why don't you just come out with it?' *Damn!*

Marley smiled again. She arched one of her perfectly shaped brows. 'Come out with what?'

He tilted his chin defiantly. 'I saw your face! When I made that announcement in the canteen, I saw the look you gave me. Go on, you may as well get it over with. It will make good practice for this afternoon, when I hold the meeting.'

'I don't know what you mean,' she assured him. 'I think you're overwrought. Maybe the pressure is too much for you. Perhaps you should call Jack to come home.'

'Don't you dare,' he said, his voice deceptively quiet.

'Dare what?'

'Imply that I'm not fit to run this place.'

Dropping all pretence, Marley turned to face him fully, hands on hips. 'Well, are you?'

Kit gaped, stunned at the nerve of her. 'Are you serious?'

'You know nothing about this company. The LuvRocks contract is massive. Okay, I'll admit, I was never very happy with it either. I think the company's tacky and tasteless, and yes, I agree with you that Carroll's should be moving away from it, and back towards our own products.'

'So, what's your problem?'

'My problem is that it takes time. You can't just decide on a whim that you want to end your association with LuvRocks! Do you have any idea how hard Jack worked to get that contract in the first place? And did it never occur to you that he did that for a reason? The factory wasn't doing too well until LuvRocks came along. If you'd bothered to research at all—'

'I did research! I'm well aware of what was happening before the dratted contract. Nevertheless, I'm determined to take Carroll's back to its roots.'

'And to hell with what Jack thinks?' Marley glared at him. 'While the cat's away, and all that. Have you even told him? Because I think someone should. You have no right—'

'I have *every* right!' Kit's voice was strained, and he could feel his heart pounding. 'How dare you lecture me? You know nothing about me, nothing about Carroll's.'

'I know a damn sight more than you do,' she began, but he banged his hand on the desk, shutting her up.

'If you knew as much as you think you do, you'd know that this company doesn't belong to Jack. It belongs to me. Jack was put in place as manager here *by me*. Do you understand that? Is that clear enough for you? I *am* Carroll's Confectionery, and what I say goes. I don't have to run anything past Jack or get his permission. Get it?'

She very obviously did get it, as she went quite pale and simply stared at him, her hazel eyes large and bewildered. Kit felt a wave of remorse as he watched her struggling to absorb that information. He'd been unforgivably rude to her, shouting like that.

'I'm sorry,' he muttered. 'I didn't mean to raise my voice. It's been a trying day.' He leaned back in his chair and rubbed his eyes.

There was quiet for a moment, then Marley said, 'I'd better get back to work.'

'Yeah, yeah.' He picked up a pen, tapping it distractedly on the desk. 'I'll be away tomorrow, by the way. In fact, I'll be away for a couple of days.'

'Right.'

They looked at each other. She seemed as shell-shocked as he felt. Kit looked away first. 'Thanks for the coffee.'

'No problem.'

Marley closed the door after her and dropping the pen he let out a loud sigh — though, whether one of regret, relief, or sheer frustration, he simply couldn't say.

CHAPTER 11

When I arrived at Fox Lodge a few days later, I found Great Uncle Charles downstairs, sitting in front of the television, hurling curses at a rather stupid contestant on *The Chase*.

'You're on the mend then,' I said cheerfully, heading into the kitchen to put the kettle on.

'No, I died in my sleep,' he replied.

Ignoring him, I busied myself making the usual weak tea for him, and extra-strong tea for myself. 'I can't stay long tonight,' I told him, as I handed him his mug.

'Well, heaven be praised,' he said. 'Good news at last.' He eyed me curiously over the mug. 'Why not? Got a date?'

'No, I haven't.' A date! Chance would be a fine thing. How long had it been?

God, I couldn't even remember.

Appalled, I searched my memory banks. There must have been someone, surely? Vaguely, I recalled a night out in Whitby, with some bloke David used to go to school with. It had been a while. Shameful, really. I ought to make some effort, I supposed, or I would end up living alone for the rest of my life. Sitting in a chair, bitter and lonely, dreaming about what might have been. Worse than Miss Havisham. At least she'd got as far as getting engaged.

'If you must know, I'm going for tea at Mum's. She's invited me, Olivia, David, and the kids over.'

'Oh? Special occasion?'

I hesitated. Should I risk telling him the truth? Was it worth the more-than-likely derision that would result if I did? Could I be bothered with yet another argument? On the other hand, it was about time that Great Uncle Charles realised there was a lot more to my mother than he gave her credit for. I hated the thought that he still remembered her as some broken, distraught woman, sobbing over her errant husband. Mum was a different person to then, and he should know that.

'She's introducing us to her boyfriend.'

'Boyfriend?' The scorn in his voice was unmistakable.

'Other half, partner, whatever you like to call it. They've been going out together for a while now, and she thought it time we all met.'

He cackled. 'God help the poor sod, getting involved with your family, that's all I can say.'

'Don't worry,' I assured him, 'we won't be introducing him to you, so it won't be anywhere near as horrific as it could be for him.'

He tutted, then put the mug on the coffee table as he was wracked with another coughing fit.

'Are you sure you should be downstairs?' I eyed him doubtfully. 'Maybe you should still be in bed.'

'No chance. I'm sick of seeing that bedroom.' He wiped his eyes and sighed. 'I'm all right. I'm eighty-nine years old. What do you want from me — cartwheels?'

At least he had the central heating on, that was something. Although, the very fact that he hadn't turned it off at the first opportunity was a bit worrying. He clearly wasn't totally well, or he'd have been at the boiler controls like a flash. 'Have you eaten?'

'Had some spaghetti hoops a few hours ago.'

'Is that it?' I sighed. 'I'll make you something. Have you got anything in the freezer?'

A quick search of the kitchen revealed he had barely anything edible in the house, before I headed back through to him.

'Who does your shopping?' I asked, feeling guilty that I still hadn't done anything about the food situation.

He looked puzzled. 'I do. Who else?'

'You know, you really ought to have a home help, or something.'

'You must be joking! I don't want anyone round here, sticking their noses in my business, thank you very much. I'm perfectly capable of taking care of myself.'

'But you're eighty-nine, and not well.' I considered him for a moment. 'Look, I'll order you a takeaway for your tea, then tonight I'll buy you some shopping online. It could be delivered tomorrow afternoon, or the day after, at least. And if I can't get a slot for tomorrow, I'll bring you a few bits and bobs at lunchtime. Okay?'

I waited for the protests, and when none were forthcoming my eyes widened. 'Are you sure you're all right? Why aren't you arguing with me?'

'Bloody hell, I can't win,' he grumbled. 'Did you want me to argue with you?'

'Of course not.'

'Well, shut up and get on with it then. I'm bloody ravenous. Order me a curry, there's a good lass.'

'A good lass?' My mouth dropped open in shock. 'Should I call a doctor?'

'Oh, bugger off,' he snapped. 'I want a chicken Jalfrezi, and make sure you use that takeaway near the school. The one between the wedding shop and the pub is well dodgy. Lots of cats go missing round there, and that's all I'm saying.'

I rolled my eyes but did as he asked. 'Will you be okay to answer the door yourself?' I asked uncertainly, thinking it really was time I headed over to my mother's, to meet that toy-boy hunk of hers.

'Ooh, I don't know. Should I ask my mummy if I'm allowed?' Great Uncle Charles waved his skeletal hand at me. 'Go on, clear off, and have a good look at this fancy man of your mother's. I want all the details when you come here next. I haven't had a good laugh in ages.'

'Takeaway should be here within twenty minutes,' I told him, determined not to rise to the bait. 'Enjoy your Jalfrezi. I'll let you know about the shopping delivery, okay?'

'Yes, fine, whatever.' He picked up his mug again. 'Thank you, Marley.'

I'd been heading into the hall but stopped dead in my tracks. *Thank you?* Since when did Great Uncle Charles ever thank me for anything?

I glanced back over my shoulder, but he was apparently absorbed in *The Chase* again, so I said nothing, just left the house and closed the door carefully behind me. Well, that was a weird experience. I hoped he really was all right, because a grateful Uncle Charles was, quite frankly, a bit terrifying.

***

As I turned into my mother's street, I saw my sister and family just ahead of me. Olivia was holding Max's hand, while David pushed Tommy in his buggy. Sam skipped ahead of them, stopping now and then for them to catch up. Olivia and David were chatting, and I saw them laughing together, as Olivia placed her hand on David's back and rested her head for a fleeting moment on his shoulder.

Watching them, I felt a lump in my throat. They were such a tight-knit family. I knew my sister and brother-in-law didn't have much money and were worn out with the stress of taking care of three young boys, but the love and warmth they shared radiated from them. Would I ever have that kind of relationship? I simply couldn't imagine it.

For the first time in my life, I felt a pang of envy for my sister, followed by a sudden lurch of panic. What if David got fed up and left? How would Olivia cope without him?

'Auntie Marley!' Sam had caught sight of me, and ran towards me, barging into my legs and nearly knocking me backwards. 'Are you going to Grandma's, too?'

'I am,' I confirmed, nodding at Olivia who waited for me with a smile on her face.

'Exciting, isn't it?'

'I'm a bit nervous,' I admitted. 'Are you?'

'A bit.'

'What on earth are you two nervous for?' said David, puzzled. 'It's the poor sod who's dating your mother that I feel sorry for. Imagine having to meet the family, knowing you're being vetted, your every word and gesture considered and chewed over.'

'There speaks the voice of experience.' Olivia laughed, nudging him. 'I remember when you went through the same thing.'

'So do I,' he said, with some feeling. 'That's why I feel sorry for him. Marley practically interrogated me. I'm surprised she didn't tie me to my chair and shine a spotlight in my eyes.'

'Don't exaggerate,' I said crossly, although I did recall that I'd sort of bombarded him with questions. Olivia *was* my baby sister, though. Someone had to look out for her.

The curtains in the living room of Mum's cottage were open, and the twinkling lights of the Christmas tree shone through the window.

'Whoever he is,' Olivia said, looking toward them, 'he's clearly done her a lot of good. I mean, this is the first year she's been in the Christmas spirit since Dad left. I never thought she'd put up her own tree and decorations again. We really need to give him a chance. Agreed?'

'I always intended to,' David said. 'Who your mother goes out with is her business.'

'And no sly comments, if he's not well-spoken,' Olivia said, eyeing me sternly. 'No snide remarks about what job he does, or trying to find out what he earns, or what car he drives. None of that rubbish, okay?'

'As if I would!'

'Oh, you would, Marley. You know you would.'

'And no comments about the age gap,' David added. 'That goes for both of you, right? Let's go in there with an open mind and a welcoming attitude.'

'I don't need telling,' I said. 'If he's that important to Mum that she wants us to meet him, well, I'm willing to give him a chance.'

'Good.'

'Although,' I added, 'that doesn't mean we should be pushovers. We need to keep a cool head and our wits about us. We can't let Mum fall for some chancer.'

'Marley!'

'Well, can we? You wouldn't want her to have her heart broken again, would you?'

Olivia took a deep breath. 'Okay. Just ... just go easy, okay?' She smoothed Sam's hair. 'Right, let's do this.'

If Olivia and I were nervous, it was clearly nothing to the mood Mum was in. Upon entering the house, via the back door, we found her in a state of near meltdown. She was still wearing her dressing gown and was wafting smoke from the oven with one hand, as she struggled to remove something from inside with the other hand, which was, thankfully, safely enclosed in a rather tatty looking oven mitt.

'Don't open the door,' she shrieked, but too late.

Sam had rushed to enter the hallway, clearly intent on heading towards the living room where the television could be heard, and almost immediately the ear-splitting sound of the smoke alarm leaping into action almost sent him tumbling over in fright.

'I've burnt my mini quiches!' Mum let out a wail that competed with the smoke alarm. 'And not only that. I've burnt my bloody hair, too. Look at it! Got caught in my tongs! Look. You can smell how singed it is. Can you see? Does it look bad?'

David winced. 'Let go of me, Max. Let me turn that racket off.'

He managed to unwrap his little boy's arms from around his legs, despite Max's shrieks of fear, and strode into the hall. He fiddled around with the smoke alarm for a moment then, mercifully, silence reigned.

'Thank God for that,' Olivia said. 'Now, what were you saying about your hair?'

'It got taffled up in my tongs,' Mum said. She slammed the tray of mini quiches on the hob and stared at us in dismay. 'Look at that. A fiver they cost me, from the freezer shop. Only fit for the bin.'

'Why aren't you dressed?' I demanded.

'Didn't want to mess up my frock, did I? Pointless now, what with my burnt hair and everything.'

'Go upstairs,' Olivia soothed. 'I'll look for something else to eat, and you go and sort your makeup out.'

Mum stared at her. 'Sort my makeup out? I've already done it.'

'Yes, we can see the mascara and eyeliner all over your face. It's kind of smudged.'

That was putting it kindly. Our mother could have played a creature from a horror film, with the grey circles under her eyes and the smell of burnt hair.

'Oh, hell.' Mum rubbed her eyes, which didn't help, and sighed. 'I wanted everything to be perfect. He'll be here in a minute.'

'Well, hurry up then,' Olivia said. 'I'm sure we can find something else to cook while you're getting ready.'

'You won't,' Mum assured her. 'I've got nothing in. Not done a big shop. Just got the quiches and a couple of bottles of wine and a twelve-pack of beer.'

'Brilliant.'

'What am I going to feed everyone with?' Mum wailed.

'How about I nip to 'chippy? I'm sure that'll go down well with everyone.'

We all turned to see Don standing in the kitchen.

'I did knock,' he said. 'No one answered, so I thought I'd come round back.'

It fleetingly registered with me that, firstly, he was wearing a suit and tie, which was most peculiar for Don, and secondly, he was in Mum's house, and why would he be there?

Before my fuddled brain could join the dots, I heard Olivia say, 'Sorry, Don, we're a bit busy at the moment. Was there something you wanted?' as Mum shrieked, 'Oh, my God! Don't look at me! Don't look at me!'

We all stared at her as she shot out of the room and bolted up the stairs. There was a moment's stunned silence, then everyone slowly turned back to look at Don.

He ran a finger around his collar and shrugged. 'Not quite the reception I were expecting, but never mind.' He nodded at the quiches. 'Reckon chippy's our best bet, don't you?'

'You!' My mouth fell open. 'You're Mum's toy-boy?'

Olivia and David exchanged incredulous glances.

'You can't be,' David said. 'You'd have told me.'

'Aye, well.' Don looked a bit shamefaced. 'Made Katie a promise, didn't I? Not 'til she was ready, she said. Begged me. What could I do? Sorry, mate.'

'But … but, how? When?' I shook my head, bewildered. 'And what do you mean, Katie? No one calls her Katie.'

'I do,' he said cheerfully. 'She likes it.'

Olivia swallowed. 'Er, let's get this sorted,' she said, taking charge, at last. 'David, take the kids into the living room and find them something to watch on the television for now. I'll shove these quiches in the dustbin. Marley, pour us all a glass of wine, or get cans from the fridge. As soon as Mum comes down, we'll make a list for the chippy, and Don and David can go.'

By the time Mum reappeared, freshly made-up and wearing a rather nice print dress, calm had been restored to the house. The boys were engrossed in some cartoon or other, and the adults were sitting round the dining room table, drinking beer or wine, and making a list of what they wanted to eat.

'You look lovely,' Don assured her, standing up and pulling out a chair for her.

Like a proper gentleman, I thought with surprise. I would never have expected such behaviour from him. I still couldn't get my head around the fact that he was my mother's mystery boyfriend. I'd never have guessed in a million years. All that time, and he'd never said a word. Hell, and I'd confided in him about my father! He wouldn't have told Mum, though, would he? Surely not?

Mum sat down and flicked her hair, rather self-consciously, over her shoulders.

'I'm so sorry,' she told us. 'This wasn't how it was supposed to be at all. I had it all planned in my mind, but everything went wrong.'

'It doesn't matter,' Don assured her, putting his arm around her. 'We're all friends here, aren't we? No need for any palaver.'

'I can't believe this,' David admitted. 'I never thought — you never breathed a word.'

'How long have you two been seeing each other?' Olivia said.

Mum and Don looked at each other, as if trying to work it out.

'About three months,' Don said finally. 'Unless you count that day at the supermarket. Then it's three months, two weeks and three days exactly.'

'Huh?'

David grinned. 'Fancy you being on a dating site, Don. I never would have believed it.'

Don pulled a face. 'Give over. I did no such thing. I haven't got the guts for owt like that.'

'It happened completely out of the blue,' Mum said. 'We bumped into each other at Sainsbury's. I was a bit frazzled, and Don helped me with my shopping, and gave me a lift home. I invited him in for a cuppa, and we had a nice long chat, and I suppose...' Her voice trailed off, and she looked at Don.

'I suppose we just clicked,' he said, smiling at her. 'I thought, even then, that I'd like to ask her out, but it were a bit awkward, what with you lot to consider. Any road, I made a point of seeking her out at work, and after a couple of weeks, I plucked up courage to finally ask her out.'

'And I said yes,' Mum said, beaming at him. 'I'd begun to think he was never going to ask me.'

'But when do you see her at work?' I said, puzzled. 'She goes in early, and it's rare I bump into the cleaning team, at all.'

'Aye, well, funnily enough, I had to go in to work early for a few weeks. Very early.' Don winked at us all and squeezed my mother's hand.

I felt a lump in my throat. There was something in the way they looked at each other that made me feel suddenly so alone. As Olivia and David grinned at each other, I realised I was the odd one out. No one looked at me the way David looked at Olivia, or the way Don was looking at my mother.

I cleared my throat. 'So, who's going to the chippy, then?'

Don nodded approvingly. 'Now you're talking. I'll go, and David can come with me. Make us a list of what you all want. It's on me. My treat.' As we all started to protest, he waved his hand at us. 'No arguments. I've said it, and that's that, so make up your minds what you fancy.'

When he and David had finally left the house, note clutched in Don's hand, Olivia and I turned to our mother excitedly.

'Oh, my God! Don! Why on earth didn't you say?'

'Do you mind?' Mum asked, sounding worried. 'I know it's a lot to take in.'

'I can't believe it,' Olivia said. 'Don, of all people!'

'Is it the age gap?' Mum frowned. 'Thirteen years is a lot, isn't it? Do you think it's too much? Do you think I'm being stupid?'

'Don't be daft.' Olivia took her hand. 'It's nothing, at all. Don's always seemed middle-aged, anyway. It's brilliant news.' She looked sharply at me. 'Isn't it, Marley?'

'Oh — oh, yeah. Great.' I was still absorbing the shock of it all. Only a couple of days ago, I'd been sitting in the canteen with Don, pouring out our family secrets, and he hadn't breathed a word. No wonder he'd been so interested.

Or was I being unfair? Don would have listened, anyway. He'd always been a friendly, kind sort of man. I was doing him an injustice, I knew it. Even so, the thought of him with my mother was a bit ... well, nauseating.

'Have you two...?'

'Marley!' Olivia gaped at me, then turned slowly to Mum. 'Have you?'

'No! I told you. He's only kissed me once. Well, kissed me properly. You know. With tongues.'

'Ugh!' I felt sick. How was I going to face my battered sausage now?

'Don, giving French kisses.' Olivia giggled. 'Well, I think it's fantastic, Mum. He's a lovely bloke, he really is. I couldn't be happier for you. He'll fit right in with this family.'

'Hey, steady on, love,' Mum said, eyes widening. 'I'm only courting him. No one said anything about him being part of the family.'

'But one day—'

'Whoa!' Mum put her hands up, as if to fend off the very suggestion. 'I'm not ready for all that yet.'

'Not ready?' Olivia raised an eyebrow. 'It's been sixteen years, Mum. How much longer do you need?'

She shifted uncomfortably. 'It doesn't always seem like sixteen years, you know. Sometimes, it feels like only yesterday.'

There was a moment's silence. I thought about my father, visiting Great Uncle Charles to beg for money. He hadn't been near nor by the rest of us. He couldn't give a damn about us. Why should my mother continue to put her life on hold for someone so undeserving?

I took a deep breath. 'Don's a good man, Mum. He's worth ten of Dad, really he is. Give him a chance, eh? Don't throw this away for the memory of someone who really doesn't deserve any consideration at all.'

Mum and Olivia both stared at me, clearly astonished.

Olivia blinked. 'Er, well, yeah. What Marley said. Don's great, Mum. Don't keep him at arm's length, will you?'

'I never had Marley down as a relationship expert,' Mum said, smiling. 'What's brought this on?'

I shrugged. I wasn't about to tell them about Dad's heartlessness. They didn't need to know.

'Just think, you know, a good man is worth hanging on to.'

Mum surveyed me thoughtfully. 'Not like you, love. Is there something you haven't told us?'

'Of course not.'

'Maybe,' Olivia said, her eyes twinkling with mischief, 'it's having Kit Carroll back in her life. Remember how she pined for him when he went to that posh school, Mum? All those years, never seeing him, wasting away through unrequited love. I reckon that's why she's never had a boyfriend. She's been waiting for him, and now that he's back, he's reawakened the romantic streak in our Marley.'

'Oh, shut up. The only thing he's awakened is worry about the future of the factory,' I said crossly, beginning to wish I'd never opened my mouth. Although, I couldn't help but notice, with some alarm, that my stomach fluttered just at the mention of his name. 'He just announces he's stopping production of LuvRocks products, and then swans off to God knows where with God knows who for a couple of days. Absolutely typical. All right for some, isn't it?'

It really rankled with me. No explanation, no lead-up. Just, 'I'll be away for the next two days. I'm sure you can cope 'til I get back.' Charming. He was the most selfish man I'd ever met.

Well, I *had* coped. I'd coped just fine. I was used to it.

'Reckon it's the *with God knows who* bit that's got her rattled,' Olivia said, nudging Mum knowingly.

'Is that right, love?' Mum looked delighted. 'Are you still carrying a torch for little Chrissie Carroll?'

'It's Kit,' I snapped, even though I never thought of him as anything but Christopher. 'And of course I'm not! For goodness sake, it's bad enough that I have to see him at work. Do you honestly think I give any thought at all to him when I don't have to? I never think about him once I leave the factory, and that's a fact.'

Except, it wasn't. More and more, the image of him looming over me as I lay on the floor of The Blue Lamp came back to me, and each time I embellished it a little further. His hand no longer just brushed my hair back but stroked my face lovingly. His eyes didn't just look at me with concern, but with something else — a look of love that sparked into desire. And Sadie's annoying cleavage didn't interrupt proceedings. Instead I experienced the feel of his lips on mine, as he bent over and kissed me.

My dreams were becoming clearer and more urgent every time. Igniting something within me that was most inconvenient, and totally unexpected. Not to mention confusing. How could I still fancy someone so much, and yet hate him at the same time?

Because I did hate him, and I would never forgive him. He was the last person on earth I should've found attractive. It was all completely baffling.

Realising, uncomfortably, that my mother and Olivia were watching me intently, I felt my face start to burn. Don's and David's return from the chip shop came at just the right time. Everyone became far too absorbed in unwrapping food to question me any further, which was a huge relief, because what on earth could I say?

'Battered sausage and chips,' Don said, handing me a package. 'Extra-large. Get your laughing gear round that, kidder.'

He was all class, I thought. Olivia was quite right. He'd fit into our family perfectly.

Chapter 12

Christopher was sitting at his desk when I popped my head round his office door early the following morning. I was a bit taken aback to find him staring intently at his laptop screen, typing as rapidly as anyone could manage with two fingers.

Why didn't he just ask me to do whatever it was he wanted? Though, of course, everything was on a need-to-know basis lately. I still couldn't quite believe that he was in charge. Properly in charge. Not just put there as some sort of puppet by Jack, but that he actually owned the place.

'Did you know?' I asked Don later. He had, after all, worked at the factory since he left school, and he was quite high up. He'd had a good working relationship with Jack, and I thought it was a fair bet that if anyone knew, it would be him.

We were standing by the vending machine in the canteen. It was tea-break time for Don, and although I had no reason to head to the canteen for coffee, not when I had facilities in the office, I'd wanted to escape the stifling presence of the boss, which emanated from beneath his door and permeated my room in a most unnerving manner.

The canteen was practically empty. Plenty of other people were having a break, too, but they'd gone outside, having a quick cigarette in the shelter that had been purpose-built for them when the new laws about smoking in the workplace had come into force.

I shivered at the thought. They must have been freezing out there. Talk about dedication.

Don collected the plastic cup from the machine, and together we walked slowly over to the nearest table, holding our steaming hot coffees carefully. 'Know what?'

'About Christopher owning Carroll's? Did you know the place wasn't Jack's at all?'

I hadn't mentioned it to him before, worrying that to do so would be indiscreet. After all, Christopher may not have intended anyone else to know about it. Curiosity, though, was getting the better of me, and besides, I could trust Don. He was practically family since dating Mum. I'd simply tell him to keep it quiet and—

"Course I knew!' He placed the cup on the table and laughed. 'Thought everyone did. Didn't take much working out, to be honest. He *is* the eldest son, after all, and everyone knows he got the house in the will, and the house and the factory have always gone to the eldest, so.... Mind you, I will admit I'd assumed he'd signed it over to Jack after he moved abroad again.'

'He owns the house, too?' That hadn't occurred to me. Knowing Christopher's feelings about the factory and knowing his determination to have nothing to do with the place, I'd simply assumed that his father had sidestepped him and left everything to Jack. When James Carroll had died, though, I'd been living in Whitby with a couple of girls from the insurance company. By the time I knew about his father's death, Christopher had already been home, and gone again. I hadn't even set eyes on him. If he'd caused any sort of gossip by handing the factory over to his brother, I'd missed the whole thing. 'What happened? Why didn't he start work here?'

Don shrugged. 'Far as I know, he wanted to continue travelling. It wasn't a big deal. I think it was all sorted very smoothly, no fuss. He had work abroad, and he never took much interest in this place, whereas Jack did, so he clearly thought the best plan was to leave his little brother in charge and go off and do what he wanted to do.'

'All right for some,' I muttered. 'Swan off abroad, while his poor brother does all the work.'

'And gets handsomely rewarded for it, don't forget,' Don pointed out. 'Doubt very much Jack did it all for love. And he got to live in the big house, an' all. Besides, Jack's happy working here, so it wouldn't have been hard to persuade him.'

'But now he's so worn down with it all that he's had to disappear abroad himself,' I said crossly. 'And Christopher comes back here, knowing absolutely nothing about the business, causes mayhem, and then swans off himself for a nice little jolly away for a couple of days.'

'Nice little jolly?' Don frowned. 'What you on about? He's been at a trade fair in Liverpool, working bloody hard to try to win us some new contracts. You've got him all wrong, Marley.'

I sipped my coffee, feeling a bit wrong-footed. 'Okay, well, he may have been at a trade fair, but that doesn't mean he knows what he's doing, does it?'

Don put down his cup and leaned towards me. 'Strikes me, you're not willing to give him any sort of chance. You weren't at that meeting the other day. I was. He's determined to turn this place around and restore it to its glory days. He's got big plans, and he's willing to learn. Believe me, he's not afraid to ask for help and advice.'

Except from me! I bit my lip, feeling even more cross. Why was he being so weird with me? It was me who should've been rude to him, not the other way around, and there I was, making every effort to be professional, in spite of wanting to slap his annoyingly attractive face every time I saw it.

'Do you really dislike him that much?' Don said. 'Or is there something I don't know?'

'It's nothing to do with whether I like or dislike him,' I protested. 'It's simply that I don't think he's good for this company, that's all. I just wish Jack would come back.'

'Aye, well,' Don leaned back in his chair and sighed, 'I'm sure he will soon enough. And when he does, let's hope we've got good news for him about this place, eh? We all need to pull together, Marley. Try to give Kit the benefit of the doubt, eh?'

Well, that was harsh. I wasn't the one being difficult, making things awkward, was I? Nevertheless, I nodded and resolved to try harder with Christopher — if only for the sake of the company.

Back in the office, I kept myself busy, noting the door to his office was firmly shut. He didn't come through or call for me at all, and the morning passed quickly.

As lunchtime arrived, I stood up, intending to head to the canteen, but a sudden impulse made me pause. I poured Christopher a coffee and knocked gently on his office door, then opened it. He didn't even look up, which annoyed me, but I forced myself to sound pleasant as I carried his cup over to the desk.

'Thought you could use a drink,' I said, a fixed smile on my face. 'It's lunchtime, you know. You really need to take a break.'

Why, I thought crossly, was my heart thumping so loudly? I wasn't scared of him!

He finally managed to glance up at me, his fingers still over the keyboard. 'Thank you.'

He sounded surprised, which cheered me up a bit.

Spotting the tired look in his eyes, a momentary stab of compassion for him hit me. So he'd been at a trade fair? I'd foolishly imagined he'd been at some swanky hotel, or spa, or something. Maybe with a woman. Did he have a girlfriend, I wondered? It would be amazing if he didn't, come to think of it. That dark hair, those liquid eyes, that rather appealing mouth....

I blinked as I realised he was staring straight at me.

'Was there something else?' he asked.

Crap! What was I supposed to say to that? *No, I was just thinking how gorgeous you still are, and how unfair it is that you're not hideously ugly, considering how cruel and selfish and arrogant you are?* Hardly.

Luckily, a phone call I'd taken earlier that morning provided a flash of inspiration for me.

'Er, yeah, I was just thinking about the staff Christmas meal.'

He frowned. 'The what?'

I sat down on the chair at the opposite side of his desk and switched on a dazzling smile. 'The Christmas meal. I was wondering when you wanted to take everyone out this year? Only, we always hold it at Miller's restaurant, and Mr Miller rang this morning to ask when we intended to confirm the final date. He's got three availabilities for us, and if you want to take a look at—'

Christopher held up his hand, silencing me. 'I have no idea what you're talking about.'

I tried — I really tried — not to feel irritated.

'Every year,' I explained patiently, 'Jack treats the workers to a hot buffet at Miller's. It's his Christmas present to them all. Mr Miller and his staff always put on a great spread. It's usually the week before Christmas, and Mr Miller is holding three dates for us, but wants us to make a final decision. Usually,' I admitted, 'it's all sorted and paid for by now, but with Jack going.... Anyway, Mr Miller's very kindly allowed us extra time, and I really think we need to get moving on this as soon as possible. Today, preferably.'

'Forget it.' Christopher's voice sounded strange.

I peered at him. 'Forget what?'

'This! This whole, treat the workers thing! We're not a charity, you know. This is a business. Tell Mr Miller he can release the dates.'

I blinked. 'You're kidding, right?'

'Of course I'm not kidding. Why would I be kidding?' He frowned. 'Are you really going to make a big deal out of this, too?'

I felt a surge of anger. 'What do you mean, *this, too*?'

'Everything's a battle with you,' he said, standing up. 'Right, if that's the way it's going to be, time to make another announcement.'

'Oh, no! You can't! Are you deliberately trying to cause trouble?' I stared after him as he walked out of the office, then ran to join him. If he was determined to commit professional suicide, the least I deserved was be there to watch. I couldn't wait to see how the workers reacted to this latest announcement.

If Christopher was nervous, or had any doubts, he didn't show it. He marched straight over to Liz and demanded that she turn off the music, as he had something to say. Liz clearly knew better than to argue for a second time. Giving him an annoyed look, she turned off her CD.

Forks dangled in the air, knives paused in spreading butter, cups halted halfway to lips, as the whole canteen stopped.

I realised I was trembling and wondered why. It wasn't my fault he was about to cause a riot. Whatever was coming to him, it was only what he'd brought upon himself.

'It's come to my attention that you're all expecting to be taken to Miller's within the next couple of weeks,' he said, his voice firm and unwavering. 'I just wanted to tell you that this won't be happening.' He held up his hand, as the wave of protests began. 'I should explain that this Christmas meal is not official Carroll's policy. It was a personal gift from Jack to you all, and as Jack isn't here, it won't be taking place this year. What goes on between you and my brother is entirely separate to factory business. My way of doing things isn't Jack's, and that's all I have to say on the matter.'

I watched, open-mouthed, as he turned and left the canteen. God, he had a death wish.

As the explosion of anger erupted in his wake, disgust and fury spread over his employees' faces. Even Don looked a bit annoyed, but then he would. He loved the hot buffet and was always first in line for the chicken wings.

Casting a quick look around, I made my decision and headed after Christopher.

He was halfway up the stairs when I caught up with him.

'What are you doing?' I grabbed his arm, pulling him to a halt.

He looked at me, then at my hand on his arm, then back at my face again.

I shivered involuntarily and cursed myself. God, he was gorgeous, but God, he was a prick.

'Are you deliberately trying to start industrial action, or something?'

His lip curled in scorn. 'They can't go on strike over a Christmas buffet. Besides, are they even in a union? Are there any unions these days?'

'You know nothing, do you?' I demanded. 'Okay, it's unlikely they'll take action over this, but can't you see how your high-handed attitude is getting their backs up? After the bombshell you dropped on them last week, about the LuvRocks contract, to then tell them they're not even getting their usual Christmas treat.... Jack would never have done this to them.'

'I'm not Jack,' he said coldly. 'My brother and I work in very different ways.'

'Clearly,' I said.

'Look, however much you like to believe otherwise, I think Jack was too soft. My way of working isn't his, and I won't be making the mistakes he did. Now, whether you like it or not, it's my choice how I run this company, and I will do things my way, not Jack's.'

'But, but...'

'But what?' His eyes locked onto mine, and I found myself staring back at them, mesmerised.

'But it's Christmas,' I finished lamely.

He continued to hold my gaze for a moment, then he lowered his head and seemed to be contemplating the step he was standing on.

'I have no interest in Christmas,' he said finally. 'As far as I'm concerned, the sooner it's over with the better.'

He turned away and ran up the stairs, leaving me standing there, mouth open, heart pounding.

No interest in Christmas? If that didn't sound like Ebenezer Scrooge, what did?

I leaned against the wall, chewing my lip thoughtfully. Olivia had been right. I was here to save someone from themselves, and I suddenly knew, without doubt, that the person I was meant to save was Christopher Carroll.

Saving *It's A Wonderful Life*'s George Bailey would seem like a piece of cake compared to this. Clarence had been let off lightly.

Chapter 13

'So, it *is* Kit Carroll you're meant to save.' Don crunched his chocolate digestive and eyed me thoughtfully. 'What are you going to do about it?'

Mum nudged him. 'Don't encourage her, for God's sake. She's daft enough.'

'I knew you wouldn't believe me,' I said, somewhat annoyed. I gestured appealingly to Don.

'See what I have to put up with? You believe me, don't you?'

Don glanced at my mother, as if asking permission to give affirmation.

Mum stared at him a moment, then burst out, 'Well, don't look at me. You're allowed an opinion, even if it is stark staring bonkers.'

'I'm not entirely sure I believe you,' Don said slowly. 'I did say, when you first mentioned the idea that you'd been brought back to save someone, that I thought it were, well...'

'Bollocks,' I reminded him, helpfully.

'Aye, well.' He looked a bit uncomfortable.

'You were right,' Mum said. 'I've never heard such rubbish in all my life.' She narrowed her eyes at me. 'This isn't like you. You're a real cynic. This is more like Olivia. She's the one with her head in the clouds. Is this her idea? Has she been watching that film again? The one with the useless angel and the miserable old bugger in the wheelchair?'

Don let out a shout of laughter. 'By heck, I've never heard *It's a Wonderful Life* described like that before.'

'Knew what I meant though, didn't you?' she pointed out.

'One of the best films ever made,' he said. 'If not *the* best.'

'I prefer *Santa Claus, The Movie*,' she confessed, leaving him to splutter in horror and cough chocolate digestive crumbs all over her sofa.

'Thanks very much for this fascinating discussion on popular culture, but what am I going to do about Kit Carroll?' I demanded, too het up to remember to call him Christopher — something I'd rigidly stuck to as a point of principle, in spite of his frequent pleas for me to call him Kit.

'He's going to bring the factory to its knees at this rate, and he's turning everyone against him.'

'Gutted about Miller's,' Don admitted. 'You can't beat their spicy chicken wings. Highlight of my culinary calendar is that.'

'Why don't we go one evening?' Mum suggested. 'Just the two of us?'

His eyes lit up. 'Ooh, sounds grand. I'll book it. Shall I see if I can get Christmas week?'

As she nodded enthusiastically, I sighed in exasperation. 'Hello? I need your help, people. Crisis here.'

'Look, Marley, if you've really been sent to save him, shouldn't you have all the answers? You're the one who died, after all. Surely, if you'd been given a mission, you'd have been told what to do.'

'That's not how it works at all,' I said crossly. 'No one told Clarence how to save George Bailey. He had to figure it out for himself.'

'Then, maybe you need to figure it out for *yourself*,' Mum said, 'and not involve us with all this crap.'

'I dunno, love,' Don said thoughtfully. 'Maybe she's got a point.'

'Oh, please. Seriously?'

He stroked his chin, as if considering the matter. 'I'm not saying Marley is an angel, or anything like that. I'm not even saying she was saved for this reason — or any other reason, come to that. I just think it were right lucky that Kit Carroll happened to be in that pub, at that moment, and knew what to do. Like, fate, you might say. And, you know, they have got history after all.'

'History?' Mum laughed. 'She had a crush on him in primary school. It's hardly Antony and Cleopatra, is it?'

I winced as my nails dug into my palms.

'Should hope not,' Don said. 'We all know what happened to those two. But the point is, Kit's clearly struggling. He may own the factory, but he doesn't seem to have any idea how to run it. He's doing his best, but let's be honest, his people skills are crap.'

'And Marley's aren't?' Mum eyed me knowingly. 'Match made in heaven if you ask me.'

'There you go!' Don winked at her. 'You said it.'

'Oh, for God's sake.' I stood up. Even I thought that was pushing it. 'I'll try to figure this out for myself. You two are useless.'

'Well, if you're sure.'

There was a definite light in my mother's eye. Clearly, she wanted to spend time alone with Don. It was a weird feeling, knowing Mum had fallen for another man, but there was no more denying it. Even with their obvious disagreement over my mission, there was something between them. An easy familiarity, an affection, a bond. They were made for each other.

Like David and Olivia, I thought wistfully.

'I'm sure,' I said. 'I'm going to see Great Uncle Charles. Make sure he's still getting better.'

'Did his shopping arrive all right?' Mum followed me through to the kitchen and opened the back door for me. Despite the fact that it meant walking around the side of the house to get to the street, no one ever used the front door. It would just have felt weird.

'Oh, yes.' I rolled my eyes. 'Not that he appreciated it. Said I'd sent him a load of rubbish that he didn't even like, and what was wrong with the budget brands? I don't know how he dare complain. It's not as if he paid for it.'

My mother's eyes widened. 'You bought his shopping?'

I blushed. 'Well, he needed food. He had nothing in, and I had no access to his account so...'

'And hasn't the tight old bugger offered to pay you back?'

I shook my head. 'He's not been well, though,' I added quickly, wondering, as I did so, why I felt the compunction to defend my miserly relative. 'I'm sure he will, when he's back to normal.'

We looked at each other. I wondered if my mother was thinking what I was thinking — Great Uncle Charles returning to normal was unlikely to result in him handing out any money, whether he owed it or not.

I sighed. 'It doesn't matter. I'll see you later, Mum. Have a good afternoon.'

It was her turn to blush, and noting the pink on my mother's cheeks, I wondered uncomfortably exactly what her plans were for the rest of the day.

Ugh! On second thoughts I didn't want to know. Was my mother finally ready to take the next step with Don? Don, of all people!

Double ugh! I didn't want to think about that either.

Hastily, I waved Mum goodbye and dashed out of the house.

***

Great Uncle Charles seemed much more like his old self as he greeted me at the door and told me I'd better not be planning on staying long because he had a book to read.

'Really? What is it?'

'*Fifty Shades of Paint and How to Watch Them Dry*. Still more riveting than a chat with you.'

'Ah, I see you're feeling well again,' I said. 'Cup of tea?'

'Go on then,' he said, shuffling into the living room. 'And don't put too much in the pot! That stuff you bought is strong enough to strip varnish. Waste of money.'

'My money,' I muttered. Heading into the kitchen, I pulled a face on seeing the quantity of dirty dishes sitting in the sink. 'I'll wash the pots first,' I called through to him.

'Suit yourself,' he replied, without so much as a hint of gratitude in his tone.

I rolled up my sleeves and began to sort out the dishes. Why couldn't he get a dishwasher like everyone else? Not that I had one myself, mind. No room for it in my poky little kitchen.

Looking round, I realised there was no room for it in his kitchen, either. Not without ripping out the units and starting again, which was just what I'd do when the house was mine. The kitchen must have been in situ for at least thirty years, I thought. Maybe even longer. It was horrible. I would have cream glossy units, when Fox Lodge belonged to me, and I'd get rid of that tatty wooden back door, and the manky old dresser beside it, and install French doors opening out onto the garden.

The garden was another thing, I thought, filling the bowl with hot water and adding a squirt of washing up liquid. It would need completely digging up and starting again. A few gallons of weedkiller would be on my shopping list, too. I imagined it finished, with new fencing, neat turf, borders of flowers, and a large decking area with superior garden furniture — not the cheap, plastic tat Mum had in her garden. I could have summer barbecues and buffets and invite people round to admire the fully refurbished house.

I tried to ignore the thought that, really, who would I invite? Olivia, David, the boys, Mum and Don? Wow. Hardly worth opening a pack of deluxe top-quality venison burgers for, was it?

'Took your time.' Great Uncle Charles put down his paper and reached for the cup I held out to him, over half an hour later. 'I could have croaked it in here for all you knew.'

'I had to wash up and clean the kitchen. It was quite disgusting in there,' I said.

'I've been ill, remember?' Although, it had to be said, cleaning wasn't something an old man of his age should be expected to do anyway, ill or not.

I glanced round, noticing for the first time the amount of dust in the place. 'I'll come back tomorrow and clean up for you. Do you have a Hoover?'

'Of course I have a bloody Hoover.' He sipped his tea. 'Mind you, not sure if it still works. Don't think I've plugged it in since nineteen-eighty-seven.'

I wasn't entirely sure he was joking. 'Okay, well, I'll bring rubber gloves and disinfectant and polish. We'll soon get this place looking decent again.'

Great Uncle Charles had a distinct gleam in his eye, which made me rather nervous.

'What is it?' I said warily.

He put his cup on the table and smirked at me. 'Who said it was anything?'

'I know that look. You look pleased with yourself, which means it's bad news for me, or some other poor sod. What have you been up to?'

He nodded over at the ancient television set that stood in the corner. 'Top of the telly. Someone shoved it through the letterbox this morning. Made most interesting reading.'

Frowning, I went over and picked up said envelope from the top of a television set that could have been a talking point on *The Antiques Roadshow*.

'To the homeowner,' I read aloud, then opened the envelope and pulled out a piece of paper. As I scanned the letter inside at record speed, my heart thudded, and I read it again, more slowly that time, making sure I'd taken it all in. 'You're kidding me! Who are these people?'

'No idea,' he said with a shrug, which belied the delight in his voice. Clearly, the whole thing amused him greatly. 'Food for thought though, eh?'

'No way!' I sank into the chair. 'You're not serious?'

'Why not? Think about it. You've said yourself, many times, that Fox Lodge is way too big for me, and this couple want it. They're keen to buy in this area, and they have two kiddies, so the house would certainly be more suitable for them than me. Or you, come to that. If it's too big for me, it's going to be too big for you, too. Maybe I should call them. Ask them how much they're willing to pay.'

My mind was in turmoil. He wouldn't, would he? Fox Lodge was at the centre of all my plans. I'd got so many ideas for it, knew exactly how it would look when it was completed. I could picture it so clearly. I loved this house. It already felt like mine. He couldn't sell it.

'You'd get peanuts for it,' I said desperately. 'Look at the state of it! It needs complete refurbishment.'

'They want a project,' he reminded me, nodding at the letter. 'Says they've been looking for a renovation project for ages, and they think this place is perfect. Just what they're after. I don't know. Who am I to stand in the way of their dreams?'

'What about *my* dreams?' I demanded, too upset to monitor what I was saying.

'What about them?' His eyes narrowed. 'I knew you were counting on it. Told you so, didn't I?'

I bit my lip. He had me there. I couldn't deny it.

He seemed to consider me for a moment, then shrugged again. 'Haven't made my mind up yet. Maybe I will. Maybe I won't. No rush to decide, is there?'

So, he was going to leave me guessing? No doubt, he'd enjoy torturing me. I felt a gloom settling on me that even the knowledge I'd used triple tea in the pot against his wishes couldn't dispel.

Great Uncle Charles leaned back in his chair and closed his eyes. I thought for a moment that he'd fallen asleep, until he suddenly asked, 'How's your own project going?'

'My what?'

'Your project. You know, to save someone. That whole guardian angel thing. Found who you're supposed to save yet?'

'Maybe. One thing I know for sure, it isn't you.'

'It's far too late to save me,' he said. 'I'm beyond redemption.'

'No one is beyond redemption,' I protested, wondering how he managed to make me feel sorry for him just by not arguing with me for once. 'Well,' I added as an afterthought, 'most people aren't, anyway.'

He opened his eyes and peered at me. 'You've found them.'

Seriously, he was almost supernatural sometimes. I'd have sworn he could read my mind. 'I may have done. I'm hoping I'm wrong,' I admitted.

'Oh? Why's that?'

'What do you care?'

'I have a very boring life. Indulge me.'

I supposed he did. Almost as boring as mine. Draining my tea, I replaced my cup on the coffee table and folded my hands on my lap.

'I think,' I confessed, wondering even as I said it why I was confiding in him, of all people, 'that I'm meant to save Christopher Carroll.'

I waited for the explosion of laughter, the sarcastic comment. Instead, he stared at me for a moment, then said, 'And why do you think that?'

Rather nonplussed, I tried to put my thoughts into words. 'He's been thrown in at the deep end with the company, and he's making a complete hash of it. And he doesn't seem very happy. Besides,' I added lamely, '*he* was the one who saved *me* from choking to death. Maybe it was fate.'

Great Uncle Charles drummed his fingers on his chair arm, lips pursed, his beady eyes fixed on me as I squirmed uncomfortably. 'So, it was Edwin Carroll's grandson who saved you? I didn't even know he was back.'

'Oh, yeah.' I nodded. 'I forgot to mention that bit. I hadn't realised who he was, but then he turned up at the factory the following Monday, and said Jack had swanned off to America for a holiday, and that he was in charge.'

'You never said.'

'You don't like to talk about the factory,' I reminded him, 'so I generally try to avoid discussing it.'

'Hmm.' He frowned, thinking to himself. 'Why would Jack Carroll bugger off to America with no warning?'

'The general consensus is that he's exhausted and needs a break, and he's desperate to spend more time with his family, since he's been working so hard.'

'And you agree?'

'I have no idea. I don't see why else he'd go. Mind you,' I added, 'I was pretty annoyed. Still am. I'm his PA, and he said nothing. I just turned up at work to find Kit in charge. Kit, of all people!'

'Who's Kit?'

'Christopher. He calls himself Kit these days. Must be trying to impress someone.' I tried hard to keep the bitterness from my voice, but my great uncle clearly wasn't fooled.

'You sound less than keen.'

'He's — he's not a nice person.'

'Oh? Why?'

I shrugged. 'Just, you know, a bit mean.'

'There's more to it than that, isn't there? Christopher Carroll, eh? After all this time.'

'What do you mean, *all this time*?' I could feel my face burning.

'Always had a thing for him, didn't you? First love is very powerful. You never really get over it. Or so I've been told.'

'How could you—?' I gaped at him. 'What are you talking about?'

'Your grandad told me all about it,' he said. 'He seemed to think this Christopher lad was good for you. I wasn't so sure. No good ever came from trusting a Carroll. Told him it would end in tears and, evidently, I was right. I would guess it ended when you were around eighteen, judging by the change in you then.'

I was speechless. It was impossible. Grandad would never have told Great Uncle Charles, of all people. I'd confided in him, when I hadn't even told my own mother, or sister. Grandad was the only one. Surely, he hadn't broken my trust, too?

'I was his brother,' Great Uncle Charles said, leaning forward and eyeing me sternly. 'I know what you're thinking. You told him in confidence, didn't you? But the thing is, he only had me, and what else were we going to talk about? You were the light of his life, the only thing that kept him going. He trusted me, and he was right to. I said nothing, did I? I kept your secret, even after your grandad died. I never knew what happened between you and the Carroll boy, but I guessed it had ended badly. You were a different person after that.' He frowned. 'What *did* happen?'

'I found out what he was like,' I murmured. 'Simple as that.'

He waited, clearly expecting me to say more. When I didn't, he sighed and leaned back again.

'Yet, you think your destiny is to save him.'

'I think,' I said slowly, 'that if I'm meant to save anyone, it must be him. He definitely needs it. Everyone else I know is doing fine. Olivia and David and the kids are happy. Mum and her new man are getting on well. You don't want to be saved, even if it were possible, which I sincerely doubt. It only leaves him. Mind you, I've a good mind to let him get on with destroying his life. Why should I save someone like him?'

'Things not going well for him then?'

'No.'

'So, what do you intend to do about it?'

'I have no idea,' I admitted. 'How do you go about saving someone, anyway?'

'You can only save someone who wants to be saved,' he said.

'I know. You've made that quite clear.'

'I wasn't talking about me,' he said. 'The truth is, people follow their own path, no matter what. You may think he's on the wrong one, but how do you know it's not the one he's meant to take?'

'Because he's miserable, angry, and very mean-spirited!'

'Maybe that's what he's supposed to be. Maybe that's his life now.'

'No!' I shook my head, appalled. 'Of course it's not.'

'How do you know? You said yourself that you'd found out what he was like. So, what was he like? Miserable, angry, mean-spirited?'

I wasn't sure how to respond to that. The old stick had thrown my own words back at me, and what if he was right?

I shook my head again. 'No, he's *not* supposed to be like that. I know he isn't.'

'But how do you know?' he persisted.

'Because — because he used to be fun! He used to be kind! He used to be gentle and generous and loving. This isn't Christopher.'

'But maybe it's Kit?'

I felt faintly nauseated.

Great Uncle Charles smiled at me — a twisted, sneering sort of smile, but a smile, nonetheless. 'You see, the truth is, maybe Kit *is* going to grow old alone. Maybe he's the sort of man who doesn't need people. Maybe he only cares about money.'

'Like you?' I gasped. 'I'm sorry. I didn't mean that.'

'Yes, you did,' he said calmly. 'That's what I am, after all. And maybe Kit is destined for the same. So maybe, just maybe, you should leave well alone, and let him grow to be the man he's supposed to be.'

I realised I was gripping the cushion of the chair and made a conscious effort to let go. 'He's not supposed to be that sort of person. I can't leave him alone. I have to save him from that.'

'So,' he said, 'how do you intend to do it?'

'I don't know,' I wailed. 'I can't exactly summon an angel, or three ghosts, can I?'

'Maybe you don't need to,' he said thoughtfully. 'What those ghosts — and the angel, come to that — did, was remind Scrooge and George Bailey of what they once had. You said Kit was different when you were together?'

'Well, yes, until ...' My voice trailed off. I couldn't tell him everything. It was far too painful.

'But when you were with him, until it went wrong, he was different. He was happy, decent? Your grandad liked him, so he must have been all right.'

'So what if he was? How does that help?'

'You need to remind him of that. You need to show him what his life was like back then, so that he can begin to realise that it could be like that again. Remind him of the good times. Remind him how to be happy.'

I gazed into the distance. 'But how? How do I do that?'

'Take him back to where it began for you both,' he said. 'Can you do that?'

'You know what? I actually think I can.' My face broke into a smile. 'Thank you! I think I know where to start now.'

'Thank God for that,' he said, picking up his newspaper and opening it with a flourish. 'Now fetch me a packet of biscuits from the cupboard, and then bugger off home.'

CHAPTER 14

I turned off the ignition and turned to face Don. 'I'm shaking.'
He laughed. 'Not surprised, all this cloak and dagger stuff.
Can't believe she agreed.'

'Neither can I! Honestly, I thought she'd tell me to sling my
hook, but she seemed really pleased at the idea.'

He nodded towards the back of the car. 'What do you want to
do with that? Are you going to show it to him this afternoon?'

I shook my head. 'I'll leave it in the boot. One step at a time.
Besides, I have to rough it up a bit first. It looks brand new.'

'That'll be cos it *is* brand new,' he pointed out. 'I were right lucky
to find it. Last one in the shop.'

'I know. I really appreciate it, Don. So good of you to spend
your lunch hour helping me out.'

'Aye, well, this is clearly important to you, so...' He sighed.
'Stomach's rumbling now. Did you hear that? Can't believe I
missed me dinner.' He opened the car door. 'Come on then. Back
to work.'

I jumped when he slammed the door shut. Outside the window
he stretched, then rubbed his poor empty stomach.

'Hang on a minute.' He probably couldn't hear me, I realised,
as I rummaged in the glove compartment. As I climbed out of
the car, Don was already a few paces ahead of me, but stopped
when I called his name.

'What?'

'Here. Found these in the car. Not much, I know, but they might head off the hunger pangs for now.'

I handed him a bag of salt and vinegar crisps, and he beamed at me. 'Just the job. Cheers for that. Hopefully, I won't pass out over the conveyor belt later.'

I frowned. 'Are you really that hungry?'

He laughed and put his arm around my shoulders. 'Don't look so worried. I can nip into canteen at break time and grab a sandwich, if needs be. Any road, let's hope this was all worth my impressive sacrifice, shall we?'

'Fingers crossed,' I agreed.

We headed towards the factory. 'Here we go then,' he said. 'Hope it all goes well, Marley. Have a good afternoon.'

'You too, Don.'

Heading upstairs, I wondered how I could broach the subject. Should I make a big announcement, or should I drop it into conversation, quite casually? Given that this was supposed to be a regular occurrence, I guessed the best bet would be to play it casual.

Christopher's door was open, which surprised me. I popped my head around it and found him standing by the window, looking out over the car park.

'Do you want a coffee before I start work?'

'You're back then?'

'Sorry?'

He turned toward me, his face impassive. 'Saw you pull up. Not eating in the canteen today?'

'No, I, er, had to be somewhere.'

'Right.'

He continued to stare at me, making me feel all hot and bothered. It was as if he knew. But he couldn't have known, could he? God, the guilt must have been radiating from me. He must see it, surely?

'That would be good. Thanks.'

'What?' I blinked. 'What would be good?'

'Coffee.'

'Oh, right. Yes, of course. Coming right up.'

I hurried back into my own office, feeling relieved to be away from his piercing gaze. What was going on? And did he always watch the comings and goings in the car park? Good job I'd left the bag in the boot, after all. I wouldn't have been at all surprised if he'd zoomed in on us all with his mobile phone, and if he'd spotted the logo of the shop on the carrier bag, it would have blown everything.

He was back at his desk when I returned, carrying the coffee. He didn't look up, but merely nodded his thanks as he stared intently at the monitor. I hesitated, my stomach churning, but then was as good a time as any, I supposed.

'Oh, by the way, do you want me to bring in the Santa costume tomorrow for you to try on?'

The expression in his eyes, as he looked up at me, was of such incredulity that I almost laughed out loud. 'I'm sorry?'

'The Santa costume. You know, for the school Nativity?' I pretended to study him thoughtfully for a moment. 'Hmm, I reckon you'll be okay. It's not exactly fitted, but maybe just in case? Oh, and you may need new boots, of course, unless you're the same size as Jack. What size *are* you?'

I knew perfectly well what size shoe he took. I remembered even that, which was depressing, when I came to think about it.

Christopher's mouth had been hanging open, but he snapped it shut and leaned back in his chair. 'Is this a joke?'

I hoped the amusement I was feeling didn't show in my face. 'A joke? Of course not! Look, you must know about the annual appearance at the primary school? Surely, Jack must have mentioned it?'

He looked dazed.

I gave an exaggerated sigh, placed my hands on the desk, and leaned towards him. 'Every year, after the children have performed their Nativity, they're rewarded by a visit from Santa, who very kindly hands out sweets, as a thank you for putting on such a great show.' I tutted. 'I can't believe Jack never said. It's ever so popular, and of course, it's great publicity for Carroll's, because all the staff and parents know who's handed out the sweets.'

Christopher's eyes narrowed. 'So, you're telling me that we give away loads of our products for free, and I have to dress up as some old, fat man in a red suit?'

'Tut-tut, no body shaming,' I said. 'It's terribly politically incorrect.'

He stood up. 'Forget it.'

'Forget it?' I folded my arms. 'You *are* kidding, right? This is something the kids look forward to every year. They're expecting you the day after tomorrow. You can't let them down.'

'Why should we hand out loads of our stuff for free?' he demanded, sounding desperate.

I ignored his evident distress, instead reminding myself that it was for his own good. 'Oh, it doesn't have to be the quality stuff. We have plenty of rejects — misshapen chocolates, that sort of thing. And we can break some of the peppermint penises up into chunks and market them as mint sweets.'

'Humbugs.'

Ha! That was the Scrooge I knew and ... worked for.

'Yes, just like humbugs,' I said, trying not to laugh. 'We'll just put them in little plastic bags, and the kids will love them. The older ones, that is. We wouldn't want any little ones to choke, would we?'

'No, we wouldn't, would we?' His eyes met mine, and I wondered if he was reliving the moment in The Blue Lamp, when he'd saved my life. He shuffled some papers on his desk and said, rather grumpily, 'We never had Santa visit us when we held *our* Nativity.'

I paused, remembering that particular Christmas vividly. It was our year's turn to take the leading roles, and Christopher had been chosen to play Joseph. I desperately wanted to be Mary and was desolate when Amy Smith got the role. She was blonde and dimpled and looked like a baby doll. Mary should be dark-haired, like me. I'd been so full of resentment and hurt that being cast as the angel had been no consolation, whatsoever. What did Joseph care for the angel? It was Mary he loved. Mary whose hand he held as they knocked on the door of the inn. Dratted Amy Smith.

'That's because it wouldn't have occurred to your father to bother with children or give anything away. Jack's not your father, and neither are you.'

He looked up at me, and I saw a brief flash of pain in the dark depths of his eyes, which made my heart thump. Just as quickly it was gone, the guard back in place again.

'The younger ones can have the chocolates,' I continued hurriedly. 'Oh, and we're donating a large box of our premium chocolates to the raffle that they always hold,' I added. 'The headmistress is ever so grateful.'

'I'll bet she is,' he growled. 'Well, she can forget it. I want no part of it. This is just another example of Jack's good nature getting the better of him. It stops now.'

I felt a flash of anger ignite inside me. 'You can't let them down! They're counting on you! Imagine how disappointed they'll be.'

'I hardly think I'd be doing them a favour. Isn't it the *politically correct* thing these days to *not* give children sweets? Handing out a load of broken rock and dodgy chocolates is hardly kindness, is it? All it will do is make them fat and rot their teeth.'

'You know, you really are in the wrong trade,' I snapped. 'If you think like that, you should have a different job.'

'Don't I know it,' he said, sounding weary.

'If you don't go, you'll drag Carroll's name through the mud. This is all about public relations, and you're ruining our reputation. Is that what you want? Are you trying to drive us to bankruptcy?'

'Of course I'm not!' He stood up, facing me, his eyes expressing as much anger as I felt. 'I'm doing everything I can to improve this company. How dare you suggest otherwise?'

'Then bloody prove it,' I said. 'If you really think putting on a costume and handing out a few sweets is beneath you, then you don't deserve Carroll's. Jack would be ashamed of you.'

We glared at each other, the tension between us ratcheting up a notch with every second that passed. My heart was jumping around in excitement. God, what was I doing? How could this high-handed attitude of his be turning me on?

But it was. No doubt about it. The temptation to reach out and stroke that raven hair was overwhelming. I had to cool things down. Quickly.

'Think about it,' I said, turning away from him. 'Let me know your decision, and I'll bring the Santa costume in tomorrow, once you've made it.'

'In other words,' he said, his voice sounding strained, 'you've already made the decision, and I just have to go along with it.'

'Pretty much,' I said, not looking back.

I walked casually into my own office, closed the door behind me, then leaned against it, trying desperately to steady my breathing.

That had been intense, and it had reminded me of things I'd rather forget — feelings I'd worked so hard to bury. But at least I'd achieved my purpose. The ghost of Christmas past was about to visit Christopher Carroll. I just hoped it would work.

Chapter 15

Kit couldn't believe he was actually doing it. As he strode into the reception of Moreton Cross Primary School — having been interrogated via an intercom and zoomed on by a rather threatening camera first — he wallowed, for a moment, in the memories it evoked.

Glancing around, he thought how small everything looked. Had it really been so tiny when he'd been a pupil there? Not much had changed. Despite the strict security measures in place, which was a sad sign of the times, it seemed exactly the same.

Noticing the cheerful paintings on the wall, he smiled to himself. He remembered the honour it had been, having your work of art selected to adorn the reception area. He'd really felt that he'd achieved something when his painting of witches and ghosts had been chosen as part of the school's Hallowe'en display.

'Mr Carroll?' A round-faced lady, with glasses on a chain around her neck and rather untidy hair, advanced towards him, hand outstretched. 'I'm so pleased to meet you. It's terribly kind of you to offer to do this. Such a generous gesture, and, of course, the children will be so happy to see Father Christmas. I understand you have a donation for the raffle, too?'

'Oh, oh, yes. Of course.' Kit rummaged in the large bag he was carrying and handed her a large, beribboned box of Carroll's Premier Chocolate Selection. 'There you go.'

'How wonderful. I hope I can resist temptation,' she said, smiling at him. 'They look so delicious they may not make it into the raffle.'

Kit gave her a faint smile and handed her a second bag. 'The sweets for the children. Can I leave them behind the desk for now? I don't really want to lug them around with me. There's a lot in there.'

'So generous of you. Of course we'll keep them safe,' she assured him, handing the bag to the grey-haired woman behind the desk.

'Is there anywhere I can change?' he asked, feeling a lurch of anxiety and dread as he spoke. Hell, he was actually going to do it. He was going to put on that ridiculous costume and get out there, making a total fool of himself.

Jack had a lot to answer for. When he called him tomorrow, Kit would certainly tell him so.

'Yes, you can make use of the staff room,' she told him. 'Of course, you don't need to do that until after the Nativity. I'll draw the raffle while you get changed, and then I'll introduce you. Is that okay?'

'If that's what usually happens,' Kit said with a shrug.

She frowned. 'Usually happens?'

'You made it!'

Kit spun round, to see Marley striding rapidly towards him. She looked flustered, casting nervous glances at the woman. 'Mrs Carlyle, so nice to see you again.'

'Goodness, I never introduced myself.' The woman tutted. 'How rude of me. I'm Janette Carlyle, headmistress at this school.'

'I gathered,' Kit said, thinking there was something wrong here, somewhere, as he felt a growing unease. Something didn't fit. Something he couldn't quite put his finger on...

'Well, if you'll excuse me, I'll just put these chocolates with the other raffle items, and then I need to check on the children. We've already had two of them throwing up with excitement — or nerves, perhaps.' Mrs Carlyle beamed at them. 'As two former pupils here, I'm sure you remember your way to the hall. We'd

be delighted if you would watch the show. It's due to start in—'
she checked her watch, '—roughly half an hour.'

'Great. Love to. Thanks.' Marley smiled and waved as the
headmistress hurried off, but Kit couldn't shake the feeling that
something weird was going on. He just couldn't figure out what.

'Come on, then,' Marley said, turning to him. 'Let's go and make
ourselves comfortable.'

'I don't think so.'

'What do you mean, you don't think so?'

Kit had caught sight of a crocodile of children, filing along the
corridor that intersected with the one he was staring down. The
image gave him a pang of despair and brought a lump to his
throat.

He thought about Farthingdale Primary. When would they be
holding their Nativity play? His nephew would miss it this year.
He imagined Tim in a shepherd's costume, or maybe playing the
innkeeper, or even Joseph. Kit had never seen him in any of his
plays. He'd rarely seen him at all, if he was being honest. Not in
real life. He'd talked to him via the miracles of Zoom and
Facetime, but it was hardly the same.

Tim was a cute kid, with Jack's dark hair and Amanda's blue
eyes, and a sprinkling of freckles across his nose. He should be
here, at school, getting excited about appearing in the play,
putting Christmas cards in the class post box, nagging his parents
to add yet another toy to his list, and singing Christmas carols in
the school hall. Instead, he was in America, miles away from
home, missing it all.

Kit's eyes blurred with tears, and he blinked them away.

'You're not changing your mind?'

Marley's voice was challenging, and he glanced down at her.
'No. No. Just, well, we've got half an hour yet. Don't fancy sitting
in the hall all that time, waiting. Do you?'

She eyed him for a moment. 'Are you okay?'

'Of course.'

'Hmm. Well, I suppose we could go for a walk around. Then
again, the kids will still be in their classrooms, getting ready.'

He nodded. 'You're right. The hall it is.'

They made their way towards the old assembly hall, nudging each other as they shared stories from their time at the school.

'Two of my nephews will be in this play,' Marley told him.

'Your nephews?'

'Olivia's kids. I have a younger sister.'

He remembered suddenly. Of course she had a sister. Come to think of it, he was pretty sure she was the one who'd begged him for help at The Blue Lamp. No wonder they had such similar eyes.

'She works at the factory.'

'She does?'

'Yes. So does her husband, David. The two eldest boys are at this school. Sam's in the reception class, and Max is in the nursery. Tommy's too young. He goes to the private nursery in the village.'

'Wow, Olivia has three kids, and so close together? Impressive.'

Marley's voice was strained. 'Is it?'

Kit cast a sideways glance at her. She seemed different all of a sudden — sort of tense. He wondered why. 'It's a shame your sister and her husband won't be here to see the boys.'

'They will be. They booked the time off ages ago, as soon as the school confirmed the dates. You have to be organised when you have kids.'

'I suppose you do.'

'You have a nephew, don't you? Jack's son. How old is he?'

'He's six.'

'Oh. What a shame he'll miss all the Christmas fun at his school.'

'Isn't it?'

Marley pulled open the door to the hall and ushered him through.

Kit stared around, wondering how many hundreds of assemblies he must have attended in that very room. He remembered sitting cross-legged on the wooden floor, staring up at the stage, listening to one of the teachers bashing on the piano keys as the kids tunelessly sang the words to some hymn or other.

To celebrate the season, a large Christmas tree stood in one corner of the hall, and the walls were decorated with paper angels, Santas, reindeer, and baubles. The children had evidently been very busy.

'I expect,' Marley said, as they made their way along the back row, before sitting down on ridiculously tiny plastic chairs, 'that he's having a whale of a time in New York.'

'New York?'

'Yes. Didn't you say he was in New York?'

'I don't think I did,' Kit said.

She was clearly waiting for him to expand on the subject, but he didn't feel able to. He didn't want to talk about his family at all, especially to her. She already brought his emotions dangerously close to the surface. He wondered again about the man who'd got out of the car with her the other day. He'd seen them talking and laughing in the car park, then the man — he was pretty sure it was one of their production managers, Don — had put his arm around her shoulders, as if he owned her.

Were they an item?

And why the hell did it matter if they were?

Marley folded her arms in a defensive gesture and stared ahead of her at the stage. So, he'd annoyed her again. Well, he was good at that, as he recalled.

He sneakily examined her profile, noting the high cheekbones, the curve of her lips, the tilt of her chin. He remembered how soft her skin had felt beneath his fingers, and how that mouth, currently set firm, felt when it yielded against his own.

When she turned to him suddenly, he jumped, startled.

'Do you really think what we had was just a teenage *thing*?'

Kit felt the heat spread from his neck all the way up to his forehead. 'What?' He was playing for time and felt a bit stupid for doing so.

'We were together for two and a half years. Don't you remember what we meant to each other at all?'

Remember it? He almost laughed. He'd spent years trying to forget it. Maybe the time for pretence was over.

'I remember,' he said softly.

She turned to face him fully. 'You do?'

Things were bubbling up inside Kit. He'd known coming to the school would be a big mistake. 'For God's sake, Marley. Of course I do. You seemed keen to downplay it, though. I thought it was what you wanted.'

'You made it sound as if it meant *nothing*. It mattered once.'

'Yeah. Once.'

She paused, then burst out, 'Do you really think I'd put it behind me that easily? I was just thrown, that's all. I hadn't seen you for such a long time, and I didn't want you to know how much it had shocked me. No way I was going to let you get one over on me.'

Kit gave a half laugh. 'I could never get one over on you.'

'You'd be surprised.' She bit her lip and turned back to face the stage. 'Well, this is awkward.'

'Isn't it?' He took a deep breath. 'How have you been? Really.'

'Oh, you know, getting along.'

'Thought you'd be married with kids by now,' he said, feeling a stab of pain at the words.

She didn't answer for a long time, and he thought she planned to ignore him. Then she murmured, 'You thought wrong then.'

'Have you been seeing him for long?'

He clearly had her full attention at that. 'Seeing who?'

'Don, is it?'

'Don?' She stared at him for a moment, then her face broke into a grin. 'I'm not with Don. Bloody hell, I think my mother would have something to say about that, if I was.'

'Your mother?'

'She and Don are, well, an item, I suppose.'

'Oh.' He really hadn't seen that coming. He was astonished, and a little afraid of the huge relief he felt at her words.

A few more people began filing into the hall, chatting and laughing as they bagged seats, took off coats, turned off their phones. A member of staff took their spot at the piano, playing a few scales. A speaker crackled.

Kit checked his watch. Fifteen minutes to go.

'I had such a crush on you.' Marley spoke so softly he wasn't sure he'd heard her correctly.

'I kind of thought it was more than a crush,' he said, trying to keep his voice light.

'I mean when we were here. When we were at primary school.'

He turned to her, amazed. 'I never knew that.'

'You weren't supposed to.'

'But I thought—' He broke off, aware that he'd almost said too much.

'You thought what?'

'It doesn't matter.'

'It clearly does. What did you think?'

What had he thought? He remembered being eleven years old, in the painful throes of first love, desperate to pluck up the courage to ask the girl of his dreams out. Marley Jacobs, the prettiest girl in the school — in his opinion, at any rate. He'd wanted to ask her out for so long, but that day had been his last chance. Term was almost over. He'd promised himself he would do it, because if he didn't, he might never see her again.

To his bitter disappointment, he wasn't going to St Hilda's with her. He was being sent, against his will, to Aidensthorpe Court, his father's old boarding school. His parents insisted it was for the best. He shouldn't mingle with the children who would one day work for him, apparently. Besides, he'd needed a good education, and his parents were far from convinced that the local comprehensive could provide that.

Deciding that it was now or never, Kit had made up his mind to ask Marley out. If he could secure her as his girlfriend before they parted, perhaps their love could survive the separation that different high schools would impose on them. Such was his naïvety in those days, he thought ruefully. Bless.

It had taken him ages to pluck up the courage. He'd lost count of how many times he'd rehearsed what he was going to say to her. In the end, he'd told himself not to be a coward, and hurried to her classroom as the final bell went, relieved to find her packing felt tips into her Spice Girls pencil case while cheerfully chatting to her best friend, Hayley. He'd stepped into the room without her noticing and hovered, waiting for his moment.

Then the world had seemed to stop spinning, when he heard Hayley say, 'So, are you going to ask Christopher out, then?'

They'd both giggled, and Marley said, 'Might do. He is quite cute, I suppose.'

Hayley nudged her. 'I knew you loved him.'

'Do not!'

'Do, too!'

Marley had flicked back her plaits and pushed her friend playfully. 'I'll probably marry him,' she announced casually, while over in the corner, Kit's heart hammered.

'Yuk. Why would you want to get married?' Hayley had screwed up her nose. 'Boys are disgusting. My brother *stinks*!'

'I know, I know,' Marley had said. 'And I don't *like* Christopher. Not like that. You know, all that kissing stuff. Ugh.'

'So, what you going to ask him out for?'

Marley had sighed patiently. 'Because he's rich, dumbo. His grandad owns that factory, and Mum says he's got a big posh house and loads of money. One day, it will be Christopher's. If I marry him, I'll be rich, too, and I might get a sports car.'

Hayley seemed to consider the matter. 'Yeah, but, still .... You'd have to kiss him and stuff. Could you do that?'

'It would be gross,' Marley admitted, 'but I've always wanted a sports car, like Ginger Spice.'

Kit had left the room, his eleven-year-old heart well and truly broken. He'd never told her what he'd heard, and he didn't know why he felt the need to tell her now. Maybe it was protection. Maybe he needed to remind himself of what she truly was and warn her that he knew her true nature. After all, that may have been the first time she'd trampled all over his feelings, but it definitely hadn't been the last.

'You're kidding me?' When he'd finished telling her what had happened that day, she looked satisfyingly stunned and rather ashamed. 'God, I'm so sorry.'

'Yeah, well.'

'But you know it was bullshit, right? I mean, you understood that I was just trying to save face?'

'Really.'

'Don't say it like that! You know it! Look, we were eleven. Boys were gross. We weren't supposed to have feelings for them. I had to have some excuse for asking you out, or my life would have been a misery. Jeez, you can't really think that, at eleven years old, I gave a damn about a sports car.'

She laughed, and Kit felt suddenly incredibly foolish.

He really had thought that. In fact, he'd cried himself to sleep, and made damn sure that he'd avoided going anywhere near her before he left for his new school, so she wouldn't get the opportunity to ask him out, and he wouldn't be stupid enough to do the asking himself.

'Anyway,' she added, 'we got past that, as I recall.'

'You think?' Kit shrugged. 'Maybe.'

'Maybe?' She frowned at him. 'What do you mean, maybe? We — we were in love, weren't we? At the time.'

'At the time.'

Marley's expression changed. She looked sullen. 'Just teenage love. Not real, of course.'

There was a tightness in Kit's throat, as dozens of children filed quietly into the room, led by smiling teachers. Their little faces were bright with excitement and joy. Oh, God.

He swallowed. 'It felt real enough to me.' Why on earth had he said that?

She stared down at her hands on her lap. 'Me, too.'

They looked at each other, and Kit noticed a sudden softness in her eyes that he hadn't seen since he'd got back. The buzz of conversation around them seemed to fade away, and he was aware only of her face, turned towards him, and the bittersweet memories it stirred within him.

The speaker crackled again, and someone tapped on the microphone.

'Good afternoon, ladies and gentlemen.'

'It's starting,' Marley murmured, then turned away from his gaze. Her face lit up suddenly, and as she waved, he realised her sister and the man who must be her brother-in-law were waving back. 'I can't wait to see the boys,' she whispered. 'Max has been practising *Away in a Manger* for ages. And Sam's the innkeeper. He's got two lines to himself!'

Kit remembered when he'd been Joseph in their own Nativity play. He'd hoped against hope that Marley would be Mary, but no such luck. Even after all that time, he found himself grimacing at the memory of that awful Amy Smith, with her blonde ringlets and sugary smile. She'd gripped his hand tightly and refused to let go as they'd stood before the innkeeper, begging him for shelter. Anyone would think she was really in labour, the way she'd clung to him. It was a wonder he'd remembered any of his lines, when all he'd been able to think about was Marley in her white gown and silver wings. She was the most beautiful girl he'd ever seen. The perfect angel.

Blinking away the memory, Kit focussed on the teacher at the piano, as she began playing the introduction to *Once in_Royal David's City*. The young children sitting at the front of the hall stood and began to sing, and his heart flipped. How was he going to cope with it all?

Doing his best to ignore his increasing distress, he concentrated hard on the performances. He remembered a programme he'd caught on the television the previous weekend, and decided to channel Simon Cowell, judging the kids' performances as if they were on X-Factor. That way, he couldn't get too emotionally involved.

Ooh, didn't really hit that high note there, son. Yes, you can sing, little girl, but you have zero stage presence. Don't hold your breath for an agent, kid.

As Mary and Joseph exited stage right, apparently to saddle up a donkey, a class of older children filed in from the left. Marley glanced at the programme.

'Oh,' she said, and gulped.

'What is it?'

'Nothing, nothing. Just, these are the children who are leaving the school next year. They'll be going to high school. This is their last Nativity play.'

Kit heard the catch in her voice, and his eyes widened in surprise. Marley, getting sentimental? Good grief.

He glanced at the children standing nervously on stage, as the teacher played the introductory strains of *O Little Town of Bethlehem* and realised that he'd only been around their age when he'd wanted to ask Marley out. They were just babies, he thought incredulously, yet his feelings had seemed so intense, so real. She'd had the weirdest effect on him, ever since the first day he'd seen her, standing in the reception class, pigtails fastened with pink plastic bobbles. How did she affect him like that? He cast a glance at her, shocked to see tears glistening in her eyes.

'Never had you down as the soppy type,' he said, nudging her gently. She turned towards him, and the distress in her face alarmed him. 'What is it? What's the matter?'

She shrugged and wiped her eyes. 'Just, you know. Christmas.'

There was more to it than that. There had to be. 'I know the singing's atrocious,' Kit joked, desperate to cheer her up, 'but it's not worth crying over.'

She sniffed and wrapped her arms around herself, as if protecting herself from something. 'I'm fine.'

'Well, you're clearly not,' he said. And he'd thought he'd be the one struggling!

'It's a difficult age, isn't it?' she murmured.

He nodded, feeling a bit bewildered by her attitude.

'Ten or eleven years old. Not quite children, not quite teenagers. Tough. And then they have high school to deal with soon. I hope,' she swallowed hard, 'I hope they have good parents, decent families to help them through.'

Was that her problem? Kit frowned. What was going on?

They sat, saying nothing, as the children performed their heart-wrenching song. Kit had barely recovered from the assault on his emotions that Marley's tears had provoked, before Mary and Joseph knocked on the door of the inn and were greeted by a little blond boy with a big grin on his face.

'It's Sam,' Marley whispered. 'Look at those dimples! That's my nephew.'

The pride in her voice was evident. Kit watched the little Mary and Joseph negotiate a bed for the night. Sam very nobly, and very loudly, informed them that they could sleep in his stable, then gave the audience a thumbs-up, much to everyone's amusement.

Suddenly, Kit couldn't see them anymore. He felt trapped, desperately blinking the tears away, terrified that Marley — or anyone else, come to that — would notice them.

'I'm sorry.'

Marley caught his arm as he stood.

'Where are you going?' she hissed.

'I can't do this.'

'What do you mean you can't do this? Do what?'

'This whole thing. This Nativity stuff.' He saw the look of disbelief in her eyes and almost crumbled. 'I can't sit through an hour or two of this. I have better things to do with my time. There's loads of stuff to do at the office. Here—' He almost shoved the bag into her arms. '—the costume. The sweets are behind the reception desk. I'm sure your brother-in-law can step in. See you later.'

'You've got to be kidding me.' The look of contempt on her face almost broke him, but he had to get away.

He pushed through the row of tutting parents and edged his way out of the hall. The walls of the corridor closed in on him, and he almost ran down it, desperate to get out of the building.

As he did so, he could almost hear one of his old teachers yelling, 'No running in the corridor, Christopher!'

Well, he was no longer a child. He was an adult now, and he could run if he wanted to.

And he wanted to.

Chapter 16

'I can't believe you fell for that!' Jack's voice was laden with amusement.

'Neither can I,' Kit said grimly. 'What an idiot. The worst thing is, I knew something wasn't right. You know when you can just feel it? I'll bloody throttle Marley.'

'I wonder why she did it?'

'To make me look a fool, why else?' He felt suddenly dispirited. She must have really hated him to plan such an elaborate ruse with the sole intention of showing him up. 'Well, that backfired, didn't it? I walked out, and she had to rope in her brother-in-law to take my place. Bet he was furious.'

The sound of Jack laughing was like a balm to Kit's wounded soul. He could take any amount of embarrassment from Marley to hear his brother's laughter. It lifted his spirits, and to his surprise, he started laughing, too.

'Sneaky little thing, isn't she?' Jack said, eventually. 'I always knew she had spirit, but this.... You *are* behaving yourself, aren't you? I mean, why would she want to show you up? What have you done to wind her up?'

'I haven't done anything.' Kit bit his lip. *Well, apart from moan about the Christmas music, refuse to pay for the staff Christmas meal out, and stop production of the LuvRocks merchandise, in spite of the factory workers' protests.*

God, they must all hate him. Were they all in on it? Did they all know about the Santa fiasco? Were they sitting in a pub somewhere, right at that moment, laughing at him?

'Are you sure? Seems a bit over the top.' Jack sounded suspicious.

An alarm bell rang in Kit's head. 'Of course I'm sure,' he said, sounding far more lighthearted than he felt. 'That's Marley for you, isn't it?'

'Is it? Not the Marley I know. She may be a bit, well, forthright, but she's professional, and a good secretary.'

'PA,' Kit reminded him, and they both laughed again. 'Thing is,' Kit said, desperate to allay his brother's doubts, 'Marley and I knew each other before. We were at primary school together.'

'Ah.' Jack sounded as if everything suddenly made sense. 'Evidently, you made quite an impression on her.'

'Evidently.' At least Jack seemed reassured. The last thing he needed was to be worrying about the factory.

'How are things?' Kit knew he should have asked earlier, but he was ashamed to admit that he dreaded these phone calls. He loved hearing from his brother, but it was never an easy conversation.

'It's going well. As well as can be expected, anyway. We're having lots of time together as a family, which I never expected.' There was a brief silence, then Jack gave a short laugh. 'It's a lot warmer here than it is there, I reckon. I mean, it's not hot, but it doesn't feel like December. Feels really odd. Not like Christmas, at all.'

Kit caught the wistful tone in his voice. 'Lucky you,' he said, in an attempt to cheer Jack up, then cursed himself. Of all the crass comments to make.

Jack didn't pick up on it. 'What's it like over there?'

'How do you think? Freezing cold, windy, grey. Frosty mornings most days, too.' He rolled his eyes. Were they really discussing the weather?

'Next year,' Jack said firmly. 'It will be a proper English Christmas for us.'

Kit's eyes filled with tears again. 'You bet,' he promised. 'We'll pull out all the stops. Biggest Christmas tree in the forest, fattest turkey in the shop, every toy on the shelves for Tim...' His voice trailed off. He didn't even know where he'd be living next Christmas. How could he make plans? How could any of them?

'Have you been in touch with Serafina yet?'

'Yeah. She's in London at the moment, but she'll be back before Christmas, and she's going to come round and start the ball rolling.'

'I'm so sorry, Kit.'

'Don't be sorry. We agreed. Hey, it's worth it, so no worries, okay?'

'You're a good bloke. I don't care what Dad said about you.'

Kit laughed. 'Hmm. Let's not even go there, shall we? Dad wasn't exactly my biggest fan.'

'Dad wasn't exactly anyone's biggest fan,' Jack pointed out truthfully. 'Miserable old sod.'

Over the telephone, Kit heard a door shut and a woman's voice calling for his brother.

'That Amanda?'

'Yeah, she's just got back. I'll have to go, Kit. I'll call you in a couple of days, okay?'

'Sure. Give my love to Amanda and Tim. Tell them — well, you know.'

'I know. Speak soon, bro, and hey,' he added with a chuckle, 'don't let Marley pull any more stunts, okay? Be firm with her.'

'I will,' Kit promised, thinking, *be firm with her?*

God, the thought of being firm with Marley put ideas in his head that had no business being there. She was still doing things to him, just as she had all those years ago. He really would have to be careful.

***

I plumped up the cushion and placed it behind Great Uncle Charles's back. 'Is that any better?' I handed him his glass of whisky, pulling a face as its pungent aroma attacked my nostrils.

'Don't know how you can drink that stuff,' I said. 'You'd be better off with cough medicine.'

'Rubbish.' He took a large gulp of whisky and smacked his thin lips together, the sunken result revealing that he wasn't wearing his teeth, yet again. 'Who wants cough medicine when a tot of the good stuff will put hairs on your chest?'

'It's not hairs you need,' I said, trying not to be repulsed at the thought of Great Uncle Charles's naked chest. 'It's vapour rub, I reckon. That cough's got worse, not better. Do you want me to call the doctor?'

He waved a hand at me dismissively. 'That's the trouble with youngsters today — no backbone. Call a doctor for a bit of a cough? I'll tell you what's to blame for this namby-pamby attitude, shall I?'

'I'm sure you're going to, whether I want you to or not,' I said with a sigh. I sank onto the sofa opposite him and waited for him to impart his pearls of wisdom.

'The NHS. That's what. Back in the good old days, people had to pay to see a doctor, so we were tougher. We didn't go running to the surgery every time we sneezed. Not like today. Nowadays, people are so soft you can't get an appointment, even if your leg's hanging off. Too many timewasters. All been handed to them on a plate, you see? If they had to cough up for treatment, they'd soon toughen up, I'll tell you.'

'Talking of coughing up,' I said, determined not to rise to the bait, 'I'll bring you some medicine tomorrow, whatever you say, and some vapour rub for your chest. If you're not better in a couple of days, I'm ringing the doctor, and that's that.'

'Oh, stop mithering, girl, and tell me how our little plan went.' He leaned back against the cushion and took another sip of whisky, watching me thoughtfully. 'Judging by that expression, it didn't go as it should. Right?'

I flushed. 'He made me look an absolute idiot,' I admitted. 'All that effort and conniving, and he cleared off. Left me to it. I had to ask David to step in. He was furious, and now I owe him a favour, which, no doubt, he will call in. I can see me babysitting for weeks ahead.' I shook my head. 'How could Christopher do that? I mean, we were just sitting there, watching the Nativity, then he jumped up, announced he had better things to do with his time, and walked out.'

'That doesn't surprise me,' Great Uncle Charles said. 'He's a Carroll. They're all the same. Selfish, miserable, self-centred swines, the lot of them.'

I was tempted to tell him that was just the description my family reserved for him. Instead, I nodded. 'Well, I don't know about that, but I saw him in a new light, I can tell you.'

He looked quite pleased about that. 'So, didn't you talk about anything? No memories evoked for him? No nostalgia trip to make him see the error of his ways?'

I tilted my head to one side, thinking. 'He did talk a bit,' I said eventually. 'He admitted he'd deliberately downplayed our relationship the whole time. Can you believe that? Out of — I don't know — pride, or something.'

'Bit like you were then?'

I scowled. 'And he told me that he'd been going to ask me out all the way back in primary school. Imagine that! I had no idea he even knew I existed back then.'

'So, why didn't he ask you out then?' Great Uncle Charles sounded highly sceptical.

My face burned. I could hardly tell him that he'd overheard me talking to my friend and assumed that I was a mercenary little brat, only after his family's money. I could well imagine Uncle Charles's response to *that*. Instead, I shrugged and said, 'Nerves, or something.'

He tutted. 'Well, this is fascinating stuff, I must say. So, basically, you went to all that trouble to remind him of how happy he used to be, and all you did was remind him that he was a coward who daren't even ask an eleven-year-old out. Marvellous work there, Marley. That should do the trick. His Christmas spirit will come flying back now, I'm sure.'

'I haven't finished yet,' I protested. 'That was just the start.'

'Cracking start,' he said, nodding sagely. 'You must be very proud.'

I tapped my fingers on the chair arm. 'Why are you so horrible?'

'It's a gift,' he said. 'So, what's next on the agenda?'

'I don't know,' I admitted. 'I have to make him see how much fun Christmas can be; what he's missing out on by being an old Scrooge. I just don't know how.'

'So, time for Christmas Present, eh? Well…' He drained his whisky glass and held it out to me. 'I'll drink to that.'

'You're an awful person,' I told him, taking the glass from him and heading into the kitchen.

'I aim to please,' he called.

I unscrewed the top from the bottle of whisky and poured him another small measure. What *was* I going to do next? Bring the Christmas spirit to Kit Carroll, somehow, for all our sakes. But how?

***

I could sense that Christopher was waiting for me to start an argument. I'd arrived at the office that morning, to find him already at work. He'd fixed me with a defiant stare, tilting his chin at me, those dark eyes flashing warning signals. Bloody hell, I'd only asked him if he wanted a coffee.

Guilt, I thought, spooning Nescafé into two mugs. He was feeling guilty, and well he should. All that money I'd forked out to hire a Santa suit, all the trouble Don and I had gone to, missing lunch to scour the shops in search of the last Father Christmas costume in Yorkshire, and offer Christopher's services — not to mention a stack of free sweets — to the primary school, just to have David plodding around muttering *ho, ho, ho,* and looking like a total plonker. Fat lot of good all the plotting had done me. Now what?

'Thanks.' He took the mug from me and placed it on the coaster on his desk. He looked at the monitor, and I turned to go, thinking I'd been dismissed.

'Did it — did it go okay? After I left, I mean?'

I turned back, giving him a look of contempt. 'Do you care?'

He looked stricken. 'Of course I care. I didn't want to let the kids down! I just —'

'You just couldn't be bothered to sit through an hour or two of them warbling Christmas carols and telling the story of the birth of Baby Jesus. Yeah, I get that. You made it pretty clear.'

He rubbed his forehead. 'It wasn't like that.'

'Oh?' I raised an eyebrow. 'So, what was it like?'

He opened his mouth, as if about to say something, but shut it again. With a shrug of his shoulders, he turned back to the computer.

I felt my hackles rising. 'If you must know, it went okay. David did his best, although he felt like a right idiot, and, of course, Sam and Max recognised him straight away. Still, the kids had fun, yanking at his beard, and they all appreciated the sweets.'

'Good. That's good. I'll catch up with David later. Thank him and apologise, all at the same time.'

'Probably best. He wasn't very happy about being dropped in it like that.'

'I know how he feels,' Christopher said, staring at me with a challenge in his eyes.

I shuffled a bit. 'Yes, well, blame Jack for that. Not my fault he didn't keep you informed.'

'Bit difficult for him to keep me informed, considering he knew nothing about it, don't you think?'

My face scorched. *Crap!*

Obviously, I'd known Christopher would find out the truth eventually, but I hadn't expected it to be so soon. What was Jack bothering to ring home for, anyway? If I was sightseeing in New York near Christmas, home would be the last place I'd be thinking about.

'Why, Marley?' He was watching me, a baffled look on his face.

'Why, what?'

'Why make all that up? Why set me up to look an idiot? Do you really hate me that much?'

'I don't hate you!' God, that had come out a bit fast. I hadn't even meant to say it. And, anyway, it wasn't even true. I did hate him. I had good reason to hate him. Why was he looking at me with those bloody gorgeous eyes, anyway? Swine.

'Don't you?' He sounded surprised. Not as surprised as I was. 'I thought, maybe, you were doing it to teach me a lesson. You know, for the decisions I've made about the factory.'

'Do you really think I'm that petty?' I demanded.

'Well, I know you disagree with the way I'm running this place.'

'I do. I've never made any secret of the fact. Even so, I wouldn't go to all those lengths just to make you feel small. God, you have a low opinion of me.'

'As low as the one you have of me?' We looked at each other for a moment, neither saying a word. Then Christopher sighed. 'Look, I know you don't approve of some of my actions, but you have to believe me when I say I'm acting in the best interests of the company. Do you believe that?'

'I believe you think you are,' was as far as I was prepared to go.

He shook his head. 'Okay, let's go with that.'

I turned to leave, but his voice saying my name forced me to turn to him once again. 'Yes?'

'I won't be in tomorrow. I have meetings all day. If you need me, I'll have my mobile on.'

I nodded. 'Fine.'

He hesitated, then burst out, 'Would you—I mean, do you want to have dinner with me tonight?'

I nearly keeled over. 'Pardon?'

'Dinner. I presume you do still eat?' He gave me a sardonic smile, and I nodded, feeling completely out of my depth suddenly. 'Great. I want to talk to you, and I don't think here is the best place to do that. How about I pick you up around half-past seven?'

'Are you serious?'

'Of course. I wouldn't say so otherwise, would I?'

I supposed he wouldn't. But dinner with Christopher? Why? And should I risk it? Given the way he made my heart tap dance faster than Ginger Rogers ever managed every time I saw him, I wasn't sure spending time with him outside work was something I should even contemplate.

And why had he asked me, anyway? He'd said he remembered the true depths of our relationship. How much did he remember? Did he remember the way he'd treated me? What he'd done? He had no idea.

'If you don't want to come, don't. It's up to you.' That was more like it. He sounded irritable while shuffling papers on his desk.

I took a deep breath. 'Yeah, okay. It's a free meal. I live—'

'Above the hairdressers on Main Street. I know. I'll be there at half seven.'

He began typing, and I knew I was dismissed. It was only as I sank, rather nonplussed, into my own chair and stared at the monitor that it dawned on me what he'd said.

How the hell did he know where I lived?

CHAPTER 17

I wasn't bothered about going out with Christopher.

All right, so I wore my best dress, bought on sale from Rochester's over a year ago and only worn once, and I styled my hair to perfection, and I applied my makeup with extra care and attention, but that wasn't because I was fussed about going out with him. It was my way of showing him what he was missing, end of story. He'd thrown me away, after all, and I was damned if I'd pass up on the chance to prove that it had been his loss. It wasn't that I cared about going on a date with him, because, after all, it wasn't a date. Just business, I reminded myself, as I dabbed my most expensive perfume behind my ears and on my wrists. Nothing more to it than that. It was probably his way of grovelling to me after being such a dickhead at the school.

Given his appalling behaviour, I reckoned he owed me the best meal in the best restaurant. Maybe The Fox and Hounds in Helmston, if he could secure a table at short notice. Or maybe we'd go even further afield — there was a well-respected and very expensive restaurant in Thornley Beck, for example. Wherever we went, I was going to choose the most expensive dishes on the menu. Serve him right.

Peering out of the window onto the street below, I told myself that I wasn't nervous. My stomach was only churning because I was excited to be going out. Not with *him*. With *anyone. Anywhere.* It had been a while.

I folded my arms, trying to stay calm. I didn't want to look all flushed when he arrived. Elegant, sophisticated, completely unfazed. That was the look I was going for.

Crap! He's here! A wave of nausea hit me when his car pulled up outside the hairdressers. He stepped out into the road, and the nausea almost overwhelmed me. God, he looked fantastic.

Leather jacket, black jeans, hair a tousled mass of raven curls....

Hang on! He hadn't shaved. There was a definite designer stubble look going on there. And he wasn't exactly dressed up, was he? He could have made a bit of effort. He began to walk towards the front door of the flat, situated at the side of the building, and I panicked. He couldn't come up. I didn't want him to see the tiny flat I lived in — not when he lived in that massive house in Farthingdale.

It would be different, I thought bitterly, if I owned Fox Lodge. I would have definitely asked him in then. Fox Lodge was far more suitable. Okay, it wasn't Fell House, but even so, I'd have been proud to show it off. This poky little place was an embarrassment.

I almost flew down the stairs and threw open the door, to find him standing on the pavement with his hand raised, as if about to knock.

'Hello.' I knew I sounded breathless. He would wonder what I was in such a rush about. *Just calm down, Marley. Focus.* The subtle citrus smell of his cologne wafted towards me on the evening breeze, and I had a momentary desire to pull him closer and inhale him. Dinner was going to be interesting.

I switched on my most dazzling smile and said, 'You're on time.'

He stared at me in a most peculiar way, then he swallowed and said briskly, 'I like to be punctual. You look nice.'

Nice? Nice! I glanced down at the burgundy lace mini dress that had cost me two weeks' wages. 'Oh, this? Had it ages.'

He didn't reply. Instead, he stuck his hands in his pockets and nodded towards the street.

'Well, my car's just over there.'

I didn't think you'd parked on the roof, I thought crossly. *Nice!* He'd better be taking me somewhere exceptional after that feeble attempt at a compliment.

'Don't you need a coat?' He frowned at me, as I pulled open the car door.

What, and spoil the look of this dress? No bloody chance.

'I'm not cold,' I said, through gritted teeth, glad the long lace sleeves covered the goose-pimples on my arms.

'Oh well, the seats are heated anyway,' he said, showing off, no doubt.

My own little car didn't possess anything as sophisticated as heated seats. When I got my inheritance, I would buy a car that would put this one to shame. Then I wondered how Great Uncle Charles was. I hoped the cough medicine I'd taken to him was working. He'd sounded terribly rough yesterday. If he was no better tomorrow, I would definitely call the doctor.

We drove off, and I leaned back in the comfortable passenger seat, feeling the warmth spread through my body and trying to quell the nerves. Would he expect me to go Dutch with the meal? I hadn't thought of that. If I was paying half, I certainly wouldn't order the most expensive dishes. Trouble was, how would I know until the end of the meal, when I'd already ordered? Maybe I'd better stick to the cheaper dishes, just in case. But then, what if I did that and he insisted on paying for the whole thing? How annoying would that be?

Unfortunately, when we'd dated before we'd been just kids. No fancy restaurants for us then. During the two years we were together, we weren't even legally allowed to drink in a pub until the last five months of our relationship. How could I tell if *Kit* was the sort of person to pay for the whole thing?

Then again, judging by his tight-fisted attitude at work, I wouldn't be surprised if he expected me to pay for both of us. After all, wasn't that the whole point of my little project? He was Ebenezer Scrooge, and when it came to money, he was meanness personified. He probably had a padlock on his wallet.

I realised we'd missed the turn-off for Helmston. Not The Fox and Hounds, then. I supposed it wasn't surprising. He'd left it far too late to book.

I felt a thrill of anticipation. Where *was* he taking me?

When he finally stopped the car, I looked at him, puzzled. 'Did you forget something?'

He turned off the engine and frowned. 'Forget something?'

Realisation dawned on me. 'We're eating at your house?'

Christopher glanced out of the window at Fell House and shrugged. 'Yeah. That's okay, isn't it? Dinner's in the oven, so you won't have long to wait. You must be starving. I know I am.'

He was cooking for us? So, he wasn't even generous enough to go Dutch over a restaurant meal? Tight git was so mean, he was actually making the food himself. Bloody hell. And I'd put on my best dress for that. I might as well have worn my jeans.

Even so, I couldn't deny a sense of anticipation as he unlocked the front door. I'd always wanted to see inside Fell House. He'd never taken me there when we'd been dating, which had been a sore subject. I'd been young and naïve and had initially believed his endless parade of excuses. As our relationship deepened, though, the niggling suspicion persisted that he didn't think I was good enough to meet his precious family.

Well, it was finally safe to invite me back, I thought bitterly, since no one else in his family was there any longer. If nothing else, maybe I could get some ideas for decorating Fox Lodge. It was a rare opportunity to glimpse how the other half lived.

The interior of the house belied the cold, stone exterior. It had clearly been decorated by a woman — Jack's wife, probably. The cushions were a dead giveaway. Men hate cushions, don't they? The sofas in his place were stuffed full of them, and they were a gorgeous collection of different shapes and patterns and textures. No man would think of that. Well, no man like a Carroll man, anyway. The furniture was solid, but modern. Lots of walnut and chrome and grey wood, and soft furnishings in white and duck egg blue.

I rather liked it. I also rather liked the delicious smell that was emitting from the kitchen. Whatever was cooking, my stomach was clearly anticipating it with relish, as it growled most appreciatively, much to my embarrassment.

If Christopher heard, he didn't comment. 'I'll just see how the chilli's doing. Sit down. Make yourself at home.'

I sat, thinking *at home* was the last thing I felt. Instead I felt tense, let down, and a bit confused. Why had I been invited here? If, somewhere in the back of my mind, I'd thought it could just possibly be a date, I'd clearly been wrong. He'd made no effort to dress up, and if he was just cooking me a bit of chilli in his own home there was definitely nothing romantic in his gesture. Which was a good thing, obviously. The last thing I needed was to fend him off all night, and I'd already rehearsed my *thanks but no thanks* speech a million times.

Even so, it left one burning question. Why invite me to dinner at all? What was he up to?

He came back through, smiling rather awkwardly, as if he, too, was wondering why he'd invited me. 'Would you like the television on?'

Was he serious? Great. I could have made myself a chilli and sat in front of the telly all night in my own flat. And I'd have had the added bonus of being able to do so in the comfort of my pyjamas, not sitting there feeling all trussed up and fake in this bloody dress. Knowing my luck, I was bound to drop chilli down the front of it, too. 'No, thanks.'

'Glass of wine?'

I kept the smile on my face, somehow. 'That would be lovely.'

'Er, red, or white? I suppose red would be better with the chilli, but—'

'White's fine. Not too dry.'

'I do have beer, if you prefer that.'

Charming. Did I look like a beer drinker? 'No, thanks. The wine will be lovely.' It had better be, at any rate. Knowing him, it would be cheap supermarket plonk, best used for washing out paint brushes.

When he handed me a glass a few moments later, I took a tentative sip, surprised to find it tasted delicious. Probably Jack's wife's, I thought.

'I'll just dish up. If you want to come through in a couple of minutes, I thought we could eat at the kitchen table? It's warm and cosy in there. The dining room's a bit formal.'

I forced myself to smile at him, thinking, *bloody hell, the kitchen table!* Why didn't he just park outside the chippy, and we could have eaten haddock and chips out of the paper, sitting in the car?

Five minutes later I sat at the table, watching him over the rim of my wine glass as he carried over plates of steaming hot chilli. A big dish of rice sat in the centre of the table, alongside a bowl of salad, and a plate of garlic bread slices. Evidently, he wasn't planning on doing any kissing. Good job we were of the same mind, I thought savagely, helping myself to a large spoonful of rice.

We ate without speaking much. What little conversation there was seemed stilted. Christopher was clearly uneasy, and I wondered again why he'd invited me. I felt awkward and wished I'd said no.

Watching him eat was pretty unnerving, though. It was quite a sensual experience, which was weird. I'd never known eating could be sexy but watching him spoon chilli into his mouth set feelings in motion that I hadn't had for so long, I'd almost forgotten I could feel like that.

I remembered the sensation of those lips pressing against mine, the way my insides had bubbled and fizzed with excitement at his touch. Of course, I'd been a teenager at the time. Nowadays, I was far more sophisticated. I sincerely doubted that he would have the same effect on me, should he try anything as foolish as kissing me tonight.

I felt a stab of dismay when he helped himself to garlic bread. Clearly, he had no intention of trying any such thing.

Furious with myself for being so disappointed, I reached over and took a slice myself. Sod him.

'I remember the last time we ate together like this,' he said suddenly.

I coughed. Why did he wait until I was swallowing my food before landing that statement on me? Anyone would think he was trying to make me choke to death again. Maybe he wanted to give me the kiss of life?

I felt myself start to blush and gulped down some wine, partly to help the garlic bread go down, and partly to ease my nerves. 'Do you?' I said at last.

'Don't you?'

I hesitated. Of course I remembered. I remembered every moment. But did he, really?

'Possibly,' I dodged.

He was holding a slice of garlic bread between his fingers, not seeming at all interested in eating it. Instead, he turned it around and around, clearly distracted, as if trying to decide whether to continue that thread of conversation.

'The Smuggler's Cave Café, Kearton Bay.'

I took another sip of wine. Okay, he remembered.

'Do you remember?' he asked.

May the twenty-eighth, just under eleven years and five months ago. 'I think so,' I said, pretending to think about it.

'You had cheeseburger, and I had beans on toast.' His eyes twinkled.

'You had beans on toast three times,' I reminded him, then cursed myself. Damn, now he'd know that I'd remembered perfectly well.

'They were small portions,' he protested, kindly not pouncing on my mistake.

'Hmm. Think the waitress got sick of us in the end,' I recalled. I couldn't help myself. I smiled, and he smiled back. 'And all that hot chocolate we ordered. In May!'

'I loved watching you get all that whipped cream on your nose,' he admitted. 'You made such a mess of it, every single time.'

I pulled a face. 'Yeah, well, sorry if I was a bit common back then.'

'You were adorable.'

I wasn't sure which of us looked more appalled at that statement. I was pretty horrified that we were travelling down such a dangerous route, but Christopher looked as if he wished he could bite his tongue off.

'I'm done here,' he said, dropping the garlic bread on his plate and wiping his hands on a serviette.

'Me, too. Couldn't eat another thing,' I agreed, and then there was no more chance of conversation, as the sound of plates clattering together and glasses being gathered up filled the air, and we busied ourselves with clearing the table.

'Do you need a hand with the dishes?' I queried.

'God, no. I'll just load the dishwasher and then I'll make us a drink. You go through to the lounge. Make yourself at home.'

I'd been half expecting to be dismissed, so I was a bit thrown, but I nodded and headed into the lounge, sinking down on the sofa and tugging violently at the hem of my dress, wishing I'd worn something a bit longer. The time ticked on, and my stomach felt most peculiar, and I didn't think it was down to the chilli.

When Christopher finally appeared, I couldn't help myself from bursting out, 'You're kidding me!'

He grinned. 'I couldn't resist. I've brought napkins, just in case.'

He handed me a mug of hot chocolate, complete with a huge swirl of cream and a chocolate flake stuck in the top. How would I ever drink that without making a mess? Was he deliberately trying to make me look a fool?

I eyed him suspiciously, but there was genuine warmth in his eyes, and I thought suddenly that he really wasn't doing it out of malice. But, that being the case, what on earth was he trying to do? I put the mug on the coffee table, reached over to pull out the flake, and put it to my lips.

His pupils definitely dilated, and I felt a fleeting satisfaction. I remembered that look. He sank onto the sofa beside me and stared at me for a moment as I nibbled the chocolate delicately, then he put his own drink beside mine and turned to face me.

'I really am sorry.'

I almost dropped the chocolate flake. God, was this it? Was this where we stopped dancing around each other at last and confronted the elephant in the room? Was he finally apologising for the way he'd behaved all those years ago?

'Yes, well ...' I began, feeling suddenly uncomfortable. It was a big deal. If he hadn't left me, would we have made it work? Still be together? Maybe...

'I should never have walked out like that.'

'No,' I said slowly. 'You shouldn't. Then again, I suppose...'

He held up his hand. 'Don't make excuses for me. It was pathetic. I have apologised to David, by the way. He was cool about it, eventually.'

David? Oh, my God! He was talking about the Santa fiasco again. I shoved the rest of the flake in my mouth and chewed violently. Swine.

'Did it really go okay? How did your nephews do?'

I swallowed the chocolate and shrugged. 'Fine.'

'It was weird, being back at the old place again, wasn't it?'

I narrowed my eyes. He hadn't got me there to talk about our old schooldays, surely? What on earth was going on? 'Yeah, it was,' I said.

'I can't believe you had a crush on me,' he continued, shaking his head. 'All that time, and I never knew.'

'Yes, well, I was just a kid,' I pointed out. 'If you'd had the nerve to ask me out, who knows what would have happened? Shame we had to wait another five years to meet up.' Although, in a way, it was more of a shame that we'd met again at all. How much simpler life would have been if I'd never set eyes on Christopher Carroll.

'Three years, actually,' he said suddenly.

'Three?' I frowned. 'We were sixteen when we met again, *actually*.'

'I saw you when you were fourteen.'

He had? 'Why didn't you ever mention it?'

He folded his arms, looking defensive. 'Because you'd have laughed at me.'

'What? Why would I have laughed at you?'

He paused, as if trying to decide how much to confide. 'Because I got beaten up in front of you, that's why.'

I gaped at him. 'You got—?'

'It was the Christmas holidays, and me and a couple of other lads who went to Aidensthorpe Court had met up in Helmston to do some present shopping. We encountered this — this bunch of weirdos on the road. They were hanging round the bus shelter on the Farthingdale road. Words were exchanged. One of them recognised my friend, and realised we were all boarding school boys, which clearly meant that we were stuck up gits who deserved to be taught a lesson. We tried to calm things down, but they weren't having it. Before we knew it, we were being kicked and punched to the ground. Yeah, I got quite a black eye that day.'

'Gosh, I'm sorry to hear that,' I said. 'But, hey, what's that got to do with me?'

'You were there. Part of the crowd.'

I was? I couldn't remember any of that. I definitely hadn't beaten anyone up. 'Are you sure it was me? I would never have—'

'You didn't actually attack us, no,' he admitted. 'You were too busy swigging cider and snogging some goth in the bus shelter. You thought it was hilarious, though. When they stopped kicking us, you jeered at us and lurched off with your boyfriend.'

'I did?' Oh, the shame of it.

'Frankly, you looked like something out of *The Munsters*.'

'My goth phase.' I closed my eyes as bitter memories flashed across my mind of one of the worst times in my life, when Dad had abandoned us, and Mum spent every day crying, and Olivia was all pale and scared. I'd hated everyone and hidden behind a mask of gothic black eyeliner and a curtain of dyed black hair. I'd been furious when Mum wouldn't let me change my name to Bellatrix. Thank God she'd held firm.

'God, I'm sorry. No wonder you never mentioned it. You must have felt like such an idiot.'

'I did at the time,' he said coldly. 'Years later, I realised that the real idiots were the bunch of yobs who attacked us for no reason other than that we went to a different school.'

'Sorry. Again.' I sighed. 'I was probably pissed. I was pissed quite a lot around then.'

'At fourteen?' he said incredulously.

'It was a bad time. My dad...'

He hesitated. 'You never really mentioned him much. Is that when he left home?'

I nodded. 'It was a bad time. I went a little bit off the rails.'

'I didn't know. I mean, I didn't realise it had affected you that badly. You never made a big deal of it.'

'There wasn't much to say. He got bored and left. Broke Mum's heart. She fell to bits and she couldn't stop crying, and then Olivia got scared and didn't know what to do, and I had to try to keep them going. It's a lot to deal with when you're fourteen, and cider seemed like quite a good painkiller at the time.'

'God, Marley, I had no idea.'

'You must have thought I was such a bitch. I'm amazed you went out with me at all after that.'

'Not half as surprised as I was,' he admitted. 'Guess there was just something about you.'

His voice sounded different — sort of soft and gooey.

Desperate to change the subject, I grabbed my hot chocolate and took a gulp. As his laughter filled the air, I realised ruefully that I'd done it again.

'Here,' he said, handing me a serviette, or *napkin* as he called it, being posh. 'Although I think you look quite cute with the cream on your nose.'

His eyes crinkled in the corners, and those soft lips were curving upwards again. Without thinking about it, I scooped up a dollop of cream and dabbed it on his own nose.

His eyes widened. 'Do you really want to start a food fight with me? I'm very good at this sort of thing. Boarding school training, remember.'

I thought about my expensive Rochester's dress and shook my head. 'Best not,' I said, half regretfully. 'You should have brought me a spoon to eat this cream,' I pointed out.

'But it's much more fun watching you trying to drink the chocolate without making a mess,' he said, his voice full of laughter.

I leaned back against the sofa, grinning at him, and he leaned back too, suddenly looking relaxed.

'I expect you're wondering why I invited you here tonight,' he said.

He wasn't wrong there. 'It did occur to me, yes,' I managed eventually.

'I need your help, Marley.'

My mouth fell open. 'My help? Seriously?' Well, there was a turn up for the books.

He grinned at me. 'Don't look so shocked. I do value your opinion, you know.'

'Really? Since when?'

He winced. 'Okay. I asked for that.'

'Yes, you did a bit, Christopher.'

He sighed. 'Please, please, don't call me Christopher. I hate it. I'm Kit now.'

'It's that important to you?'

'It is. Christopher—' He paused. 'Christopher was the name my father gave me. Kit's who I am.'

I felt a stirring of compassion for him. Clearly, he had major issues with his father, and I could well relate to that. 'Okay. Kit it is.'

He smiled. 'Thanks. I like the way you say that.'

I felt an ominous tingling and cleared my throat. 'So, my opinion on what, *Kit*?'

The softness left his eyes, and he made an obvious effort to look business-like. 'Thing is, Marley, I have some news for the staff, and I don't think they're going to be happy. I want your advice about how best to put it to them.'

My heart sank. 'Oh, God. What now?'

'Don't say it like that!'

'Well, what do you expect? They're already fuming about the staff Christmas meal, and then there's the LuvRocks contract.'

'What are they saying about that?' His voice was sharp.

I shrugged. 'What do you think they're saying? That you're a complete moron to throw it away like that. Okay, most of us wanted to get back to making our original products anyway, but talk about throwing the baby out with the bathwater.'

'It was the right decision,' he said, sounding grumpy.

'So you say, but come on! Some of them are worried that you're going to make us bankrupt at this rate. It's all right for you, sitting here in your posh house. Some of us have rent to pay, or mortgages. Some of us have bills and families — children...'

'I know that. I don't want them to worry. I really don't.'

He took a sip of hot chocolate and sighed. I wondered how he managed to drink it without getting cream all over his face. Typical.

'Thing is, Marley, I don't want to do things the way Jack did. Don't get me wrong,' he said quickly, as I began to protest, 'I'm very grateful to him for the way he took over the company, and for how hard he's worked. The LuvRocks contract was absolutely the right thing at the time. Thing is, it's not the right thing for Carroll's anymore. The staff can hate me if they like, but that's my decision, and I'm not about to change my mind.'

'So,' I said, rather huffily, 'what's the latest bombshell you're about to drop?'

'The Christmas bonus.' He took a deep breath. 'There won't be one this year.'

I couldn't believe what I was hearing. My fingers tightened around the mug. 'You *are* joking?'

He shook his head. 'I'm not, I assure you. You see, what you have to understand—'

'No! What *you* have to understand is that it's Christmas! We always get our bonus, and we expect it. We count on it. I mean, some of the staff count on it. It helps with the Christmas presents for their kids, or the food bill, or visiting relatives, or the extra heating for the winter. They're used to it. You can't just withdraw it without warning.'

'I *am* warning them. That's what I want you to help me with.'

'You call two and a half weeks warning? They'll be expecting it in their next pay packet! Jack always gives it to them before Christmas. You can't do this.'

He frowned at me. 'Are you reliant on this bonus, Marley?'

I shuffled, annoyed at his question. 'Of course not. I mean, it helps, obviously, but I'm not as reliant on it as some of the others. They have responsibilities after all. Husbands, wives, elderly parents...'

'Children.'

I bit my lip. 'Yeah. And children.'

He looked down, swirling the drink in his mug for a moment. 'I'm sorry. I understand that it's come as a shock, but if you could help me, so I can break it to them gently—'

'You must be kidding me.' I slammed my mug down and stood up, my anger bubbling over. 'You got me over here just to get me to do your dirty work for you? Forget it. I wouldn't help you if you were the last person on earth.'

'Marley!'

'We're not at work now, and I can say what I bloody well like. You're a disgrace. These people work hard for you, all year round, and their graft has enabled you to go off and travel the world, living like a king, while they scrimp and save. The least — the very least — you could have done for them was to take them out for a thank-you meal, but oh no. Even that was too much trouble for you. Now you're dropping this on them, as if they haven't got enough to worry about. Well, you can do this on your own. I'm having no part of it, and when you do tell them, I shall make it bloody clear that I totally disagree with you. Thanks for the chilli.'

'Where the hell are you going?' His voice reached me as I headed for the door.

I looked back at him, my lip curled into a sneer. 'Where do you think? Home.'

He stood up. 'I'll take you. You haven't brought a coat.'

'You will *not* take me,' I said. 'I'd rather freeze to death.'

'Now you're being stupid,' he said.

'On the contrary, I've just wised up. I *was* stupid, because for a brief moment, I actually thought that maybe you were the man I fell in love with all those years ago. But that man never really existed, did he? He broke my heart, trampled all over my feelings, and left. That's who you really are. A man who just doesn't care. I'll get a taxi, thanks very much.'

'Broke your heart?' Kit was staring at me, his face pale. 'What do you mean, broke your heart? We—'

'Forget it,' I snapped. 'It's ancient history. You know what, I really wish I *had* forgotten you. How much easier my life would be if I had. In fact, I wish to God I'd never met you.'

His hand was on my arm, but I wrenched away from him.

'Marley, please wait. Let's talk about this.'

I made sure I slammed the front door extra hard on the way out.

God, it was freezing. I was a fool. I could have been sitting in his nice, warm car, instead of tramping the streets of Farthingdale looking for a taxi. My temper had got the better of me. He knew just which buttons to press, but then, he always had. I couldn't believe that he'd denied breaking my heart. No one was that stupid. He must have known.

My shoulders sagged suddenly. Except, he didn't know, did he? Not all of it anyway. I shivered, wrapping my arms around myself as I walked. The taxi office wasn't far away, thank God. At that time of year, it shouldn't be too much of a wait for a car.

My eyes blurred with tears, and I rubbed them away fiercely. It was the cold air that was causing them. It certainly wasn't emotion. So, he'd acted all innocent and bewildered. Big deal. What sort of man was he anyway? Cutting the Christmas bonus and expecting me to tell the staff about it? He must think I was stupid.

I *was* stupid. He was right about that at least, because I'd actually thought I could change him. Make a difference. Remind him of the man he used to be when we'd first met. Well, I was on a hiding to nothing there. He hadn't been a man then. He'd been a boy. A little boy. And inside he was still a little boy — a childish, selfish, cruel little boy.

If only Jack would come home, I thought. Jack would make everything right. He wouldn't let this happen. *Jack!*

Jack would never allow Kit to scrap the bonuses. If he knew, he'd be furious. I'd bet he had no idea about it, and probably didn't even know about the LuvRocks contract either. I'd ring Jack and tell him what was going on.

I felt suddenly much better. Okay, Kit may have been in charge, but it was Jack who'd won the contract, Jack who'd been running the factory for years. He wouldn't just let his brother destroy everything he'd worked for without a fight.

Kit was about to get a very nasty shock, indeed.

Chapter 18

It was a relief going into work, knowing that Kit wasn't around. I didn't think I could have faced him, after what had happened the previous night.

Glaring at the closed door to his office, I made myself a coffee and sat down, wishing I could ring Jack right now, while I had the nerve. A quick check on Google, however, confirmed that it was the early hours of the morning in New York, so I would have to wait until after lunch to call him. I only hoped I would still have the nerve.

As the morning wore on, I could feel my resolve start to falter. Was it fair to involve Jack when he was on holiday? He clearly needed a break from work, and would it be right to let him know how things were playing out at the factory in his absence?

Then again, I reasoned, was it fair to keep him in the dark? To let everything he'd worked so hard for just slip away?

Plus, there were the workers to consider. I knew for a fact that Olivia and David counted on their bonuses. It wasn't a huge amount of money, but it came in very useful around Christmas time. I was certain they weren't the only ones to rely on it. Surely Jack would realise that and force Kit to reinstate it. Even if it was too late to save the LuvRocks contract, he could at least make things easier for his employees.

As my mind fought a constant battle, it became difficult to concentrate on my work. I kept remembering the expression on Kit's face, and the pleading look in his eyes when he'd tried to persuade me to tell the staff for him. As I replayed our conversation in my mind, I realised, with a guilty start, that he hadn't actually asked me that at all. All he'd wanted was my advice on the best way to go about telling them. He was going to do the deed himself. I'd overreacted badly.

By lunchtime, I'd more or less made up my mind not to involve Jack at all. When Kit got back tomorrow, I'd simply sit him down and force him to listen to reason. He wasn't a monster after all.

Was he?

The canteen seemed quieter than usual when I queued for lunch. A subdued air floated among the staff, and even Don wasn't wearing his Santa hat.

'What's up with everyone?' I put my plate of risotto on the table and eyed Olivia curiously. 'Even Liz has lowered *Now Christmas* down to *loud*. It's usually playing at *deafening roar*.'

'Everyone's pretty fed up,' she said with a sigh, prodding a rather dismal-looking lamb stew with her spoon. 'There doesn't seem to be much Christmas spirit in here these days.'

'Well, it's not surprising, is it?' David said, as he and Don dropped down beside us, each carrying a plate of steak and kidney pudding with chips and peas. 'Everyone's feeling pretty hard done by, what with the Christmas buffet being cancelled, and all the confusion about LuvRocks. And look around,' he added, waving his fork in the air. 'Not exactly overloaded with Christmas decorations, are we?'

Jack usually roped in members of staff to decorate the canteen and public areas of the factory with festive trimmings. There was always a tree in the entrance foyer, too. This year, the whole place was bare and looked very sorry for itself. Trouble was, even if Kit had agreed to decorating the place — and God knows, that was highly doubtful — I knew for a fact that Jack had thrown most of the stuff away last year, declaring it well past its sell-by date and promising that he would buy new decorations the following year. Well, it *was* the following year, and I was pretty certain that he'd done no such thing. Great. Things just went from bad to worse.

'I'll have a word with Kit,' I said impulsively.

God, had I really said that? As if he'd care about Christmas decorations, and hadn't I enough to deal with already?

However, looking around and seeing the obvious discontent on everyone's faces, I thought, with increasing gloom, how much worse they would feel once Kit broke the news about the bonus. If they were already this fed up, how bad would it be after that little bombshell?

My stomach churned. He couldn't do it to them, he just couldn't. I would have to call Jack. I had no choice. In the meantime, there was something I could do to cheer them all up.

Liz raised an eyebrow when I asked her to turn off the music, but there were no arguments from her. Nervously, I surveyed the clearly surprised staff and raised my hands, appealing for their attention. They all stopped talking when I cleared my throat.

'It's just a couple of weeks until Christmas,' I began, 'and this factory is sadly lacking in any festive spirit. Unfortunately, Jack threw out all the decorations and the tree last year, as he fully intended to replace them with new ones. I'm sure we can all agree that they were looking a little shabby.'

Shabby was an understatement. They were donkey's years old, and had been a source of embarrassment, frankly. They were so tatty, I'd have been ashamed if I'd been Jack, but then, men were often oblivious to those things and, let's be honest, no one there had much taste.

'Anyway, it's pretty obvious that Kit Carroll has other things on his mind right now.' *Didn't he just!* 'After all, this is all quite new to him, and it's been a lot for him to deal with, so I think he can be forgiven for forgetting about such things, which, I'm sure, must be very low on his list of priorities.' *Yeah, his main priority at the moment being to screw us all out of our bonuses without causing a riot.* 'So, I think we should take matters into our own hands and decorate the factory ourselves after the shift finishes.' *And before he gets back tomorrow and tries to stop us.* 'What do you say?'

There were some nods and a general mumbling of approval.

'Where are we getting the new decs from?' some bright spark called. 'Left us some money in the kitty, has he?'

'Ha! A generous donation from our new boss?' Another man shook his head. 'Doubt that very much.'

'What I was thinking,' I said loudly, as they all began to mutter to each other, clearly still rankled that they were missing out on their all-you-can-eat buffet at Miller's, 'is that, maybe we can go home and find any spare decorations we have and bring them back here? I know I have some baubles that I can bring, and I'm sure, between us, we can all find enough stuff to make a difference to the canteen and the foyer, at least. Am I right?'

'And why the hell should we do that?' demanded a sour-faced woman with alarming turquoise eyeshadow. 'I'm buggered if I'm forking out for something that the bosses should pay for.'

There was a muttering of agreement.

Don stood up. 'That's as may be,' he said. 'Fact is, though, Kit Carroll's new to this lark, and he obviously hasn't given the matter any thought. Jack's not here, and he's not likely to be back any time soon, so if we want this place to look a bit brighter and cheerier, it's up to us. You can argue all you like about whose responsibility it is, but the question remains: Do we want to make this factory Christmassy or not? Up to us, I reckon, and I, for one, am all for it. Now, I've got a box full of tinsel, and I'm happy to bring that in. Anyone else got owt going spare?'

'I can bring some holly,' someone called. 'Got tons of the stuff growing in my garden.'

'I'll pop to the shop and buy some balloons,' someone else offered.

'I've got loads of spare baubles,' someone else admitted. 'I'm always buying new ones every year, and I can't fit them all on my tree. I'll bring them in.'

'We haven't got a tree, though,' David pointed out. 'Not much use bringing baubles without a tree.'

There was silence for a moment, then someone shouted out, 'I've got an artificial tree in me loft. The wife wanted a change this year, so she's got one of them white trees. Looks bloody awful, but since when do I get a say about owt? Anyway, it means our old green one's just sitting there in its box doing nowt. I'll fetch it after work.'

'Fabulous,' I said, despite thinking, *God what sort of tat are we going to finish up with?* There would be no colour co-ordination whatsoever.

Still, needs must.

'You might as well get them lights back from Mum,' Olivia murmured to me, as I sank back into my seat a few minutes later, having established that just about everyone was willing and able to bring something back to the factory after work. 'You know, those posh clear ones that you bought her last year.'

'Might be a bit of a problem with that,' Don said, shaking his head. 'Safety regulations, and all that. Anything electrical ought to be tested.'

'It's fine,' I said. 'I bought them from Rochester's last December. They cost a fortune and they're top quality.'

'Even so...' He seemed to think for a minute, then said, 'I know someone who's a qualified electrician. I'll get him to pop by after work and check them out. Don't want factory to go up in flames, do we?'

'And we don't want to give Kit Carroll an excuse to make us take the whole lot down either,' I admitted. 'Fair enough, Don. Thanks.'

Fearing the factory was going to look like a tacky nineteen-seventies department store Santa's grotto, I headed back to the office after lunch and sank into my chair, eyeing the phone nervously.

I shouldn't really put everything on Jack. He was on holiday, after all. Then again, it was his own fault for leaving his brother in charge. I mean, of all people!

Although, thinking about it, maybe he'd had no choice. Maybe Kit had insisted, and since he owned the place, Jack could hardly refuse. No, it was still no good. Whichever way I looked at it, I couldn't get past the fact that it was Jack who'd swanned off to America on holiday, leaving us all at his brother's mercy, so in the end, the buck stopped with him. It was his responsibility to sort the mess out.

I looked through the address book on my desk and found his mobile number, then I picked up the receiver and jabbed the buttons, biting my lip as I punched out his number.

It took four rings for him to answer, and he sounded astonished to hear my voice.

'Marley? This is a surprise.' A moment's hesitation, then, 'Is something wrong?'

Well, I hadn't rung him to chat about the weather, had I? 'I'm sorry to disturb you on your holiday, Jack. I really am. I just didn't know what else to do.' Taking a deep breath, I launched into my story, leaving nothing out. The LuvRocks contract, the Christmas buffet, the bonus, Kit's high-handed attitude, and how he'd managed to anger the staff.

Jack listened in silence, not interrupting once. I began to wonder if he was still there.

'So, you see, I had to tell you what was going on, because you know how the staff rely on the bonus, and it's not fair that, just because Kit's got a bee in his bonnet about us making traditional chocolate and rock, he's jeopardising our future and the future of this factory. You worked so hard to get the LuvRocks contract. You must see that he can't just throw it away on a whim.'

More silence.

I chewed my lip anxiously. 'Jack? Are you still there?'

'Yeah, yeah. Still here.' He cleared his throat, and I sighed.

'You're narked I rang you, aren't you?'

'What? No, no. To be honest, Marley, I kind of wish you'd rung sooner. I need to talk to Kit, clearly.'

I heaved a sigh of relief. 'That would be great.'

'Marley?' Jack's voice sounded strained, and I felt a pang of regret that I'd burdened him with it all when he should've been enjoying himself Christmas shopping with his family in New York.

'Yes?'

'Can you — will you be kind to Kit?'

My mouth dropped open. 'What?'

'Just … just go easy on him, okay? He's got a lot on his mind, and he's been dropped into all this with very little warning. He's doing the best he can so, please, just support him. For me?'

Well, honestly! At the end of the day, it was quite clear that it was a case of family comes first. Whatever Kit had done, Jack was going to be on his side. What a waste of time my trying had been.

'But the factory! The LuvRocks contract! The—'

'I know, I know. I hear what you're saying, and I understand, honestly. But just be on his side, will you? He's a good man, Marley. The best.'

Talk about deluded. It was clearly a battle I couldn't win. 'But you'll talk to him about everything?'

'Oh, yes.' His voice sounded different suddenly, more determined. 'I will definitely be talking to him. You can count on that.'

'Fair enough.' Thank God for that. He sounded a bit more like the old Jack, and I felt a stirring of hope. Maybe he would do something, after all. 'I'm sorry to have bothered you, Jack.'

'No worries. Thanks for keeping me informed.'

'Merry Christmas, Jack.'

'Merry Christmas, Marley.'

I replaced the receiver and leaned back in my chair, suddenly uncertain what to think or do.

Jack was going to tackle Kit about the way he'd been behaving, so it was all in his hands now. His problem. Nothing more I could do.

But I had to be kind to Kit? Support him and be on his side? Huh! As if Kit had ever needed me to be on his side.

A memory of the previous night flashed into my mind. *I need your help, Marley.*

I felt an uncomfortable twinge of guilt but dismissed it. I'd done what I had to do. Jack and Kit could sort it out between themselves. I was done.

***

'I've got to hand it to the lad. He's no spendthrift, is he?' Great Uncle Charles cackled with laughter, then broke into another spasm of coughing.

I'd been about to remind him that the scrapping of the workers' Christmas bonuses was no laughing matter, but his health made me frown in concern. 'That cough's not getting any better. It seems to have come back even stronger. I'm calling the doctor.'

'Are you buggery!' He waved his hand at me, his face cross. 'I'm fine. You call any quack round here and it will be the last time you set foot in this place.'

His expression relaxed, and he smirked at me, a sudden gleam in his eye. 'Mind you, it might be the last time, anyway, if I decide to sell up to the Martins.'

'The Martins?' My heart thumped. 'Is that the couple who wants to buy Fox Lodge? Have you had any more dealings with them?'

'I may have.' He shrugged. 'It could be that they've been here for a wander around and have decided it's just what they're looking for. It may be that they can't wait to move in. It may be that we've just got to agree on a price, and then it's all systems go.'

'You wouldn't!' My voice was faint. 'You haven't. I mean, you didn't.'

'You seem to know a lot about me,' he observed. 'Who says I wouldn't, haven't and didn't? Maybe I would, have and did. If you must know, they knocked on the door yesterday, and I let them have a look at the place. Nice couple. Come from London. Sold up their house, and they're renting in the village for now, so they're cash buyers, and they've got plenty of it. Big plans for this house.'

I shook my head, feeling sick. 'So, that's that?'

'Never agreed anything,' he said. 'Just let them look. Said I was still thinking it over.' He leaned forward, observing me closely. 'Not having a very good week, are you? Fancy him expecting you to break the news to the factory workers about cutting their bonus. What a gutless coward. Typical of a Carroll.'

I felt a pang of guilt. 'He didn't actually ask me to tell them,' I backtracked. 'He asked me to help him decide the best way for *him* to tell them.'

'Same difference.' He rubbed his nose thoughtfully. 'And has he told them, yet?'

'He wasn't at work today,' I said. 'Had meetings all day apparently. I don't know.' And I'd dropped him in it big time with Jack. How was he going to react to that when he found out? I shrugged helplessly. 'It just feels as if we take one step forwards and two steps back.'

He would be furious with me, and how would he react when he saw the factory?

My worst fears had been confirmed when the staff rolled up at the gates an hour after leaving work, with an assortment of the tackiest, cheapest decorations I'd ever seen — and, believe me, I'd been dragged around enough awful pop-up Christmas shops with Olivia to recognise tacky when I saw it. The canteen looked like a pop-up Christmas shop itself, with tinsel draped everywhere, balloons in every corner, and awful foil garlands draped across the room. Someone had even brought a battery-operated Santa who yelled *ho ho ho* before dropping his trousers and revealing a large and very rosy behind. I'd tried to get them to take it home again but had been drowned out by yells of protest. Apparently, it was funny.

I'd had a bit more success with the foyer, where a six-foot artificial Christmas tree was decorated with a mixture of ancient baubles that had probably been around in the sixties, and an assortment of plastic snowmen, reindeer and angels that I guessed cost around six for a pound on a market stall. At least the lights added some elegance, and I'd donated a rather beautiful silver star to sit on the top. Plus, I'd added my Rochester baubles, although it quite broke my heart to see them sitting among such tawdry neighbours. It was like asking the Duchess of Cambridge to share a flat with the characters from *Shameless*.

Frankly, I'd been appalled, but seeing the smiles on everyone's faces had kind of made up for it in a most unexpected way. Mum and the other cleaners had joined in, and we'd all worked together to give the factory the Christmas spirit it had been sorely lacking. Even the security guards had helped.

A few of the staff had nipped into the village, returning with food from *The Leaning Tower of Pizza*, and it had turned into quite a party. Remembering the laughter and teasing that had gone on, and the cheers that went up when the lights were finally switched on, after being checked over by Don's pal, I felt a warm glow inside. Against all odds, it had been fun. I hadn't enjoyed myself so much in ages.

'Were you disappointed?'

I blinked, confused. 'Disappointed?'

'Well, he asked you out for dinner.' Great Uncle Charles's eyes bored into mine. 'You must have wondered why. Maybe you were expecting something a bit — you know — romantic.'

'Romantic? With Kit Carroll? I hardly think so.'

'Wouldn't be the first time, would it?'

'That was years ago. I told you, we were just kids. Anyway, never mind Kit Carroll. What are you going to do about Fox Lodge?'

He sighed and leaned back in his chair. 'I told you. I'm thinking about it. Don't make my head hurt with your mithering.' He closed his eyes and fell quiet.

I picked up my cup and sipped my tea, my stomach churning. As if having to face Kit tomorrow at work wasn't bad enough, I also faced the prospect of losing Fox Lodge before it was even mine. I replaced the cup and rubbed my eyes. I was tired and feeling rather stressed out by it all. Maybe I'd join my uncle and have a nap.

'It's not good this, is it?' he said suddenly.

I jumped, not expecting him to speak. 'What's not good?'

'You, being like this. Your grandad would be very unhappy about it.'

My mouth fell open. My uncle was talking about Grandad without being prompted? It had never been known before. And what would he be unhappy about? 'I don't know what you mean.'

Great Uncle Charles opened his eyes. Pieces of flint stared back at me, wizened old lips pursed tightly as he watched me shrewdly. 'Don't you?' he said at last.

'No, I don't,' I said, feeling uncomfortable and annoyed, all at the same time.

He tapped his bony fingers on the chair arm. 'Does it never strike you as somewhat depressing that the only thing you have in your life, the only thing that gives you any interest, is a house? And not even your own house. My house. This house.'

I swallowed. 'I don't—'

'Don't say you don't know what I mean again,' he said crossly. 'How old are you, girl?'

'Thirty. What's that got to do with anything?'

'How old's that halfwit sister of yours?'

I glared at him. 'If you mean Olivia, she's twenty-seven.'

'Twenty-seven. Three years younger than you, yet she's married and has three kids. Three kids!'

'She started young,' I said defensively.

'Yes, she did. Too bloody young. Daft bint. Even so, at least she got off the starting line. More than you did.'

'Not everyone wants to get married, or have kids,' I pointed out, my stomach churning harder until I felt sick. 'It's not compulsory.'

'Too right it isn't. And good luck to anyone who doesn't,' he said. 'Plenty of other things to fill your life with. Friends, travel, a career.... You, on the other hand, have this house.'

I blinked away unwelcomed tears, feeling a fluttering of unease. 'What are you saying?'

'When you were a little girl, your grandad had such high hopes for you. He thought you were wonderful. The sun shone out of your arse, as far as he was concerned, and nothing I could say would sway him. Personally, I thought you were an obnoxious little brat, but that's beside the point. I did, at least, think that your ambition would take you somewhere in life. Instead, you just stagnated. It's shameful.'

'How would you know what I have going on in my life?' I demanded.

'Because you come here — out of the goodness of your heart, I'm sure,' he added with a smirk, 'and you struggle to find anything to tell me. Oh, I get the odd bit about your mother, and snippets about those nephews of yours, and a few thinly-veiled hints about how poky your flat is. That's pretty much it.'

'Maybe I don't want to tell you everything,' I protested.

'I'm sure you don't. But knowing you, if anything different happened to you, you'd be telling me about it. You couldn't help yourself. Look how you banged on about that choking thing in the pub, as if it was the most exciting thing to happen to you in years, which it probably was.'

I couldn't give him an honest answer to that. He was right. I simply stared at him, unable to look away, as much as I wanted to.

'You've got a poxy job as a secretary in a poxy factory—'

'PA,' I interrupted forcefully.

He tutted. 'A secretary, in the one place you always insisted you'd never work. You've gone on one package holiday abroad, to my knowledge, to Benidorm with some girls from the insurance company you worked for. You shared a flat with those girls for two years. Then the insurance company goes bust, and what happens? Did you continue sharing the flat with them? No, you moved home. Did you ever see those girls again? If you have, you've never mentioned them. You never mention any friends, come to that. You don't go out, do you? Your life revolves around your family, and your dreams of living in Fox Lodge. That's it. What a tiny world you inhabit.'

I studied my nails. God, he was right! Truthfully, I'd only moved in with Lois and Jen from work because they'd been desperate for a third flatmate to help cover the rent, and Olivia had challenged me to leave our mother and stand on my own two feet. I hadn't enjoyed living there at all. I'd hated it. And I'd only agreed to go to Benidorm because they'd roped in Jen's cousin and needed someone to share a room with her, and I hadn't enjoyed that either. I found the whole experience tacky and knew that they were well aware of the fact.

When the insurance company went bust, Jen had found a job in her hometown of Scarborough and moved home, and Lois had moved in with her boyfriend, leaving me to head back to Moreton Cross. I hadn't heard a word from either girl since. We hadn't even exchanged addresses.

'The only good thing you ever had going on in your life was Christopher Carroll. Now he's back, and all you do is fall out with him and bang on about this house. Something wrong with you, girl?'

I gaped at him. 'It's not my fault he's so obnoxious, is it? And I'm not banging on about this house. All I'm saying is, you should be careful before you go ahead and sell it. It's a lovely house. At least, it could be if someone spent some money and time and love on it.'

'Someone like you, you mean?' Great Uncle Charles narrowed his eyes. 'Or maybe the Martins? After all, does it matter who restores the old place, as long as someone does?'

I folded my arms, trying not to sulk. He was just trying to wind me up, and I refused to let him succeed.

'This Carroll chap,' he said suddenly. 'Strikes me, you need to up your game.'

'What do you mean by that?'

'I mean, if he's scrapped the bonus, stopped the Christmas buffet, admits he can't wait for Christmas to be over, walks out on a Nativity play — not that I can blame him — and tears up a lucrative contract, then he's got serious problems, and you need to do something fast. This has to be down to you, you know. I mean, it's the third time he's come into your life. There has to be a reason for that.'

I leaned forward, suddenly eager. 'Actually, it's the fourth.'

He raised a rather scary, antenna-like grey eyebrow. 'Oh?'

'I also saw him again when I was fourteen, and I never even knew.'

'How could you not know? You *were* sniffing glue, weren't you? I always suspected it.'

'I did not sniff glue,' I said crossly. I cleared my throat. 'I was pissed on cider, though. Well,' I added defensively, as he gave me a smug look, 'I was going through a rough time. Dad had just gone. You remember.'

'Right. So, you'd been celebrating?'

I glared at him. 'I was getting drunk to forget. Except, the only thing I forgot was meeting Kit, which is ironic really. Apparently, I was with a gang, and then some of the boys beat him and his mates up, and I didn't do a thing to stop them.' *Because I was too busy snogging some loser in the bus shelter,* I added silently.

He tutted. 'Charming, I must say. Mind you, it only makes me more certain. He got his head kicked in, and he still wanted to go out with you. Four times you two have been thrown together. Fate wants you to do something. Why else would it put him in exactly the right place, at exactly the right time to save your life?'

'Hang on! You're actually taking me seriously?' It didn't make sense. 'You're the biggest cynic going. Why would you believe in all that fate stuff?'

Was it a good, or bad, thing? With Uncle Charles acting as if I was meant to save my Scrooge-like boss, it made it seem more real, more urgent. 'And what do you care about saving him, anyway?'

'I couldn't give a monkey's about any Carrolls,' he admitted. 'Even so, you need that job, and so does your mother and your sister. The way he's going, he's going to drive it into the ground, and then you're all going to expect me to give you handouts. It's in my best interests to make sure that dratted factory keeps going.'

'Right.' I might have known there'd be something in it for him. 'Although, you're completely wrong, if you think Mum or Olivia, would come cap in hand to you. They'd never ask you for anything. Not in a million years.'

'Huh. You think? In my experience, it's surprising what people do when money's at stake. Pride goes well out of the window, along with reason and loyalty, and everything else.'

There it was again, that slightly wistful tone. I wondered what was behind it. 'So, what do you want me to do about it?' I said.

'Crack on with the plan to change him, of course. Take him back to the decent chap you claim he used to be. Now, you've tried Christmas Past and that didn't go down too well. Reckon it's time for Christmas Present. Show him how much fun Christmas can be. Not that it is, of course,' he added, shuddering, 'but you have to convince him otherwise. Get him a present. Stir his emotions. You need to fill him so full of Christmas spirit that he wants to share it with everyone else. To do that, you have to touch his heart. You remember how to do that, I suppose? After all, you love Christmas so much. If anyone can do it, it's you.'

'How do you know I love Christmas?' I demanded. I'd certainly never discussed it with him.

He rolled his eyes. 'You always did. When your gran was alive, your parents were kind enough to take you to see her and your grandad every weekend, remember? Your grandad used to tell me how excited you got every year, chattering away about Christmas from around the middle of September. Then, when your father left and you made sneaky visits to see your grandad, he told me how you'd taken over from your dad, organising Christmas for your mum and sister. It's obviously important to you, so all you have to do is pass that feeling onto Christopher.'

'Kit,' I said, without thinking. I was too absorbed in other thoughts about my mixed feelings towards Christmas. Great Uncle Charles would be astonished if he knew the truth. It was true, I had always loved the festive season, but for many years, it had become a distraction. Something to focus on to ease the pain that always seemed ten times worse at that time of year. It had, I was forced to acknowledge, become something of an obsession.

He eyed me curiously. 'Kit now, is it? Thought you didn't approve of that?'

'Well, maybe I understand his reasons for changing his name a bit more now,' I said uncomfortably.

'Oh, and what were they?'

I wasn't sure I had the right to tell him. Then again, he never saw anyone, so he was hardly going to blab it around, was he?

'Because of some bad feeling between him and his father. He seems to think that Christopher connects him to his past and he doesn't want that connection.'

Great Uncle Charles frowned. 'So, he's escaping his past? Maybe not such a good idea to try to drag him back there, then. Seems like it has bad memories for him.' He coughed again. 'Not that I can blame him,' he wheezed, eventually. 'Who'd want to be tied to someone like James Carroll? As bad as his father, from what I heard. Maybe the lad's not such a lost cause, after all.'

Maybe not, I thought. There'd been definite pain in Kit's eyes when I'd mentioned his father before. I wondered why. I'd never seen the two of them together when we'd been a couple. Kit had refused point blank to tell his parents about us, saying it was our business, and there was no need for them to know. Even Jack didn't know about us. He'd been away most of the time, at Kit's old boarding school, and besides, Kit said he was just a kid and wouldn't understand. I'd tried very hard not to push him about the matter, but it had hurt. It hurt a lot. If I wasn't good enough for his family, what sort of future did we have together?

Well, none as it turned out.

Why, I wondered, had we ever got together in the first place? He'd certainly had no reason to want me, given what I'd recently been told. I hid a smile, thinking how he'd actually believed that I only wanted to go out with him when I was eleven years old because I wanted a sports car. A sports car! Honestly, how gullible was he? Although, to be fair, Hayley had believed it, too, and she'd been my best friend.

If only he hadn't heard me that day, he might well have asked me out there and then, and then I'd have had someone to confide in, to turn to when Dad left. I might never have gone off the rails and become so bitter, so lonely.

I thought about that day when Kit had been beaten up by my friends. They weren't really my friends, to be honest. They just knew how to get hold of alcohol, and that was all I needed from them at the time. They didn't ask questions, didn't want to know anything about me. I hid behind black hair dye and a mask of heavy makeup, and they didn't care a bit. It suited me fine.

Poor Kit. He was a very forgiving person really. He must be, because he'd known who I was that day we met up again in

Helmston, and he'd not let it put him off. He hadn't even mentioned my shameful behaviour.

I rubbed my arm, remembering that day when I was sixteen years old. It was a few days before Christmas, and I'd gone into Helmston to wander around the market and seek out any last minute bargains. Christmas, even at that tender age, had become my responsibility, and I wanted it to be perfect for Mum and Olivia.

Christmas had flavoured the air: the scent of pine from the lorry load of Christmas trees on sale, the tempting aroma of roast turkey and stuffing sandwiches coming from a nearby stall, roast chestnuts, and hot mince pies, which were being devoured by a crowd of people who acted as if they hadn't tasted food for months.

I'd felt my stomach rumble and stopped, wondering if I could be bothered to queue to buy a sandwich. I didn't even have time to make a decision, as I found myself tumbling to the ground, having been knocked over by someone who clearly hadn't been paying attention to his surroundings.

'God, I'm really sorry.'

A hand took hold of mine. I pushed back my hair and peered up to see a boy, around my own age, looking down at me, quite anxiously. As he'd pulled me to my feet, I glared at him, feeling stupid and humiliated.

'Why didn't you watch where you were going?' I snapped, brushing the back of my jeans, then tightening the grip on my shoulder bag. Well, he could have been anyone. For all I knew, the whole thing was a scam designed to put me off my guard, while he grabbed my bag and ran. Although, to be fair, he needn't have helped me up if that was the case, and he did look quite remorseful.

'I wasn't paying attention,' he admitted. 'I was too distracted by the smell of that roast turkey.'

Despite my annoyance, I couldn't help but smile. 'Me, too,' I confessed. 'Smells fab, doesn't it?'

His face broke into a grin and his eyes twinkled.

My stomach flipped in sudden recognition. Those eyes!

'Are you — are you Christopher Carroll?'

His smile dropped, and he stared at me. 'Marley? Marley Jacobs?'

We both gaped at each other. 'Oh, my God.'

I'm not sure which one of us said it. Maybe we both did. We both seemed pretty stunned to meet again, that was for sure. Given that the last time he'd seen me, I'd been an angry drunken goth, maybe it wasn't surprising that he hadn't recognised me. Not that I'd realised that at the time, of course.

'How have you been?' I remembered feeling all trembly and nervous, talking to him, though he'd seemed pretty cool once he'd got over the shock of seeing me.

Later, he confessed that he'd been all churned up inside, but I would never have known that from the way he shrugged and replied, 'Oh, you know. Fine. How about you?'

Funny, but we'd both completely forgotten about those roast turkey sandwiches, as we began walking through the market together, talking and catching up. It was as if we already knew each other, somehow, which in a way we did, but not like that. It was as if we'd been best friends, or something, and we really hadn't been. There was a bond. It felt right. Like it was our time at last.

He'd told me all about refusing to stay on at the boarding school to do his A levels — much to his parents' fury — and how he'd finally managed to convince them to allow him to do them at the local college instead. I'd eagerly informed him that I was attending the same college. I'd started there in September and was doing a two-year secretarial course. We'd both agreed it was a coincidence that we were at the same place every day, and how funny it was that we'd never bumped into each other.

'I'll keep an eye out for you,' I'd promised.

He'd shook his head, his eyes looking deep into mine. 'We'll have to make firmer arrangements than that, don't you think?'

My insides had swished around as if they were on the waltzers, and I'd nodded and bashfully agreed that we would.

Christopher had eventually steered me over to a little van selling drinks and bought us both a hot chocolate. It was the first time he saw me get whipped cream on my nose, and he'd laughed at me. I'd got all huffy, but he'd dabbed the cream away, then leaned over and kissed me, very gently and quite shyly.

Oh, that kiss! I remembered it so clearly. The Christmas lights that were strewn across the marketplace dimmed into darkness by comparison. He lit me up, he brought me to life. It sounded very dramatic, when I thought about it, but it was true. It was how it'd felt. From that moment on, Christopher Carroll was my world.

'What are you smiling at?' Great Uncle Charles's curious tone brought me back to the present.

'Just remembering some stuff,' I mumbled.

'About Kit Carroll, I presume, judging by that soppy look on your face.'

I shivered. How had Kit and I drifted so far apart? How had we reached the point where he could just walk away, leave me behind? The young man I'd known then was so different to the one I knew now. The teenager who'd led me around that market, so pleased and eager to be in my company, who'd enjoyed the Christmas build-up, who'd dabbed cream from my nose and kissed me so tenderly, wasn't the sort of man who would abandon his girlfriend, break all his promises, then return years later to bring the family business to its knees.

What had gone wrong?

'I can't give up on him,' I murmured. 'The old Kit is still in there somewhere. I just have to find him.'

Great Uncle Charles sighed. 'Then hurry up and get on with it, girl. It's nearly Christmas. You're running out of time.'

This, I thought grimly, wasn't for the sake of the factory and all its workers. It wasn't even for my family, or for Jack and his family. This was all about Kit.

Maybe, at some level, it always had been.

Chapter 19

There was a most annoying voice in Kit's ear. He kept trying to ignore it, but it persisted, whining at him in an irritating tone, repeating the same words, over and over again.

He opened one eye and blinked sleepily. Silence. All was darkness. Had he been dreaming?

Deciding he had, he closed his eye again and hugged the pillow, too tired to give the matter further thought.

'This is your brother calling. Warning, warning, this is your brother calling. Pick up the phone. It's your brother!'

'What the—?'

Both Kit's eyes snapped open, and his heart hammered in fear. That was his mobile, the ringtone he'd assigned to Jack. But why would Jack be calling at that time of night? Oh, God.

He sat up and scrabbled on the bedside table for the lamp. As light flooded the bedroom, he spotted his mobile phone lying face down on the floor. What the hell was it doing there? He must have knocked it off the table during the night. He'd not looked at it all day yesterday. He'd been so stressed about the meetings that he'd accidentally left it at home, and then he'd been too tired to check it when he finally went to bed.

He reached down and grabbed the phone.

'Jack?' He was breathless with anxiety. 'What is it? What's happened?'

There was a silence that seemed to stretch for eternity, then Jack's voice said, 'It's okay, Kit. Everything's fine at this end. Sorry if I panicked you. I should have thought.'

Kit took a deep breath and leaned back against the headboard. 'For Christ's sake, Jack. You do know it's—' He glanced at the alarm clock on the bedside table. '—just gone one in the morning. Bloody hell! What are you doing, ringing me at this time?'

'I've been trying all day. Where have you been?'

Kit rubbed his eyes. 'I didn't have my phone with me. I was in meetings, then I fell asleep downstairs. Only woke up at half eleven, and my phone was upstairs the whole time. Sorry. What's so important if everyone's okay? Everyone *is* okay? I mean, nothing—'

'Everything's as it should be here, Kit. This is about you, and the factory.'

Kit's mouth went dry. What had he heard? 'Go on.'

'I had an interesting phone call today.'

Phone call? Had Colin been in touch with him? Their solicitor? Didn't accountants and solicitors have some sort of code of confidentiality? Or was it someone else? Had someone who knew Jack seen *The Gazette*? Someone in the know had obviously grassed him up. Damn. How was he going to reassure his brother?

'Don't you want to know who rang me?'

'I daresay you're going to tell me.'

'I am. It was Marley.'

Marley! Kit's eyes widened. 'What the hell is she playing at, ringing you up? She knows you're in America.'

'On holiday.'

'Yeah. On holiday. I'm sorry, Jack. What did she want?' And then he remembered. The argument the previous night. Her fury and disgust with him about the bonuses. But she wouldn't, would she? She wouldn't go behind his back like that, surely?

'Oh. Let me guess. I'm the big bad boss who destroyed Christmas. Right?'

'Something like that. I really didn't like what she told me, and I couldn't get hold of you for an explanation, so I got in touch with Colin. I knew he'd know if there was a reason for your strange behaviour, and sure enough, he did.'

'He told you?'

'Yep.'

'Everything?'

'I'm really hoping so. Surely to God there can't be any more. Or can there?'

Kit sighed. 'I'm sorry. I'd really hoped to save you from all this. You've got enough going on.'

'But, Kit, this is my problem, too! For God's sake, it's my fault. All of it.'

'It's not your fault, don't be stupid. How could you know that Halliwell & Stephenson was going to go bankrupt?'

'I should have been prepared. It's not as if I wasn't suspicious. They hadn't paid us for months. As soon as they started fobbing me off, I should have scaled down production and done some serious investigating, but I was so preoccupied with everything else. I really took my eye off the ball. I'm so sorry.'

'It was my fault, not yours. You had enough to do, and I should have come home sooner and taken this place off your hands.'

There was quiet for a moment, then Jack said, 'How bad is this?'

Kit hesitated, wondering how much to reveal. He supposed the cat was out of the bag, anyway, thanks to bloody Marley and her big mouth. 'Fairly bad. Colin doesn't think we'll be able to get anything back, and there's barely enough in the accounts now to cover the wages for January.'

He heard the sharp intake of breath and wished, with all his heart, that he could have kept the news from Jack, but he couldn't lie to him. Not when he was aware of the demise of LuvRocks.

'Has Serafina been in touch yet?'

'She'll be here in a few days. She seems really positive about the whole thing, so that's looking good.'

'I should hope she is. She's been angling for this for years.'

'Yeah, well. Looks like she'll get what she wants.'

'I really am sorry, Kit.'

'It doesn't matter. It doesn't mean anything to me anyway. Never did. It's you and Amanda who'll suffer again.'

'Oh, we can sort something out, no problem. It's hardly the most important thing we've had to deal with, is it?'

'I guess not.'

'Nowhere near in fact. What I don't get is, why haven't you just told the factory staff the truth? You've got them all hating you and blaming you and thinking you're a real tightwad. Why haven't you explained the situation?'

'Because I'd rather they hated me and thought I was a miser than worry all Christmas about not having a job in the new year, that's why. They're going to have to know soon enough, but for God's sake, let's let them enjoy their Christmas first. It's the least we can do.'

'You're a good man, Kit. I wish Marley realised that. You should at least tell *her* what's going on.'

Kit laughed. 'Oh, yeah, because she's so trustworthy, isn't she? Can't believe she went behind my back like that and rang you.'

'She was worried sick about the factory, and worried about your behaviour. Tell her the truth, Kit. Let her help you. You need someone on your side.'

Kit didn't answer. He didn't actually trust himself to speak.

'If this thing with Serafina goes ahead, will that fix our problems?' Jack's voice was quiet, and Kit considered, for a moment, bluffing his way through the conversation and assuring his brother that of course it would. But only for a moment.

'It will pay off what we owe the suppliers and keep us going for a few months, but unless we come up with some drastic solutions, we'll be in the same position this time next year, if not before. The truth is, we need to increase output drastically and pull in some money from somewhere. Even the big names are struggling. What chance has a small company like Carroll's got these days?'

'I wish I could be with you to help.'

'Don't be daft. I've been to some trade fairs and conferences. I've got some people interested. Something might come of it.

And I had a promising meeting yesterday with a potential customer. Could be really lucrative, if it comes off. We'll just have to wait and see.'

'We don't have time to wait and see though, do we? That's what you're telling me. We have to get more people interested in the place, and in our products. We need a branding rethink and a marketing campaign. Have you been in touch with Clarke & Howell's? Gina usually works with us, and she's excellent.'

'And very expensive,' Kit pointed out. 'Marley already suggested her, and she wasn't too impressed with me when I said I'd do it all myself.'

'Well, you can't really blame her,' Jack said, sounding far too reasonable for Kit's liking. 'She hasn't a clue what we're dealing with, and she must think you're a complete Scrooge. You have to tell her, Kit. No way around it.'

'I won't tell her anything,' Kit insisted. 'I don't trust her, and she's just proved I was right not to, by telephoning you and dropping all this on you.'

'She was thinking of Carroll's,' Jack said.

'She was thinking of her Christmas bonus and some pathetic designer dress she wanted, you mean,' Kit growled. His anger towards Marley was growing by the minute. How could she have been so sneaky? And why was he so upset about it, anyway? He should have expected something like that from her. 'Look, it's the middle of the night, and I'm knackered. I have to be at work at eight, so I'll get off now and call you tomorrow, okay?'

'Will you? Promise?'

'I just said so, didn't I?'

'I mean it, though, Kit. I have enough going on here.'

'Which is why I didn't want you to know!'

'But now that I do, I'll only worry more if you don't keep me informed every step of the way. Don't make me play guessing games, okay? I want to know everything. Swear it.'

Kit rolled his eyes. 'Hell, Jack, you'll be asking me to make a pinky promise next.'

'I'll make you cross your heart and hope to die if I have to. Now, promise.'

Kit sighed. 'I promise.'

'And you haven't got your fingers crossed?'

In spite of himself, Kit couldn't help laughing. 'How old are you?'

Jack chuckled. 'Okay, I believe you. Night, 'bro.'

'Night, Jack. Take care.'

Putting his mobile on the bedside table, Kit switched off the lamp and lay back down, staring up into the darkness while his mind replayed the conversation.

It was no use. He needed to sleep. He was exhausted, and he had to be at the factory early. He had a long day ahead of him, and that awkward encounter with Marley to get over.

As if her overreacting so badly and storming out of the house hadn't been bad enough, he had to tackle her about her unbelievable lack of loyalty towards him, and her underhanded behaviour. Great.

Sighing, Kit pulled the pillow over his head. He had a feeling he wouldn't be getting much sleep at all that night.

CHAPTER 20

I wasn't looking forward to going into work. As I approached the factory gates, my stomach turned over in dread. No doubt Jack would have been in touch with Kit already, and as if that wasn't bad enough, I hadn't seen him since that embarrassing night at Fell House.

At least the foyer looked half decent, I thought, as I passed the glass door and glanced in. The Christmas lights had been switched on by Claire in reception, and the tree didn't look anywhere near as tacky as I'd remembered. Then again, I wasn't standing too close to it, was I?

I wondered if Kit had already arrived, and if he'd noticed what we'd done. Wait 'til he saw the canteen. He was going to flip his lid.

Oh well, might as well be hanged for a sheep as a lamb, as they say.

I wasn't sure if he was in or not, as his office door was firmly shut when I sneaked into my own office. Closing the outer door quietly behind me, I hardly dared to breathe. The longer I could put off the evil moment, the better. I was even willing to sacrifice my first coffee of the day in case the sound of the kettle alerted him to my presence.

I switched on the computer, wincing at the faint whirring sound it made, and unbuttoned my coat as I waited for it to start up. After hanging my coat on the hook, I picked up my bag, but almost dropped it in fright as my mobile started to ring. Heart hammering, I fumbled around inside the bag, desperately trying to locate my phone to turn it off. Who the hell was calling me at that time of the morning?

'Having fun?'

I stopped my frantic dash to silence my phone and turned slowly, to see Kit standing in the doorway, mobile phone clutched to his ear. He gave me a rather forced smile then ended the call he was making. Immediately, my phone stopped ringing. He put his mobile in his pocket and folded his arms, leaning against the doorframe.

'How did you get my number?' Stupid question, really. It would have been in the file box containing all staff contact details. Hardly difficult to find, even for him.

He raised an eyebrow. 'Seriously? That's all you have to say to me?'

I hesitated, wondering whether to play dumb or brave it out. I decided on the latter course of action. I'd done nothing to be ashamed of, after all. 'If this is about me refusing to help you—'

'Oh, I think we both know it's about more than that. My office. Now.'

I glared at him, but he'd already turned his back on me and was heading over to his own desk. How rude. I stomped in after him, determined not to let him see how rattled I felt.

'Close the door, please.'

'Yes, sir.' Bloody hell, it was worse than school!

'Take a seat.'

I sank into the chair and faced him across the desk, wearing what I hoped was a defiant expression.

'So, have you anything to say about your behaviour?'

I stared at him incredulously. 'Who are you? Mr Matthews?'

Mr Matthews had been our headmaster at Moreton Cross Primary. He'd been a fairly affable chap, but of course, we'd all been quite wary of him back then. He was authority after all, and in those days, that actually meant something. Not like today's whippersnappers.

'I'm your boss. Sometimes, I think you forget that.'

'Fat chance,' I muttered.

'Marley!' His eyes flashed at me, and his hands gripped the edge of the desk. 'This isn't a game. I'm bloody furious with you.'

'And I'm bloody furious with you,' I retorted. 'What did you think I'd do, Kit? Just let you walk all over the staff as if they don't matter? Let you destroy Carroll's without trying to do something to stop you? I had to act before it was too late, and Jack was the only option I had left. You drove me to it, so don't try to make me feel guilty.'

'You had no right to contact Jack! I told you about the staff bonus in confidence. I thought I could trust you. Well, I won't make that mistake again.'

'I know how you feel,' I snapped. 'Hurts, doesn't it? But you live and learn.'

We glared at each other.

'You have no idea what you've done. Jack should never have been dragged into all this. It wasn't fair of you.'

'Oh, boo-hoo,' I said, past caring what he thought, or about Jack's feelings. Kit's face was all rage and fury, sparks flashing in his dark eyes, his mouth tight set beneath the twitching of a muscle in his jaw. He'd never looked more fabulous, quite honestly, and my hormones leapt about all over the place, until I wasn't afraid any longer. Frankly, I just wanted to pounce on him.

'Poor Jack. Did I interrupt his holiday? How inconvenient for him.'

'You're an absolute bitch, do you know that?' Kit snarled.

'I'm not sure a boss is supposed to say that to an employee. I think there may be laws against it.'

'Marley, I'm warning you...'

'Warning me? You honestly expect me to feel guilty about disturbing Jack, while he's swanning around New York with his glamour-puss wife, buying up half of Macy's — no doubt for little Prince Timothy — while all your employees are going to be scrabbling around, hard-pressed to afford a bag of sprouts for Christmas, now you've even stopped their bonus? Tough luck.'

'For the last time,' he said, through gritted teeth, 'he's not in bloody New York, and stop being such a fucking cow.'

My eyes widened. 'I beg your pardon? Don't you dare talk to me like that! And, okay, so he's not in New York. Big deal. California, then, star-spotting in Hollywood, or wherever the hell else he's swanned off to, enjoying himself while we all struggle on, coping with Ebenezer Carroll here.'

'Florida, actually.'

I laughed bitterly. 'Oh, well, this just gets better and better. Taken Tim to meet Mickey Mouse, have they? Bully for them. My nephews probably won't even get a Disney DVD this Christmas, thanks to you, never mind a trip to Disney World. How the other half live, eh?'

Kit had gone very quiet. He clutched the desk as if his life depended on it. I folded my arms, waiting for him to explode. Even I had to admit, I'd gone too far. I'd be lucky if he didn't sack me.

To my astonishment, he suddenly let out a long breath, as if he'd been holding it in for ages, then leaned forward and rubbed his eyes. I watched him, feeling a bit uncomfortable. Why wasn't he yelling at me? Instead, he looked … broken.

After what felt like forever, he looked up at me, and my heart sank when I saw tears glittering in his eyes.

'Kit, what is it? What's wrong?' I forgot all about my anger and was at his side in an instant, my hand on his arm.

He swallowed, staring up at me without speaking, as if he didn't even know how to begin.

'Kit, you're scaring me.' I grabbed my chair, pulled it round to his side of the desk and sat next to him. It was as if all the years peeled away as I reached for his hand. He didn't pull away, just stared down at it, then back up at me.

'It's Tim,' he said eventually. 'He's — he's very ill. He has a brain tumour. They've been battling this for months, Marley. That's why they're in America. Tim's having proton therapy at a specialist clinic in Florida. He's been through hell. They all have.'

It was like that moment in films, when someone finds out something shocking and everything around them fades out and there's just a huge close-up of their horrified face. That's exactly how I felt right then. The world just seemed to stop, and there was just Kit with his sad eyes and weary voice, and me and my guilt and shame. I felt cold as ice.

'Oh, God,' was all I could manage, and even that took me some time. I realised he was gripping my hand tightly, and I squeezed his fingers, trying in one small gesture to communicate how sorry I was, how terrible I felt, how sad I was for Tim and his family. 'Is he? I mean, how bad ...'

Kit let go of my hand and stood, wandering over to the window, where he stared down at the car park, hands in pockets. I watched him, saying nothing. I didn't know what else I could say.

'Jack seems to think it's going well. The NHS funded it, so there must be hope. They wouldn't do that if they didn't think it would benefit him, would they?'

I nodded. 'Well, that's good then, isn't it?'

He turned to face me again. 'Yeah, that's good. It's just, it's not pleasant is it? And he's already been through so much this year, and he's all that way from home, and it's Christmas...' His voice caught, and I bit my lip, longing to go to him and put my arms around him.

'Why didn't Jack mention it?' I murmured. 'All these months, he's not said a word.'

'He didn't want them to become *that family*. You know what it's like when people get ill. Everything becomes about the illness. He wanted to feel normal. He wanted to be able to come into work and put it all behind him, just for those few hours each day. If you'd known, it would have been there between you the whole time. I can understand that, can't you?'

'Yeah. Yes, of course I can.' No wonder Jack had been looking so exhausted lately. He must have been worried sick. All those months of watching his little boy suffer like that, all that pain and worry and fear. And I'd rung him in the middle of Tim's treatment to pour all that stuff about the factory onto him, on top of everything else. I felt sick with shame.

'I'm so sorry,' I said. 'Really. I'm sorry for all the things I've said about Jack not caring. I'm sorry for ringing him up and bothering him with all this, and I'm sorry for not being there for you.'

He looked a bit nonplussed. 'For me? What do you mean?'

'You've carried all this worry about Tim, and you've had to deal with the factory and knowing nothing about how to run it, and all I've done is make things more difficult for you. I'm so sorry, Kit, I really am.'

He walked over to me and put his hand on my shoulder. 'You didn't know what was going on, so how could you possibly be responsible for all this? I should have told you sooner. It's done now anyway. We have to get on with it. I've told Jack everything's okay and not to worry. I just want him to concentrate on Tim.'

'Of course,' I said. 'How long will he be over there?'

'He'll be back around the middle or end of January,' Kit said. 'All being well.'

His eyes gazed into mine. They were full of sadness, determination, fear and defiance, all at the same time. It was a potent mixture. I put my hand to his face and stroked his cheek with my thumb.

'It will be all right,' I whispered. 'You'll see.'

He lifted his own hand to his face and covered mine with it, still staring at me. For a moment, neither of us moved, not even to breathe. Then we were together, and all the years fell away, as his mouth met mine and he kissed me for the first time since we were eighteen-year-olds, with all our lives ahead of us, and nothing but love and hope and dreams before us.

The kiss seemed to go on forever, yet at the same time, it was over far too soon. We stepped back from each other, and Kit seemed as stunned as I felt.

My mouth felt bruised. My fingers brushed my lips. I could have kissed him all day. How did he feel, though? Was he regretting it? Would he tell me that should never have happened? I waited, half afraid of what he would say, and too scared to speak and break the spell.

He sank into his chair, looking rather dazed, while I stood, stomach fluttering as I waited for his verdict.

'That wasn't supposed to happen,' he said eventually.

'No.' I felt my spirits sinking. He regretted it then. I'd known he would, somewhere inside me. That was why I hadn't wanted to be the first to speak. I hadn't wanted that magical moment to be over. And with his words it was, and I felt awkward, embarrassed. How were we going to work together again after this?

Even so, it was probably for the best. We had so much baggage between us, after all. So much had gone wrong in the past, and it would never work again. You should never go back, everyone knew that. I bit my lip, wondering, *what now?*

'I'd forgotten how good you are at kissing,' he said.

I lifted my head and saw the smile playing on his lips and the sparkle in his eyes. My heart thumped.

'You're pretty good yourself,' I said.

He shrugged. 'Where does this leave us, Marley? I mean, what did it *mean?* Was it just about feeling sorry for me? About Tim? Or...'

I stared at him helplessly. The truth was, I didn't know. After everything he'd done, after the terrible way he'd let me down, after all I'd been through, how could I let him back into my life? It wasn't as if we even got on, was it? We'd done nothing but bicker since he'd come back. Yet, there was no denying the attraction between us. It flared and simmered every time we were together. But was that enough? How could we just pretend the past had never happened?

'I'm guessing you're regretting it,' he said heavily. 'I can see in your face that you think it was a big mistake.'

'Don't you?' I asked, surprised. I felt a stirring of hope and pushed it down firmly.

'No,' he said, after a moment's hesitation. 'Truthfully, I've wanted to kiss you since the moment I saw you walk into The Blue Lamp. Of course, you had to go and ruin the moment by dying.'

I wanted to laugh, then I remembered Tim and the laughter dissipated. 'You hid it well,' I said instead. 'You seemed to feel nothing but contempt for me.'

'You do push my buttons,' he admitted, 'but maybe that's because you're special. No one else has ever been able to wind me up the way you do. But no one else has ever made me feel the way you do either.'

'But after everything that went on before...'

'We had something good once, didn't we?' His voice sounded almost pleading.

'Yes, we did. But then...' I sighed, the memories tumbling back and filling me with pain and dread. 'They always say you should never go back to an old love. If it ended, it ended for a reason.'

'Do you really believe that?'

His eyes, those beautiful dark eyes, bored into mine, and I swallowed.

Did I?

The phone rang, and I jumped.

Kit cursed under his breath and snatched up the receiver. 'Yes? Okay, Claire, put him through.' He covered the mouthpiece with his hand and whispered, 'It's Ethan Rochester. I have to take this. Can we talk later?'

I nodded, wide-eyed. Ethan Rochester was the owner of Rochester's Department Stores. What on earth would he be calling Kit about?

A picture of a Jenny Kingston handbag floated before my eyes, and I sighed. As if I'd ever own one of those. Time to come back down to earth.

I closed the office door behind me and headed over to the kettle. I needed a strong coffee and a few moments to gather my thoughts. My lips still tingled from that kiss, and I wondered how the hell I could resume normal working relations with my boss after this.

The true question was, was a working relationship all I wanted from him? And if not, how could we ever get past everything that had happened before?

And how, with whom he'd become, could I bear to have any sort of relationship with a man who put Ebenezer Scrooge to shame?

CHAPTER 21

'See the smiles you've put on everyone's faces?' Don beamed at me, as he paused in his mission to devour a plate of stew and dumplings within five minutes flat. 'Makes a big difference, doesn't it? All these trimmings, I mean.'

I glanced around at the silver, gold, blue, red and purple shiny mess that the canteen had become and sighed. 'I suppose so.'

'You suppose so?' He waved a spoon at me, dripping stock all over the table, and shook his head. 'Now, what's up? You were right as rain, last night. Even had a smile on your face at one point. Your mum wanted to take a photo. Now look at you, gone all mardy again. What's to do?'

I kissed my boss, and now I think I've gone and fallen for him all over again, in spite of the fact that he broke my heart, I can't trust him, and he's the meanest man in town.

'Nothing,' I said. 'Still doesn't feel like Christmas does it? I mean, considering it's less than a fortnight away. There's just something missing.'

'Yeah,' he said, suddenly gloomy. 'Miller's spicy chicken wings, that's what.'

'You're going with Mum, aren't you?'

'Oh, aye, but it's not the same as the Christmas buffet, is it? That's a tradition. Christmas is made up of traditions. Take one away and nothing feels the same.'

I considered that for a moment. He was right in a way, even though I'd never particularly enjoyed the Christmas all-you-can-eat buffet at Miller's. The all-you-can-eat tag seemed to trigger some weird effect in many people, who took it as a personal challenge and went all out to empty the restaurant of anything edible within its walls. It was quite disgusting to watch, and certainly brought out the worst in the factory staff. Even Olivia had been known to have three main courses and two puddings, and David — well, better not to think about David and that memorable occasion with the chicken satay. Ugh. Even so, without the staff meal, something did feel wrong. Christmas wasn't Christmas without a works party, and Kit needed cheering up, too.

I looked around thoughtfully. I needed a distraction, something else to think about. Kit needed reminding that Christmas could be fun, in spite of everything that was going on in Florida, and the staff needed to pull together again. It had been an amazing atmosphere last night. We needed more of that, especially since they were yet to hear the news about the bonus.

Time for another announcement.

It didn't go down well at first. There were lots of protests that it wasn't up to us to organise a party — that it was management's job. They had a point, but as Don pointed out, it was either we did it, or no one did it. Did they want a party or what? Turned out they did, however sour-faced some of them looked about it.

'Right,' I said. 'Tomorrow lunchtime. Everyone can bring something to eat or drink. I'll pin a sheet of paper on the noticeboard, and you can all write down what you want to bring so we don't end up with ten thousand sausage rolls and nothing else. Liz, have you any other CDs apart from *Now Christmas*?'

Liz nodded eagerly. 'Oh, loads. Plenty of party songs, too. We'll soon have everyone up and dancing.'

'Brilliant.'

'What about misery guts upstairs?' asked someone. 'Is he gonna put a spanner in the works, or what?'

'I'll speak to him,' I promised. 'I'm sure he'll be fine about it.'

'Oh, aye? Believe that when I see it,' said another man, and as they all jeered and laughed,

I felt torn.

I wanted to defend Kit, to tell them what he was going through, with his nephew being so poorly, but on the other hand, I could well understand their anger. He'd not behaved well towards them, and they'd be even less happy when they found out about the money. He'd brought it on himself really. I could only hope that the party would give them all a chance to heal and meet on better terms. Maybe, just maybe, Kit would change his mind and pay the bonus after all.

Fingers crossed.

I wasn't particularly looking forward to mentioning the party to him, but in the event, it was quite easy. He was smiling when I walked into his office, carrying a mug of coffee and a plate of chocolate biscuits, and he seemed much more relaxed.

'Just the job,' he said, taking the snack from me and nodding his thanks. 'I haven't had time for lunch, so this will fill the gap nicely.'

'You should have had a proper meal,' I said. 'You need to eat.'

'Oh, there's plenty of time for that when I get home.' He eyed me ruefully. 'I've still got loads of chilli in the fridge. I'll just warm that up.'

I blushed. 'Sorry about all that,' I began, but he waved his arm, brushing my apology away.

'It's forgotten.'

'You look a lot happier,' I observed. 'Has this got something to do with the phone call from Ethan Rochester?'

He grinned. 'Yeah, it has. Sit down, Marley.'

I did, wondering what had happened.

'When I was at the trade fair in Liverpool, I got talking to Kirsty Benson. She's a buyer for Rochester's Department Stores. She was telling me that Ethan Rochester is keen to support smaller local producers in his food halls and has been trying to find a decent chocolate manufacturer for his York store. I sent her some samples of a few of our lines, and she showed them to Ethan.'

'I take it he approved?'

'He definitely did. Must admit, I was quite shocked that he rang me personally. He told me he's aiming for Rochester's to be a champion for the small companies, rather than the major producers whose products you can find anywhere. Carroll's is definitely in the running to supply the York store, which would mean we'd also have our products available through the Rochester's website. He says they have a very popular gift category, and they'd be included in that. It apparently gets a lot of hits all year round, though it's especially popular at Valentine's Day, Easter and Christmas. He wants me to meet up with him and take him some different chocolates. A taster session, if you like.'

'Meet up with him? You're going to London?'

'God, no. He lives locally — just a few miles from here, actually. He seems like quite a nice chap. Much more informal than I'd expected. He says his wife is a chocolate expert, and he wants her to try them. I dunno, maybe she's a confectioner by trade or something. Anyway, I'll be visiting Moreland Hall in a few days, armed with a selection of our premium chocolates.'

'That's great news!'

'It is. Fingers crossed. Although, it's a shame that, even if we get the contract, it's come too late for this Christmas.'

'But we'll be quids in next Christmas,' I pointed out brightly. 'And who knows where it might lead?'

His smile faded a little. 'Yeah.'

I wondered if he was thinking about Tim, and whether he'd be around for next Christmas.

'I have some news for you, too,' I said, thinking it best to strike before his good mood dissipated entirely. 'The staff have decided that, since the Christmas buffet at Miller's has been cancelled, they'll organise their own party here.'

'Here?' He frowned. 'What do you mean, here? And what sort of party?'

'It won't cost you a penny,' I said hastily. 'Everyone's chipping in with food and drink — non-alcoholic, of course. And we're going to hold it tomorrow lunchtime in the canteen, so work won't be affected at all.'

He looked unconvinced. 'And they're willing to do that, are they? Pay for everything themselves.'

I sighed. 'They want some sort of a do, Kit. If this is the only way they're going to get one, then they're willing to make it happen. All they need is your permission. Is that too much to ask?'

He tapped his fingers on the table for a moment, then shook his head. 'No, it's not. But look, tomorrow lunchtime is out. Tell them we'll have it around three tomorrow afternoon, and we'll close production early.'

'What? Are you serious?'

'Absolutely. You're right. They deserve this. And I'll bring some beers and wine as my contribution. It's Friday, so they'll have the whole weekend to recover. Okay?'

'Great.' I smiled at him, feeling a flickering of hope. Was the Christmas spirit finally returning to Kit Carroll at last?

***

'When did all this happen?' Kit gazed around the glammed-up canteen in surprise, and I grinned up at him.

'We did it on Wednesday night. Everyone chipped in and brought stuff from home. I know it's not the classiest display in the world, but it's better than nothing.'

'I saw the tree in the foyer, but I didn't realise.' He shook his head. 'I feel terrible.'

I was glad he felt terrible, in a non-vindictive way. It meant that, just maybe, my plan was working, and the old Kit was coming back. 'Why?'

'I don't know. All this effort everyone's making, and I have to tell them about their bonuses. It's not going to go down well, is it?'

'You're not telling them today?' I said, alarmed. If I could just persuade him to hold off until the next day, he might well change his mind. It's surprising what an afternoon spent eating and drinking and chatting with people can do to someone. I had high hopes that he'd start to see his staff as real people, and determine to pay them what they were due, after all.

Relief seeped through me when he said, 'Of course not. Let them have their party and forget about everything else for the day. I know I could use a break from real life.'

People were clearly wary of him being there at first, but when they saw the crates of beer and bottles of wine that he'd brought along, they soon relaxed. As they tucked into egg and cress sandwiches and chicken drumsticks, their hostility, softened by comfort food and alcohol, melted away. Soon they were laughing and joking with Kit as if they were old friends.

Part of me was relieved. The other part of me thought how fickle people were, and how easily bought. I was quite sure I would never have forgiven him so easily if I hadn't been on a mission to save him. And if I hadn't known about Tim, of course.

I wondered how he was getting on in America. I thought of Jack and what he and his wife must have been going through. Things were never what they seemed. People went through the most awful experiences, and no one else ever knew about them.

'Come on, our Marley!' Olivia's face was bright pink, as it always was when she'd had something alcoholic. 'Come and have a dance with me.'

I shuddered. Some dreadful ancient song called *The Bump* was playing, and people were doing the most extraordinary thrusts with their hips in time to the music. 'No thanks.'

'Oh, go on. Even you can manage this. It's dead easy, and it's a laugh. Come on!' She grabbed my hand and pulled me into the middle of the canteen, where everyone was bumping to their heart's content.

Mortified, I made a half-hearted attempt to join in, feeling totally ridiculous. I was pretty sure Olivia was deliberately bumping me so hard that I'd fall over, and I kept a close eye on her hips and put in a few hefty bumps myself. She laughed and bumped me back, and before long we were both whacking each other hard and trying to keep our balance, while giggling helplessly at the same time.

'Can anyone join in, or is this a sisterly thing?'

I turned my head, still laughing, to see Kit standing beside me, and blushed to my hair roots.

How embarrassing!

Olivia squealed gleefully. 'Feel free. We can attack her from both sides!'

'Well, that's hardly fair,' I protested, but too late.

Kit had taken up position, and between them I was thoroughly battered and bruised by the end of the song. Luckily, there was only a couple of choruses left, or I'd have likely ended up with a fractured hip.

A much faster, rather frenetic song started to play, and a cheer went up from some of the older ones. Kit, Olivia and I looked at each other, baffled.

'Now you're talking! A bit of Mud,' yelled someone. '*Tiger Feet*!'

Immediately, a whole line of people formed, doing a rather ridiculous stepping movement and laughing delightedly as the rest of us stood around, puzzled.

Deciding I'd danced quite enough, I turned back towards the tables, which had all been moved to the edge of the canteen.

'You can't sit down now,' Kit said, grabbing my hand. 'We have to try this out!'

'I've never even heard of it,' I pointed out.

'Me neither, but it looks like a laugh. Come on. It's Christmas!'

Was he serious? And what the hell had happened to him? I'd created a monster.

Reluctantly, I fell into line beside him, and placing my hands on my bruised hips, I began to copy the movements of the enthusiastic oldies who were having the time of their lives.

Kit got the hang of it pretty quickly and had clearly won over even the most cynical of the staff. A middle-aged operative called Sheila was bopping away beside him, laughing up at him and encouraging him in his efforts to emulate her steps. Unless she was just drunk. That seemed likely, given the scarlet flush on her cheeks and the hazy look in her eyes. What was Kit's excuse, though?

Was it, I thought suddenly, that he wanted to put all his worries behind him? That he was so intent on forgetting about Tim for one day that he was throwing himself into the party heart and soul? If so, who could blame him? Not me, and it seemed that the staff were willing to give him another chance, so that would help.

A weight lifted from my shoulders, and in its place landed a new feeling of optimism. When the song finished, I felt quite sorry. Not that I had the chance to feel sorry for long, as the velvety tones of Bing Crosby suddenly began, and Kit, after hesitating for just a moment, put one arm around my waist and took my hand to dance with me, as the crowds melted away.

We swayed gently to the music, and I put my head on his shoulder, allowing the magic of *White Christmas* to wash over me. My eyes closed, and I let myself drift away, back to those days when I was so innocent and so much in love with this man I could hardly think straight. The scent of Kit's aftershave wafted over me, his hair silky against my cheek. I sighed with pleasure, then remembered where I was and realised that a lot of people would be watching us with great curiosity. Kit and I hadn't said a word to each other the whole time we were dancing. We must look very odd.

'I've bought you a Christmas present,' I informed him, determined to bring us both back to the realities of the present day.

'Have you?' He smiled down at me. 'That's very kind of you.'

To be honest, I'd bought it for David, but I'd decided that he would never appreciate it. It was a tie from Rochester's and would be wasted on someone who lived in *Game of Thrones* t-shirts, or football jerseys, whereas Kit attended meetings and had to wear a suit. The tie would be used regularly and would look very smart. I'd have to think of something else for my brother-in-law.

'I may have got you something, too,' Kit murmured.

I shivered with delight, as images of a gold bracelet, or posh perfume, or a Jenny Kingston handbag floated before my eyes. Best not to look too eager though.

'Really? You didn't have to.'

'Neither did you,' he said. 'I figured I owe you.'

A shadow passed over me. He could never pay me back for what he owed me. No fancy gift could make up for the fact that he'd abandoned me, just when I'd needed him most.

His hand reached out and stroked back my hair, just as it had that night at The Blue Lamp. I looked up into those dark eyes and crumbled inside. How could he possibly still have such an effect on me? No one else had ever come close. Maybe no one else ever would.

When Kit got collared by a group of men intent on discussing football, and I finally made my way over to the table, Olivia pounced.

'Oh, my God!' She looked so excited, I feared for her heart.

'What?'

'Don't you *what* me, Marley Jacobs. You and Kit! You were practically sealed together over there. What's going on?'

'Nothing's going on,' I said. 'We just danced to *White Christmas*, that's all.'

'So did loads of other people,' she said. 'Didn't see them superglued together, though.

Everyone's talking about it. Mum's going to be furious that she missed this.'

I glanced around nervously. 'Where is Mum?'

'Outside with Don. Don't ask. Seems love is in the air tonight.'

'Yuk.'

'Don't say yuk like that when you and the boss are clearly involved.'

'Involved! Don't be ridiculous. Honestly, Olivia, you and your imagination.'

She put her hand on my arm. 'It wasn't my imagination, Marley. Trust me. I saw the way he was looking at you. The bloke's smitten. Be kind, eh?'

The irony of her statement didn't escape me. Me, be kind to Kit? She had no idea.

I glanced across the canteen, my eyes seeking him out. He was standing in a corner talking to a group of three or four men, bottle of beer in one hand, sausage roll in another, and he looked utterly beautiful.

As I watched, he turned his head and glanced around the room as if looking for something. His gaze fell on me, and he stared at me a moment, then his lips curved into a warm smile before he turned back to resume his conversation.

My heart belatedly decided to do *The Bump* all by itself. What was I going to do? This wasn't how it was supposed to go at all. I was meant to bring back the spirit of Christmas to this modern-day Mr Scrooge, not rekindle an old relationship that had almost destroyed me.

Things were getting way out of hand, and the worst thing about it was, I knew without doubt that there was a big part of me that was delighted. How, I wondered, half-terrified, half-thrilled, would it all end?

***

I asked myself that same question a couple of hours later, as I stood outside the front door of my flat, hands in pockets, not daring to look up as Kit stood beside me, not saying a word.

He'd insisted on walking me home. We'd both had a bit to drink so couldn't drive, and though we could have got a taxi, it hadn't seemed to occur to us at the time. Thankfully, my flat wasn't that far from the factory, although how he'd then get home to Farthingdale was another matter.

As we'd walked, we'd discussed the biting cold weather, how soon it would be Christmas, how happy Mum and Don looked together, how awful the egg and cress sandwiches tasted, as well as the merits of nineteen-seventies party music as opposed to the grinding tunes of the nineties, whether *White Christmas* was the definitive festive song, and if Nigel from packing seriously believed no one knew that he wore a toupee. Anything, in fact, apart from the thing that was hanging between us the whole time. What was happening to us? And where did we go from here?

Standing outside the flat, my mouth seemed dry with nerves. What should I do? Should I ask him in for coffee? Should I say goodnight? Would he kiss me? Did he even want to kiss me? If he did kiss me, how should I react? And had I tidied the flat before I left for work?

The flat! God, what would he think to that poxy little flat? It was miniscule compared with Fell House. He'd laugh at it, laugh at me. Maybe I should just say goodnight already and forget the whole thing.

His arms went around me, and I tried — I really tried — to keep a clear head. But the clean, soapy smell of him enveloped me, the warmth of his body, the familiarity of his touch, the sheer longing to be safe within his embrace again. It was too much to resist. I leaned against him, glad to be home. It didn't seem to matter what the flat looked like anymore.

'Come in for a coffee,' I murmured.

His eyes were searching, a question in those dark depths. 'Are you sure you want to make me coffee?' he said, his voice sounding thick with emotion.

I gave him a half smile, then pressed my fingers to his lips. 'I think I may be out of coffee,' I admitted. 'But it doesn't really matter, does it?'

He hesitated, and I saw a range of emotions flit across his face. He was clearly as torn and confused as I was. Neither of us knew what the hell we were doing, or whether it was a good idea to continue down this path — that much was obvious.

Strangely enough, it was a comfort to know that he wasn't that confident, after all. That wherever we were heading, we were doing so together, as lost and scared as each other.

I reached up and kissed him gently, and his hand cupped the back of my head, and the pressure on my lips increased, and then there was no more time for worrying, or wondering, or questioning. Whatever was going to happen seemed inevitable. And at that moment, I was glad.

CHAPTER 22

Kit stayed the entire weekend. He popped home for some fresh clothes and toiletries but wasn't gone long. He got a taxi straight back to my flat and, to be absolutely honest, we spent most of the time in bed. He hadn't been scornful about the flat at all, even though I'd apologised for how tiny it was. He'd just looked at me in surprise, as if he hadn't even noticed, then went back to making us scrambled eggs in my bijou kitchen, which was probably the same size as one of his cupboards.

On the Sunday morning we just lay there, arms around each other, my head on his chest, a smile on my face as he gently played with my hair, and we reminisced about the good times, carefully avoiding all talk of how our previous relationship had ended.

We talked about the Christmas Eve we'd spent with Grandad, having our own early Christmas Day together at Grandad's suggestion, and how Kit had had his first whisky that day, and how awful my first attempt at Yorkshire puddings had turned out, and how Grandad had laughed and said not to worry, the lumps in the gravy would take our minds off how bad they tasted.

'He was such a lovely man,' Kit remembered. 'I still miss him, even now.'

I loved him for that. He was quite right. I thought about Grandad every single day, and the fact that Kit had thought so highly of him made me feel all warm and happy inside.

'I miss him, too,' I said.

He kissed the top of my head. 'It was awful when he died. He was far too young. I know how badly it affected you, and of course, your mum didn't understand why, and you could hardly explain it to her, since she didn't even know you were still in touch with him.'

'But I had you,' I pointed out because it was true. Kit had been a tower of strength for me in those dark days. He'd held me while I cried and attended the funeral with me, holding my hand while I struggled to keep it together. After that, our relationship had deepened and matured, somehow. We'd shared something that bonded us, and it felt, to me at least, that we were no longer just boyfriend and girlfriend, but partners. Real partners.

'I'm sorry I wasn't there for you,' I murmured. 'When your dad died, I mean.'

He fidgeted a bit, clearly uncomfortable with the topic of conversation. 'Doesn't matter.'

'But he was young, too. It must have been a terrible shock.'

'It was, but if I'm honest, I can't say I grieved as much for him as I did for your grandad. Does that sound awful?'

'Well, no. I suppose not. I'm just a bit taken aback. I had no idea things were so bad between you.'

'Didn't you?' He sounded surprised. 'I thought you realised. Why did you think I never took you back to meet him?'

I hesitated, not sure how much I should reveal, or how deep I wanted to delve into past hurts.

'Honestly? I thought you were ashamed of me.'

He pulled away from me and stared at me in horror. 'You didn't!'

My face burned with embarrassment, and I lowered my gaze, staring intently at the dark hairs on his chest which, to be fair, was no hardship at all.

'What else was I supposed to think? I asked you loads of times when I could meet your family, and you kept fobbing me off, saying they had no need to meet me and that our relationship was our own business.'

'Because it was! Christ, Marley, you really thought...' He shook his head and pulled me close again. 'You must have been so hurt.

It wasn't like that at all. I just didn't want him spreading his poison to you. He didn't like anyone, and he made damn sure they knew it. Plus, I was afraid he'd turn you against me.'

'How on earth could he do that?' I said, incredulously.

'He never had a positive word to say about me,' he muttered. 'He'd have made damn sure you knew what a failure and a disappointment I was. I didn't want you to think badly of me.'

'Badly of you? Why on earth would I listen to him?'

He shrugged. 'He had a way of getting under your skin. Making you believe the worst. I know he made me believe I was a failure. It took me years to shake off the feeling that I was a complete waste of space. I don't know that I entirely have if I'm being honest.'

'But you proved him wrong,' I said. 'You went abroad and got a great job and made a success of your life.'

He laughed. 'Not in his eyes. It depends how you measure success. If I'd gone to university when he asked, and then learned the ropes in the factory and stayed on there, maybe I'd have had a chance. Going off to work in the third world with a variety of charities didn't even begin to pass muster.'

I sat up. 'Charities? You worked for charities?'

He raised an eyebrow. 'Didn't you know?'

I'd assumed he worked for some holiday company, or some big business overseas. It hadn't occurred to me that he'd been working for a good cause. Of course, I'd wanted to think the worst of him, and I'd certainly not risked making enquiries about what he was up to. It would have been far too painful to know.

I shook my head, and he sighed and sat up too, pulling the duvet around us to fend off the cold December air. I hated sleeping in a hot bedroom and never had the radiator on in there.

'After we — I mean, the first time I went abroad, before uni, I volunteered for a charity in West Africa. Then I came back after a year, did my duty at university, got my degree. Dad fully expected me to start work in the factory, but I had other ideas. I couldn't stand the thought of working beside him every day, so I found a job in South America, working with indigenous children in Peru. We were trying to educate them and make sure they got schooling, got off the streets, basically to empower them. There's so much trafficking there, and poverty, and the kids are expected to work, rather than go to school.' He shook his head sadly. 'It really is another world.'

'I had no idea,' I whispered. 'So, you've been in Peru, this whole time?'

'Oh, no, not the whole time. I went to India and worked to help the street children over there for a few years. I was contemplating my next move when I got the call from Jack about Tim.'

'You were in India when he called you?'

'No, I was back in Peru. I was just about to start walking the Inca Trail for charity when he told me what was going on and asked if I could come straight back after I'd finished, which I did. Hence the Yeti look.'

I stared at him in awe. 'You're amazing.'

'No, I'm really not. Jack's amazing. He carried the burden of Tim's illness and the factory all that time, without bothering me about it. I had a lot of time to think while I was walking and, believe me, I've been pretty selfish. I've basically done what I wanted to do with my life, and not given a thought to the people who needed me at home. My brother and his family, the factory workers .... They were all my responsibility, and I was so busy with my own life, I didn't give any of them a second thought.'

'But you were doing good,' I protested. 'You were being totally unselfish.'

'Not as unselfish as you might think,' he said. 'Like I said, I had a lot of time to think on that walk, and it occurred to me that I'd had my reasons for doing what I did, and they weren't all about making the world a better place. A lot of it was down to me, trying to feel better about myself, trying to earn my place in the world, trying to prove the old man wrong. He did a real hatchet job on my self-confidence, Marley. I can't even begin to explain it. All I know is, by throwing myself into good causes, it eased some of the pain, somehow. I could look in the mirror and feel a bit worthier. So, you see, I'm no saint. Far from it.'

I didn't know what to think anymore. He'd spent years working to make the world a better place for people, so I couldn't exactly

call him selfish, could I? On the other hand, he was right. He'd
not given a thought to the people who'd needed him. He'd
mentioned Jack and his family, and everyone at the factory, but
he'd not said a word about me. It was as if he'd given me no
thought at all. But I'd needed him. Perhaps I'd needed him most
of all, and he'd abandoned me.

'You've gone very quiet,' he said, taking hold of a strand of my
hair and twirling it around his fingers. 'What are you thinking?'

I almost said it, but I knew if I did the moment would be ruined.
The reckoning was coming though. At some point, we had to
discuss what had gone wrong, why he'd done what he did. He
needed to explain himself. I deserved that, at least.

There were things I had to tell him, too, and I wasn't looking
forward to it. But if I started to pick at that thread right then, the
whole picture could unravel. The truth was, I didn't want it to
unravel. I was happy. It was the best weekend I'd had in years,
and I couldn't bear to let it go. Not just yet.

I smiled at him. 'Just wondering what you've got me for
Christmas.'

He laughed. 'You'll never guess in a million years, and you'll
have to wait to find out. But there are other things we can enjoy,
in the meantime.'

I raised an eyebrow in mock surprise. 'There are? I can't imagine
what they'd be.'

He slid down the bed, pulling me with him. 'Well,' he
murmured, holding me close and gazing into my eyes, 'allow me
to demonstrate.'

***

Kit buttered his toast and put the knife in the sink, then sat
down at the folding table in the corner of the kitchen. He looked
around him, smiling to himself at the neat and tidy flat. It was
small, there was no escaping that fact — God knows, Marley had
apologised for its size a million times, as if it was a crime to have
a small house — but it was pretty, cosy and felt like home. He

preferred it to Fell House, any day. That place had never felt like home.

It had been purchased as a status symbol by Edward Carroll in the late nineteenth century — a stone, square house with a grey slate roof, large sash windows, high ceilings and original fireplaces in almost every room, including all of the eleven bedrooms. In Edward's day, the house had been full of children — seven, in all — plus an assortment of servants, and various house guests. It had sent out a clear message to his competitors and the community that he was a man of standing and wealth.

Lately, it was just a drain on expenses, and a bit of an embarrassment. Kit had never liked visiting his grandparents there, and had been devastated when his father inherited it and moved his family in. He couldn't wait to see the back of it.

Talking of which .... He picked up his mobile phone and glanced at the message from Serafina. Tomorrow evening. Well, that was something. At least it would get the ball rolling, although he wasn't at all certain things would move quickly enough. She'd been enthusiastic on the phone, assuring him that it was a done deal, and not to worry, but he couldn't help it. It had been years since she'd last been at Fell House. Things could still go badly wrong, so he wasn't counting on anything. Not even the Rochester account, as much as he wanted to.

He chewed his toast, hoping Marley wouldn't be much longer. Her tea was getting cold. He could hear her moving around in the bathroom, and the sound brought a warm glow to his heart. He couldn't believe he was actually sitting there in her flat, having had the most perfect weekend with her. All his doubts and worries had been pushed to one side. She was amazing, and he knew the feelings he'd had for her all those years ago had never really gone away. All their differences seemed to have been forgotten. Was there a chance for a happy ending, after all?

She walked into the kitchen looking like a different person. Gone was the tousled hair and makeup-free face. Her hair was neatly straightened, she was carefully made-up, and the body that Kit had thoroughly enjoyed seeing all weekend in all its naked glory was encased in a smart black pencil skirt and white shirt. Back to being Marley, the secretary.

Oops, PA, he corrected himself mentally, with a wry smile. He supposed he was Kit the boss again. Except, it wasn't time for work yet, and they were still technically off-duty.

'What are you smiling at?' she said, slipping into the chair beside him and picking up her mug of tea.

'You,' he said, dropping a kiss on her cheek.

She laughed and stroked his face, before returning the kiss. 'Thanks for the tea and toast. I could get used to this.'

'You could?'

The question hung in the air between them, and Kit felt suddenly awkward. He wished he hadn't said that. It was too soon. He'd scare her off.

'Back to reality now,' she said with a sigh, clearly avoiding the subject.

He took a sip of tea. 'I suppose so.'

He wanted to ask her, *where do we go from here? What happens now?* Somehow, he couldn't make himself do it. What if she politely informed him that it had been a one-off, never to be repeated?

There was still something overshadowing them. He could feel it. He just didn't know what it was, and he didn't know how to ask. He turned his thoughts to work and felt a dread descending.

'I'm not looking forward to today,' he confessed, taking another bite of his toast.

Marley sipped her tea. 'Why not? Come on, it's nearly Christmas. Cheer up. You're everyone's friend after your amazing dance show at the party on Friday.'

He managed a smile. 'Yeah, but for how long? I have to tell them about the bonus today. I can't put it off any longer. Doubt I'll be anyone's friend after that.'

Marley's face fell. She put down her mug and stared at him. 'You're going ahead with it? After all that?'

He was puzzled. 'All what? And of course I'm going ahead with it. I told you.'

'But I thought—'

'What? What did you think?'

She pushed her plate of toast away, untouched.

He stared at it, a sudden nausea in the pit of his stomach. 'What's wrong?'

'I thought, after the fun we all had on Friday, that you'd change your mind.'

'Because of a few sandwiches and a beer or two? Do you really think it works like that?'

She glared at him. 'Because you might finally have seen them as real people, instead of just numbers on a spreadsheet. I thought, if you got to know them, got talking to them, that you'd realise they were decent people and might rethink your money-grabbing attitude.'

'My...' Kit's mind whirled. My God, was that what she thought of him? 'So, you think I didn't see them as real people before? What sort of man do you think I am?'

'I don't know,' she snapped. 'You're a bundle of contradictions. You're happy to spend years helping the poor in third world countries, but when it comes to your own staff, you treat them like dirt. Aren't they poor enough for you? Or doesn't it count when it's your own pocket the funds are coming out of?'

Kit's mouth fell open. 'Is that what you really think of me?'

'What am I supposed to think? You can't do this to them. It's mean and petty!'

'Mean and petty? Bloody hell, Marley, say what you think, won't you.'

'Well, what do you expect? I'm so — so disappointed in you.'

The voice echoed back down the years. His father's voice. *You're such a disappointment, boy. You'd run the factory into the ground if it was left to you. Too bloody soft, by half. You need to toughen up!'*

Kit felt cold inside. He pushed his own plate away and stood up. 'I'm going to work. Are you coming?'

Already expecting her to refuse, he wasn't in the slightest bit surprised when she shook her head. 'I'm going to see my uncle first. He's not well. I should have visited him over the weekend. I'll make my own way to work.'

Kit grabbed his overnight bag and pulled on his jacket. 'Right, well, I'll see you at the office.'

'Yeah.'

Feeling sick, he headed down the stairs and unlocked the front door, then stood for a moment outside on the main street, taking deep breaths of cold, December air.

That was that then. He'd seen the contempt in her face, and it had just about finished him off. He'd seen that look so many times in his own father's face. Ironic, really. His father had always accused him of being too soft, yet Marley was accusing him of being too harsh. He couldn't win.

He could have told her his reasons, he supposed. Maybe he should have told her. Jack certainly seemed to think he should. But Marley was a family girl, and she had a sister, a brother-in-law and a mother who all worked at the factory, not to mention Don. She would feel obliged to tell them the truth about the precarious state Carroll's was in, and then that would spread all round the factory. He had to keep it quiet, at least for a while. He wanted them all to have a worry-free Christmas. Maybe, just maybe, a miracle would happen before the new year. He owed them all that much at least.

If that cost him his relationship with Marley, maybe that was the price he would have to pay.

Chapter 23

I wasn't in the best of moods when I arrived at Great Uncle Charles's house. I couldn't believe that Kit was going ahead with his plans to cut the Christmas bonus. I'd stupidly and naïvely believed that he would change his mind, once he got talking to the staff and bonded with them. I should have known better. Mr Scrooge wouldn't change his miserly ways that easily.

Frankly, though, after everything that had happened, I couldn't imagine what else I could do to show him the error of his ways. If the weekend we'd just spent together hadn't made him want to be the man he used to be, then what would?

My steps slowed as I trudged up the path to the front door. Feeling defeated wasn't a mood I wanted to face Great Uncle Charles in, and he'd no doubt make it worse by having something to say about my total failure. Great.

The door was locked, though that wasn't surprising so early in the morning. I knocked several times, but there was no answer. He was probably avoiding me, winding me up. The world felt out to get me that morning.

Cursing, I stomped around to the back of the house, moved the pot, and retrieved the key.

The house was cold inside — freezing cold. It actually felt even colder than it did outside, which was a bit weird. For the first time, a seed of doubt formed inside me. Was he okay? It was deathly quiet in here.

I wandered into the living room, but there was no sign of him. A half-eaten pot noodle sat on the coffee table, its congealed contents alarming me and filling me with shame. He'd not even managed to finish that meagre meal. Had he been eating properly at all over the weekend? I should have visited him sooner, instead of going to parties and rolling around in bed with Kit.

I would make it up to him. I'd cook him a proper breakfast, get that heating on, and then make sure he got a hearty evening meal, cooked with my own fair hands.

While climbing the stairs, I called his name. I didn't want to alarm him, walking in on him in his bedroom. Reaching the airing cupboard, I flicked on the boiler, relieved to hear it click into action. At least the heating seemed to be working.

When I knocked on his bedroom door, though, there was no call for me to come in or, more likely, to bugger off.

Tentatively, I pushed open the door. Great Uncle Charles was in bed. His duvet had landed on the floor, and I scooped it up, horrified at how cold he must have been. Laying it over him, I felt a churning of dread in the pit of my stomach. He looked terrible. His eyes were closed, his face was grey, and his breathing was rapid and shallow. I placed my hand on his forehead. He felt clammy, despite the cold air, which had wrapped itself around him in place of the bedding.

I glanced at my watch. If I rang the doctor, there'd be no chance of a visit before lunchtime. I wasn't at all sure I could wait that long. I wasn't sure Great Uncle Charles could, either.

'All about the money, you know.'

I jumped as his reedy voice cut through the quiet. 'It's all right, Uncle. Go to sleep. I'm going to get help.'

'You're a good girl, Marley. Always a good girl.'

I stared at him in disbelief. He was being kind about me? But at least he knew who I was. That was something, wasn't it?

'Don't let him go, Marley. He's not like them. Don't be alone.'

I bit my lip. 'I won't. Don't worry about all that now.'

He kicked at the duvet, his breath coming in short gasps. 'But I love you. I love you. Please don't do this. Please .... Please don't leave me. I need you.'

Tears filled my eyes as I stood up and hurried down the stairs to telephone for an ambulance. Something was dreadfully wrong with Great Uncle Charles, and it was all my fault. I'd abandoned him in his hour of need, and it seemed I wasn't the only one.

***

I called Kit. He sounded quite sharp at first, not that I could blame him.

'Where are you? You do know you're nearly an hour late for work?'

'I'm sorry. I won't be coming in today. I—'

'For God's sake, Marley. How unprofessional is that? So, you don't approve of my decisions. Tough. Live with it. You have a job to do, and you should be here. Unless, of course, you've decided to move on?'

A note of hesitancy moved into his voice at that point, and I tutted impatiently. 'Just shut up, Kit.'

'Pardon?'

'Look, this has nothing to do with you, or us, or the factory. It's my uncle. He's seriously ill.'

'What? God, I'm sorry, Marley. Where are you?'

'At the hospital. I had to call an ambulance.' My voice wavered. 'He's — he's really poorly, Kit. They suspect pneumonia, and it's all my fault.'

'How is this your fault?'

'I should have visited him sooner. I promised I'd call round earlier, but I stayed away all weekend. I feel terrible.' Tears rolled down my cheeks. 'I let him down. He could die.'

'He won't die.' The uncertainty in his voice belied his words, though. 'I'll be right there.'

'There's no need,' I said. 'Besides, you have a job to do, don't you? Can't put it off any longer.'

'Already done it.' His voice sounded grim. 'I'm hardly Mr Popular around here at the moment. I'll be with you as soon as I can.'

'What, just so you can get out of everyone's way?' I sniffed, feeling angry and hopeful all at the same time. I was annoyed that he'd done what he'd said he would do, and part of me resented the fact that he just expected me to want him with me. On the other hand, I *did* want him with me. He'd been a massive comfort to me when I'd lost Grandad. I needed him beside me again. I could hardly expect my family to care, could I?

'No,' he said. 'Not because of that. Because I want to support you. Is that okay with you?'

I wiped away the tears and nodded. 'Yes, please,' I said, my voice small. 'I would really appreciate that.'

His tone softened immediately. 'I'll be as quick as I can. Promise.'

In the event, he was there within three quarters of an hour, which was pretty good going, considering he'd brought along David and Olivia.

'What are you two doing here?'

'Why wouldn't we be here? Kit told us what's happened and offered to bring us. Don's gone to fetch Mum. Can't believe you didn't call us, Marley.'

'I didn't think you'd be bothered,' I admitted.

'He's still family, whatever we think of him,' Olivia said. 'Besides, *you're* bothered. We'd be here for you, even if we hated Great Uncle Charles, which we don't. I definitely don't like to think of him so ill. I was going to visit him at the weekend, for Christmas. I feel bad now. He'll be okay, though, won't he?'

I stared at her, stricken. Truthfully, I couldn't say he would be, having seen the state of him. He'd been mumbling some pretty weird things before the paramedics had arrived and placed an oxygen mask over his face. I couldn't make head nor tail of most of the stuff he'd said, but what was clear was that the rumours were true. Great Uncle Charles had definitely loved someone once, very much. And that person had left him and broken his heart.

Was that when he'd become such a bitter man, driven only by the pursuit of wealth?

He'd left Moreton Cross when in his early twenties and gone to Leeds, where he'd eventually built up a hugely successful construction company. He'd sold it off on reaching retirement age and had moved back to Moreton Cross to spend his twilight years with his younger brother. Grandad had once told me that he'd been very different when he was younger, and that I shouldn't judge him too harshly, as I had no idea what he'd been through. Evidently, he was quite right. I wished with all my heart that I'd been more understanding towards him. Kinder. Though, God knows, he hadn't made it easy to like him.

'Marley? He *will* be all right?' Olivia reached for David's hand and squeezed it as she waited for my reply.

I took a deep breath. 'He has severe pneumonia. He's very poorly. It's not looking good.'

Kit put his arm around me and drew me towards him. 'I'm sorry,' he murmured, kissing the top of my head.

David and Olivia exchanged glances.

'Coffee, anyone?' David said hastily. 'Tea? There's a vending machine down the corridor.'

We all agreed a cup of tea would be just the job — more, I think, for something to do than because we actually wanted a drink.

We'd just settled into chairs in the waiting area, clutching our plastic cups, when Mum and Don came rushing in. Mum hurried towards me and put her arms around me, almost knocking the tea out of my hand.

'Why didn't you call me, love? Are you okay?'

'It's not me that's poorly, Mum,' I reminded her.

'I know, but you go to see him a lot. And he's all you have left of your grandad, after all.' I gaped at her, stunned that she'd even given any thought to that aspect of our relationship.

She ruffled my hair. 'What? You think I didn't know that you kept in touch with him? Do me a favour, Marley. I'm your mum. I always know.'

Not everything, Mum. You definitely don't know everything.

She cuddled me, and I quickly passed the cup to Kit before any more hot tea could land on my lap.

'I'm sorry, love, I really am. I should have been there for you when your grandad died, but I was too angry and bitter with your dad. It coloured my judgement, and I really let you down. I'm so sorry. It wasn't your grandad's fault, any of it. I should never have listened to your dad.'

'Dad only hated Grandad because Grandad saw him for what he was,' I said. 'When Grandma was alive, he kept his mouth shut, and let her believe the best in their son. When she died, Dad must have known that Grandad wouldn't put up with his lies any longer. He was probably worried that Grandad would tip you off about what Dad was really up to. He couldn't risk that, so he turned you against him. Grandad was lovely, Mum. The best man in the world.'

'I'm sure he was, love. I'm sorry you went through all that alone. I just wish I'd been there for you.'

I risked a sideways glance at Kit and wanted to say, *I wasn't alone. I had the second-best man in the world right beside me, every step of the way, and here he is again, just when I need him.* Although, he hadn't always been there when I needed him, had he? And I didn't think now was the time to reveal the depth of the relationship Kit and I had shared — not with Great Uncle Charles so ill.

The nurses allowed us in to see Uncle two at a time, for short periods. He looked dreadful. His face was grey, his wispy hair plastered to his head. Beneath his closed eyes, an oxygen mask covered his face. He had tubes coming out of his arms, which didn't surprise me, considering I'd heard the nurse telling Mum about *complications*.

'He's nearly ninety,' Mum had said gently. 'You've got to be prepared.'

But I wasn't prepared. As I looked down at the old man, who'd been such a big part of my life since Grandad had died, I knew I wasn't ready to let him go. I would have given anything to hear him snapping at me about my ulterior motives for visiting him or telling me off for making the tea too strong or making some sly comment about Olivia's baby-making prowess, and my own lack of anything meaningful in my life.

Kit squeezed my hand. 'I'm sorry, Marley.'

'Don't write him off just yet,' I said desperately. 'He's a lot stronger than you think. He'll pull through this, you'll see.'

Back in the corridor, I announced that I was heading to Fox Lodge to get Great Uncle Charles some things.

'What things?' Mum said.

'What do you think? When he wakes up, he's going to be furious that he's stuck in that hospital gown. I'm going to bring his pyjamas, and his glasses, and a newspaper for him to read, and his favourite biscuits. Bet you anything you like that he'll moan about the food in here.'

They all looked at each other, and I wanted to scream at the expression on their faces: *You don't know him like I do! He won't let this beat him. He's tougher than he looks.*

Instead, I said dully, 'Can someone give me a lift, please?'

A chorus of voices obliged, but strangely enough, I knew exactly who I wanted to take me home. 'Kit, you need to get back to the factory. David, can you drop Mum home before you go back to work? Don, thank you. I'd really appreciate the lift.'

Kit looked at me, clearly hurt. I couldn't deal with him right then. I couldn't think about anything but sorting out Great Uncle Charles's belongings and bringing them straight back to him.

'You've done enough for me today,' I told him. 'Seriously, I appreciate it, but you need to be at work. I'll be fine with Don.'

Don put his arm around me. 'Come on then, love. Let's get off to Fox Lodge, shall we? Don't want the old man sitting there in that gown when he wakes up do we? Let's give him some dignity, eh?'

And that, I thought, following him out of the hospital towards the car park, was why I needed Don right then. He'd go along with whatever I said, without trying to talk me out of it, or prepare me for the worst like the others. It was why he'd spent his entire lunchbreak finding a Father Christmas outfit for Kit, even though he thought my whole mission to save him was completely barmy. He was a good man, and perfect for Mum. At that moment, I didn't want reason, or kindness, or sympathy. I just wanted someone who would let me believe.

***

'So, this is Fox Lodge,' Don said, as I pushed open the front door and ushered him inside.

The heating was still on. Great Uncle Charles would be furious if he knew.

Don looked around him, while I waited anxiously for his verdict. 'It could be a cracking place, this. I can see why you love it so much. Make a smashing home when it's done up.'

I could have hugged him. Mum and Olivia thought it was just a gloomy old pile of bricks, but Don could see the potential, just as I could. Even so, I would far rather have Great Uncle Charles at home, sitting in his chair, newspaper in hand, trying his best to ignore me, than his house, however gorgeous I could make it.

The thought shook me. I'd had no idea how fond of him I'd become. I wished with all my heart that I'd realised it sooner. Maybe if he hadn't thought I only cared about the house, he'd have softened towards me, too. Maybe we'd have got on better.

Well, I thought, squaring my shoulders determinedly, when he got home things would be different. I'd tell him how much he mattered to me. We'd make a fresh start. Get to know each other properly. There was so much I wanted to know about him, and it wasn't too late. It wasn't.

We headed upstairs to his bedroom, and I opened the top drawer of his chest of drawers, pulling out several pairs of pants and some socks.

'He'll need a couple of pairs of pyjamas,' I said, placing the underwear on the bed. 'Hope he's got some clean.'

I assumed they'd be in the next drawer, but they weren't. Instead, there was an assortment of shoes lined up, all neatly polished.

Don wrinkled his nose in bewilderment. 'Why keep shoes in a drawer? Funny old stick, isn't he?'

'You could say that,' I said, smiling. 'He has his own ways, and they're always right. Everyone else is wrong.'

I closed the drawer and tried the bottom drawer, relieved to see several pairs of stripy pyjamas folded up neatly. I pulled a couple of pairs out and then peered back into the drawer. 'What on earth's that?'

Don wandered over to stand beside me and stared into the depths of the drawer.

'Looks like a scrapbook,' he announced, quite unnecessarily. My question had been rhetorical. I could see for myself what it was. The question was, should I look inside it?

Don looked down at me as I crouched beside the open drawer, trying to decide what to do.

'He won't thank you for it,' he said. 'It's private, Marley.'

'I know. I know that.' But I bit my lip. It might be my only chance to find out what made Great Uncle Charles behave the way he did, what made him tick. Grandad had said a lot had happened to him, and that he didn't used to be like that. What had changed him? If I could find out what had happened, maybe we could build a better relationship when he got home. He need never know that I knew, after all.

Without another thought, I pulled out the scrapbook and rushed over to the bed.

Don tutted and shook his head. 'You sure about this, love?'

'Quite sure,' I said firmly.

The scrapbook was old, its pages stiff. I stared down at the newspaper cuttings and frowned. They were just about the last thing I'd expected. Don sat beside me, and we turned the pages in silence, my mind whirling.

'By heck,' said Don at last. 'It's like a history of Carroll's.'

'But I don't understand,' I said. 'Great Uncle Charles hates Carroll's. Why has he been collecting all this information about it?'

Don went back to the beginning of the scrapbook and looked through it again. 'It's not a history of Carroll's really. It's a history of Edwin and Dorothy Carroll. Look, it starts with their engagement announcement, and goes right up to the birth of James Carroll. Then it stops. This whole thing only covers about five years.'

I examined the cuttings and photos again. He was quite right. The first cutting was all about how delighted both parents were that Edwin Carroll was engaged to be married to Miss Dorothy Enid Brocklehurst. Dorothy was, apparently, the daughter of a Whitby solicitor, and was rather attractive.

I stared down at her face, noting the sparkling eyes and the dark curls, and realised with a start that I was looking at Kit's grandmother. How strange that Great Uncle Charles had a picture of her in a scrapbook. Not just one picture, I realised. He'd collected press cuttings of their wedding, and a photograph of them posing with their only child, Kit's father, James. He also had various newspaper snippets about what was happening at Carroll's during that time, and details of parties the couple had attended.

One photo particularly caught my eye. It was a picture of Fell House, complete with dozens of posh cars in the drive, and an article about the swanky party that the couple had hosted after James's christening, and the local dignitaries who were his godparents, and how happy and how much in love the couple clearly were. After that, the scrapbook was empty, although there were several pages he could still have filled. What did it mean?

Don shook his head. 'Seems to have had a bit of an obsession with them, doesn't he?'

The fog was lifting. 'Dorothy Carroll,' I murmured. 'That's what went wrong. That's what changed him.'

'Sorry?'

'Grandad said he'd been badly hurt, and it had changed him. That he didn't used to be the way he is. Don't you see? He clearly loved this Dorothy Carroll, or Brocklehurst, as she was, and she chose Edwin Carroll over him. Great Uncle Charles probably thought it was his money she'd gone for. That's what made him so bitter, and that's why he went off chasing after a fortune of his own. No wonder he hates the Carrolls and that factory. Edwin was at school with him and must have known how he felt about Dorothy. No wonder Great Uncle Charles says you can never trust that family. Poor man. He must have been heartbroken.'

Don sighed. 'What a waste of life. He could have found someone else, instead of sitting here, brooding over something he couldn't have.'

'But if she was the love of his life, how could he ever get over that? She abandoned him for money. She chose the lifestyle over him!' I thought of Kit. He'd abandoned me, too. Okay, he'd gone off to do good, but could I trust him? Could you ever trust a Carroll?

'Now, Marley, you don't know that she abandoned him for money, or anything else for that matter. You don't even know if she was aware that your uncle was in love with her. It might have been a secret crush, for all you know. And who's to say she didn't genuinely love this Edwin Carroll?'

'Huh. I very much doubt it. From what I've heard, he was horrible.'

'And your uncle's all sweetness and light?'

I glared at him. 'He was, until she broke his heart!'

'By heck, there's no shifting you when you've made your mind up, is there? All right, love, if you say so. We may never know the truth of it, so there's no use falling out over it. Let's put this back and get his stuff packed for the hospital, eh? Don't go upsetting yourself.'

But I was upset. If Edwin Carroll hadn't been so selfish, if Dorothy Brocklehurst hadn't been so greedy, Great Uncle Charles might have had the life he deserved, and he may have turned out as lovely and kind and sweet-natured as Grandad. I could well understand his hatred for the family. Hadn't I felt it myself all those long years, when Kit had left me all alone, after all his promises?

Don put his arm around me. 'This has really got to you, hasn't it? What is it, love?'

I put the scrapbook beside me on the bed and rubbed my face wearily. I was so tired of everything. I wasn't sure I could carry the burden of the past on my own any longer, and Don was so kind and so straightforward. I leaned into him as he patted my arm, just like a dad should have done.

'You can tell me,' he said. 'I won't say a word.'

I knew that. I had no doubts about him at all. So, slowly, hesitantly, I told him about Kit. I told him about my childhood crush on him, how he'd wanted to ask me out, but hadn't dared, how he'd overheard my conversation with Hayley and misunderstood. I told him about my goth phase, and how I'd unwittingly been party to Kit's total humiliation, and about our meeting again in Helmston Christmas Market, and the start of our relationship. I told him about our secret meetings at Grandad's, and how Kit would never take me to Fell House, and how I hadn't told Mum and Olivia about our relationship because of Mum's fragile state. I told him how close we'd become, especially after Grandad died, how Kit had supported me through it all, how much I'd loved him, how I'd believed him when he said he loved me.

'Well, I'll go to the foot of our stairs,' he said, shaking his head. 'I had no idea. You and Kit, eh? Mind you, you can see the lad's smitten with you. Saw it straight away at the hospital. By heck, you kept that quiet, love. All that stuff about saving him, was that just a cover to spend time with him?'

'Definitely not!' I protested. 'Actually,' I added thoughtfully, 'it was Great Uncle Charles who encouraged me most with that little plan. Kept telling me that Kit was the best thing that ever happened to me, and that I'd only been happy when I was with him. He said I changed after Kit and I split up.' I frowned. 'It doesn't make sense. Why would he want me to save a Carroll, after everything that family did to him?'

Don sighed. 'I hate to say this, Marley, but have you ever thought that maybe what he was really trying to do was save you?'

My eyes widened. 'Save me? From what?'

'From being like him. From being alone. From having nothing in your life but this house. Look, you told me before how he's always having digs at you about Olivia and the kids. From what you've just said, he clearly believes that you'll be happier if you and Kit rekindle your romance, so don't you think that what he was really trying to do was give you a reason to become involved with Kit again? And maybe, just maybe, he wants you to focus on something other than money and Fox Lodge? Maybe he thinks you need to remember the past, just as much as Kit needs to.'

I was about to deny the possibility that Great Uncle Charles would ever have been that deep, but the words died on my lips. It made sense. And, given what I'd just seen in that scrapbook, I realised there was far more to him than I'd imagined. He had a heart. He understood love. He understood pain and loss and rejection. Maybe he really had done all that for my sake, after all. It was more likely than wanting to help a Carroll.

I thought of Dorothy. Kit was the image of her. How could I look at him again, knowing he was the double of the woman who'd destroyed my uncle's life?

'Sometimes,' I said, tearfully, 'the past isn't something you want to remember.'

Don nodded. 'True enough. On the other hand, sometimes we have to remember, so that we can learn from it.' He squeezed me gently. 'What went wrong between you and Kit, love? Sounds like you were a really close couple. What changed?'

'He changed,' I said bitterly. 'I thought we were happy, Don. I was making plans. In my head, it was all arranged. Kit would go to university, then he'd start working at the factory with his father, preparing for the day he'd take over. We'd get engaged, married, have a family.' My voice cracked, and I buried my face in his chest.

Don stroked my hair. 'But it never happened.'

'No.' I sat up and wiped the tears away, my voice harder as the memory seared through me. 'You see, Kit failed to mention that he had other plans entirely. He wanted a gap year. He didn't want to go to university straight away. He planned to go abroad, travel.'

'Nothing wrong with that, love,' Don said gently.

'Really? Don't you think he could at least have had the decency to tell me himself?'

'You mean he didn't?'

I shook my head bitterly. 'One of Mum's cleaning team at the factory also cleaned at Fell House. Mum came home one day, full of gossip, about how Audrey said there were ructions with the family because of Christopher's rebellion. Apparently, he was refusing to do what his father insisted he had to do, and there was a massive row going on. James Carroll was furious, because he wanted Kit to get his degree and then learn the ropes at Carroll's as soon as possible, but Kit had informed him that he wanted to get some life experience first and had no plans to work at the factory for the foreseeable future. *Life experience*!' I tutted in disgust. 'Can you imagine how that felt? He hadn't said a word to me, and there was Mum chattering blithely on about it all, thinking it was so funny that James Carroll had been disobeyed for once, and I was just sitting there in shock.'

'So, I'm guessing you confronted him?'

'Too right I did. I was livid.'

'And did he have a good reason for not telling you first?'

'He said it had all snowballed without him meaning it to. He said it was an idea he'd been mulling over, but his father had got on his high horse about something, and he'd just blurted it out in anger, and of course, his father put his foot down immediately, which just made Kit dig his heels in and refuse to budge. He said the more his father insisted he do as he was told, the more the idea appealed. By the time I spoke to him about it, he'd made up his mind, and there was no shifting him.'

'So, what did you do?'

'What do you think I did? I was furious. I told him he couldn't go, and what about all our plans?' I blushed at the memory. 'He said *what plans?* Like he hadn't even thought about getting married and taking over the factory.'

'Hang on. Are you saying you hadn't actually discussed the future with him?'

My face burned. 'Well, no, but it was a given, wasn't it? That's what happens when you're in a relationship.' Besides, how many times had he assured me he loved me with all his heart, that he would always love me?

'But you were only eighteen, love. Far too young to think about all that. No wonder the lad panicked.'

I glared at him. '*He* panicked? How the hell do you think I felt?'

'I don't know. Why don't you tell me? Why would you panic just because he was going away for a year? If he said he was coming back to do his university course after that, wasn't that good enough for you? It was only a postponement of twelve months. Was it really that bad?'

'You don't understand.'

'What don't I understand, Marley?' Don's voice was kind, and I realised I was crying again.

'I was scared. I thought he wouldn't come back.'

Don sighed and nodded. 'Aye. Like your dad, you mean?'

'All those rich, brainy kids on a gap year. What if he met someone over there? What if he wanted to stay with them, rather than come home to a boring college kid?'

'So, you broke up with him, rather than risk it?'

'I didn't break up with him!' I said. 'He left me. He said we had no future together, and he walked away.'

'Why would he do that?' Don sounded confused. 'Didn't the lad try to reassure you?'

I chewed my lip, remembering. 'He asked me to go with him,' I said eventually.

Don frowned. 'Eh? He wanted you to go abroad for a year with him?'

I nodded, wrapping my arms around myself, as if to protect myself from the memory.

'Then you've lost me, love. Clearly, he didn't want to break up with you. The lad was offering you the chance of a lifetime. Why didn't you go with him?'

I rocked back and forth for a moment, feeling sick. It was all too painful. There were some things that I couldn't explain, not even to someone as understanding as Don.

'Marley? Why didn't you go with him? A year abroad, a chance to discover new things together. Think of the memories you'd have made, the bond you'd have forged. Why would you turn that down?'

'Because — because I didn't fancy it.' I saw the look on his face and tried to justify myself. 'He was talking about trekking through jungles, living in tents, that sort of thing. I mean, he really wanted to cut himself off from civilisation and rough it, as if there's something noble about that way of life.'

Don gave me a look. 'So, you turned him down 'cos you didn't fancy camping?'

'I didn't fancy living like some primitive being in the middle of nowhere, with no real sanitation, and God knows what dangers lurking.'

'And that's what you told him?'

'More or less.' I shivered. 'I said I didn't see any reason to live in a tent for a year, and that it didn't make you a better human being to go without a flush toilet.'

Don let out a long breath. 'Right. I can see what went wrong now. What did he say to that?'

My anger burned brightly again. 'He said I was a spoilt little princess. He said that everyone was right about me, and that he should have known what I was like. He honestly thought I was only with him because he was a Carroll. He said all I wanted was to trap him, so I could live in luxury all my life, and that I needn't think he was going to lock himself in a prison just so that he could provide me with the lifestyle I wanted. He told me we were finished, and that I could find myself some other mug to sponge off.'

'Right.' Don stood up and replaced the scrapbook in the bottom drawer. 'So, quite a bitter break-up then.'

You have no idea. I tucked my hair behind my ears. 'You could say that.'

'But that's the past. Clearly, he's changed his mind about you, or why would he become involved with you again? And you've obviously forgiven him.'

I stared at him dumbly, and his eyes narrowed.

'You *have* forgiven him, haven't you?'

When I didn't reply, he reached for my hand. 'If you can't forgive him, there's no future for you, Marley. You must see that? All right, harsh words were spoken, and the break-up was painful, but that's all gone now. You were just teenagers. All them hormones sloshing around must have played havoc with your reasoning. He probably regretted what he'd said the minute he left.'

'But he still left,' I muttered. 'And he came back for university after a year and didn't get in touch. He came back from working abroad, for his father's funeral, and never contacted me. If Jack hadn't gone to America, I'd probably never have seen him again. What kind of love is that?'

'You never tried to contact him either, I presume?'

I hadn't even thought about it. 'It was up to him. He was the one who left me.'

Don tutted. 'I don't know. Seems to me, you two need your heads banging together. Come on, love, let's get this stuff back to your uncle. Them hospital gowns are proper draughty round your vitals, you know.'

We picked up the pyjamas and underwear and headed downstairs. As Don took my uncle's belongings to the car, I went over to the heating thermostat and turned the temperature down a little, just to keep the chill off the place without burning too much gas. Great Uncle Charles wouldn't thank me if he received a huge gas bill in January.

Looking around, I felt a warmth towards him that I'd never experienced before. He'd be home soon, and then we'd build a better relationship. I couldn't wait to get to know him properly.

Smiling, I closed the front door of Fox Lodge behind me.

CHAPTER 24

Serafina closed the door of the final bedroom and turned to Kit, her eyes bright. 'Perfect. It's even better than I remembered.'

Kit felt a surge of hope. 'So, you think it's suitable? You're still interested?'

'Absolutely. This house will make a wonderful luxury development. I can see at least six or seven apartments here, and with landscaped gardens and such a beautiful location, I can't imagine I'd have any trouble shifting them.'

'And what we said about Jack?'

She smiled. 'One apartment included in the price for Jack and Amanda, as part of the deal. I haven't forgotten.'

Kit sagged with relief. 'Thanks, Seffy.'

'What made you change your mind?' She followed him downstairs, the scent of her expensive perfume wafting over him as they walked. 'After all these years, I'd given up.'

'I need the money,' he admitted, opening the door of the sitting room for her and ushering her inside. 'The factory needs a major cash injection, fast. This was the only way.'

'You really shouldn't tell me that,' she reproached him, shaking her head playfully. 'It puts me at an advantage. How do you know I won't use that information to haggle the price down?'

'Because I've known you since we were teenagers,' he responded, smiling, 'and I know you'd never do that.'

'Curse my kindly nature,' she said, eyes twinkling. 'So, would you like to look over the contract?'

'You've had one prepared?' He stared at her, astonished. 'But how did you know you'd still want the place?'

'I've wanted Fell House for a long time,' she said. 'If you remember, my father wanted it, too, but your father wouldn't even contemplate it. Of course, Daddy wanted it for different reasons. He visualised himself living here like a lord of the manor. I only ever saw its investment potential. Tell me, Kit,' she leaned forward, handing him the papers that she'd removed from her bag, 'does it bother you? The fact that this will no longer be in your family? Or that it will be divided up into apartments?'

Kit rolled his eyes. 'You must be joking. I have no interest in, or affection for, this place. All it holds are memories of arguments, bitter silences, and a lot of misery. I'll be glad to be rid of it.'

'Yes, I remember your relationship with your father was never easy,' she said with a sigh. 'I always felt sorry for you about that. I loved my own father so much, and always felt you missed out.'

'My father wasn't like yours. He was cold and strict. He and my mother were a good match. She was selfish, hard, and not in the slightest bit maternal. Still isn't. Do you know, she hasn't once set eyes on Tim? Her own grandson. Too busy, apparently. Yep, she was the perfect woman for Dad. I don't think they gave a damn about each other, to be honest. Mind you, it seems to be a Carroll family trait. My grandparents despised each other. Like my parents, they slept in separate rooms and barely spoke. Lovely examples of marital bliss, I must say.'

'But Jack and Amanda are happy?'

Kit hesitated, thinking of Tim and everything his brother and his wife were going through. Happy wasn't the word he'd use to describe them at that moment. 'They're solid,' he compromised eventually. 'I think they'll last the course.'

'And what about you, darling? Anyone special on the scene?'

Kit eyed her warily, wondering how much to confess. Truthfully, he wanted to talk to someone about it, and he didn't have anyone else. He could hardly pour it all onto Jack's shoulders, after all.

'I've been sort of seeing someone,' he said carefully.

She squealed with excitement. 'Really? About bloody time. Thought you'd taken a vow of celibacy. Who is she?'

He stared at the contract, not really seeing it. 'Her name's Marley, and—'

'Marley?' She clapped her hands, leaning forward eagerly. 'Not *the* Marley?'

'You remember her?' Bloody hell, he'd honestly thought she'd have forgotten all about her.

'How could I forget? I spent an entire year mopping your tears and listening to you drone on about that awful gold-digging, selfish, conniving bitch. Remember?'

Kit flushed. 'I was very young, and probably a bit too harsh about her.'

She shook her head. 'From what you told me, she deserved everything she got. Are you sure about this, Kit? What on earth made you give her a second chance?'

How could he explain? In a strange way, he hadn't had any say in the matter. It was as if he'd been waiting for Marley to give *him* a second chance, even though it was she who'd hurt him. From the moment he'd seen her at The Blue Lamp, it was only a matter of time really. He knew he'd forgive her anything, even the way she'd used him back then.

'She's changed. Grown up.' He really hoped he was right about that, though little doubts still niggled at him.

'Oh? What makes you think that?'

He put down the contract and considered the matter. 'She really cares about other people. She's my secretary now, believe it or not.' He felt a sudden warmth, thinking how Marley would be giving him an indignant look and reminding him she was his PA, *actually*. 'And she's been worrying about the factory staff. Things haven't been easy here, Seffy, I won't lie. I had to make some unpopular decisions, like scrapping the Christmas bonus, and not taking them all out for their traditional meal. She was really angry with me for messing them around like that. She's been giving me quite a hard time about it, actually,' he added with a laugh.

'I take it she doesn't know the trouble the factory's in?'

He blushed again. 'No. I haven't told her.'

'And why's that?'

'I didn't want her to tell the rest of the staff. Didn't want them all worrying about their jobs, especially over Christmas. She has family working there, and she may have felt obliged to tell them.'

'Are you sure that's the only reason?'

'What do you mean? What other reason could there be?'

She leaned back against the sofa, eyeing him sternly. 'You're sure you just don't want her to know you may not be as financially secure as she imagines? Frightened she'd suddenly find you a less attractive prospect?'

'It's not like that!' His denial sounded hollow, even to his own ears. Wasn't that what had nagged away at his subconscious all this time? The voice that whispered in his ear, even while he tried to drown it out with protests that she wasn't like that anymore, that the feelings between them were real? Marley had got what she'd always wanted, after all. She was dating the boss of Carroll's Confectionery Factory — sort of. Wasn't that what she'd planned, way back when they were besotted teenagers?

At least, he'd been besotted, he remembered bleakly. She'd soon shown her true colours when she realised he wanted more from life than to run a sweet factory. She hadn't wanted to be with him when he went to Africa. She hadn't wanted to embark on a real adventure with him, to share the experience of a lifetime. She'd thrown it all back in his face, going on about the lack of luxury, and how she wouldn't be seen dead in a tent. And at that, he'd told her they were over, hurling insults at her in a panicked attempt to get her to change her mind, to tell him she loved him and would happily go anywhere with him, whatever the conditions. But she hadn't. She'd simply stared at him, all wide-eyed and pale, and told him to go then. So, he had.

Seffy had been one of the other gap year students on the project, and they'd bonded very quickly. She'd had the patience of a saint, quickly becoming his confidante, and never complaining when missing Marley had overwhelmed him at times and he'd had to fight the urge to rush back home to make it up with her. Marley had never got in touch with him, and he'd guessed she'd found someone else.

He'd gone home a year later to start uni and had wanted to find her but hadn't dared risk the rejection. Then, on a night out with some fellow students in Whitby, he'd seen her with a man. It was nearly Christmas, and she was slow dancing with some denim-clad bloke. He'd seen the expression on her face. She'd looked a million miles away, and he'd felt sick with jealousy and hurt, and gone straight home.

He'd never attempted to find her again and had pushed her to the back of his mind. Or at least, he'd tried to. Marley had a habit of forcing her way forward at the most inconvenient moments. He'd never really been free of her.

Truthfully, he didn't think he wanted to be free of her. He had to believe in her. What choice did he have?

'She's going through a hard time at the moment. Her great uncle's seriously ill.'

'I'm sorry to hear that,' she said, 'although I don't see what that's got to do with anything. Just be careful, Kit, that's all. I'd hate for you to go through all that heartbreak again. On the other hand, if she genuinely has changed, I couldn't be more delighted for you. I'd like to meet her one day.'

He smiled faintly. 'Would you like a drink?'

She shook her head, blonde hair bobbing. 'No thanks. Peter's taking me out for dinner. It's our wedding anniversary.'

'God, I'm sorry, you should have said. You could have come another day.'

'Not at all. This house is the best present I could ever ask for,' she said, standing up and smoothing her skirt. 'Have a look through the contract, then show it to your solicitor. Any problems or queries, get in touch with me.'

'I'm sure there won't be,' he assured her.

She laughed and held out her hand. 'Pleasure doing business with you, Mr Carroll.'

'Likewise, Mrs McCoy.'

She released his hand and threw her arms around him. 'It's been lovely to see you again, Kit. I have missed you. You must let me know how it goes with Marley. I really do hope it all works out.'

'Thanks, Seffy.' He smiled and showed her to the front door.

'Don't forget,' she said, 'any problems, just call me.' She leaned forward and kissed him gently on the cheek. 'Take care.'

'See you soon,' he promised, and waved as she rushed over to her car, clearly keen to get out of the freezing evening air and into the warmth again. He stood on the step, waving until her car cleared the drive and disappeared from view, then turned to go back inside.

'Kit?'

He spun around, shocked. 'Marley? What the hell are you doing here?' God, she looked frozen, and so pale. She was standing by the wall, just staring at him. 'What's wrong? What's happened?'

'Great Uncle Charles.' She swallowed. 'He died a couple of hours ago.'

Kit slumped against the door. 'Oh, my God. Marley, I'm so sorry.' He shook himself, realising suddenly that he was freezing, so she must be even colder. 'Come in. It's like ice out here.'

She didn't move, still staring at him. 'Who was that?'

'What? Oh, you mean...' His voice trailed off. She was looking at him most peculiarly. 'Her name's Serafina. We're old friends. Known each other since we were teenagers.'

'I don't remember you mentioning her before,' she said, teeth chattering.

He frowned. 'You wouldn't. We met in our gap year. She was in Africa with me, working on the project I told you about.'

'And you're still in touch?'

He shifted, feeling in the wrong, but not knowing why. 'She became a good friend. We got on well.'

'Clearly.'

Her eyes were boring into him, and Kit felt a spark of annoyance. What was she insinuating? And did it matter, given that she'd just lost her great-uncle? Surely, she had better things to think about? 'Are you coming in?'

She turned and started to walk towards the gate.

Kit glared at her. 'I said, are you coming in?' he called.

'No thanks. I just wanted you to know about Great Uncle Charles. Goodnight.'

Kit was about to run after her, to stop her from leaving, to make her listen, but a growing weariness stopped him. Why was it always so difficult with her? Why did she always seem to believe the worst of him? Obviously, she'd seen Serafina kiss him, put two and two together, and made a million out of the scenario. That was Marley all over. How much had she really changed?

He walked into the house and slammed the door behind him. Maybe Seffy was right. Maybe he was being stupid trusting her after the way she'd behaved. And if he was being honest with himself, how much did he trust her anyway?

Wasn't the truth of it that he'd just been waiting for her to revert to type? Didn't he know, deep down, that when she found out how broke he was, she'd run a mile?

Kit sank into the sofa and stared with unseeing eyes at the contract on the coffee table. Why the hell had he ever got involved with Marley Jacobs again?

More importantly, how could he ever stop loving her?

CHAPTER 25

Mum offered to have the wake at her house. I had thought to prepare something at Fox Lodge, but I didn't have the heart. Besides, the large rooms in that house would only emphasise how few people attended Great Uncle Charles's funeral. I had no doubt that, apart from immediate family, there would be no one, and in the end, I was proved almost entirely correct.

Mum, Olivia, David and Don had been granted the day off work to attend, and we stood in solemn silence as the coffin was carried into the crematorium. Great Uncle Charles wasn't religious and had requested a humanist service, which seemed fitting.

As we filed indoors, following the pall bearers, I couldn't help but remember Grandad's funeral and contrast the two. The church had been packed with all Grandad's friends and acquaintances, and I'd felt so proud to know how loved he'd been, and how popular. This room was tiny, but it was still practically empty. I felt an unbearable sadness for Great Uncle Charles.

How different things could have been, if only he'd never loved a Carroll.

There was, I thought bitterly, a great lesson to be learned there. You couldn't trust them. They would always abandon you in the end. Here I was again, all alone and let down by Kit Carroll. I deserved all I got.

Hearing the door open and close behind me, I glanced around and noticed, to my surprise, that there were a couple of other people sitting in the pews behind me. I had no idea who they were.

My eyes widened when I realised it had been Kit who'd just entered the chapel. Dressed in a black suit and tie, he looked very serious and — I couldn't deny it — devastatingly handsome. My heart thumped, and I turned away, furious with myself. What was he doing here anyway? It had nothing to do with him.

The ceremony went by in a blur. There were a couple of readings by the humanist official, and two of Great Uncle Charles's favourite pieces of music were played. I wouldn't have known what to choose, but he'd left instructions. The funeral was to be carried out exactly as he requested, and who would dare to disobey Great Uncle Charles?

I watched through blurry eyes as the coffin disappeared behind the curtain. His last journey. I'd never got the chance to tell him how sorry I was for all that he'd been through, how much I wished we'd had the chance to really talk, how much he meant to me, and how much I regretted that I hadn't realised that until it was too late.

Afterwards we filed outside, and the two men who'd been sitting behind us came up to us and shook our hands. They commiserated with us and explained that they used to work for Great Uncle Charles in Leeds, and that he'd been a well-respected boss who treated his workers well, and ran a tight, but fair, ship.

'He was well thought of,' they said, 'and he'll be sadly missed by those who remember him.'

'Who'd have thought it?' said Mum, shaking her head in astonishment, when they wandered off, having politely declined her offer to come back to the house for a glass of something alcoholic and a bite to eat.

'Just shows you,' Olivia mused. 'There's good in everyone, after all.'

I glanced over at Kit, who was talking to Don. He looked pale and was shivering. He wasn't the only one. The air was bitterly cold, a coating of frost covered the ground. Mum had slipped and almost fallen over on her way into the chapel.

Christmas was just days away. Olivia was hopeful that there would be snow in time for the big day, but I doubted it. A white Christmas was the stuff of fairy tales and soppy songs, and real life had a habit of being a massive let-down.

Mum looked at me, then at Kit, then back at me again. 'What's gone on between you two?' she whispered.

'I don't know what you mean.'

'I think you do. You were all over each other at the hospital, now it looks as if you're not even speaking. What have you done?'

'Well, I like that! Why do you assume it's me that's done something? For your information, he's an absolute dickhead, and I should have known better than to get involved with him.'

'He's a tight git,' admitted Olivia. 'I'm struggling to forgive him for cutting our bonus. Made things very difficult for us this year. I must say, I thought you'd have gone for someone flashier. Can't imagine him putting his hand in his pocket for a Jenny Kingston handbag for you.'

That reminded me. He must have gone over to Moreland Hall to take Ethan Rochester and his wife the chocolate samples. I wondered how that had gone? Was there any news on the contract?

I wanted to ask him but had no intention of doing so. I supposed I'd find out at some point, along with everyone else at the factory.

I remembered the present he'd left for me at the flat. It was a sealed envelope with a bow stuck to the front. Hardly a handbag. Unless it was a gift voucher? Maybe he'd thought I would prefer to choose my own gift?

I wondered if I should give it back to him. Not that I wanted my own present back. I'd given him the parcel containing the tie at the weekend, and he'd taken it home with him, promising to put it under the Christmas tree.

When I'd laughed and pointed out that he didn't have a Christmas tree, he'd sworn he would decorate the house especially. Somehow, I doubted he'd bothered. There had been no sign of twinkling lights through the windows of Fell House the other night when I'd stood outside, watching him kiss that woman. Or rather, watching that woman kiss him. So, he knew her from Africa? Hadn't I feared that he'd meet someone over there? How involved had they been? Had he forgotten me so quickly? I'd bet, as soon as he arrived there, he'd not given me a second thought.

I blinked when Kit suddenly loomed over me. As my eyes met his, all the blood pooled in my feet.

'I'm really sorry, Marley.'

Was he? For what, exactly?

'I know he was all you had left of your grandad. I wish you'd had more time together, really I do. I want you to take the rest of the week off. Come back after the Christmas break.'

'There's no need—'

'Yes, there is. Compassionate leave. Everyone's entitled to it, and you're no different. You've been through a lot, and you need some time to deal with it.'

I nodded. 'Thanks.'

'Marley…' His voice was appealing, as if he wanted me to just forget about everything that had happened. 'Can we go somewhere and talk?'

My teeth clattered together. 'I have the wake to go to. I can't just abandon that.'

He glanced around, his expression clearly pointing out that there was hardly anyone there who would object. 'I just think we should discuss things, don't you?'

Those soft, dark eyes seemed to stare into my very soul, and I wanted suddenly to launch myself against him and sob my heart out — for Grandad, for Dad, for Great Uncle Charles, for us, for ... everything.

'I suppose we should,' I murmured eventually, swallowing down the huge lump in my throat. 'Fox Lodge, tomorrow night?'

After a small pause, he nodded. 'Fox Lodge, tomorrow night. Around seven?'

'Fine.'

'I'll see you there,' he promised, then moved away to give his condolences to my family, and to make his excuses that he was going straight back to work.

Watching him walk away, I just didn't know what to think anymore.

Don appeared beside me and draped his arm around my shoulder. 'Don't know what's gone wrong between you two, love, but remember what your uncle wanted, eh?' he whispered. 'Don't throw everything away again. Don't be alone. Give him a chance, Marley.'

'Come on, you two,' called Mum. 'Back to ours. There's a table full of food to be eaten, and I expect you all to do your bit and clear the lot. I didn't spend twenty-four quid at the freezer shop for nothing.'

CHAPTER 26

With the heating on full at Fox Lodge, I wandered into the kitchen and filled the kettle, thinking sadly that I could make the tea as strong as I wanted. There was no one to stop me, anymore. There was no one to stop me doing anything. I was, in the words of Great Uncle Charles's solicitor, a very wealthy young woman.

Despite all his threats, my uncle had left me Fox Lodge after all, along with the fairly substantial sum of money from the sale of his construction company that hadn't gone on his house. He hadn't exactly been a big spender, so there was plenty of it. I could do anything I liked really. Take a year off work and go travelling. Spend next Christmas in New York. Certainly, there was more than enough to turn Fox Lodge into the home of my dreams.

I heaped three spoonfuls of tea into the teapot and sighed. It seemed wrong to even be thinking about doing anything to Fox Lodge right now, with Great Uncle Charles so recently gone. He must have cared about me after all. Apart from small sums to my mother and Olivia, I'd inherited everything.

My sister hadn't seemed in the slightest bit surprised and had shrugged it off when I told her I was sorry.

'What for? You went to see him all the time. I barely saw him from one year to the next. Who else was he going to leave it to? Besides, I'm chuffed to bits that he left me and Mum five grand each. That was a real surprise. We're going to have a smashing

Christmas after all. Kit Carroll can stuff his Christmas bonus up his turkey's arse.'

She'd laughed and hugged me, and I knew things were all right between us. There was no bitterness, no resentment. I was very lucky to have my family. After all, they were all I had in the world.

Glancing around that crematorium yesterday I'd realised that, like Great Uncle Charles, I would barely have anyone who'd want to say a final goodbye to me. The dismal funeral had been a glimpse of my future, and it had filled me with a dread that no amount of money could shift.

I poured two mugs of tea and had just carried them into the sitting room when there was a knock on the door. Kit was bang on time.

He followed me into the room and sat down when I indicated the sofa.

I took the chair opposite — Great Uncle Charles's chair — and eyed him suspiciously.

'Your tea,' I said, nodding at the mug on the coffee table between us.

'Thanks.' He reached over and picked up the mug, cradling it in his hands and making no attempt to drink it. 'Lovely and warm in here,' he said, sounding nervous. 'Absolutely bitter out there.' He glanced around. 'So, this was your uncle's house?'

'It was,' I said. 'It's mine now.'

He raised an eyebrow. 'Yours? He left it to you? Wow.'

'There's a lot to do to it, of course,' I said hurriedly. 'It's not as classy as Fell House, but it will be beautiful when I've renovated and furnished it. It's a lot of work, but I'm looking forward to it.'

'Right. Right. It's not far from my old home — where me and Jack lived with Mum and Dad before Grandad died, and we moved into Fell House.' He glanced down at his tea for a moment, then back up at me. 'There's nothing between me and Seffy, Marley.'

I felt my throat tighten. 'Who said there was?'

'I saw it in your face, and in your actions, ever since you saw us that night. You've pulled away from me again. She's just a friend.'

'A friend you made after you abandoned me.'

He stared at me. 'I didn't abandon you! How can you say that?'

'Because it's true.' There, it was out in the open, this huge thing that had been between us the whole time. 'You said you loved me, but you left anyway, even though you knew I didn't want you to go.'

'But I wanted you to come with me! I *begged* you to come with me! I didn't want to leave you, but you knew I had to go. The way things were between me and my father—'

'Which you never mentioned before then,' I pointed out. 'As far as I knew, you were one big happy family.'

'Jesus, if you couldn't pick up the clues about our relationship from the things I'd said, or the way I'd kept you away from him for two years, there was something wrong with you. Maybe if you'd actually cared enough about me to pay attention to me, instead of plotting and scheming to become Lady of Fell House, you'd have realised how bad things were, and how desperate I was to get away from him.'

I couldn't believe it! 'Lady of Fell House? What the hell do you mean by that?'

'You,' he said, sounding bitter. 'That's what you wanted, isn't it? That's the reason you went out with me. Money. You thought I was your ticket to a posh house and that sodding sports car you always wanted.'

'Bloody hell, not the sports car again! I was eleven years old! Are you insane? If you really believed I only went out with you for the money, why go out with me at all?'

'I've often asked myself that very question,' he snapped.

We glared at each other. Well, this was going well.

'Maybe I should just —' he began, then broke off at a loud banging on the front door.

I stood up. 'I don't know who that would be,' I said, a bit nervous.

It was dark outside, after all, and everyone local knew Great Uncle Charles had passed away. Did they also know I was the new owner? It could be anyone.

'Do you want me to get it?' Kit asked, as if reading the anxiety in my face.

I drew myself up, determined not to show him I needed him. 'It's fine. I'll go,' I assured him, but added, 'You wait there,' as an insurance policy. I didn't want him clearing off home and leaving me with God knows who.

As I pulled open the front door, it was as if someone had pressed rewind on my life. I stared in shock at my father, who stood on the doorstep, a cheery smile on his face, as if he'd just popped round for a cup of tea and hadn't been missing from my life for the last sixteen years.

'Marley, love. Don't you look all grown up!'

Considering I'd only been fourteen the last time he saw me, it was no wonder that I looked grown up to him. I *was* grown up. I was thirty years old. For some annoying reason, though, I no longer felt it. As I looked into his eyes, I was fourteen again, and I couldn't think of a single thing to say to him. I just stared at him, completely tongue-tied.

He grinned at me. 'Bit of a shock, eh? Look, are you going to invite me in? Only, it's bloody freezing out here.'

I blinked and stepped aside. 'Yeah, yes, of course. Come in.'

Kit half stood as I led my father into the sitting room.

Dad stopped, eyeing Kit warily. 'Have I interrupted something?'

'Not at all,' I said firmly. 'Dad, this is Christopher Carroll. Kit, this — this is my dad.'

The two men gaped at each other, and it was hard to say who looked most surprised.

'Christopher Carroll? Well, there's a turn up for the books,' Dad said eventually. He turned to me, clearly puzzled. 'Are you two together then?'

Kit and I shuffled awkwardly.

'Perhaps I should leave you both to it,' Kit said. 'You must have a lot to talk about.'

I'd been about to say that was probably a good idea, but my father got there first. 'That's right. Me and Marley have things to discuss in private, so if you don't mind.'

Something snapped inside me. Who the hell did he think he was, acting all high-handed like that? He couldn't just waltz back into my life and take over. As Kit moved towards the door, I put my hand on his arm. He looked at me, surprised.

'Sit down, Kit,' I said. 'Whatever my dad has to say to me, he can say it in front of you.'

Clearly my expression revealed my inner thoughts, because after a moment's hesitation he sat down again.

Dad tutted. 'Like that, is it? Fair enough.'

He sat down on Great Uncle Charles's chair, which infuriated me, forcing me to sit beside Kit on the sofa. I watched him as he glanced around the room, his gaze taking in the paintings on the walls and the dusty ornaments on the sideboard. I could practically hear him totting up how much they might be worth.

I could have saved him the trouble. He'd be lucky to get a tenner for any of them at a car boot sale. Great Uncle Charles didn't hold with spending money, and everything he'd furnished his house with was from junk shops or markets, a fact he'd always been extraordinarily proud of.

My anger grew as Dad settled himself into the chair and said, 'Could murder a cup of tea, Marley. Stick kettle on, love.'

'What do you want, Dad?'

His eyebrows knitted together. 'Well, that's charming. Some welcome, I must say.'

'Welcome! What sort of welcome do you expect? You've been gone for sixteen years, for God's sake. You vanished off the face of the earth, without so much as a goodbye kiss. You think I'm going to just rush into your arms and tell you how much I've missed you?'

'Well, haven't you missed me?'

'You're unbelievable! What the hell do you care anyway? If you'd wanted to know how I felt about you leaving you could have asked me any time during the last sixteen years. But you didn't, did you? You couldn't be bothered to come and see me. Why ask the question now?'

'I've been busy,' he whined. 'It hasn't been an easy time for me, either, you know. I had lots to do, and time just slipped past without me realising it.'

'You found the time to visit Great Uncle Charles and beg him for money, though, didn't you?'

I watched the wheedling look slip from my father's face, replaced by anger. 'He told you that?'

'He did. He also told me that he refused you point blank. Is that why you're here? You've heard about his will, and you've come to beg me for the money he wouldn't give you.'

Dad stood up, all softness gone from his voice. 'It's a bloody disgrace. He had no right leaving you that money. It should have been mine, by rights. I was next in line. You got well in there, didn't you? Creeping round him to make sure you got everything.'

'If you mean I visited him regularly and took care of him, then yes, I did.'

'Took care of him! Rubbish. You didn't give two hoots about the old devil. Who would? If you visited him, it was for one reason only, and we both know what that was. You're a chip off the old block, Marley, so don't sit there all high and mighty, acting as if you're better than me. We both know you were after his cash, and it paid off. Well, now you owe me, and I want what's mine.'

Tears rolled down my cheeks, and I wiped them away, furious for showing any weakness to this loathsome man. How had I ever loved him? How had I ever thought he was the perfect dad? Why had I spent so much of my life missing him, and grieving for him?

'I cared about Great Uncle Charles,' I managed, my voice cracking.

Kit took hold of my hand and squeezed it, and I made no attempt to remove it from his grasp. I needed his strength.

'Cared about him?' Dad gave a contemptuous laugh. 'As if anyone could care about him. He was a vile creature. Why do you think no one ever visited him? He was mean and bitter. Rotten through and through.'

'He was wounded!' I cried, outraged at the attack on my uncle's character. He wasn't around to defend himself, after all, and my father had no room to criticise anyone else. 'He loved someone very much, but she left him for another man. It broke his heart, and he never got over it.' I was aware that I was sitting beside the grandson of the very woman who'd broken it, too. It felt weird. What a crazy day it was turning out to be.

To my astonishment, Dad burst out laughing. He sat down in the chair again and rubbed his eyes. 'Broke his heart? Left him for another man? Is that what he told you?'

I felt the colour drain from my face. 'He didn't tell me anything,' I admitted. 'I found his scrapbook.' I looked apologetically at Kit. 'I'm really sorry, but it seems Great Uncle Charles was in love with your grandmother. She clearly didn't feel the same way, or she left him for a better prospect. Great Uncle Charles wasn't wealthy then, you see, but … but your grandfather, Edwin, was. She left him for Edwin. Uncle kept a scrapbook of cuttings about their engagement, their wedding, their life together. Right up until your father's christening, then he just stopped. I guess he'd accepted that it was truly over once there was a baby involved. He must have given up. That was around the time he moved to Leeds and started his construction company. I think,' I took a deep breath. 'I think he threw himself into work and decided to make his own fortune to show your grandmother what she'd missed, what she'd given up. He obviously loved her very much.'

Kit stared at me. 'Are you sure about this, Marley?'

'Positive,' I said. 'I'm sorry. I'm sure she loved your grandad, too.'

He shook his head. 'There was no love between them,' he told me. 'They slept in separate rooms and barely said a word to each other. When Grandfather died, my grandmother seemed relieved, if anything. It wasn't much of a love story.'

'That's so sad,' I wailed. 'If she'd stayed with Great Uncle Charles, they may have really made each other happy. If she'd only waited, instead of going where the money was.'

'Yeah.' Kit sighed. 'Money. Everything comes down to money, in the end.'

We looked at each other, and the bitter accusations he'd thrown at me hung between us. Was that really what he thought I was? Some little golddigger? Clearly, my father thought the same.

I felt completely defeated and worn out. What had I become, that this was the image people had of me? Well, if that was what they wanted to believe, let them. I was past caring.

I realised suddenly that Dad was laughing again. 'Honestly, our Marley, you and your imagination. What a load of tosh. You still haven't clicked on, have you? My God, the old goat really did fool everyone. Well, I know the truth, and it isn't half as pretty as the picture you've just painted.'

'What do you mean?' I demanded.

'This may come as quite a shock to both of you,' he said, leaning forward and rubbing his hands in obvious glee. 'My uncle was in love, all right. Very much in love. And the feeling was mutual. But he wasn't in love with your grandmother,' he added, nodding at Kit. 'I'm sorry to say, he was in love with Edwin. It was your grandad he was involved with, and they carried on right after he got married, an' all.'

Kit's mouth dropped open in shock.

I glared at my dad. 'And how would you know that?'

He shrugged. 'Found some letters, years ago, that he'd written to Dad, explaining why he'd buggered off to Leeds. He was afraid Dad would disown him if he knew the truth, but clearly that never happened. When I confronted Dad with them, he went mad. Told me to keep my mouth shut, and that I'd had no business rooting around in his stuff. Tried to make out that Uncle Charles did the noble thing, walking away from Carroll when the baby was born and putting it all behind him. Huh! Noble! No choice, more like.'

'I can't believe it,' Kit murmured. He glared at Dad. 'Is this a joke? How do I know you're telling the truth?'

'You don't, but this is what happened. Your grandad and Marley's great uncle were at school together, and their relationship started when they were in their teens. After the war, they got together properly. Now, I've only got my uncle's side of things, but according to those letters, they were besotted with each other. Of course, they had to keep that secret. Illegal, for one thing, and think of the scandal! Anyway, it seems suspicions were being raised, and Edwin's father decided it was time that his son was married off, so they selected some woman from Whitby, and Edwin was more or less, ordered to propose. Poor cow. She was like a lamb to the slaughter. No idea what she was getting involved with.' He chuckled. 'No wonder they had separate rooms. Bet he had to pretend she was Uncle Charles, so they could conceive your dad.'

I could feel Kit trembling with rage, and I couldn't blame him. I put my hand on his arm, trying to soothe him.

'They carried on after the wedding,' Dad continued. 'Edwin convinced Charles that nothing would change, and that he had no feelings for his wife, whatsoever. Then Charles found out that Dorothy was pregnant, and that was that. Your grandad insisted that it was my uncle's choice to walk away, for the sake of the baby and for Dorothy, but I reckon he was just jealous and pissed off that Edwin was having it away with his wife, after all. Anyway, he buggered off to Leeds and threw himself into building his company, and the rest, as they say, is history.'

My mind whirled. It had never occurred to me that Great Uncle Charles had loved a man, but thinking about it, it explained his bitterness towards Edwin Carroll and his loathing for the factory. Edwin had clearly had to do his duty — take over the business, marry, produce an heir. The factory had come between them after all.

I remembered the wistful look in Uncle Charles's eye, and the regretful tone in his voice when he'd told me that I'd be surprised what people would do for money. But it wasn't all about money, I thought suddenly. In another era, Edwin might have made a different decision entirely, but back then, it would have been dangerous for two men to have a sexual relationship. He could have gone to prison. They both could. And they would have been shunned, vilified. I couldn't entirely blame Edwin for choosing an easier path. It was just a shame that three people had suffered so much because of it.

'I expect this has come as quite a shock to you, too,' Dad said, nodding at Kit. 'Not the sort of thing that you'd want people to know about, is it? I mean, with Carroll's being so respectable.'

I couldn't believe what I was hearing. Was Dad honestly trying to blackmail Kit?

I held my breath as I watched Kit, his face stony, eyeing my dad with obvious contempt.

'It wouldn't bother me in the slightest,' he said eventually. 'No one with a shred of decency cares about that sort of thing anymore. Tell the world and his wife, for all I care. You can't hurt anyone. The three people who were involved are all gone now. Do your worst.'

Dad paled. 'I wasn't threatening you,' he whined.

'Weren't you? Good job, really. The police take a dim view of blackmail,' Kit said coldly.

I'd had enough. 'Just get out,' I said.

Dad's eyes widened. 'Get out? You don't mean that, Marley. You're my little girl.'

'I stopped being your little girl a long, long time ago,' I said. 'I wasted more than half my life pining for you, wishing you'd come back, wondering what I'd done wrong and why you'd abandoned me. Well, now I know. You abandoned me because you didn't care about anyone but yourself. You didn't care that you broke my heart, or Mum's heart, or Olivia's heart. You didn't care that we were flat broke, and Mum had to take on five cleaning jobs to keep the roof over our heads, or that she cried herself to sleep every night for years, or that you left behind two scared little girls who didn't know how to make her feel better, and were worried every day that we'd lose our home. You haven't even asked how Mum is. How Olivia is. You're disgusting. Just go.'

'What about my money? You can't say it's not mine by rights, Marley,' he said, sounding angry. 'I'm the next in line, not you. That should have gone to me.'

'But it didn't,' Kit said, standing up and looming over him. 'It went to Marley, because Marley stuck around. Marley visited her great uncle. Marley cared about him, and he knew that. That's why he left it to her. He could have left it to you, to her sister, or to a local cat's home, for God's sake, but he chose Marley. That says to me that he knew she loved him, and that the feeling was mutual. So, do as she says and clear off. You won't get your hands on her money, and she doesn't need you messing with her head. You've done enough damage, don't you think?'

Dad scrambled to his feet. 'So, that's what you think, is it?' he demanded, jutting his chin out defiantly.

The emotions tumbled around in my head as I recalled the days when he'd been my hero. My daddy. The first man I ever loved, and the first man who walked away from me. The man standing before me was no hero. He didn't deserve the affection I'd once felt for him. He'd broken my mum and left me to mend her. I didn't need him anymore. I didn't want him anymore.

'That's exactly what I think,' I said. 'Goodbye, Dad.'

He opened his mouth to speak, but no sound came out. I turned away from him, as Kit led him to the front door and showed him out. Hearing the key turn in the lock, I sank down onto the sofa again, feeling numb.

Kit joined me and took my hand. 'Are you okay, sweetheart?'

Sweetheart! He hadn't called me that before. I realised I was trembling. 'Yeah. Just — you know.'

He nodded and let out a long breath. 'Well, that was quite a shock all round. Who'd have thought it?'

'Does it change how you feel about your grandad?' I asked.

He gave a short laugh. 'I don't really feel anything about my grandad, and that hasn't changed at all. He wasn't the nicest chap to be around, from what I remember. I was only little when he died, but I've no fond memories of him. Grandma was okay, I suppose, though not exactly one for cuddles and kisses. I guess I feel sorry for her now. She must have had a very unhappy and frustrating life. They both must have. It's sad. How about you?'

'Me?'

'Does it change how you feel about your uncle?'

I considered the matter. 'I think it makes me love him a little bit more, and it certainly helps me to understand him better. They were different times. He must have lived a half-life, really. How different things would be today.'

'Yeah, I know. Weird, isn't it?' He shook his head. 'All that pain, and all that love wasted. Such a shame.'

I wrapped my arms around myself, shivering, despite the heating being on full.

'Marley, what we were talking about before your father arrived...'

I turned away from him. This was the man who thought I was only with him for his money. All the love I'd felt for him, all the longing for him, everything that was between us, had just been destroyed. He'd cheapened our whole relationship. No wonder he'd found it so easy to walk away from me all those years ago.

That's the reason you went out with me. Money.

He knew nothing.

'Can we do this another time, Kit?' I said wearily. 'I've just discovered the truth about Great Uncle Charles, met my dad for the first time in sixteen years, and learned that he really isn't the man I'd built him up to be. It's a lot to process.'

He looked disappointed but didn't argue. 'Of course. Another time.' He stood up. 'I'll see myself out, Marley. Take care.'

I nodded and sat quite still, as he walked away. *Another time.* I think we both knew, deep in our hearts, that time had just run out. There was nothing else to say.

***

'It's fabulous news, Jack. Such a relief. You must be over the moon.'

'You could say that.' Jack's voice was loaded with laughter. 'Amanda had a good cry this morning. She's been brilliant through all this — so strong. I couldn't have got through it without her.'

'You're both brilliant. Tim's lucky to have such great parents, and it's fantastic that the treatment's going so well. You'll be home before you know it, and then you can start to live properly again. All of you.'

'What will I be coming back to, though?' A cautious note had entered Jack's voice, and Kit sighed.

'Don't worry about all that. Just concentrate on getting through the rest of Tim's therapy.'

'I told you, Kit. I don't want you keeping anything from me. Besides, I need to know what's happening. Have we a home to come back to? Will I have a job? Did you meet up with Serafina?'

Kit relaxed a little. There, at least, he had some good news for his brother. 'I did. She loved the house as much as ever and made me an offer there and then. I got our solicitor to check over the contract, and he was happy with it. I signed today. Serafina now officially owns Fell House.'

'Wow!' Jack let out a whistle. 'It's what we were hoping for. Kind of sad, though.'

'Not as sad as you might think,' Kit reassured him. 'I had it written into the deal that you were guaranteed one of the apartments for free. You and Amanda and Tim will always have a home at Fell House. All right, it's not the entire house, but from what Seffy described, the apartments are going to be amazing. I think you'll love it.'

'Christ, Kit, I don't know what to say.'

'You don't need to say anything. Call it a Christmas present,' Kit said, grinning.

'But I haven't even got you a present,' Jack complained. 'I haven't had time to think about it.'

'You just gave me the best Christmas present in the world,' Kit assured him. 'Knowing Tim's on the mend is the best news ever. I don't need anything else.'

'So, what about the factory? Will the money from the sale put things right?'

Kit must have hesitated just a fraction too long.

Jack pounced back in with, 'Don't keep things from me! I want to know the truth. You promised, remember.'

'I know, I know. The money from the sale will pay the bank what we owe them, and not a moment too soon, as they're getting very demanding. It will also clear the bills from our suppliers, and that should leave us with enough to pay the wages for a few months. After that, who knows?'

'Shit.' There was a long sigh. 'So, then it will be back to square one?'

'Not necessarily. I had a meeting yesterday with Ethan Rochester.'

'Who?'

'Ethan Rochester? You know, Rochester's Department Stores?'

'Oh, God. Of course. Why on earth did you meet up with him?'

Quickly, Kit filled him in with the news about the York shop.

Jack whistled. 'But even so, meeting the big boss himself? Doesn't he have minions to do that sort of thing for him?'

Kit laughed. 'I know. I couldn't believe it, either. He invited me to dinner at his house, and we had a really pleasant, informal evening. I took along some samples, and he got his wife to taste them. Turns out she's a huge fan of our chocolate. Told me she has a serious addiction to our Caramel Choc Bloc.'

'They sound a nice couple.'

'They are. Ethan was bouncing his baby son on his knee, and his little sister was running around causing havoc, and his wife sampled every chocolate and told me, after tasting each and every flavour, that it was her new favourite. We had a lovely time.'

'So, did you get the contract?'

Kit sighed. He thought it best not to tell his brother the whole story. Informal the meeting may have been, but Ethan wasn't stupid. Far from it. He'd known all about their involvement with Halliwell & Stephenson and was aware that the company had crashed. He wanted to know how the loss of the LuvRocks contract had impacted on Carroll's, and whether his investment in the company would be secure, should he choose to give them the contract to supply York.

Kit had considered embellishing the truth but decided in the end that honesty was the best policy. Ethan had clearly appreciated that, but it would no doubt throw a spanner in the works. They weren't guaranteed anything. Far from it.

'Not yet. He's going to let me know. I would have said yes, judging by how well we got on, but for all I know, he might have invited a dozen other manufacturers along and done exactly the same with them. It's just a question of wait and see.'

'Will the contract be enough to pull us through?'

Kit considered the question before answering. 'Not on its own,' he said. 'It will help, but we're going to have to find other customers, new sources of income. I don't want to be so heavily reliant on one contract ever again.'

'After LuvRocks, I can't say I blame you,' Jack said, sounding sheepish. 'I really am sorry about that.'

'You did what you thought was best,' Kit said firmly. 'It's past and done. Forget about it.'

'When I come back,' Jack said, 'what's going to happen? With us, I mean? Are you planning on staying?'

Kit leaned back in his chair, closing his eyes. 'Would it bother you if I was?'

'Hell, no! I'd love it.'

'Really? I wouldn't cramp your style?'

Jack laughed. 'Are you kidding? Are you seriously considering it?'

'More than that, Jack. I've made up my mind. I've done my travelling. Now I want to stay put and try to turn Carroll's around. We have a long way to go, and I don't honestly know if we'll make it, but I want to do everything I can to save the place. No idea where I'm going to live, though. May end up sleeping on the office floor.'

'Don't be daft. You can move in with us. It's the least we can do.'

'I think that might be a bit too much, don't you? Much as I love you, I don't think I could be with you twenty-four hours a day. It might just finish me off.'

'Point taken. Well, you'll find somewhere, I'm sure. I'm just so glad that you're staying. I look forward to working for you.'

Kit's eyes snapped open. 'You won't be working for me, Jack. You'll be working *with* me. Partners.'

'Are you serious?'

'Absolutely. I've already spoken to our solicitor about making it official. You've earned your share in this factory, which is more than I've done. But I intend to start earning it. From now on, it gets my full, undivided attention.'

'Hmm. Well, I'm thrilled that you're staying, and I'm grateful for the partnership, Kit, truly I am, but don't get like Dad, will you?'

'Like Dad?' Kit felt his hackles rising. 'As if!'

'He thought about nothing but the factory. I don't want you to have nothing in your life but that place. Time you found yourself a girlfriend, if you ask me. You need some fun and a bit of love in your life.'

'Plenty of time for all that,' Kit said, lightly. 'I'm only thirty. No hurry.'

Jack laughed. 'Just as long as you bear it in mind,' he said. 'I met Amanda when I was just a teenager, and I'm glad about it. We've had so many years together. Don't leave it too long, eh?'

'Oh, get back to your lovely wife and your sickeningly happy marriage,' Kit said, trying to sound jokey. 'Give Amanda and Tim my love and tell them I can't wait to see them. I'm counting the days.'

'We are, too,' Jack said quietly. 'Take care, bro. And thank you. Thanks for everything.'

'No need to thank me. A half share in a failing factory is hardly anything to get excited about. I may just be saddling you with a half share in a pile of debts, so I'd hold off on those thanks, if I were you.'

'We'll make it work,' Jack said. 'Together. I'll head to the shops as soon as I can and send you an amazing Christmas present. Promise.'

Kit laughed and ended the call. He didn't need any Christmas presents. His nephew's good health was all that he wanted. Anything else was just the icing on the Christmas cake.

He thought about the one present he *had* received. He shouldn't really have opened it, but he'd been unable to resist. It was from Marley, and it was a smart tie — from Rochester's, ironically. It had probably cost a small fortune, and it meant absolutely nothing whatsoever to him. Typical of Marley. It was all about the designer name. She really didn't know him at all.

He wondered briefly what she would make of the present he'd got her. She would probably hate it.

It just showed the difference between them, he thought sadly. They were miles apart. How had he ever thought it could work? The physical attraction between them was as strong as ever, but it wasn't enough. The simple fact was, he didn't trust her. She'd proved over and over that it was money that motivated her, and love had played no part in her relationship with him. Why had he been so determined to ignore that? He would never deny the truth to himself again.

Chapter 27

I knew David would call in the favour I owed him before long, and sure enough, I was roped in for babysitting duty.

'You made me dress up as Santa,' he reminded me when I pulled a face. 'The least you can do is watch the kids, while me and Livvy go out and have a nice meal.'

'How cosy,' I said. 'Just the two of you?'

Olivia looked a bit awkward. 'We're going with Mum and Don. You don't mind, do you? Don's managed to change his booking at Miller's to a table for four instead of two. We thought it would be nice to have a bit of adult time before Christmas, without kids hanging around.'

I felt a pang of jealousy. I was being pushed out, all because I was single. Seeing Olivia's anxious face though, I smiled. ''Course I don't mind. I don't fancy spending an evening watching Don and David pig out anyway. Bad enough every day in the canteen. Enjoy yourselves.'

Tommy was in bed, fast asleep, but I'd been lumbered with Sam and Max, who were so hyped up about the rapidly-approaching big day that they wouldn't have slept even if I'd put sleeping tablets in their cocoa, which, of course, I would never do. Mind you, I did think it would be worth a prison sentence at one point, as they clambered over the sofa, squealing and fighting and demanding biscuits and drinks, a look at the toy catalogue, a game on my mobile phone, and a piggy back ride around the living room. The Christmas tree nearly went over twice. My nerves were in shreds.

'Don't you two ever get tired?' I demanded, slumping in exhaustion onto the sofa, after having deposited Max safely back on the ground.

Sam shook his head. 'Nope. Can we watch a film?'

'Shouldn't you be in bed?' I said grumpily. 'I'd love some peace and quiet.'

'If you let us watch a film, we'll be quiet, won't we, Max?'

Max thought about it for a moment. 'Maybe.'

I had to admire his honesty. 'Okay. One film, then bed. What do you want to watch?'

They considered the matter carefully. Each made several suggestions, which the other dismissed. Finally, Sam shrieked, 'Willy Wonka!'

Max jumped up and down on his knees. How did he find the energy? I felt drained just watching him. 'Yeah, Willy Wonka!'

Seriously? I had to sit and watch a film about a sodding chocolate factory and its weird and wonderful owner? Great.

'If I let you watch it, you promise to go straight to bed afterwards?'

'Promise,' they said, all solemn-faced, wide-eyed and innocent, as if chocolate wouldn't melt in their mouths.

Doubting they meant it, but having no choice, I duly obliged and pushed the disc of *Willy Wonka and the Chocolate Factory* into the DVD player. At least it might give me around an hour and a half of peace and quiet.

No such luck. Sam and Max chattered the whole way through, sang along to every song, and bombarded me with questions.

'Marley, you work in a chocolate factory, don't you? Like Mummy and Daddy,' Max said.

I nodded gloomily. 'For now,' I muttered.

'Do you have Oompa-Loompas there?' he queried.

I shook my head. 'No Oompa-Loompas.'

'Daddy said you had Oompa-Loompas!' Sam shrieked. 'Where have they gone?'

I shrugged. 'Sacked for being naughty,' I told them. 'There was a lot of fuss about it. The Oompa-Loompa union almost went to the papers.'

Clearly, my wit was wasted on them because they stared at me in bewilderment.

'I think,' I said gently, 'that your dad was having you on. No Oompa-Loompas at Carroll's.'

'Then, who makes the chocolate?' demanded Sam.

'The factory workers. People like your mum and dad.'

'And you?'

I gave him an icy stare. 'Certainly not. I'm a PA. I work in the office.'

'You know the sticks of rock you make,' Sam began, 'how do you put the words inside them?'

'It's an interesting process,' I said. 'You have to make the letters individually, and you should see how big they are to start with.'

'How big are they?' said Max, sounding curious.

I held up my hands to show him the rough size of the letters. They shrieked with laughter.

'Don't be silly,' Sam said. 'That would never fit inside a stick of rock.'

'Ah,' I told him, 'but you have no idea how big the sticks of rock are at first.'

Their eyes widened. 'Show us.'

I held my hands apart and said, 'Longer than this. They're enormous. You'd never believe it.'

'Then how,' said Max, 'do they end up so small?'

'They're put into machines and rolled. The rock comes out the other end like a long sausage, and then it goes onto a table and is rolled and cut by hand. It's still quite soft then, but it hardens up very quickly, so you have to be quick.'

They looked at each other, clearly not certain that I was telling the truth.

'Cross my heart, hope to die,' I assured them.

They turned back to the television, where Augustus Gloop was currently stuck halfway up a pipe.

'Do you have a chocolate river at your factory?' Sam asked.

'No. Afraid not.'

'You don't have much there, do you?' he said.

'I want to see the rock being made,' Max shrieked.

I covered my ears with my hands and winced. 'Shush, Max, for goodness sake. If you wake Tommy, I'll cry.'

'I'd like to see the geese that lay the Easter eggs,' Sam admitted.

'No geese either,' I said, feeling more and more like the Grinch. 'Your mum and dad make the Easter eggs, and they're very clever at it.'

'Really?' They both looked quite impressed.

'I want to work in the factory when I grow up,' Sam said.

Max yawned. 'Me, too.'

It was on the tip of my tongue to tell them that, surely, they could think of a better career than that. As I watched them, though, their little heads bobbing as they fought off sleep, blond hair tousled, all neat and cute in their Batman pyjamas, I had second thoughts.

I looked around the cosy living room. The toy catalogue lay open on the floor, the pages ringed with all the toys the boys had requested. The Christmas tree was strewn with a jumble of shop-bought and handmade decorations, pride of place going to a Santa made from a cardboard tube — Max's contribution from nursery. There were dozens and dozens of cards pinned on every wall, and covering every available surface, and tinsel draped over the huge, framed photograph of David, Olivia and the boys that took up most of the chimney breast.

David and Olivia had achieved all of it by working in the factory. It wasn't a designer home. It wasn't a large home. It wasn't even a particularly tidy home. But it *was* a home, and it was full of laughter and noise and love. What more could I hope for, for my own nephews? What more, when it came down to it, could anyone hope for?

Feeling the pang of loss all over again, I wondered if it would ever really go away.

Sam closed his eyes, and I gently ruffled his hair. 'Come on, sweetheart,' I said, scooping him up in my arms. 'Time for bed.'

CHAPTER 28

'Are you actually serious? London?' Mum put her arm through Don's and stared at me, clearly upset.

'Bit of a sudden decision isn't it, love?' Don said. 'I mean, it's Christmas Eve the day after tomorrow. Cutting it a bit fine.'

'I've always wanted to spend Christmas in New York,' I said truthfully, 'but it's not possible. I'd never get a visa in time, for one thing. I looked online and London looks amazing with all the lights and the department stores and markets. I've never been there before, and it will be an experience.'

Don whistled. 'London, though? Proper expensive there, you know.'

'That hardly matters,' I reminded him. 'I can afford it, so why not?'

'But it's Christmas,' Mum said, clearly bewildered. 'You should be at home, with us. It won't be the same if you're not here.'

I felt a warm glow inside, grateful that she felt that way. I knew I would miss her, too. I'd miss all of them. But I needed to get away and think things over in peace. The guilt was eating me away, as Dad's words kept coming back to haunt me. *You're a chip off the old block, Marley.*

Kit's assertion that I'd only been with him for the money hurt more than I could express, and I kept remembering how I'd promised to look after Great Uncle Charles, then spent the entire weekend in bed with Kit, forgetting all about a lonely, sick old man. His death was on my conscience, and I just didn't know what to do any more.

Knowing Kit was just a short walk away from my flat every day didn't help either. I needed to get far away from him and all the painful memories he stirred up. London wasn't as far as New York, but it would do for a while.

Mum gave me a helpless look, but said, 'Well, if that's what you want. I'll go and find your presents. You can, at least, take them with you to that London.'

As she hurried upstairs, Don fixed me with a piercing stare. 'So, go on. What's to do?'

'I don't know what you mean,' I said, feeling the tell-tale heat spread through my face.

'This has something to do with Kit, I'd bet my last penny on it. What happened?'

'Why do you think anything happened?'

'Oh, come on.' He rolled his eyes, exasperated. 'Let's not play them games, eh? Look, he were looking at you like a lovesick puppy one minute, and the next thing we knew you were standing miles apart not talking. You don't go from one thing to the other without something happening. What were it?'

I sighed. 'I don't honestly know how it all went so wrong.'

Mum lumbered down the stairs, dragging two big bags of presents. 'There you go, love. At least you'll have something to open on Christmas morning, even if you won't have your family around you.'

I blinked away the tears. 'What the heck are all these?'

'Christmas presents! What else?' She tried to smile, but I could see she was upset. 'Some from me and Don, and some from Olivia and David and the boys.'

'But that's far too much,' I protested.

She waved my protests away. 'We had a bumper budget this year, with our unexpected inheritance. Decided to blow a whole stack of it on Christmas. And why not? You only live once, don't you?'

I put my arms around her. 'Thanks, Mum. Love you.'

She patted me on the back. 'Love you, too. Have a smashing time, love. Ring me up on Christmas morning, won't you?'

'I will,' I promised.

Don cleared his throat. 'Right, well, I'd best help you to the car with this little lot. Dead icy out there. Don't want you falling and breaking your neck, do we? Wouldn't want you to miss out on that London.'

He collected the bags and I waved goodbye to Mum, then followed him out onto the road, where he began to pack the boot of my car with the presents.

'So, go on,' he said, after checking that Mum hadn't followed us. 'What happened?'

'Do you really want to know?' I said, knowing that he'd insist he did.

It took me a good ten minutes to tell him everything, while we both faffed around in the boot, moving things around so Mum would think we were still busy sorting the presents if she looked out of the window.

When I'd finished, Don gave a big sigh and slammed the boot shut. 'No wonder you're all over the place. Attacked on all sides, eh?'

I could have hugged him. He, at least, understood how I felt.

'Reckon Kit feels the same,' he said, stroking his chin thoughtfully.

I glared at him. 'I thought you'd be on my side.'

'Strikes me, love, that you and Kit are on the same side.'

'And how do you work that out?'

'Oh, come on, you're not that daft. Look, it's pretty obvious that he loves you to bits, but he thinks you only care about him for the money. He doesn't trust that you love him more than cash. You love him to bits, too, but you have serious abandonment issues. You can't get past the fact that he walked out on you. Not your fault, entirely. I mean, he *did* walk out on you, even though I shouldn't imagine he sees it that way. In his eyes, you chose comfort over love. Hard for *him* to get past *that*. In your eyes, he did exactly what your father did. He left you. You don't trust that he really loves you and won't abandon you again. Hence your willingness to believe there was something between him and that woman, even on the flimsiest evidence. You'd already made up your mind he wouldn't hang around, and she just fitted what you'd already imagined. Obvious, really.'

I stared at him. 'Who are you? Sigmund Freud?'

'Just an ordinary bloke who doesn't have any major issues, which gives me an uncanny ability to step back and see the issues others are having, especially those I happen to care about a lot. You know what you need, don't you?'

'A holiday in London,' I said.

'No. You need to collar that bloke of yours, sit him down, and thrash this out, once and for all. You'll never get any peace if you don't.'

I bit my lip. 'I can't. There's too much — I just can't.'

He shrugged. 'Fair enough. If you'd rather spend Christmas all alone in some fancy hotel room, then go ahead. Don't think it will make you feel any better, though. The only thing that's going to bring you peace of mind is sorting this mess out. And I'll tell you another thing. Until you sort this gold digger stuff out, you'll never enjoy a single penny of this money, and Fox Lodge will mean nothing to you. So, there you have it.' He held up his hands. 'Now, I've said it, and that's that. No more on the subject. Whatever you decide to do now is your business.'

He put his arms around me. 'You be happy, kidder. That's all I ask. Merry Christmas, Marley.'

I swallowed down the tears. 'Merry Christmas, Don. Look after Mum for me, won't you?'

He winked. 'Goes without saying. Love of me flipping life, she is. Don't you worry about her, I'll make sure she's all right. Always.'

He would, too. I knew it. I smiled and climbed into the car, wondering briefly how all the presents were going to fit into my tiny living room. I hadn't moved into Fox Lodge yet, and as I drove away from Mum's house, I reflected on my plans to move in after the New Year. I would start renovating then, too. I'd already picked up several brochures for new kitchens, fitted wardrobes, and flooring specialists.

Truthfully, though, I'd barely glanced at them. Don was right, I couldn't enjoy the money. Dad's opinion of me no longer mattered, but Kit's did. It mattered more than anything.

I pulled over and stared at my reflection in the rear-view mirror. What was I doing? How could I ever move on if I didn't sort it out with Kit, once and for all?

He'd hurled some pretty vile accusations at me, and I could sort of understand why. But he hadn't acknowledged how much he'd hurt me, and he needed to know that he really had. It was time he knew what he'd done.

It was time he knew it all.

***

Kit cursed as the parcel tape twisted in his hands. He wasn't having much luck with it. Every time he tried to tear a strip off, it managed to get all tangled up, and he had to pull it off the box and start again. He supposed it was his own fault. He should have been more patient. It would probably help if he could be bothered to go and find the scissors.

Glancing around, he totted up how many boxes he'd managed to fill so far. Sixteen. That meant he had four boxes left to unfold, and he hadn't even packed up half the house. This was going to be a major challenge. He'd have to order more boxes, for a start.

There was no hurry, really. Seffy had assured him that he had at least a couple of months before he needed to think about moving out. 'We probably won't even start to look at it until early spring. Don't forget, we'll need planning permission, although that shouldn't be a problem. I know it's a Grade Two listed building, but our architect is very skilled at knowing what the planners are looking for and ensuring all renovations are sympathetically carried out. Besides, we're creating multiple homes for several families in an area where housing is at a premium. We've never had a problem before, and I can't foresee any now.'

It would at least give him time to find a rental property. More importantly, it would give Jack and his family time to find somewhere to stay until their new apartment was ready to move into. That was the priority. With everything they'd been through, Kit was determined that they should come home to a decent home. He'd already left Jack's details with several property agents in the area. As for himself, anything would do, as long as he could get to the factory within a reasonable time.

As soon as he found something suitable, he was out of there. He wouldn't be waiting for Seffy and her developers to move in. The sooner he put Fell House and all its bitter memories behind him, the better. It was time for a fresh start. From now on, his life would revolve around Carroll's and his family. Nothing else mattered.

He wrenched the parcel tape off the box and threw the roll onto the floor, fed up with the whole thing. His back ached, and his mouth tasted of adhesive from where he'd bitten off endless strips of the tape. He leaned back in the chair and gave a heavy sigh. Any visitors would never know it was just two days until Christmas. There was nothing remotely festive in the house.

Then again, Kit didn't feel remotely festive himself. In fact, he was battling to stay positive. There were too many unresolved issues in his life for him to feel settled.

The Rochester contract was still only a possibility. He'd heard nothing from Ethan Rochester, either way. The future of the factory hung in the balance. Even with the contract, the company's continued existence was far from certain.

Then there was Marley.

Kit closed his eyes. He'd been determined not to spare her another thought, but as was always the case with her, she insisted on making guest appearances in his mind at every given opportunity. Deep down, he knew that if things had worked out with Marley, the other stuff wouldn't seem so dire. With her, he'd always felt that anything was possible. Instead, all that loomed before him was hard work and uncertainty.

At a knock on the door, Kit reluctantly opened his eyes. Whoever it was could go away. He wasn't in the mood for visitors.

With his next breath, the vague hope that it might be someone with news of the contract had him getting to his feet. He could use some good news. Fingers crossed.

The last person he'd expected to find on his doorstep was Marley. She was all wrapped up in a thick quilted coat, almost like a duvet. A fake fur-trimmed hood shrouded her face, so her features were barely visible, and she had her arms wrapped around herself as though even such a heavy coat wasn't keeping her warm.

Her voice, though, was strong and determined. 'We need to talk.'

'Come in, why don't you?' he muttered, as she pushed past him and entered the hallway.

God, now what?

Part of him was annoyed that she had the nerve to just storm over and act as if she had every right to bug him, after everything that had been said. The other part of him was so thrilled to see her that his stomach leapt in joy at the sight of her. Honestly, that annoyed him even more. Even his own body betrayed him when it came to Marley.

She pushed her hood back and looked at him, a trace of nerves in her eyes. Clearly, she wasn't as confident as she was trying to make out. Standing there she looked so fragile that his annoyance melted away like chocolate left beside a candle.

'What is it you want, Marley?'

'You said I only wanted you for your money. You practically accused me of being a cold-hearted little gold digger.'

Kit ran his hands through his hair, exasperated. 'For Christ's sake, are you seriously telling me you've come here for another argument? I can't do this anymore, Marley. Enough already.'

'Oh, no, you don't.'

She pushed open the sitting room door and stormed in, not even seeming to notice the boxes that were strewn all over the place, as she plonked herself down on the chair and glared up at him. 'You don't get to say all those things about me and ignore the stuff you inflicted on me. The way you let me down.'

'Let you down?' Kit's anger bubbled over, and he dropped down opposite her, his hands clasped tightly together as he leaned forward. 'How the hell did I let you down? All I wanted was to take a year out of uni and go abroad, see a bit of the world. What was wrong with that?'

'But you didn't even discuss it with me first! You never even mentioned it. I thought you were going to do your degree, then work in the factory. I thought we had a future together.'

'Oh, I know you did,' he said bitterly. 'Put me in a suit and tie, sit me behind a desk, and reap the rewards. Never mind what I wanted, as long as Marley got what she wanted.'

'And what exactly did you think I wanted, as if I didn't know!'

'You wanted what you've always wanted — money! You wanted designer clothes, and a flash car, and the big house. Oh, you could quite see yourself sitting here in Fell House, couldn't you? It wasn't me you cared about at all.'

He felt a pang of guilt when tears spilled down her cheeks. How the hell did she manage to rile him up so much one minute, then make him want to take her in his arms and protect her the next? That was some gift she possessed.

'Don't cry,' he said gruffly.

'How could you say that?' she said, her voice sounding hoarse and strange. 'I loved you so much. And yes, I did visualise living in this house, but only because it was your home. I wanted to be with you, more than anything. I wanted a future with *you*.'

'I wanted a future with you, too,' he admitted brokenly. 'But you couldn't even wait a year. You couldn't support me in the one thing I asked.'

'You should have told me,' she sobbed. 'I had to find out from one of my mum's workmates. How do you think that felt? I didn't matter to you. If you'd really cared about me, if you'd really thought about building a future with me, you'd have discussed it with me first. Told me how you felt. You just presented it as a done deal and expected me to be happy about it.'

Kit bit his lip. She had a point. 'I'm sorry. I was eighteen — just a stupid, selfish kid. I got something in my head, and that was that. I was so busy trying to get one over on my father that I never even thought to discuss it with you. I just assumed you'd go along with whatever I wanted. I'm truly sorry, Marley.'

She pulled a tissue from her coat pocket and wiped the tears away. 'I loved you so much. You broke my heart when you left, and you broke my heart again when you accused me of only being with you for the money.'

Kit had no idea how to explain things to her. The way she was reacting, he may just make things worse. Then again, could they be any worse?

He took a deep breath. 'I suppose, if I'm honest, I always thought, deep down, that I wasn't good enough for you, so it was very easy to imagine that money was your main incentive for being with me.'

Marley shook her head. 'Don't be stupid. Why would someone like you think he wasn't good enough for someone like me?'

'Because, when you've spent your entire life being told by someone who's supposed to know everything, someone whose opinion you're supposed to value and respect, that you're a waste of space and will never make anything of yourself, it kind of stays with you. Even if your conscious mind argues that he's talking rubbish and insists you're worthy, your subconscious clings to those little seeds of doubt that he's planted. My father never thought I was good enough to run Carroll's. He thought I was too soft. He hated the fact that I liked reading, and that I'd rather be curled up with a book than outside playing rugby. He used to get so angry when charity appeals on the television upset me. Said I was pathetic. Wanted me to *man up*.'

He sighed. 'You know, thinking about it now, I wonder if he had an inkling about his father and, in his prehistoric way, was trying to make sure I didn't turn out the same way. If my father knew Grandfather was gay, my God! It would have been the worst thing he could imagine. Maybe that's why he was so tough on me. Who knows? The point is, he destroyed my self-confidence. I thought I was worthless. How could someone as beautiful and smart and funny as you possibly be interested in me? Much as I wanted it to be true, I suppose deep down, the doubt persisted that it was the name and the fortune you wanted.'

'But all that time we were dating, surely you realised that I loved you? I thought we had something really special!'

'We did.' He sat forward, his eyes pleading with her to understand. 'For the two and a half years we were together, I swear to you that, most of the time, I believed in you. In us. It was just now and then .... Little things you'd say. But when you refused to come with me to Africa, it all came flooding back. I couldn't believe you wanted me to do what *he* wanted. It felt like the ultimate betrayal.'

'That's how *I* felt,' she admitted. 'Like you'd totally betrayed me and everything we meant to each other.'

'But it was only for a year, Marley,' he pleaded. 'Why was that too much to ask?'

She chewed her lip, staring at the boxes on the floor, but clearly not registering them.

'Because,' she said at last, 'I was scared. It felt like you were abandoning me, and I was terrified you wouldn't come back, like...'

'Like your father?' Kit looked up to the ceiling, shaking his head softly. It all made sense, really. But at eighteen, he would never have been able to work it out, even if he'd known how deeply her father's leaving had affected her, and he hadn't known, because she'd hardly mentioned it. 'But if you were afraid of that, why didn't you come with me? I wanted you to. I begged you to. We could have had such a wonderful experience together.'

'I couldn't.' Her voice was small but determined.

Kit felt a coldness come over him again. 'Because you couldn't bear to rough it in a tent in a jungle. Wasn't that how you described it? You say you just wanted to be with me, but not enough to give up the luxuries of home, right?'

'I couldn't go with you, Kit,' she said, and there was a thread of steel in her tone as she tilted her chin towards him defiantly.

'Because you're a princess who couldn't give up her comforts to be with me.'

'No, Kit,' she said finally. 'Because I was pregnant.'

The world seemed to swing on its axis. Kit's heart thudded. 'What did you say?'

Marley wiped the last of her tears away and sat up straight, suddenly calmer. 'I couldn't go with you because I was pregnant. I'd only found out for definite a couple of days before you dropped your little bombshell. The signs had been there for weeks, but I kept ignoring them, pretending it couldn't be true. I was almost three months pregnant when you left. So, you see, how could I possibly go to Africa with you and live in a tent for a year? It was never an option.'

Kit stood and began to pace, dodging boxes as he went. His mind was a whirlwind of confusion.

'But — but why the hell didn't you tell me?'

'I was going to. Then I heard that you were leaving, and I panicked. I wanted you to stay, but I wanted you to stay for the only reason that mattered — because you wanted to be with me. When you started hurling abuse at me, calling me spoilt and selfish and greedy, I just couldn't bring myself to tell you. I thought, if that's what you really think of me, how can I tell you that I'm having your baby? You would accuse me of getting pregnant on purpose, of trying to trap you. I couldn't bear you to think that. I heard my father throw that at my mother so many times. I didn't want to hear *you* say it. When you walked away, I really thought, deep down, that you wouldn't go through with it. That you'd think again, and tell me it was a horrible mistake, and you wanted to stay with me. But you didn't.'

'Oh, Marley. I'm so sorry.' Kit crouched down before her and took her hands. 'But the baby? What happened to the baby? Did you—'

'I lost it.' Her voice broke again, and fresh tears welled up in her eyes. 'I'd just had my first scan, and everything seemed okay. I was trying to pluck up the courage to tell Mum, and then—' She shook her head, dabbing furiously at her wet face. 'I told her I'd stayed at my friend's house, but I was in hospital. I lost a lot of blood, you see. It was a nightmare.'

Kit buried his head in her hands, unable to bear looking at the pain in her face any longer. 'I'm so sorry. I'm so sorry.'

She freed one hand from his grasp and tentatively stroked his hair. 'It's all right. I know.'

He couldn't suppress his sob. 'If I'd known, I would never have left. You have to believe me.'

'I know that, too,' she said. 'But it wouldn't have worked, would it? I'd have always wondered if you resented staying. It would have hung between us, destroyed us.'

'I wouldn't have resented you.' He looked up at her finally, anguish tearing at his insides. 'I would never have resented you, or our baby. I loved you. I spent the entire year I was away missing you and pining for you. Seffy was my confidante. She listened to me when I wanted to talk about you, and she didn't make fun of me when I cried. She was a really good friend, but that's all she ever was. There was never anyone but you, Marley.'

'I thought you'd have forgotten all about me,' she admitted.

'Never. I wanted to look for you when I got home and started uni. I was trying to pluck up the courage to call you, but then I saw you dancing with some bloke in a club in Whitby, and I realised you'd moved on. I knew I had to let you go, somehow.'

She frowned. 'What bloke? I never really dated anyone after you left.' Her expression changed, and she said, 'Oh! There was someone who David knew. He did take me out a couple of times around Christmas.' She shook her head. 'It was nothing. I wish you'd come over to talk to me.'

'I would have done, but you looked so dreamy. I thought you must have been mad about him.'

She gently cupped his face. 'It was Christmas. It would have been our baby's first birthday. I was grieving.'

They stared at each other, then his arms went around her, and they clung to each other, crying for their lost child, the wasted years, the pain they'd inflicted upon each other without ever meaning to.

***

Much later, Kit handed her a mug of coffee and sat down beside her on the sofa she'd moved to. She was looking around her, quite bewildered, as if she'd only just noticed the chaos in which she was sitting.

'What's going on? What's with all the boxes?' He noted a hint of panic in her voice. 'Are you leaving again?'

He smiled reassuringly at her. 'Only out of this house, not the area. I'm staying on permanently at the factory. Jack and I are going to be partners and work together.'

'That's brilliant. I'm so pleased for you both. How is Tim?'

'He's doing well, really well. It's looking hopeful.'

She nodded. 'I understand now, about the Nativity, I mean. Why you couldn't face it. I'm sorry I gave you such a hard time. It must have been awful being surrounded by all those little children, when your own nephew was going through so much.'

'It was,' he admitted. 'I really tried to hold it together, but—' He broke off as a memory stirred in the recesses of his mind. 'Oh, God,' he murmured.

'What is it?'

'The Nativity! I've just realised. I thought it was weird at the time, but it never occurred to me .... You got all upset and emotional about the class of eleven-year-olds. Our baby — he'd be eleven now, wouldn't he?'

She nodded. 'Yes. It's pretty tough to think about. Can't imagine me being a mum to an eleven-year-old, can you?'

'Yes,' he said quietly. 'I can.'

She sipped her coffee, looking a bit flustered.

'Does Olivia know? Your mum?'

'No one,' she confessed. 'I didn't want them to know. I guess it's kind of like Jack, not wanting anyone to know about Tim. I wanted to go back to normal, pretend it never happened. I couldn't deal with the sympathy and the tears. It would have just about finished me off.'

'But it must have been hard, especially when Olivia started having children.'

'It was, but I focused on other things instead.' She sighed. 'I think that's when Fox Lodge started to become an obsession. I wanted my own home, and I wanted it to be beautiful. Olivia had the whole motherhood thing nailed. I had to be something else, find something else to fill the emptiness. Sounds pathetic, doesn't it?'

'Not at all. I understand now.'

'And all the insecurities you talked about, when you were a kid. I had them, too. After Dad left, everything felt so precarious. Mum was a bag of nerves and fell to pieces, and Olivia was completely overwhelmed with it all. It was a real struggle to keep the house, and money was so tight. I never knew what I would walk into when I got home from school, whether Mum would be having one of her good days, or would be in bed, sobbing her heart out. I opened the bills, so I knew what was going on. I knew we were behind with the rent. I had to be really tough on her in the end, which made me hate myself. I think I just pictured Fox Lodge as the antidote to such an insecure childhood. I thought, owning that big house, filling it with pretty things, would make everything go away. I'd have my future all neatly contained within those four walls, and no one would be able to hurt me ever again.' She gave a short laugh. 'I know I sound like a crazy person.'

'You don't, Marley. Really, you don't.'

She smiled at him, and his insides fizzed with love and joy.

'So, what's with the boxes and the house move? Is Jack staying on?'

'In a manner of speaking.' He quickly explained about Seffy's purpose for being at Fell House, and how his brother was guaranteed an apartment there.

'But why are you selling?' she said curiously. 'It's been in your family for years. Seems a shame.'

He hesitated. Maybe there'd been enough revelations for one day. On the other hand, wasn't right now the ideal time to tell her the truth? A day for getting everything out in the open?

He put down his coffee cup and turned to her, feeling a knot of anxiety in his stomach.

'There's something I have to tell you, Marley. You're not going to like it.'

And out it poured — the whole, unpalatable truth about Carroll's Confectionery Factory. Marley listened, her face composed, not interrupting once, as he told her the sorry state of affairs.

When he'd finished, he watched her carefully.

She sipped her coffee, then said, 'You should have told me. I could have helped. At least supported you.'

When he didn't reply, she burst out, 'I thought you were just mean! I thought you didn't care about the factory staff, and all the time you were trying to protect them. You would rather they thought the worst of you than worry about their jobs over Christmas. God, Kit.'

'The point is, they're going to find out. The truth about Halliwell & Stephenson will hit the news very soon. They'll soon realise that LuvRocks is bankrupt, and then the questions will start. Did they owe us money? Is that why I stopped production? What sort of financial state has that left us in? They'll start to worry about what's going to replace it. When they thought I'd chosen to drop LuvRocks, they probably assumed I had a Plan B. When they know it was forced upon me, they'll think the worst, and they'll be right.'

'All those people,' she murmured. 'All those jobs. We *have* to get the Rochester contract.'

'Even if we do, it won't be enough to sustain us.'

'But it will give us some breathing space, and it will be a start!' She shook her head. 'I can't believe you've carried this all alone.'

'It's nothing compared with what you've carried alone,' he said gently.

She hugged herself, biting her lip as she looked away from him.

He watched her for a moment, then said, 'Where does this leave us, Marley?'

She looked back at him, eyes wide. 'What do you mean?'

She must know what he meant, surely? He wanted to ask her if it made a difference, if losing the factory would change how she felt about him, but he couldn't bring himself to do it.

'Would you like to pop over on Christmas Day for a drink or something? I mean, I know you're probably having dinner at your mum's.'

She stood up, and he realised she was shaking. 'Actually, I won't be here. I'm going to London. I'm staying in a hotel, having Christmas dinner there.'

He frowned. 'Alone?'

She nodded. 'Yes. I — I just fancied doing something different. I've never been to London. Never really been anywhere. It will be an adventure.'

Her voice trailed off, and he wondered what she was thinking. Clearly, he didn't figure in her plans at all. He shrugged. 'That's great. I hope you have a fabulous time.'

'I'll be back just before New Year,' she assured him. 'I'll get back to work and we'll try to figure out a plan of action for Carroll's.' She watched him, eyes wide. 'If — if the worst comes to the worst, if the factory *does* fail, what will you do? Head back to Peru, or wherever?'

'No,' he said firmly. 'My place is here, whatever happens. Besides, I'm not throwing in the towel just yet.'

She chewed her lip, her mind clearly working overtime. What was she thinking? She looked pale, he thought. Something was clearly bothering her.

'I must go,' she said suddenly.

'Sure.' He nodded, trying to sound enthusiastic. 'I'll see you then.' He showed her to the front door, and she pulled up her hood, ready to brave the freezing cold outside once more.

'Well, I guess this is it.'

'I guess it is. Merry Christmas, Kit.'

He leaned over and gave her a quick kiss on the cheek, his heart thudding. 'Merry Christmas, Marley.'

Then she was walking down the steps and towards her car, faster than was likely wise on the slippery ground.

Kit closed the door behind her, unable to bear watching her any longer. Wondering what the hell had just gone wrong between them, he tried desperately not to believe the worst. Had his fears come true? Was she having second thoughts, now she knew the truth about the factory?

But then he recalled the look of fear in her eyes when she'd noticed the boxes, the note of panic in her voice when she thought he might leave again if the factory failed.

The truth was, he realised, it was time that he stopped believing the worst of her. She was clearly still struggling to trust him, and what she needed, more than anything, was to believe in him, to have faith that he wouldn't walk away from her ever again.

How would he ever make her understand that he'd never abandon her, though? Just what would it take to prove to her that he had never stopped loving her, and he never would?

CHAPTER 29

I lay back on the bed and stretched out my arms, revelling in the luxury of the super king-sized bed, with the most comfortable mattress I'd ever slept on. Seriously, it was like falling asleep on clouds. I yawned and blinked, staring up at the chandelier in the middle of the ceiling, and wondered how I would top this experience.

Mum had been adamant that I'd be scared in London, all on my own, and when she discovered that I'd booked into Fenbrooke's Hotel, not far from Oxford Street, she'd warned me that I'd find it far too posh and overwhelming. *'Them sort of places aren't for people like us,'* she'd advised. *'You'll feel like a fish out of water, our Marley.'*

'You would, perhaps,' I acknowledged. 'I intend to revel in every moment of my stay. Besides, it's just a stone's throw from all the best shops, and I want to visit them all. I'm going to have the time of my life.'

I meant it. It would be the experience of a lifetime. I was going to have such fun. Of course, when I'd booked it, I hadn't known that Carroll's was in such dire straits. That, I thought gloomily, had really taken the gloss off the whole thing. Still, I wasn't going to think about that. Not today.

I sat up and looked around me, at the room that was almost as big as my entire flat at home. It was Christmas Eve, and I had — I glanced at my watch — five hours to make the most of Oxford Street, Regent Street, Bond Street, and anywhere else I could manage. Yesterday afternoon, I'd had a fun time at Carnaby

Street, then afternoon tea in the hotel, served by staff who treated me as if I were royalty. Today, it was time to hit the department stores, and I didn't have that long left to do so. Time to get on with it.

The doorman touched his hat in deference as I sailed past him on my way out. I smiled and nodded, and after ascertaining that I didn't need a taxi, he wished me a pleasant day.

London was a picture — a thing of beauty. Maybe it was the festive lights, and the noise, and the excitement. Maybe it was because Christmas was within touching distance, and everyone was looking forward to it, but there was a feeling of expectation and joy in the air. My previous shopping experience had been limited to small cities like York and Oddborough, and I'd thought they were busy enough, but London was something else entirely. I'd never seen anything like it, and I could only gasp in astonishment at the sights and sounds and smells of the capital on Christmas Eve.

It was difficult, however, to window shop. The streets were packed, and it was hard to get close enough to browse. I kept a tight hold on my handbag, mindful of my mother's chilling advice that London was full of muggers and nutcases and that I should keep my wits about me or suffer the consequences. Even Don had warned me to concentrate, avoid eye contact with anyone, and to make sure I always looked as if I knew where I was going and what I was doing.

'If they get the scent of fresh blood, they'll swoop. You mark my words. Northerners are easy prey down there.'

I'd laughed at them both but swamped as I was by wave upon wave of shoppers, I began to feel a bit nervous, and their warnings suddenly didn't sound so far-fetched. Gripping the strap of my bag very tightly, I tried to look as if I made this journey every day, and strode determinedly down the street, dodging people who looked as if they were on a mission, and trying to fight the tide of flesh, in order to make my way inside at least one of the department stores.

Three hours later, I was washed up on the steps of Rochester's, exhausted and drained. I could have wept with relief. Here, at last, was something familiar. The Oxford Street branch was far larger than the one in York, but it was recognisable.

I fought my way inside, landing in the warmth and calm of the perfume department, where desperate-looking men were seeking advice from smart sales assistants as to which scent their partners would be thrilled to find under the Christmas tree the following morning.

The gentle strains of orchestral music soothed my frazzled nerves, and I headed to the coffee shop where, after queueing for almost twenty minutes, I finally managed to buy a caramel latte and a mince pie, for the price of a three-course meal at The Blue Lamp, and sank into a chair, grateful to take the weight off my feet. Classy and expensive my new boots may have been, but it had definitely been a mistake to go shopping in them when they were less than a week old.

At the next table, a young couple were discussing their plans for the evening.

'I'll make sure she has a bath around seven, then she can watch *The Polar Express*. By the time that's finished she'll probably be sleepy, anyway, so we should be able to get her to bed. If we allow two hours for her to fall asleep, that should give us just enough time to retrieve the presents and get them set out before midnight.'

'Great.' The man laughed. 'That should give us all of four hours to sleep, before she wakes up and shrieks at us that Father Christmas has been, and it's time to get up.'

The woman rolled her eyes. 'Aw, well. It's Christmas. What do you expect? I bet you were the same.'

'I was,' he admitted. 'Although, I already knew what I'd got. I used to sneak into Mum and Dad's bedroom every year and check out the presents hidden in their wardrobe. They always stuffed them in there before they got around to wrapping them. I never had a single surprise after the age of seven.'

'Serves you right,' she said. 'If Anastasia did that to us, I'd throttle her.'

'We wouldn't be so stupid as to keep them in the wardrobe,' he pointed out.

'Gosh,' she said suddenly, 'you don't think she's ever looked in the sauna, do you?'

They looked at each other, clearly horror struck, and I smiled wistfully before taking another sip of my coffee. That could have been Kit and me, discussing getting our child's presents ready for the morning, if only things had worked out differently. I couldn't help but wonder what sort of parents we'd have made. Not the sort who'd keep toys in a sauna, for a start. Not ones who'd even have a sauna for that matter.

I found myself half wishing that Anastasia had enough wits about her to check in there, then reproached myself for being so mean.

Glancing at my watch again, I pulled a face. I didn't have long, and there was one thing I really had to do. I'd promised myself this treat for long enough. I wasn't going to be thwarted at the last minute.

Gulping down the rest of my latte, I grabbed my bag and pushed my way out of the heaving café towards the escalator, passing the confectionery department as I did so. Out of the corner of my eye, I saw a display of chocolates. All the leading brands were there. I wondered if, one day, Carroll's chocolate would be on sale in the York branch. I could only hope.

Pushing the thought away, along with all the other thoughts it led to, I headed downstairs to the one place I'd been determined to visit. The handbag department.

There they were — Jenny Kingston handbags, in all their glory. That was what I'd dreamed of. A Jenny Kingston handbag, I'd decided, would be the start of everything. It was the first thing I'd determined to buy when I finally got some money. After that, it would be new clothes, a new car, a complete refurbishment of Fox Lodge, and a trip to New York. I'd had it all planned for such a long time. And finally, there I was, standing in Rochester's swanky London store, with the pick of those bags before me, and enough money to achieve my first goal, but everything had changed.

There were so many to choose from, but I quickly fell in love with a simple cream bag with a tiny blue butterfly in one corner, and JK stamped on the front in gold lettering. I flinched a little when I handed over my credit card and parted with the best part of six-hundred pounds but told myself I was worth it. I deserved it. If I deserved nothing else, I was going to get this handbag and I would not beat myself up about it.

After fighting my way back to the hotel, my new handbag safe in its Rochester carrier bag that I vowed to never throw away, I hobbled back to my room. I sank onto the bed, pulled off my boots, and rubbed my poor, aching feet. It had been a day to remember, but with it done, I had more important things to worry about.

Rummaging in my pocket, I pulled out a piece of paper and scanned the number written on it. For a moment, I held the paper to my chest, a million emotions tugging at me. Then, taking a deep breath, I leaned over and picked up the receiver.

Time to make someone's Christmas very happy indeed.

The concierge very kindly booked me a taxi to the station, just half an hour later. 'I'm very sorry you had to cut short your stay, Madam,' he said, sounding as if he actually meant it. These hotel staff certainly knew about customer service, I'd give them that.

'Thank you,' I said. 'I'm afraid it couldn't be helped. Still, it's not all bad. It's snowing back home, according to my weather app. Looks like we're having a white Christmas after all.'

He smiled at me. 'Then I wish you a very merry, white Christmas, Madam.'

A few minutes later, the doorman held open the door of the taxi for me. 'I hope you enjoyed your stay here, Madam.'

'Oh, I did,' I assured him, as I climbed into the back seat. 'It's been the experience of a lifetime.'

'I'm very glad to hear it. Merry Christmas.'

'Merry Christmas,' I said, closing the car door.

As we drove away, I realised with sudden horror that I hadn't tipped either him, or the concierge. Was I supposed to tip them? I had no idea. I guess I wasn't as knowledgeable about such matters as I pretended to be. Not that it mattered, anymore. I was leaving London well behind me.

It was Christmas Eve — and I was going home.

CHAPTER 30

Mum's voice was anxious. 'I'm ever so sorry to bother you, Christopher, really I am, but it's our Marley. No, no, she's not in London anymore. She turned up back here, out of the blue, last night. I know! Caught the last train back to York and drove home in all this snow. Madness. Well, that's my point, really. She's not herself, not at all, and I was hoping you'd come here and speak to her. No, really, she keeps talking about you. I think she's having some sort of meltdown, and I don't know what else to do. Will you come? I mean, I know it's Christmas Day and everything, but — you will? Oh, you are a good lad. Thank you so much. See you soon.'

She put the receiver down and turned to me, looking quite annoyed. 'That poor lad. He sounded distraught. You are cruel, Marley.'

'Oh, give over, Katie,' Don said, hooking his arm around her. 'This is dead romantic, this. Besides, what are you looking so miserable about? You've got what you wanted — all your family together for Christmas Day, and a bonus guest to boot.'

'Oh, heck,' she wailed. 'I'll have to give him some dinner, won't I? I hope it will stretch.'

'If not,' Don said, winking at me, 'you can give him some of mine. I'm willing to make that sacrifice.'

Luckily, she didn't seem to notice his amusement. She was far too busy rummaging around in the freezer and totting up portion sizes.

Don and I left her to it and headed back into the living room, where chaos had descended with the arrival of Olivia, David, and the boys. The floor was strewn with torn wrapping paper, and Don and I had to gingerly step over piles of games and toys, terrified of breaking anything.

Tommy waved his new xylophone at me, before bringing it crashing down onto the carpet, while Sam and Max sat happily playing with their Power Ranger action figures, their faces smeared with chocolate from their selection boxes.

'Bit early for sweets, isn't it?' I said, nodding at the empty wrappers on the floor. 'We haven't even had dinner, yet.'

Olivia rolled her eyes. 'You try stopping them on Christmas morning. It's part of the fun, anyway. Rules go out of the window today.'

'Besides,' Don pointed out, 'having seen what's in store for us for Christmas dinner, I'd advise them to fill up on Milky Ways while they can.'

David laughed. 'Let me guess. Frozen turkey, frozen Yorkshire puddings, frozen stuffing balls, frozen vegetables, frozen mashed potatoes, and gravy made from granules and boiling water.'

'Be fair,' Olivia said. 'She's using the water from the veg since it's a special occasion, rather than just boiling the kettle.'

'Bless her,' Don said, shaking his head. 'I wish she'd let me cook the dinner, but she was adamant that she was going to treat us all. Treat us all! Reckon we'll be looking for a takeaway that's open later tonight.'

'Don't be mean,' I said. 'To be honest, I hardly notice her cooking these days. It's become normal. Besides, you're going to have get used to it, now that you're making an honest woman of her.'

He beamed at me. 'And you don't mind? About me and your mum getting married, I mean.'

Olivia and I looked at each other in amusement.

'Why on earth would we mind? It's the best news ever. We're so happy for you both.'

I meant every word. I'd finally let Dad go, and his shadow no longer hung over me. We were a family without him. We didn't need him, and Mum deserved someone as wonderful as Don.

'And that engagement ring you gave her was beautiful,' Olivia said. 'You have very good taste. Unlike David here,' she added sternly. 'A slow cooker! I mean, I ask you. And after I treated him to that X Box, too.'

David looked sheepish. I wondered how Olivia would have reacted if he'd bought her the same present that Kit had bought me. I'd finally opened it that morning, tearing open the envelope in eager anticipation, to discover a certificate and card, thanking me for my generosity and informing me that a borehole, which would bring clean water to an entire village, had been gifted on my behalf, and wishing me a very merry Christmas.

I'd stared at the message in disbelief for a moment, then a smile had spread across my face. If that wasn't typical Kit, I didn't know what was. I wondered what he'd made of his Rochester's tie and almost giggled at the thought. What had I been thinking? As if he'd care about that!

Olivia looked across at me, her eyes shining. 'What are you grinning at?'

I shook my head. 'Just thinking about stuff.'

'About Kit, you mean.' She rubbed Sam's chocolate smeared hands with a baby wipe and tossed it in the bin, then put her arms around me. 'I can't believe you came home from that swanky hotel in London for all this.' She waved a hand across the messy living room in disbelief. 'You must really have it bad.'

I glanced across at Don, and he gave me a sympathetic smile. Arriving at Mum's last night, I'd sat them both down and told them the truth about the factory, and about everything that had been going on between Kit and myself. I hadn't mentioned the baby, though. I knew it would hurt Mum that I hadn't told her at the time, and she would only be upset that I'd gone through all that alone — not to mention the fact that she'd lost a grandchild without even knowing about it. I couldn't put all that on her. I'd made them promise not to tell Olivia and David, or anyone else for that matter, about the true state of affairs.

Don hadn't seemed too surprised, to be honest. '

Thought it were something like that,' he'd confessed. 'Kit Carroll's far too smart to do something as daft as throw away a lucrative contract for no good reason, especially when he had nothing to take its place. I guessed he'd had no choice in the matter. Been worrying meself sick about it, to be honest, and I'm not the only one. There have been mutterings. I appreciate that he was trying to save us the stress over Christmas, but we're not daft. Well, some of us aren't, any road.'

'What happens now?' Mum said, sounding anxious.

'Ah,' I'd replied. 'Now, that's where you come in.'

'Marley,' Mum had entered the living room, and was peering anxiously out of the window, 'does this chap of yours drive a black car?'

'That narrows it down, love,' Don said, grinning. He stood up and, dodging the boys' assorted presents, made his way over to stand beside her. 'That's him, all right.' He turned to me and gave me a thumbs-up sign. 'Action stations, Marley. You're on.'

***

Kit's mouth felt dry and his heart thumped as he knocked on the front door of Marley's mother's house. What was he about to walk into? A meltdown, Mrs Jacobs had said. What sort of meltdown? How bad was it? Was it his fault? Had he pushed her too far, made her remember things that were so painful, she should have been allowed to forget them?

He wondered how she'd coped with the grief all those years. He'd only had a few days to process the fact that he'd almost become a father. It felt raw to him. He couldn't imagine how she'd got through it all, and the fact that she'd had to go through it without him filled him with shame. How could she ever forgive him?

He almost stopped breathing when the door opened, then his eyes widened in shock at Marley standing on the other side. She looked fine. Hell, she looked more than fine, she looked beautiful.

Kit's eyes scanned her in appreciation, then he remembered the phone call and felt ashamed all over again. 'Are you all right? Your mum said—'

She laughed and took hold of his arm, pulling him inside the hallway. 'It's freezing out there. Look, you're covered in snow already.' She brushed the flakes of snow from his shoulders and touched his damp hair, very briefly. 'Come in and get warm.'

Bewildered, he allowed himself to be half dragged into the living room, where a scene of devastation met his eyes. The room was how he imagined Santa's grotto would look if he employed hyperactive elves. To his astonished eyes, it was all tinsel, glitter, wrapping paper and scattered toys.

In one corner of the room, the television blasted out some Christmas cartoon, although no one seemed to be paying any attention to it. David sat on a chair, peeling a satsuma, and seemed oblivious to the chaos. Olivia busily scrubbed a little boy's face with baby wipes. Two other little boys were dressed in Batman costumes and were wrestling, with alarming ferocity, on the carpet. Someone had trodden chocolate into the rug — at least, he hoped it was chocolate.

Don, wearing a grey cardigan, navy blue slippers, and a green paper hat from a cracker, looked far older than someone in his late thirties, but was beaming as if he'd won the lottery, and Marley's mum was busy asking anyone and everyone if they fancied a glass of snowball, apparently unwilling to take no for an answer, as if refusing a snowball on Christmas Day was illegal.

'Merry Christmas, Kit,' Don said, standing up to shake his hand. 'Would you like a beer? Or do you fancy a hot drink to defrost you before dinner?' He leaned forward and whispered, 'Trust me, when you've tasted Katie's cooking, you'll wish you'd chosen alcohol.'

'Tasted...' Kit blinked, not knowing what to think. 'I don't understand. I thought you said Marley was ill,' he said to Mrs Jacobs.

She had the grace to blush. 'Now, be fair, Christopher. We couldn't leave you sitting in that big empty house all alone, now could we? Not on Christmas Day.'

'And if I'd just invited you, you would never have come,' Marley added. 'You'd have made some excuse, and I couldn't risk that.'

He shook his head, as the reality of the situation finally sank in. 'There's nothing wrong with you? You concocted the whole story, just to get me over for dinner?'

She smiled softly. 'Not just for dinner, no. I have something to ask you.'

Olivia clapped her hands together. 'Right, boys. How about we build that snowman now?'

There were shrieks of delight from all three children, followed by a general rush to find boots, hats, gloves, coats and scarves.

David looked quite disgruntled. 'Do we have to? It's cold out there.'

'That's the point,' Olivia said brutally. 'Shift your bum off that chair and come and have some fun with your sons.'

Sighing, David heaved himself out of the chair and dropped his satsuma peel in the bin. 'You coming to help?' he asked Don.

'Fat chance,' Don replied. 'I'm going to be in the kitchen, helping Katie defrost the food. Them Christmas dinners won't microwave themselves you know.'

Mrs Jacobs blushed and slapped him on the arm, and together they hurried into the kitchen. Olivia herded David and the children into the garden, the door closed behind them, and silence fell upon the living room.

'It may look like a battlefield,' Marley said cheerfully, 'but at least we can hear ourselves think now. Sit down, Kit.'

Kit dropped into a chair, feeling dazed. He'd been sitting alone in that gloomy old house less than an hour ago. It had been so quiet he could hear the clock ticking, and he'd fully expected to spend the entire day on his own, watching the odd programme and trying not to dwell on the appalling mess he'd made of his life.

From that, he'd gone to standing in a cosy, untidy home, about to be served what promised to be a most interesting meal, and surrounded by a noisy, loving family. And he was with Marley.

He could hardly believe it.

'I thought you were in London,' he said. 'What made you come home?'

She sat down on the sofa, curling her feet beneath her. He watched as she twisted a strand of her glossy chestnut hair between her fingers, just as he'd done that Sunday morning while lying in her bed, holding her close. It seemed like a million years ago.

'London was fabulous,' she said. 'A bit scary, but fabulous. I had a brilliant time. I finally got a Jenny Kingston handbag from Rochester's on Oxford Street. I'm so thrilled with it. I've promised myself one of those bags for years.'

'Great.' He had no idea what a Jenny Kingston bag was, but clearly it meant a lot to her.

'Thanks for the borehole, by the way,' she said.

His eyes narrowed, as he scanned her face for annoyance, but she was still smiling, and her eyes were twinkling.

'Thanks for the tie,' he replied.

She looked at him, and suddenly they were both laughing.

'I guess,' he admitted, 'a borehole wasn't top of your Christmas wish list.'

'It never even occurred to me,' she said. 'Still, I looked it up on the charity's website, and I was pretty impressed. It gave me a surprisingly warm glow to know that a whole village will now have clean water because of us. It's a great present. Better than a tie, anyway. I can't imagine what I was thinking.'

'Maybe you were thinking that your ideal man would be a smart businessman who wore designer ties,' he said ruefully.

She shook her head. 'I actually bought it for David. I only gave it to you because I didn't have anything else.'

He laughed. 'Charming. Although, in a strange way, that makes me feel better.'

'Do you want a drink?' she asked him. 'Don offered, but then drifted away.'

'In a minute, maybe.' His hands twisted in his lap, unsure what was going on. 'What's this really about, Marley?'

'Okay. Cards on the table.' She leaned forward, face suddenly serious, and Kit felt his guts twist with nerves. 'I have a proposition for you.'

'Oh? What sort of proposition?'

'The sort of proposition that may just be the answer to all your problems.'

He sincerely doubted that, but he smiled, anyway. 'That would be good.'

'Wouldn't it? I'm not joking, Kit. I want to invest in the factory.'

Kit's face dropped. 'What?'

'I said—'

'I heard you. What do you mean? What are you talking about?'

She sighed patiently. 'You know Great Uncle Charles left me most of his money? Well, I want to put it into the factory. You need a cash injection. I have the cash. What do you say?'

His mind raced. Was she serious? 'But why? Why would you do that?'

'Because I believe in Carroll's. Because I believe in you.'

She unfurled herself from the sofa and walked towards him, crouching down at his side. She held up her mobile, and he peered at the screen, confused.

'What's that?'

'Online banking app. See that figure at the top? That's what I now have sitting in the bank, and I'd like to put it all into the factory.'

'Bloody hell!' He shook his head. 'I'm sorry, Marley. I can't let you do that. That money's for you. It's what you've wanted for so long.'

'Yes, that's true enough. And you know what, I had a taste of the high life this week. I stayed in the swankiest hotel in London — well, one of them. I had a fabulous time, completely guilt free, and I treated myself to my handbag and afternoon tea, and some new boots, and even a facial and massage. It was brilliant. But I don't want to waste the rest of it on that. The fact is my family depends on Carroll's. I felt so guilty that Mum and Olivia got so little in the will. It didn't seem fair. This way, I get to help them.

I get to help everyone who works there. The factory needs money, and I've got it. Let me do this.'

'I can't. It's too risky. I won't let you invest all that capital when there are no guarantees that you'll get it back.'

He broke off as his mobile began to ring in his pocket. He tried to ignore it, but she stood up.

'Take that,' she said. 'It might be Jack. You'll want to talk to him, today of all days.'

Giving her an apologetic look, he took the phone out and glanced at the screen, then went pale. 'It's Ethan Rochester.'

'Oh, my God!' Her face lit up with excitement. 'Answer it, quickly.'

Hands shaking, Kit tapped the screen, and said, quite nervously, 'Hello, Kit Carroll speaking.'

Marley's eyes bored into him, as he listened intently to what Ethan was telling him. At first, he couldn't grasp what was being said, and with everything that Marley had just landed on him, it all seemed very jumbled in his mind. Then the fog lifted, and he gasped. 'What did you say?'

Ethan laughed. 'Do you think you can handle it?'

Kit stared at Marley, who was practically hopping up and down with impatience. 'Yes. Yes, I know we can.'

'That's all I needed to hear. We'll be in touch in the New Year. Sorry to disturb you on Christmas Day, but my wife insisted that I put you out of your misery. She's a bit soppy like that.'

Kit heard an indignant 'Oy!' in the background, and Ethan laughed again. 'I'll leave you to enjoy the rest of your day. Merry Christmas, Kit.'

'Merry Christmas. And thank you.'

As he put the phone back in his pocket, Marley practically pounced on him.

'Well? What did he say? Have we got the York contract?'

He shook his head. My God, what a day it was turning out to be. 'Not exactly.'

Her face fell. 'Oh. Well, what then?'

He looked up at her, dazed. 'Ethan wants to launch Rochester's own brand of chocolate products, and he's been searching for a manufacturer for some time. He wants Carroll's to make them.'

She sank down onto the floor beside him, her expression showing that she was as stunned as he was. 'You're kidding.'

'No. No, I'm really not.' It was beginning to sink in at last. 'It will be right across the board, Marley. All his stores will stock them, as well as the website. He wants a full range of premium chocolates, Christmas confectionery, Easter eggs, the lot.'

'My God, it will be massive.' She clapped her hands together. 'So, now will you accept my offer?'

He reached over and took hold of her hands. 'It's still just one contract, and after what happened with LuvRocks .... I know that Rochester's is a big company, but you never know. It's still a risk.'

'Which is why I want you to think about my next proposition,' she said. 'The other night, I babysat for my nephews. They bombarded me with questions about the factory. They were convinced we employed Oompa Loompas and had a chocolate river, but that's beside the point. Thing is, they were fascinated to know how we made the rock and the chocolates, and it got me thinking. What if we held factory tours? What if we set up parts of the factory that could take visitors who could see demonstrations of chocolate making? Maybe we could take school parties, that sort of thing? We could even get the kids making their own sticks of rock. And we could set up a shop on the premises, selling our own products to visitors. We could even open a café, perhaps, at some point.'

Kit considered the matter. 'It sounds like a really good idea,' he conceded, 'but it would take loads of work. The factory would have to be reconfigured. There'd be insurance to think about and more staff, and advertising. It would take a huge investment.'

'Which is what I'm offering.'

He smiled at her gently. 'You're wonderful for offering, Marley, and I think your ideas are fabulous, but I'm afraid it would take more even than you have in the bank to get this up and running, and I'm not sure how my bank would react to the idea. I mean, we could certainly approach them if I can get Colin to draw up a decent business plan, but even so.'

To his surprise, she stood up and climbed onto his knee. Wrapping her arms around his neck, she looked deep into his eyes and said, 'I know that, which is why I've made sure I have a lot more to offer you than what's in the bank.'

He wasn't sure what was making his heart race more — the promise of an end to the factory's troubles, or the fact that she was curled up on his knee, her body close to his, the scent of her perfume making him quite dizzy with longing.

'I'm not following,' he said faintly.

'It's quite simple,' she said. 'I've sold Fox Lodge — at least in principle. Don't worry, though, it's a done deal. The couple who've bought it have been after it for quite a while, and they're cash buyers. No chain, you see. They've been living in rented accommodation while they looked for a project. Fox Lodge is everything they wanted, and they were willing to pay top dollar for it. I called them yesterday, and they're over the moon. So, you see, I have plenty of money to invest in the factory tour idea, and I think it's going to work. How about you?'

'How about me?'

'Do you think it's going to work?'

He looked into her beautiful hazel eyes and saw the faint trace of anxiety in them. Brushing back her hair, he kissed her gently on the lips, and she responded immediately. For a few moments, Kit completely forgot what they'd been talking about.

As they finally pulled away from each other, she said softly, 'Well? Do you?'

He stroked the soft hollow of her cheek and nodded. 'Yes,' he said. 'I really think it could work.'

'And what about the factory?' she said, smiling mischievously.

Kit swallowed. 'Marley, are you sure about this? About us, I mean? Because I don't think I can go through all this again. We seem to go one step forward and two steps back. The other day, when I told you about the factory, you couldn't wait to get away. I thought for a moment that—'

'That I didn't want you anymore because you weren't the rich businessman I'd assumed you were.'

'I'm sorry,' he said, feeling ashamed. 'It was only for a moment.'

'It's okay, Kit. I understand that. We need to learn to trust each other, and I really believe we can do it. The truth is, when you told me about your financial problems, I had a moment of panic. Not because you had no money, but because I knew what I had to do. I knew, in that moment, that every plan I'd made over the last few years was going to be swept aside, and it scared the life out of me. I wasn't scared of giving up the money. I was scared that you meant so much to me that *not* giving you the money wasn't even an option. I knew that giving up Fox Lodge was huge. I'd built an entire future around it, and yet, all I wanted was to seal the deal with the Martins as quickly as possible so that I could help you. I guess my future is with you. Not some house.'

He tapped her playfully on the nose. 'Still went to London, though, didn't you?'

She laughed. 'Too right. I thought, if I'm doomed to live in poverty for the rest of my life, I'm going to have one weekend in a swanky hotel, and a bloody designer handbag to show for it. It's the least I deserved.'

'You won't live in poverty,' he promised her. 'I'll work night and day to make this work. Carroll's will be a success.'

'And I'll work right beside you,' she promised.

'You really think you can give up Fox Lodge?'

'I really do. Mind you, given that you've sold Fell House, I really hope you can cope with living in my tiny flat. I know it's miniscule after what you're used to, but we can make it work, can't we?'

'You want me to live with you?'

She blushed, very prettily. 'I'm sorry. I sort of assumed you would.'

He was silent for a moment, then he shook his head. 'I can't live with you, Marley.'

She pulled away a little, her face scarlet. 'Oh. Right.'

As she tried to climb off his knee, he wrapped his arm around her waist and held her securely.

'Wait a minute. I've listened to your proposition, now it's time you listened to mine.'

He rummaged in his jacket pocket and pulled out a small velvet box. 'You're not the only one who wants to make an investment in our future,' he said softly. 'The borehole wasn't your only present. I want you to know how much I love you, and I want you to believe that I'll never abandon you. My future is with you, or it's no future at all. Will you marry me, Marley?'

He held his breath as she stared down at the diamond engagement ring, nestling in its satin bed. It felt as if she was never going to answer him.

'For God's sake, hurry up and say yes, you idiot!'

They both jumped and looked round, astonished and rather embarrassed to see the entire family standing in the doorway, faces rosy from the cold, clothes dotted with snowflakes. They had eager expressions on their faces as they waited for Marley's answer.

Kit looked at Marley, and she looked back at him.

'Yes,' she said, smiling. 'Of course it's yes.'

'God, I love you so much,' he told her and pulled her to him, burying his face in her hair, while the family whooped with excitement.

'Must check on dinner,' squealed Mrs Jacobs, while David ushered the boys in with stern warnings to keep away from the chocolate.

'Aw,' Don said, plonking himself down on the sofa and reaching for a can of beer. 'Now, that's what I call a happy ending.'

'What else would you expect at Christmas?' said Olivia dreamily. 'I said you were saved for a reason, Marley, and there it is. You were brought back to be with Kit. It's like a Christmas miracle. Nice ring,' she added, nodding approvingly as Kit slipped the diamond solitaire onto Marley's finger. 'Shouldn't you make a speech, Kit? I seem to recall Marley bullied David into making one when we got engaged.'

Marley wrinkled her nose and mouthed *sorry* to Kit. 'Take no notice. You don't have to say anything, honestly.'

'The microwave's pinged,' Mrs Jacobs said, rushing back into the living room. 'Dinner's nearly ready! Ooh, our Marley, what a lovely ring. Maybe he's not such a miserable old Scrooge, after all.'

Marley looked horrified, but Kit laughed as he looked around at the big, happy family that he had become a part of.

'There's really only one thing I can say to that,' he said. He pulled Marley close and beamed at them all. '*Merry Christmas, and God bless us— every—*'

But he didn't get to end the quotation. As Don and David groaned, Mrs Jacobs yelled, 'Corny!' and Olivia threw a cushion at him in disgust.

Marley, however, shut him up in the way she knew best, and Kit decided he didn't have to finish that sentence after all. He already knew he was blessed, and this was going to be the merriest Christmas ever.

The End

To find out more about Sharon Booth and her books visit:

https://linktr.ee/sharonboothwriter

Acknowledgements

Saving Mr Scrooge was tricky! Because the storyline dips frequently back into the past, it was essential that I didn't confuse the reader about what was happening and when. And, with Marley being the character who really needed saving, I was faced with creating a heroine who wasn't always nice. Certainly, she had her flaws, and I've read enough 'How-To-Write' books to know that the main character should, above all else, be likeable. How to make someone who had a selfish streak a mile wide and was — on the surface at least — pretty shallow, likeable?

Luckily for me, I have a team of beta readers who, as ever, were on hand with plenty of feedback, advice and opinions. Of course, they didn't always agree with each other, which did make for some confusion and cause me some head-scratching, but generally it was all very useful. I certainly couldn't have done it without them, so huge thanks and much love to Jo Bartlett, Alex Weston and Julie Heslington, who are absolute superstars. Thanks also to Pat Posner, who cast a look over the story, spotted typos, made some sharp observations and gave me huge encouragement. Thank you so much, Pat!

Back in the spring of 2017, my lovely daughter and daughter-in-law took me to the John Bull Factory near Bridlington, so that I could immerse myself in the world of the Carroll's Confectionery business. I even had a go at making a stick of rock. Trust me, it's harder work than it looks! I also had a wander around their fantastic shop and couldn't resist their rose creams and violet creams. Yummy! Thank you so much, Jemma and Sarah, for always being willing to ferry me around, and for happily accepting my (often weird) requests.

Huge gratitude to Berni Stevens, for her fabulous cover design. I love it!

Special thanks to all of you who are reading this book. I appreciate each and every one of you, and I hope you enjoyed *Saving Mr Scrooge*. If you did, perhaps you'd consider leaving a short review on Amazon? It doesn't have to be more than a few words and it really does make a difference.

Finally, to my husband, Mr E, who puts up with so much from me, and is always ready and willing to take me off to different areas of Yorkshire, researching locations for my books, is always super proud of me, cheers when I'm doing well, encourages when I'm feeling low, and uncomplainingly brings me cups of tea and snacks while I'm locked away upstairs writing. You really are a star, and I appreciate you more than I can ever say.

Wishing you all a very merry Christmas!

Sharon
xxx

More from Sharon Booth

Resisting Mr Rochester (Moorland Heroes 1)

Cara Truelove has always been a romantic, burying her head in books and dreaming of being swept off her feet by her very own Brontë hero. When she was a gullible teenager, she believed boyfriend Seth to be a modern-day brooding Heathcliff. Fourteen years later, when Seth has proved to be more like Homer Simpson, Cara vows never to fall in love again, and turns her back on romance for good.

Leaving Seth behind, Cara secures a job as nanny at Moreland Hall on the Yorkshire Moors, but is shocked to discover her new employer is none other than the tall, dark, and disturbingly handsome Mr Rochester.

Her resolve to be more level-headed is soon tested when strange things begin to happen at Moreland Hall. Why is Mr Rochester's mother hidden away upstairs? What are the strange noises she hears from the attic? Why is the housekeeper so reluctant to leave her on her own? And where is Mr Rochester's mysterious wife?

As events unfold, Cara knows she must keep a cool head, curb her imagination – and resist Mr Rochester at all costs.

After all, one Brontë hero in a lifetime is more than enough for any woman. Two would be downright greedy.

Wouldn't it?

Belle Book and Christmas Candle (The Witches of Castle Clair 1)

Do you believe in magic?

Sky St Clair doesn't, and growing up in Castle Clair, a small town renowned for its mystical past and magical legends, she never felt she belonged.
Sky got away from Castle Clair as soon as she could, but when a run of bad luck leaves her homeless and jobless, she has little choice but to accept her sister Star's invitation to return home for the festive season.
When Star has an accident, Sky finds herself running the family's magical supplies shop. Wands, crystals, pendulums ... really? It's a tough job when she doesn't believe in the products she's selling, but how can she? Magic isn't real, no matter what her deluded siblings think.
Jethro Richmond doesn't believe in magic either. In fact, he doesn't believe in anything much anymore, which is proving to be a bit of a problem for a writer of fantasy novels. With a self-constructed wall around his heart as high as Clair Tower, and his dreams as ruined as the town's ancient castle, he's lost all hope of repairing his tattered career. The last thing he needs is to get involved with a family like the St Clairs, and no matter what a certain little black cat seems to want Jethro has no intention of spending any time with Sky or her unusual sisters.

But this is a strange little town and, as the residents prepare to celebrate Christmas, Sky and Jethro might just discover that in Castle Clair, anything is possible. Even magic

A romantic comedy with a magical twist!